W9-CNC-964

A CHOIR OF CROWS

A CHOIR OF CROWS

Candace Robb

CRÈME de la CRIME

This first world edition published 2020
in Great Britain and the USA by
Crème de la Crime an imprint of
SEVERN HOUSE PUBLISHERS LTD of
Eardley House, 4 Uxbridge Street, London W8 7SY.
Trade paperback edition first published
in Great Britain and the USA 2021 by
SEVERN HOUSE PUBLISHERS LTD.

British Library Cataloguing in Publication Data
A CIP catalogue record for this title is available from the British Library.

ISBN-13: 978-1-78029-126-0 (cased)
ISBN-13: 978-1-78029-724-8 (trade paper)
ISBN-13: 978-1-4483-0445-5 (e-book)

All Severn House titles are printed on acid-free paper.

Severn House Publishers support the Forest Stewardship Council™ [FSC™],
the leading international forest certification organisation.
All our titles that are printed on FSC certified paper carry the FSC logo.

Typeset by Palimpsest Book Production Ltd.,
Falkirk, Stirlingshire, Scotland.
Printed and bound in Great Britain by
TJ International, Padstow, Cornwall.

For the Medieval Women's Choir of Seattle –
to sing with you is a joy surpassing reason,
and especially for Marian 'Molly' Seibert, my inspiration.

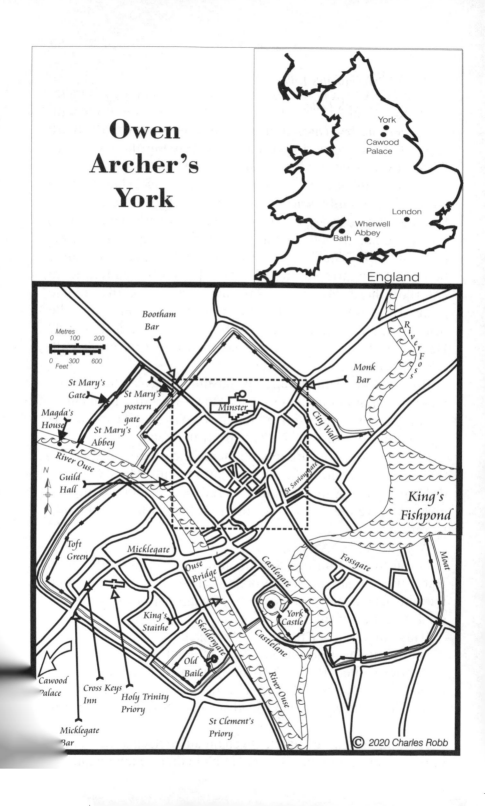

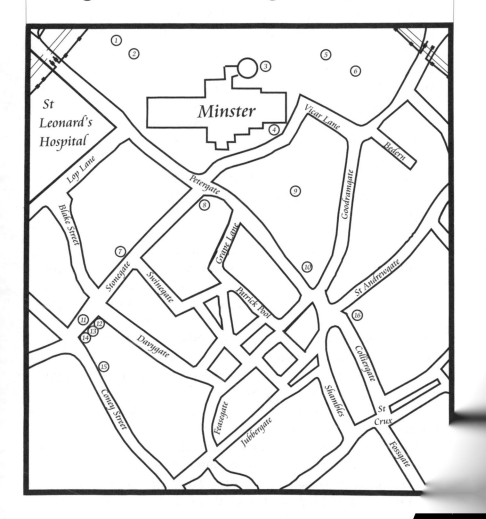

1. Archbishop's Palace
2. Mason's Lodge
3. Chapter House
4. Deanery
5. Chancellor's House
6. Jehannes's House
7. Farfield's House
8. Dale's House
9. Bedern
10. Hempe's House
11. St Helen's Churchyard
12. Lucie and Owen's House
13. Lucie's Apothecary
14. York Tavern
15. Swann House
16. Poole House

The marvels of God are not brought forth from one's self. Rather, it is more like a chord, a sound that is played. The tone does not come out of the chord itself, but rather, through the touch of the Musician. I am, of course, the lyre and harp of God's kindness.
Hildegard of Bingen

ONE

Minstrels & Players in a Hall of Power

Cawood Palace, early December 1374

Holding their pikes upright so they no longer threatened the new arrivals, the guards stepped aside to allow the players entrance to the great hall of Cawood Palace. A collective sigh rippled through the company as they exchanged encouraging nods, and, with a flourish of drums and recorders, stepped lightly through the carved doorway making a merry sound. Ambrose strode forward, arms outspread to show off the elegance of his fur-lined cloak and robe as he intoned a song celebrating the harvest.

Late for that, but with little time to prepare he had chosen a tune in both his and the players' repertoires, and one that lent itself to such a procession – a good tempo and a range in which he could project his voice above the clatter of their instruments. The grandness of the gesture was key, not the theme: a jubilant noise to delight the lords gathered here. Tomorrow, as the nobles feasted in the hall, that would be the time to turn their heads with new lyrics in praise of the rising power of the Nevilles in the North.

For the new lord of Cawood Palace was a Neville, and the occasion was a gathering of Alexander's kinsmen before his imminent enthronement as Archbishop of York in the great minster. Already consecrated archbishop in Westminster Abbey earlier in the year, he would now take his official seat. When Ambrose had learned of this gathering, the most powerful among the Nevilles here to instruct their ecclesiastical cousin on the temporal significance of his position, he had set about finding a way to witness it, in hopes of overhearing something of use to His Grace Prince Edward. For he had no doubt much would be said – the Nevilles had used their influence, including a not inconsiderable amount of wealth, to win this honor for Alexander, and now they would expect him to make it worthwhile, to prove himself worthy of the high position – second most powerful churchman in the realm. The impression he made on the city of York and the many religious houses therein, especially the chapter of its glorious minster, must be one of strength, but tempered with grace – he must assure the dean and chapter and all the clergy in his care that he meant to be a magnanimous master.

It remained to be seen whether Alexander Neville could play the part. His career so far would argue otherwise. Even across the south sea in the French court Ambrose had heard tales of Neville's tantrum over a bishopric in Cornwall, an ugly dispute that had begun over a decade earlier and dragged on for years.

And now, as Ambrose strode into the great hall of one of the palaces that came to Alexander as part of the archbishopric, he studied the proud faces, noticed signs of strain. No doubt partly inspired by the setting. Cawood seemed a neglected property. Judging from the stained whitewash on the gatehouse and weedy state of the yard, the previous archbishop, John Thoresby, had paid little attention to its upkeep. Why had this gathering been called here? Why not Bishopthorpe, the palace close to York and much favored by Thoresby? Ambrose guessed that this was meant to be a secret gathering. Which was, of course, why he risked being here. He might win the prince's ear with news of the Nevilles' strategy for the North.

At least the hall was brightly lit with torches and a large fire in the center – for it was not yet fitted with a hearth. The light was not kind to the musicians' colorful garb, emphasizing the faded areas, the worn patches on the velvet, the oft-repaired seams. The contrast with Ambrose's own costly robes and the elegantly garbed guests was striking, and the nobles gazed on the players with a mixture of amusement and impatience. A few smiled and moved to the music, but most began to turn away, resuming their conversations. At least no one started at Ambrose – he believed himself unknown to the Nevilles, though he had performed before some of them on occasion years earlier. Before France.

Enough of this mundane fanfare. Time to entice the guests with a taste of what they might expect on the morrow. The company's leader, Carl, awaited the signal to begin. Nodding to him, Ambrose approached a fair youth who stepped forward upon hearing the opening notes. Matthew was the requisite comely player relegated to the female roles, at present valuable for the angelic voice, and the ethereal beauty to match – slender as a willow wand, graceful, with a mass of spun gold curls surrounding pale eyes and features kissed by innocence.

'Shall we give them a taste?' Ambrose whispered in French.

With a smile of anticipation so breathlessly sweet Ambrose thought his heart might shatter to look on it, the youth straightened, took a deep breath, and intoned the beginning of the duet, a playful argument about whether it is preferable to spend a delightful night with a mistress and possibly not even make love, or to proceed quickly to the act and move on, picking the flower and leaving the fruit. *Amis, ki est li meulz vaillans: / Ou cil ki gist toute la nuit / Aveuc s'amie a grant desduit / Et sans faire tot son talent, / Ou cil ki tost vient et tost prent / Et quant il ait fait, si s'en fuit, / Ne jue pais a remenant, / Ains keut la flor et lait le fruit?* The courteous lady (Matthew) seeks to persuade with descriptions of tenderness, but the man (Ambrose) is too keen on his own argument to listen to hers.

As Matthew sang the note before Ambrose's entrance, their eyes met. Sweet Jesu. Ambrose responded in his soft baritone, playing the part of the lusty, sardonic knight. Their voices shaped a dance of persuasion and arrogance, the lady remaining sweet, the man stubborn and certain of his right to pluck and run, until he insisted on cutting her off and having the last word.

As they began, the room went coldly quiet, but after one lewd comment the rest of the performance was punctuated by bawdy commentary. When a flourish made clear that Ambrose had won the argument, the song was met with shouts, stamps, and whistles, and audible sighs from the ladies. The players took up the tune as they were led out of the hall to their quarters for the night, leaving a promise of more delight on the morrow. Ambrose had gambled on Sir John Neville's reputation for just the sort of behavior championed by his part in the song, and he had won. God be praised.

He looked round as the company passed through the kitchen, seeking a potentially cooperative member of the household, someone who might know a place from which he might eavesdrop on the hosts of the gathering.

They were housed in the undercroft beneath the huge kitchen, sharing the space with casks of wine against the walls and salted meats hanging above them. It had been made clear that should they think to sample the wares, they could forget the generous purse they had been promised. Carl took charge, warning that pilfering would not be tolerated. He was a large man skilled with a knife, and the others, though loudly letting him know the insult cut deep, withdrew to see to their costumes for the morrow. After all, they might well be content with the barrel of ale provided them. And the cold repast. There was no need for his bullying, they muttered amongst themselves.

Ambrose wondered at how little they knew themselves. After a few tankards of ale they would find the stores irresistible. Anyone would.

He chose a corner away from the others, removed the velvet hat, and set it aside with his elegant cloak, letting his long white hair flow free. Placing his crwth on his blankets, he dusted it, then drew out the wax tablet on which he had written the lyrics composed for the occasion. Just the words – the tune was in his head and his fingers. He read it through, then set it aside to tune his instrument.

'Might we rehearse?'

Ambrose thoughtlessly touched the youth's chin, an affectionate gesture that he immediately regretted as Matthew pulled away.

'Forgive me. I was startled . . .'

Matthew shook his head. 'I should have announced my presence.' Placing a small bench near the blanket, the youth sat down, signaling that no more need be said. Ambrose was trusted.

Blessed be. Sitting cross-legged on the blanket, Ambrose plucked out the primary tune on the crwth. Matthew attended, leaning in toward the sound, nodding, pale face radiant with excitement. Softly vocalizing the notes, then adding more, exploring elaborations, playing with the tune. This was not random play. Every note suited the mode in which Ambrose had composed the piece. Where had the youth learned modes? A religious house? Curious, he tried another tune, in another mode. Frowning, fair hair falling over the pale eyes, and then a smile, and an exploration of notes rising, falling, turning back on themselves – one note out of the new mode quickly corrected with a shake of the head. Ambrose had come to realize the youth's secret, but was there more, this knowledge, the familiarity with French lyrics? He yearned to ask, but he must say nothing. A conversation might be overheard. Quietly he instructed Matthew in using elaborations only when they enhanced the lyrics. *Ah, I see.* A lift of the chin, a gesture. That gesture – how was anyone fooled? Yes, Matthew was meant to emphasize the feminine, yet what lad could do it so effortlessly when not performing?

Ambrose had noted an undercurrent amongst the players, a tension. Carl kept a sharp eye out for Matthew. Yes, the man knew. How long could he hold the illusion cast over his players? It was a wonder he'd managed thus far – for Matthew had clearly sung with them a while.

Out of the corner of his eye Ambrose noticed two of their fellows rising, ambling over toward them.

'Once through the song, Matthew,' he said. The lyrics were not as polished as Ambrose would like, but they would do. He counted on the wine flowing at tomorrow's feast – perfection would be wasted on the mighty. All they wished for were celebrations of the family's victories, their increasing power.

Matthew sang the tune with a few flourishes enhancing the piece. Perfect recall of the lyrics. Excellent.

'Well done.' Ambrose nodded to Matthew. 'Enough for tonight. Now to sleep, and rest your voice.' He nodded to the pair who had come forward. 'All our voices.'

'It is a pleasure to sing with you, Master,' said the youth.

'And with you.'

'Did you leave any ale for me?' Matthew asked the two idling nearby.

'Oh aye, and you've earned it, pretty lad,' said one. He nodded at Ambrose. 'The minstrel's taken a liking to you. Watch yourself, lad.' Though they were the danger, not Ambrose.

He shook his head as if he could not be bothered with such talk and fussed with his crwth, placing it in a soft case and setting it on his pack, then made as if to go out to relieve himself.

Once outside, seeing no one following, Ambrose doubled back, slipping into a doorway indicated by the kitchen wench who had a weakness for singers. Down the corridor to the curtained alcove, she had said. And there it was. He slipped within and pressed his ear to the boarded-up aperture.

'Ravenser? I do not think you will make much headway with him, Alexander. Thoresby's nephew – he thought to succeed his uncle. He is not likely to befriend you.'

Ambrose did not recognize the voice. He bent down to a chink in the boards, but the speaker had his back to him. A dark, well-padded jacket embroidered in bright colors, the seams picked out with silver thread.

'Yes, I had heard. My secretary tells me that Ravenser is well thought of amongst the clergy in the city . . .' Such a nasal quality to the archbishop's voice. No wonder he railed against his destiny. Was it not enough that his appearance lacked pleasing proportions and grace? He was cursed with beady eyes, a wide nose, and a tiny mouth in a broad, jowly face, his body thick and graceless. He moved with a ponderous, flat-footed gait. An impressive voice might have done much to mitigate such misfortune, especially paired with a composed delivery, as if all the world were his to rule. A good actor might create a powerful illusion. But Alexander Neville had no such talents.

'A word in the right ear . . .' The mystery man spoke in a soothing tone. Here was one who knew how to shape the air round him. 'You know how it is done. Be at ease. We have not brought you so far only to abandon you.'

'Brought me?' A bleat that hurt Ambrose's ears. What horror to have that amplified in the soaring spaces of York Minster. Pray God the man did not speak above a whisper

in that sacred place. And might he never attempt to sing . . .
'Do you insult me?'

A dramatic sigh. 'I remind you that you are nothing without
the support of the family, Alexander. Nothing.' The voice was
cold. 'Do not trip over your pride. Our purpose is to unite the
North in protecting the realm against all that threatens.'

'You have made yourself plain. But do not forget, I have
the ear of the Holy Father.'

'Mark me, he will soon test you, tug on your strings to
see whether you dance to his measure. Remember to whom
you owe your allegiance – your kin. And King Edward.'

'He is the Holy Father.'

'And he favors the French. Never forget that. Now. What
has your secretary learned of the dean of York Minster?'

'Cardinal Grimaud regrets that he is unable to make the
journey north in winter. But we met at Westminster. He seems
indifferent. A proud, stubborn man . . .' A petulant sigh. 'God
save me from these overbearing clerics.'

A startled laugh that the man hardly bothered to mask with
a cough. 'And the sub-dean acting as dean in his absences?
John of York, I believe.'

'Absences? I am not certain the cardinal has ever set foot
in the city.'

'You grow tedious. The sub-dean? Dean John?'

A petulant scowl. 'A simple mind, easily dominated. You
grow tedious as well. I am more concerned about Jehannes,
Archdeacon of York. He presents himself as a gentle, unworldly
man. But I am warned that one does well not to underestimate
him. He sounds a pious bore.'

'And the lay men of influence? This John Gisburne might
be of use. Yet having met him – I would prefer a more palat-
able man in our confidence. He is the sort to make an enemy
with each breath. And it appears he considers himself above
the law. Someone needs to teach him his place. What did
Prince Edward's man Antony of Egypt think of him?'

'My secretary Leufrid found Antony inscrutable. He was
courteous to Gisburne, no more, no less.'

'What of the late John Thoresby's spy, the one-eyed
Welshman?'

'Archer? He's now captain of bailiffs for the city. And
Prince Edward's man in the city, his eyes and ears in the
North, they say. He entertained Antony in his home. Geoffrey
Chaucer as well.'

Owen Archer's position with the prince was precisely why
Ambrose had come north.

'I am aware Archer has the favor of the prince's household.
What do we know about him?'

'The city sought his protection. He's said to be a clever
bloodhound, still a fine archer – he was captain of archers for
Henry Grosmont before the loss of an eye, then his spy.
Grosmont educated him to the latter position before he died.
By all accounts he's Gisburne's nemesis. At some point the
merchant crossed Archer and all the city awaits the day
Gisburne is made to pay, and pay dearly.'

'So Archer has enemies.'

'Other than Gisburne?' Ambrose wished he could see black
jacket's face, read the expression that lit up Alexander's face.
'Oh. Yes, I see.'

Ambrose settled himself to hear more. His distasteful
interlude with the kitchen wench had been worth it.

As the company proceeded into the hall Ambrose cringed
at the fog of greasy smoke in the great space, the rising
odor of sweet wine, roasted meats, and sweat. And the noise!
It was not the worst he had experienced, but that did not
make the prospect any less daunting. To sing with his
lungs filling with smoke – he would suffer tomorrow. At
least he need not fret about the rough lyrics – few would
hear them.

His heart lightened when Carl directed them to ascend to
a gallery overlooking the feast. Closer to fresh air, at a slight
distance from the fire and the noise. Better. The steep wooden
steps were a challenge with the instruments, the man before
him stumbling, almost knocking the crwth from his grasp.
Ambrose's quick reflex saved it.

'How will they hear us?' Matthew whispered as Ambrose
joined the youth.

'Those who wish to will find a way.'

And, lo, as soon as the musicians struck up a jig, faces lifted to see whence came the sound.

'Ah,' breathed Matthew.

'Just so,' said Ambrose, staring directly into the eyes of Sir John Neville, Knight of the Garter, Admiral of the North, Steward of the King's Household, he of the gorgeous silver-seamed jacket. So the archbishopric of York was that important to the family that Alexander's eldest brother took time away from his military activities and duties at court to attend this meeting. Suddenly what Ambrose had conceived as a fortuitous opportunity to gather a tidbit of gossip that might be of use had become a far more dangerous ploy than he had intended. John Neville's cool gaze chilled him. Ambrose did not recall having been introduced. But he was glad the velvet hat covered his long, lustrous white hair, just in case Neville had seen him at the French court. He had certainly heard much about Neville there. He, in turn, might have heard of Ambrose, who was known as the silver-haired troubadour. God help him. He was glad he had decided to play an instrument that had been of no interest in France, the Welsh crwth.

The song ended, and the players fanned out to make room for Ambrose and Matthew in the center. Lifting his crwth, Ambrose teased out the melody, giving Matthew the pitch.

The pure voice rose up in praise of the Nevilles, Ambrose answered. John Neville's eyes crinkled in delight.

God be praised. Perhaps that was all his concern, that the entertainment be suitable and pleasing to the ear.

While his companions busied themselves preparing for the performance, Ambrose had gathered the belongings he would not be needing and taken them to a spot he had found beside the gatehouse. A break in the wall, narrow, but he was still slender and agile, God be thanked. An overturned barrow covered his pack. Now, as the players were settling for the night, having drunk deeply and eaten their fill, Ambrose lay awake fully dressed, even to his boots, listening to the rustling, the stumbles and slurred apologies. He might simply slip out as if heading out to relieve himself but for his instrument and the blankets. So he waited.

The danger lay in waiting too long, and he must have fallen
asleep, for he came alert of a sudden, heart pounding, with a
vague sense of someone thrashing about. Was that a cry? He
lay still, holding his breath. There. A muffled cry, a grunt of
warning. He sat up and blinked to adjust to the unhelpful light
from a torch by the door, flame dancing in a strong draft.
Someone hunched over Matthew's pallet. Real? He quietly
collected his things, donned his hat, and rose, gathering his
cloak about him. His instrument case securely hanging from
his shoulder, he crept toward the sound, and, seeing that he
was right, reached out and yanked the naked man away from
Matthew, tossing him aside. Ambrose would never be considered strong, but he knew how to make use of surprise, and
the awkwardness of a swollen cock. A loud thud, a curse, then
silence.

'Get your things and come with me,' Ambrose whispered,
offering Matthew a hand.

'I can manage,' the youth muttered, scrambling up, gathering
blankets, clothes, a pack, turning back with a curse for the
boots that had been kicked away.

'I have your boots. Hurry!'

They picked their way among the players, some cursing,
others merely turning over and resuming their snores. No one
seemed to be chasing them. Near the door, Ambrose noted
Carl was not on his pallet. It had not been him attacking
Matthew, so where was he?

At the door to the kitchen garden, Ambrose gestured for
Matthew to stay back while he checked for a guard – or Carl,
then took Matthew's things and proffered the boots. 'Best to
start out well shod. It will be a long walk.'

Bending over the boots, the youth glanced up. 'You mean
to go with me?'

'I planned to leave tonight. You are merely an unexpected
encumbrance.'

'I can manage.'

'We waste time. Come.'

As they began to move across the courtyard two figures
approached from the fields, a bare-assed man tottering after a
woman who yanked him along by his member. Carl and the

assistant cook. Ambrose felt a laugh rising and covered his mouth as he backed farther into the shadows. As the two passed nearby, Ambrose felt the heat of the woman's fury. Near the door to the kitchen she let go of Carl. He stumbled forward. She kicked him aside and disappeared within. Carl groaned. Grabbing Matthew's hand, Ambrose hurried on. Clouds hid the moon, forcing them to move with care down the paths. But Ambrose had planned for it, walking the route several times, learning the contours, the obstacles – like the thorn hedge.

Near the gatehouse he froze in mid-step as a guard called out a challenge. But it proved to be directed at a rider who approached the gate from the road. God watched over them. The distraction would give them the cover they needed.

A forceful knock on the door. 'My lord!'

Sir John kissed the wench tenderly – a woman bedded is a dangerous creature should she feel used and discarded. 'Forgive me, my beauty.'

With a sigh, she slipped from beneath the sheets. John groaned at the vision, her curves caressed by the candlelight, in full view as she wrestled her simple gown over her head, dropping over that lushness. She blew him a kiss and scampered out, trading places with Pit, the man he had set to watch the players, especially the minstrel in the squirrel-lined cloak and robe. The elegance of the clothing had been his mistake, and his choice of instrument. Few played the crwth. Fewer yet with such a voice, and clothes unmistakably the work of tailors for the French court. And the intensity with which he had regarded those gathered in the hall – Sir John included. He'd not needed the curvaceous kitchen wench to tell him of the man's interest in hearing 'what the nobles said amongst themselves' to know he was a spy. But who had hired him? At one time or another Ambrose Coates had been rumored to be the lover of every man in the French court – and a few women. Or was he now spying for someone in the English court? Of late John had been on the Scottish border, too far afield to stay current with court gossip.

Pit slouched to the bedside, keeping his eyes averted as if fearing he might see his lord's nakedness.

'You had best have news after so rudely interrupting my pleasure,' John growled, more for the sport of seeing the man even more discomfited. Whence came these fine sensibilities in hired brutes? It was ever the same, a taste for all but a certain vice. Pit feared naked flesh, and pleasure. Pain, blood, splintered bones, guts spilling from sliced velvet, gouged-out eyes – nary a flicker of unease. But show him a woman's bare breast or a cock wet with sex and the man blanched and bowed his head.

'The minstrel and the fair-haired lad, milord. They have gone. Left all the rest asleep.'

'Have they?' John smiled to himself. 'You know what to do.'

'Alive?'

'Alive if you catch him on the road. I should like to know who sent him. But if you follow him into a town or guarded manor . . .' John paused, considering how likely it was that Pit and his fellows could be discreet. 'If you might be seen dragging him away, dispatch him in the shadows, leave him to die.'

'And the lad?'

The beautiful youth with the voice of an angel. Were the pair lovers? If so, the youth might know much, might be able to carry out the minstrel's mission.

'The lad likewise.'

Pit managed to bow even lower as he backed from the room.

'Take as many men as you see fit. And some horses – they took no horses, I presume?'

'No, my lord,' Pit mumbled at the door. 'They were on foot.'

'Do not disappoint me.'

'May God bless this mission.'

John almost laughed out loud. 'God has little to do with such work. Get on with it!'

When the door closed he lay back, contemplating the bed curtains. The kitchen wench was a delicious piece of flesh, but now, should the minstrel be found dead and she hear of it . . . He would order her death on the morrow. Tempting to send for her and enjoy her once more before his man took her away. Or he had that slow-acting poison . . . Rising, he knocked on the door, and when his manservant answered he told him to send for the wench. 'And bring more wine.' She would find her death in a fine claret. A kindness.

TWO

A Fell Night, An Angel's Voice

York

At the dying of the year the minster stonemasons worked a short day, heading for home as clerics gathered in the choir to chant the prayers of nones. As soon as the yard no longer rang with the hammering of chisels on stone and the dust settled, the poor crept out of their makeshift hovels on the north side of the great minster to light their fires against the deepening dark.

Brother Michaelo stepped out of Archdeacon Jehannes's house. In honor of the first snow of the season he wore an old cloak over the tattered habit he donned to perform his penitential service, his feet clad in boots rather than his customary sandals. He need not add frostbite to his penance. In one hand he carried a horn lantern, in the other a basket of food for the poor. Already the minster's immense bulk obliterated any last glimpses of the fading sun, but as Michaelo moved along the great windows the sanctuary lights over the altars in the chapels and in the choir lit his way, those with stained glass casting odd colors on the muddy snow. His exhaled breath swirled round him, a fragile cloud, and by the time he hurried up to the west door he was shivering. He jerked his head in a cursory nod to a man standing without as he swept past him into the relative warmth of the nave. At least here he was not battered by the rising wind. He stood still, closing his eyes, listening to the last notes of the psalms. A momentary silence ensued, then the rustling and shuffling of the men departing through the door of the lady chapel.

As he turned toward the lady altar, Michaelo noticed two men standing in the south aisle, heads bent close as they talked. One of them struck an arresting figure with flowing white hair and clothes cut with attention to the drape of the fabric in the French fashion. He had graceful hands with long fingers; in one hand he clutched pale leather gloves, lightly resting the other on his companion's shoulder. The other man was so enveloped in a heavy cloak, with a hat covering his head beneath his hood, that Michaelo did not recognize him until he shook off the hood to scratch his ear. Ronan, who had been Alexander Neville's vicar. As with a vicar whose canon passed away, he was secure in his position for life, and sought after by clerics from the powerful to the humble desiring his knowledge of their new archbishop. He could afford such a warm cloak, though it was far more modest than his companion's.

No doubt they were discussing preparations for the enthronement. All the minster close was obsessed with plans for the event. The elegant one seemed to be reassuring Ronan, now and then looking round, as if expecting someone. Or did he not wish to be overheard? He need not worry. Michaelo saw no one about at the moment, too far from the crowd in the transept and the clerics in the choir, and he himself could hear nothing. Ronan's companion was not familiar – Michaelo would not forget such a man, and yet whenever he turned a certain way a memory stirred. Long ago. Perhaps . . . Michaelo closed his eyes, attempting to catch the memory, but already it was gone, and the elegant one was rising with a grace that bespoke a much younger man. It was then that the two men did something most peculiar. Each removed his cloak and held it out to the other, their expressions solemn, though it seemed Ronan's mouth turned up a little as he handled the costly cloak. He certainly had the better part of the exchange. Now the elegant one bowed and strode away, Ronan's dark sheepskin-lined cloak billowing round him as if he might take flight.

The vicar fussed with his acquisition, burying his face in the fur, then looking up with such pleasure Michaelo guessed it was perfumed. As he moved to leave, the vicar glanced down at the floor, bent to pick something up, and turned as if to call to his companion. But the stranger was gone. With a shrug, the vicar turned the object round in his hands – soft, yielding, a scarf or a hat, then shrugged and removed his plain felt hat and replaced it with what he'd rescued from the floor. He took care with the placement of the dark velvet hat, winding its trailing piece of velvet round to secure it in place. Smiling to himself, the clerk tucked his discarded hat under his arm and shuffled away. Was there a flicker of movement toward the transept? No, Michaelo must have been mistaken. The clerks and others who worked in the north transept were gone for the day.

Shrugging at the odd encounter, Brother Michaelo continued to the lady altar, where he knelt with a sigh of contentment, bowing to his devotions.

Michaelo sat with the dying Mary Garrett through the night until a lad returned with the healer Magda Digby. A light shone in Mary's eyes at the sight of Dame Magda, and she cried out her relief, humbling Michaelo. For all his prayers, he had not the gift to comfort the dying. As he stepped out into the snowy yard he heard shouts off to his right, toward the chapter house. Pulling up his hood, he turned away from the sound, bowing his head to the blowing snow as he hastened round the west front of the minster. The wind reached icy fingers into his hood, stinging his ears and freezing the lashes over his watering eyes. He tried to warm himself by imagining how he would soon sit before the fire – Anna the cook would already be up – with a cup of hot spiced wine, perhaps some fresh bread and cheese. He should fast and take communion, but as he had not slept he would compensate with a brief prayer in the minster on his way. As he changed direction he stumbled into a drift of snow beneath which something hard bruised his shins. Muttering a curse he brushed the snow away from a long wooden sledge. Left by the stonemasons, he guessed, in their haste to find shelter and warmth. Who could blame them?

Stepping through the flimsy door over the entrance to the unfinished lady chapel he faltered, caught by an unexpected sound curling within the howling wind. A voice. An angelic voice singing *Missus est Angelus Gabriel a Deo in civitatem Galilææ, cui nomen Nazareth*. An Advent hymn – appropriate, but at such an hour, and alone? He thrust back his hood so that he might gauge whence came the sound. The transept? No, that would echo and cut the immense silence of the overarching stones. This came from behind a door. The chapter house? He was hurrying in that direction when something did cut the silence – the jangle of keys on a ring approaching from the south transept. Shining his lantern to his left, he saw Theo, the precentor's man, lit by his own lantern as he hurried across toward the chapter house.

'God in heaven, what madness has descended upon us this night, a man fallen, someone singing in the chapter house. What? Who dares intrude—' Theo halted, peering at Michaelo. 'Out of my way, brother,' he called, hurrying on, the keys and the rude command sacrileges in this holy place.

Michaelo followed on his heels. Reaching the door of the chapter house Theo paused, breathing heavily while he bent his head to fumble with the keys.

. . . *de domo David, et nomen Virginis Maria* . . .

'You said a man had fallen,' said Michaelo. 'Who? Where?'

'From the chapter house roof. Or so it would seem. The snow did nothing to cushion his fall. Now hush. Between that bleating and your questions I cannot think.'

It seemed to Michaelo that unlocking a door that Theo locked and unlocked daily should require little thought.

'Dead?' he asked.

'Indeed.'

Ave gratia plena . . .

'Are you such a dolt you cannot appreciate such a voice? Bleating indeed.' Michaelo huffed.

'On such a night, it can only be the voice of the devil,' Theo growled as at last he managed to turn the key and push wide the door. While he crouched to retrieve his lantern, Michaelo lifted his own and stepped past him into the echoing space. Theo shouted for him to halt, but Michaelo paid no heed, continuing until his light illuminated the singer.

Now he stopped as he beheld a vision. A tall, ethereally pale youth with flaxen hair stood in the middle of the space with arms outstretched, slowly turning round and round as he sang . . . *benedicta tu in mulieribus* . . . In his right hand he held a dagger, as if warding off an attacker. Only when he faced the light did he discover his audience, going silent and still, and dropping his arms. Michaelo stepped closer, wrinkling his nose at the state of the youth's clothing – stained and torn, his face smudged, his hair wild. He stank of sweat and fear. Another step and Michaelo noticed how the hand holding the knife shook, and what might commonly repel him made him wish to protect this soiled angel. It occurred to him that if Theo believed this youth to be in Michaelo's charge he might release him without fuss. Though what he would then do with the lad, well, no time to think of that now.

'So that is where you were hiding. You have been missed.' Michaelo hoped his tone and words expressed just enough affectionate irritation. 'I pray you, if you would permit me to deal with him . . .'

Theo regarded him with distrust, then recognition. 'Brother Michaelo. I am relieved to hear you know the intruder.'

Michaelo nodded. 'You see why he forbids you to go forth after twilight without escort? And the chapter house – the dean and chapter will not tolerate such an intrusion. Come now. Your uncle awaits us.'

'But the man fallen from this very building—' Theo began.

'I assure you, this lad is no murderer,' said Michaelo. An assumption, for of course he did not know, but he sensed – perhaps it was the smell of the lad. And how would a man sing so beautifully after committing such a sin?

At first, the youth stared with mute puzzlement, then asked, 'My uncle?' Another pause. Michaelo searched for something to save the ruse, but at last the youth gave a wan smile. 'Did Master Ambrose send you? God be thanked!' As quickly as the smile appeared, it dissolved into a grimace. 'I beg your forgiveness. I was locked in. I managed to sleep a while, but I was so cold. And frightened. I remembered that Master Ambrose said a mere whisper can be heard across this space, so I hoped a song might be heard without. I thought a shout might bring armed guards, whereas a song . . .' He lifted a slender hand to his heart and bowed to them. 'I pray you, forgive my trespass.'

Spent the night here? Slept? His clothes suggested a different tale, damp, as if recently outside. On the roof? The lies gave Michaelo pause, but his instinct to protect held. He looked at Theo. 'Is it not customary to ensure this room is empty before securing it for the night?'

'I have never before found anyone within. Who is Master Ambrose?'

Michaelo held out his hand to the youth. 'A dagger offers poor protection against the dark. I will take that.'

The youth hesitated.

Michaelo stepped closer.

With a mumbled, 'I thought to protect myself,' the youth surrendered the weapon, but shaking with such violence that Michaelo caught the dagger as it fell from the slender hand.

'Protect yourself?' Theo lifted his lantern, looked round. 'I see no one else. And I don't understand. You sang for help, then meant to resist?'

'You might check up above,' Michaelo suggested to Theo.

Theo took a step back. 'I am not armed.'

'I am so cold!' The youth hugged himself.

No wonder, in wet clothing. 'Find help,' said Michaelo. 'I will see to the lad.'

'They say you now work with Captain Archer,' said Theo. 'Fetch him.'

Michaelo bristled that the man would presume to order him about. 'It is you who failed to search the chapter house before securing it for the night. See to yourself.'

'I pray you.' Beginning to slump, the youth clutched Michaelo's arm.

As he put his free arm round the youth's torso to support him, Michaelo's hand encountered the rounded breast of a young woman. God help him. He bit off an apology. The young woman continued to crumple.

'Take this.' He thrust his lantern at Theo, who took it without argument.

'Is he ill?'

'God knows,' Michaelo muttered. Remembering the sledge he had uncovered near the outer door, he thought he might assist her that far. Putting both arms round his charge, he whispered to her, 'Help me. If I ask this bumbling fool for help he, too, will discover your sex. It would go better for you if you summoned up all your remaining strength and helped me get you to safety.'

He felt her try to recover, but the effort increased her now almost continual tremors and her flailing attempts to gain a footing worked against his efforts.

'I pray you, do not fight me. If you can help me get you to the outer door, there is a sledge. I can pull you to safety.'

Apparently she understood and eased her struggle, leaning into him. With her feeble assistance he managed to get her across the transept. How was it she'd sung with such strength when now she could barely keep her eyes open? Had he imagined it? Was Theo right, this was the devil's work? In his heart, Michaelo did not believe it. He must believe God was working through him. Or her.

They were heading down the aisle along the choir when Theo caught up, panting, his keys clanging. 'I heard something within. The sound of someone on the steps.'

The woman gripped Michaelo's hand.

'Did you have the sense to lock them in?' Michaelo asked.

Theo said nothing.

'Fool.'

'More the fool to walk into danger unarmed.'

'How is locking the door walking into danger?'

With a sniff, Theo demanded to know where Michaelo intended to take the youth.

'To his lodgings,' said Michaelo.

'Not to his uncle?'

Michaelo cringed at his own confusion. 'Precisely.'

'This Master Ambrose?'

Michaelo was saved by the sound of the outer door opening. Two clerks bustled in, each carrying a lantern. Behind them was Master Adam, the precentor.

Theo held up the two lanterns. 'Master Adam.'

'What are you doing here?' the precentor demanded. 'Who is this?'

Michaelo and Theo interrupted each other trying to explain.

Adam waved them to stop. 'One of our vicars has been murdered and a stranger lies dead, all in the minster yard. The stranger is believed to have fallen from the roof.' He gestured up above them, then leaned close to the woman in Michaelo's arms. 'What do you know of this?'

'Nothing, God help me.' Her voice little more than a croak.

'What is wrong with you?'

'He is quite weak,' said Michaelo. 'I have all I can do to hold him upright.'

'Injured?'

'I do not know.'

'Take him to Captain Archer. Tell him to hold him under suspicion of murder.'

'Murder?' Michaelo said. 'Look how he shivers, how he can barely stand.'

Adam brushed the hair from the woman's eyes. 'So fair. Were you defending your honor, son?'

The woman hid her face in Michaelo's shoulder.

'Two men attacked him? Is that what you think?' asked Theo.

Adam stepped back, shaking his head. 'I cannot believe it of Ronan.'

Ronan. Michaelo inwardly crossed himself, remembering the exchange of cloaks. He yearned to ask if he meant that the murdered vicar was Ronan, but he dared not cause more delay. His strength was giving out. 'Theo heard someone up above,' he said. 'You would do well to investigate while I escort this lad to the archdeacon's lodgings.' Jehannes, Archdeacon of York, surely the precentor would accept his authority.

'Not there. Captain Archer's house.'

Michaelo opened his mouth to protest that Owen's children were ill, it was no time to impose on him, nor was he responsible for crimes in the minster liberty. But what was the alternative?

'Help him,' Adam ordered one of the clerks. 'Theo, check the chapter house. Now!'

With much muttering Theo handed Michaelo's lantern to one of the clerks and turned back to the chapter house.

'There is a sledge just outside the door,' said Michaelo to the clerk. 'I will pull the lad on it while you light the way.'

A nod. God be thanked he did not insist on helping carry Michaelo's charge.

Outside, he directed the clerk to the sledge and had him brush off the accumulated snow, then settled the young woman on it. Blinking against the blowing snow, Michaelo pulled up his hood, then bent to the young woman, advising her to hold onto the sides of the sledge.

The clerk warned him to step back as a group of men rushed past, lanterns swinging in their haste to follow others disappearing round the east end of the minster. Shouts echoed from somewhere in the minster yard.

Two men dead, one possibly Ronan. Had he been mistaken for the white-haired man? Michaelo crossed himself and prayed that he was not delivering a murderer to Owen and Lucie.

THREE
Sanctuary

As Owen stoked the kitchen fire he heard the maidservant stirring on her small bed behind the corner screen. Before she could ask, he said, 'Hugh's fever broke in the night. All three children are now on the mend.'

'God be praised.' Kate's voice broke with emotion.

The children's illness had spread so quickly from Gwen to Emma to Hugh that their nursemaid had fled, certain it was pestilence, the memory of nursing her mother the past summer only to lose her and her brother too recent. *I cannot bear to watch the children die.* No matter that Owen's wife Lucie, an apothecary, assured her it was catarrh, that the healer Magda Digby agreed. Lena could not be consoled. Truth be told, they had all worried that the worst might happen. But Lena's panic had silenced the rest. No one dared breathe their worry, for fear it might somehow conjure the death. Kate's tears – he now heard her weeping – were no surprise to Owen. He, too, had wept for joy.

'No need to rise just yet,' he said. 'Your mistress and the children are asleep. Only Alisoun and I are wakeful.'

Magda Digby had suggested that her apprentice Alisoun Ffulford bide with them as long as they needed her. Formerly nursemaid to the two eldest, she was a favorite. She had swept into the nursery with a basketful of remedies and treats, humming as she assisted Lucie and Owen with calm competence and singing to the children as she rocked them to sleep. The songs were familiar to Gwen and Hugh from their earlier years, inspiring comforting memories for all in the house. Gwen gamely attempted to croak along though she must all too often stop and gasp for air, unable to breathe through her swollen nose. When Emma's fever broke, her first conscious act was to giggle at the sounds coming from her big sister.

Alisoun seemed able to go without sleep for days, giving Lucie time to rest. All in the household trusted her, even Owen, who had found her difficult in the past.

But even Alisoun could not hasten the children's recovery, could not allay their worry. The dread of pestilence was ever-present. Lucie and her first husband had lost their only child to the scourge.

Hours earlier, in the haunted time before dawn, Owen had held his son, his face buried in the boy's fiery hair, praying for God to spare Hugh. 'Take me, O Lord, take me.' When the boy wriggled in his arms, Owen had tightened his grip, thinking he had gone limp and was slipping from his arms.

'Da.' The sound was little more than a sigh. But then damp fingers touched Owen's cheek. Opening his one good eye, he found his son watching him. 'Thirsty,' Hugh lisped. Was there ever such a wonderful sound as his son's voice? Ever such a tender touch?

Owen had called for Lucie, and she was at his elbow in a heartbeat, cup in hand, whispering endearments as tears fell down her cheeks.

'Is Hugh awake?' Gwen had whispered from her cot.

'Yes, my sweet,' Alisoun said. 'His fever has broken.'

A moment so precious . . .

A knock on the door startled Owen from his thoughts. Wiping both his eyes – even the sightless one shed tears – he resettled the patch over his left eye and rose, crossing the room in a few strides.

Kate slipped out from behind the screen. 'That might be Mistress Merchet with bread and ale. She's brought them every day since the children fell ill.'

Opening the door, Owen began to announce the news and stopped. It was not Bess Merchet, but Brother Michaelo and someone swathed in a cloak, leaning heavily against the monk for support.

'Forgive me, Captain,' said Michaelo, breathless.

'God's blood, Michaelo, you are not bringing sickness into our home?'

'I would not have come, but the precentor insisted you hold this poor pilgrim until—' His companion began to slide out of his grasp, the hood falling away to reveal a fair young woman.

'What madness is this?' Owen muttered as he caught her up in his arms and carried her to a pallet that Kate had already retrieved from the corner and was piling with cushions.

'Poor woman. Ale or broth?' Kate asked as she helped Owen peel away the damp cloak and remove the woman's boots.

'Brandywine, then broth.'

Owen studied the woman. Worn boots, much-mended stockings, and tunic – a man's tunic, her fair hair cut short. Her eyelids flickered now and then, and when Owen first began removing her boots she had kicked out, but his whispered reassurances quieted her. Or she was too weak to continue struggling. He noted that her stockings were surprisingly wet, the dampness elsewhere on her clothes. An icy draft reminded him of Michaelo, who still stood in the doorway.

'You do me no favor sharing the fire with the garden. Step inside and close the door. Did you walk her here?'

'No. Pulled her on a stoneworkers' sledge. I left it in the tavern yard.'

While Michaelo fussed with his boots, Owen tucked blankets around the woman and debated whether to call for Lucie or Alisoun. But his wife was finally enjoying some much-needed rest, and Alisoun had charge of the children. Kate knelt to the woman with a bowl and spoon.

'She has been passing for a man?' he asked as the monk came to crouch beside him.

'She is as you see. Captain, I would not have brought her here – your children – but her disguise fooled the others and – I sensed a desperation.'

'Hugh's fever has broken. Lucie is resting at last, as I soon hoped to be.'

'Forgive me.'

'You said the precentor says I am to hold her?'

'Master Adam. Yes.'

'Why? And by what authority?'

'It is a long story.'

Owen rose. 'Let us leave Kate to her task.' Noticing how

the monk winced as he tried to rise, Owen reached down to assist him. 'She struggled?'

'No, but she is so weak that she was of little help moving down the aisle and out of the minster. I did not want Theo or Master Adam's clerks to assist. As I said, I thought it best they continue to think her a young man.'

'The minster?' Fetching the jug of ale and bowls, Owen sat down beside Michaelo, near enough to the fire, but far enough from the young woman that they might not disturb her. 'Begin at the beginning.' He poured for both of them.

'Where to begin?' Michaelo sat quietly for a moment, then described his night with the dying woman, Magda's belated arrival, the walk home, the men's shouts, the woman's singing.

The tale raised many questions, but Owen allowed him to finish, and then said nothing for a few moments, ordering his thoughts. Difficult after days with little sleep. The men's shouts – so at least one of the deaths might have occurred before Michaelo and Theo entered the chapter house.

'Adam thinks the woman did all this? Murdered a vicar in the minster yard, entered the chapter house, climbed the steps, pushed someone off the roof, or the other way round, and then burst into song?' A clever ruse if one had the strength. But the woman could not keep her eyes open. Had she induced the stupor?

'Struggling with someone up on the roof – he implied she might have fought someone off. So fair . . .'

'You think the vicar might be Ronan? What do you know of him?'

'A piece I forgot. Before I went to Mary Garrett I saw him in the minster with a stranger.'

Owen listened with interest as Michaelo described the exchange of cloaks. Neville's vicar and a stranger. 'Was Ronan wearing the cloak when murdered?'

'I do not know. Nor am I certain it was he.' Michaelo had stared down at his cup while he gave his account. Now he sat up sharp. 'She asked if Master Ambrose sent me.'

'Ambrose?' Why did the name take him back to the description of the fine cloak? 'Tell me again about Ronan's encounter. Everything you can recall about the stranger.'

Michaelo described the flowing white hair, the cloak in detail.

'French, you thought?'

Michaelo smiled. 'Not a thought. I know the fine tailoring of my country of birth.' He was of a noble Norman family, a point of pride. 'Yet he seemed familiar. Something in the way he moved, how he gestured with his hands. Beautiful hands. One can see he takes good care of them. Pale leather gloves.'

Beautiful hands. Gloves. A man who had been in France. The name. Owen felt the familiar shower of needle pricks across his blind eye. But this morning it was hardly a premonition of trouble to come – trouble was here. And he believed he might know this Ambrose, an old acquaintance who had of late resided at the French court.

'Who is this?' Lucie spoke from the doorway to the hall.

Owen rose. 'Forgive us for waking you.'

'I heard chatter down in the street. A death at the minster. A vicar?'

'Two deaths,' said Owen. 'The vicar apparently murdered, the other fallen from the chapter-house roof.'

Lucie crossed herself and greeted Michaelo, who had risen and now bowed and apologized for the early call. Owen noticed that she did not assure him that it was never too early to call. Not a good sign. Wrapped in a heavy mantle, she had paused in the doorway, observing them with eyes bruised with worry and exhaustion. 'And our guest?' Her voice lacked warmth, as did her eyes as she joined Owen on the bench. He offered her his untouched cup of ale. She took a drink. 'Who is she?'

'We do not know. Michaelo found her locked in the chapter house.'

'Did he?' She rose, asked Michaelo to excuse them for a moment, and motioned to Owen to follow her to the hall.

As soon as the door closed behind them, she demanded he tell her what she had missed.

'You are angry,' he said.

'Not yet.'

He told her all she had missed, then waited as she paced to the garden window and stood facing out. A decade of loving her had him tuned to her moods, the clues in her posture, her breath, even where she chose to stand – or sit. When at last she turned to him he was not surprised by her stiffened jaw, the hot spark in her eyes.

'Our children are on the mend, yes, but they are weak and only beginning to heal, we have lost our nurse, we are both weary to the bone, as is Jasper, who has been sole apothecary in the shop for days while winter ailments spread through the city. Why did Brother Michaelo agree to bring her here when he knows how it goes with us? What right has a minster canon to order you to take responsibility for this woman?'

All good questions. Owen sat down on a bench at the bottom of the steps to the solar, put his head in his hands. God help him, why was he even considering sheltering the young woman?

'When I carried her in, something . . .' He shook his head. 'She is so weak.'

With a sigh, Lucie joined him. 'Mother in heaven, is this the moment you have chosen to test what Magda calls your clear-seeing?'

Was it? He thought not. '*You* are clear-seeing. God woke you to wake me from my confusion. You are right to question my judgment.' He straightened with a sigh. 'I promised nothing. Yet. But that was my intent. And now, hearing your questions, I wonder whether lack of sleep has robbed me of all wit.'

'Yet she is here, and neither of us is so cold-hearted as to send her away.' She took his hand, pressed it to her cheek, looking into his eye.

'No, though I would have it otherwise this once.'

'We would not wish to be otherwise, my love. Do you sense harm in her?'

'How can I know? She sleeps. I have not even seen her eyes.' He rested his forehead on Lucie's head a moment, searching his thoughts. There was something, but did it come from her? 'I sense a void, as if she has lost everything. Yet there is a spark in her, warmth, steadfastness. How I see this I cannot say. Nor do I know whether to trust it.'

When Lucie did not respond, Owen straightened, found her watching him with a slight smile. 'I will watch and listen, and see whether I agree with you and Michaelo.'

'Do you think he, too, senses it?'

'He would not have risked your ire if he did not.'

He wished he might scoop her up and take her to bed. His mind traveled back over the long days and nights, the pain of watching their precious children struggling for breath, the constant coughing, the nightmares. 'You must sleep.'

'You as well, my love. The time will come. For now we must return to the kitchen. Perhaps when she is dressed in something more appropriate she will seem less strange to me. If you would carry her up to my aunt's bedchamber.'

Her elderly aunt had resided with them until her death in the summer.

'Are you certain?'

'She will be safe there.'

They had barred the small window and put an outer lock on the door to keep her elderly aunt from wandering at night.

'Bless you,' he whispered as he followed her back to the kitchen.

The monk nodded by the fire. Owen need not disturb him until he had moved the woman up to the solar.

She roused a little as he lifted her. 'God help me,' she moaned.

Lucie touched her cheek. 'You are safe here. We are taking you up to a bed in our solar, next to the children's bedchamber. Sleep. Heal.'

A tear coursed from the woman's eye to her temple as she fought to open her eyes. For a breath she succeeded, gazing up at Owen, then Lucie. The palest blue. 'Who . . .?' Her eyes closed and she went limp. Owen carried her up to the small chamber, holding her until Lucie drew down the blankets, then setting her on the soft mattress.

'Go back to Michaelo, find out all that he knows. I will undress her,' said Lucie.

'Shall I send Kate up to help?'

'No need. I grew accustomed to this with Aunt Philippa at the end.'

Owen kissed her forehead and withdrew with a whispered thanks.

*   *   *

Michaelo started awake as Owen eased down beside him. 'The woman. Where—?'

'Up in the solar where she will be safe and at ease.' Owen took a long drink of ale. 'Here is the problem. I am no longer the keeper of the peace in the minster liberty. The dean and chapter still resent me for acting as such under Thoresby's charge, so I must have a care. Now if they should come to me, request my aid, I will assist them. Until then, for the safety of my family, I need to learn what I can about the young woman and why she is in York.'

Owen had of late assumed two roles, one as Prince Edward's spy in the North, and one as the captain of the city bailiffs, called on to resolve incidents requiring the skills he had honed as Archbishop Thoresby's spy – crimes of a complex and violent nature, crimes that might endanger the city at large, or the realm. Both the prince and the mayor and aldermen welcomed the dual role, as, to his surprise, did Owen. After a year of mourning John Thoresby, he had undertaken an investigation at the request of an influential family in York. He'd been startled by the ease with which he resumed the work. He had missed it. But without the authority and connections to power that the archbishop had conferred on him, he had felt at sea.

As the prince's eye and ears in the North, Owen was expected to provide regular reports to the royal household, which required a secretary. And who better for the job than the late archbishop's personal secretary, Brother Michaelo? What Owen had not expected was Michaelo's keen powers of observation.

'I pray you, tell me all that you have noted about her,' said Owen.

Michaelo took a drink of the ale he had set aside. 'She was singing a particular hymn for Advent,' he said. '*Missus est Angelus Gabriel.* That and how she holds herself – I believe that she is either a professed nun or at the least convent-educated. How she phrased the lyrics – she understood the words, took care to express the meaning. What I am trying to say is that the song has become a part of her, as if she has sung it many times. I do believe she has taken vows.'

'Do you think we can trust her?'

'I cannot say. I know too little. But it was plain when I found her in the chapter house that she was frightened. Not of me, but – someone lurking above?' He paused, as if deciding whether or not to mention something. 'She said she'd slept there, curled up, afraid, but her clothing was wet, and she had smudges of mud and perhaps blood on her face, hands – I thought she might have fallen. But I noticed nothing that might account for her sudden weakness.'

'Lucie will be able to tell us of any wounds and other injuries. She told you someone was above?'

Michaelo considered. 'No, it was Theo. He thought he heard something. But the knife. I forgot the knife.' He drew a dagger out of his sleeve and handed it to Owen.

'You forgot something like that up your sleeve?'

'I often carry things there.'

Owen studied the weapon. The wooden hilt was cracked, a small piece missing, the sharp edges not yet smoothed. 'You might find some splinters in your arm.' And might he find a piece of wood up on the roof of the chapter house? He thought it worth a look.

Michaelo's expressive brows drew together. 'Whether the danger she fears comes through this Master Ambrose she mentioned, or if he was her protector, I have no way of knowing. Nor can I say whether or not she had been up on the roof.'

'I see your point.' A man on the roof of the chapter house, a woman found inside, two such unusual incidents must be connected. And now, knowing that her clothing had been wet when Michaelo found her, it did beg the question of her part in the man's fall. 'What else have you noted about her? Is her speech that of the North?'

Michaelo raised his eyes to the ceiling as he considered. 'No. I would say the south of England. Well spoken.'

'If you are correct about her vows, an important question is why she left the nunnery. If this Ambrose is who I think he might be, and is the white-haired stranger who traded cloaks with Ronan, she did not leave for his sake. He shares your nature regarding women.'

Michaelo met Owen's gaze. 'If you are right about his identity, I would say, seeing the way he rested his hand on Ronan's shoulder, it might have been true of the vicar as well.'

So Ronan preferred to lie with men rather than women. 'That might be helpful.'

Michaelo's thin lips curved into a smile. 'Soon you will wonder how you ever managed without me.'

Though Owen grinned, he agreed. Thoresby had once referred to his choosing Brother Michaelo as his personal secretary as donning a hair shirt, a penance. And for ten years Owen had believed that to be Michaelo's worth. But in the past month he had discovered that Michaelo had been, instead, Thoresby's bloodhound. He might never have discovered the man's worth had Archdeacon Jehannes not urged him to try him out as a secretary for his correspondence with Prince Edward.

'But I cannot be much help with the woman,' said Michaelo.

'Your observations are helpful.'

'But I have burdened you.'

'Perhaps you did well to bring her here, though this is not the day I would have chosen to take in a stranger. If necessary we will find lodgings elsewhere once she is on her feet.' Owen paced to the garden window. Dawn crept close, softening the darkness, revealing a branch here, a portion of the wall that had shed the night's snow there. He wondered what animal had climbed the wall. Too small a space for a man, God be thanked. They must be alert to danger until they knew more about their uninvited guest. He turned back to Michaelo. It occurred to him that the monk himself looked as if he had not slept. 'Tell me again how you came to be in the minster before dawn.' His weary brain was not as sharp as he would like.

'I watched over Mary Garrett until Dame Magda could come to her. I was on my way to bed when I heard the men shouting, and then the singing.'

'Mary Garrett is one of the poor in the minster yard?'

Michaelo nodded.

'Did you notice anyone about?'

'I did not move from her side.'

'So Magda arrived not long before you encountered this woman and heard the shouts?'

'Yes. You are thinking Dame Magda might have noticed something as she came through the minster yard. I can escort you there.'

'You sat with Mary Garrett through the night?'

'I did.'

'You should retire to your lodgings, and some well-earned sleep.' As Michaelo assured him he often went without sleep, Owen interrupted. 'Had you expected Magda sooner?'

A sniff. 'I did. The lad I sent in the night to summon her returned alone. Said she would be delayed. She gave no reason. The boy said he'd heard another voice in her house when he knocked on the door, but she did not invite him in, so he could not see who it was. A man, that is all he knew.'

Owen closed his eye, chasing the sense of an idea gathering strength, that this Ambrose had found his way to Magda's home, and he had been the cause of her delay. If he was the man Owen knew, he and the healer were old friends. He had been one of the few people in York to befriend her son, Potter Digby. He had looked beyond her late son's odd appearance and his work as the archdeacon's summoner and noticed his voice, a strong middle range. When Ambrose and his lover needed to flee, Magda had come to their aid. His lover might have taught him how to avoid the locked gates after dusk. One who knew the tides and the mudflats might avoid waking the guards at the gates by slipping down the bank and creeping upriver along the oozing mud. A dangerous route, but if Ambrose had been desperate enough to exchange cloaks, he might risk it.

'You think to find this Ambrose at her home?' asked Michaelo.

Uncanny how quickly the monk had learned to fathom Owen's thoughts. Chilling to think there was nothing quick about it, that he had seen into Owen's mind through all the years serving Archbishop Thoresby.

'I will be disappointed if I do not find him there.' Owen rose. 'I must see if Lucie needs assistance, then we will go.'

A bow. 'I will await you here by the fire.'

*   *   *

Lucie met Owen on the landing and drew him into their bedchamber. 'One of Aunt Philippa's gowns might fit her.' Her aunt had died a few months earlier. 'She was tall.'

'Injuries?'

'After I cleaned the mud and grime from her I found fresh bruising on her wrists, her right hand, arms, shoulders, neck, chin, mouth, ankles, and legs. Grazing on one knee as if she fell on it. The back of her right hand has a darkening bruise, her knuckles are scraped, two of her fingernails are torn, one of her fingers might be sprained for it does not curl like the others. Nothing serious, but all signs of a struggle with someone much stronger than she is. The marks on her wrists and ankles suggest she was bound. There is a cut on her ankle bone that might have been caused by a knife slicing the bonds.'

'As fresh as last night?' He told her what Michaelo had said about the condition of her clothes.

'Yes. Poor woman. I did not notice anything that would suggest her attacker ravished her, but I cannot be certain.' They exchanged a pained look. 'So what now?' she asked.

'I want to talk to Magda. I have a feeling about this Master Ambrose, and, if I am right, he might have gone to her.'

'You are thinking Ambrose Coates?'

'Am I mad?'

She touched his cheek. 'We shall see.' She went over to her chest of clothes, crouching down to open it. Glancing back at him, she asked, 'If it is him, will you bring him here?'

'No. I will not risk him in our home, at least not until I know why he is here. Even then . . .'

She nodded. 'You do not have a sense of him as you do this woman.'

'I've not seen him in years.'

'The musical instruments he left behind. It would be good to give them to him. I could use the space in the workroom.'

'How did that come to mind?'

She pulled out a wool gown, then stood up, shaking it out. 'I am reminded of him whenever I tidy the workroom.'

Unable to take all his precious instruments on his flight from York, Ambrose had entrusted them to Magda Digby, who had asked Lucie to keep them safe in her workshop. Lucie did all she could to keep the workroom warm, yet not too warm, dry, yet not too dry, so it was a suitable home for the sensitive items.

He leaned against the wall, watching Lucie change into the warmer gown. 'You are going to work in the shop?' The hearth in the apothecary workroom did little to warm the small shop front.

'If Alisoun can spare me for an hour, I thought to spend a little time there. Jasper has been alone for most of the past fortnight.'

'What of our guest?'

'I will slip a sleep draught in her ale.'

'Clever.'

'The man's clothing – she runs from something.'

'Michaelo thinks a convent.'

'I would understand why a woman might do that.' Lucie had been sent to St Clement's Priory, a Benedictine nunnery outside the city walls, after her mother died. And often attempted escape. 'Once she feels at ease, which rest might afford us, she may confide in us. Tell us who she is, why she is running. From whom. From what.' She shrugged. 'Or she may remain a cipher.'

'You might warm yourself distilling some elixir to free her tongue.'

Lucie looked over her shoulder to make sure he smiled, chuckling when she saw that he did. 'If only it were so simple. So you distrust Ambrose?'

'How can I know? He has been away a long while. And you must admit he has ever attracted trouble. If this is him, he has certainly brought it this time – a man falling from the chapter-house roof, a vicar's murder, and this young woman dressed as a man, clearly having suffered an ordeal last night. I will be interested to hear what you might learn of her.'

'A riddle. I accept the challenge.' She touched his arm. 'And do consider the instruments. If Ambrose intends to work, he will need them.'

'So you trust him?'

'I did not say that.'

Owen was about to follow Lucie's lead in donning warmer clothing when he was interrupted by someone pounding on the door that opened onto Davygate. Glancing out the narrow window above it, he saw his friend George Hempe, a city bailiff, and Adam, precentor of York Minster. The chapter had wasted no time.

'Come round to the kitchen,' he called down, trying to keep his voice low. All this fuss would surely wake the children. Indeed, that they were not yet wakeful worried him. As soon as he saw George and Master Adam move on to the garden gate, Owen finished dressing and went to check on the nursery.

He found Lucie in the doorway, speaking softly to Alisoun, who held baby Emma in her arms, rocking her.

'Is she an angel?' It was Gwen's sleepy voice, and there she was, his raven-haired first-born, tugging on her mother's skirts, Alisoun softly explaining that while she was distracted with Hugh, Gwen had slipped out of bed and gone to the room in which the woman slept.

Their guest's skin pale as if carved from candle wax, her flaxen hair – he could see why his daughter thought the woman a divine being.

'How is my beloved?' Owen crouched down and held out his arms to Gwen.

She came shuffling over and hugged him tightly. 'Has she come to take Hugh to heaven?'

Lucie knelt to them, a protective hand on her daughter's back. 'No, my love, Hugh is out of danger.'

How could she be so certain? Owen prayed Lucie was right, but he still feared for his son, for all three of them.

'He is sleeping off his victory over the fever,' Lucie said. 'You shall see. The woman is our guest.' She leaned over to Owen, kissed his cheek. 'Have faith in the healers in your household, my love.'

'Forgive me. My mind believes, but my heart fears.'

She touched his scarred cheek. 'I know. But Hugh's forehead is cool, and his breathing is quiet. I am confident.'

He kissed her. 'We have visitors. Hempe and Master Adam, the precentor of the minster chapter.'

'Then you must go now,' she said. 'Find out what George and the precentor have come to ask of you.'

'Will you come down?'

'I will.' Lucie took Gwen's hand, and, with a kiss, commanded her back to bed.

'Mistress Alisoun will sing to me?' Gwen asked.

'I will indeed, Mistress Gwenllian,' said Alisoun, nodding to the two on the landing as she closed the door.

FOUR

Deaths on a Snowy Morn

'I pray you forgive this early call, Archer.' Hempe was stomping the snow from his boots on the stone step outside the door. 'There are two bodies in the minster yard, and Master Adam has requested your help. The mayor has approved.'

The precentor had perched on the bench inside the door, struggling with his boots while casting a doleful eye at Kate, who was filling a jug with ale. An important man in the chapter, responsible for the vicars choral and for the liturgy, Adam was keen on being respected in the city. Of course all here would be respectful and hospitable, but in this household a man removed his own boots unless he was unable to do so himself.

Lucie pressed Owen's hand. 'Your first official assignment as captain of bailiffs,' she whispered.

'I was not so eager as this.'

'Nor I. We may regret your decision.'

'I pray you, take my seat near the fire,' Michaelo suggested as Adam padded toward the hearth in his stockinged feet.

The precentor thanked him and sat down with a grunt. 'You are good to receive us, Captain, Dame Lucie. Brother Michaelo was just telling us of your children's illness. It is difficult to watch the little ones suffer. I will pray for them.'

'I believe we are past the worst of it, God be thanked,' said Lucie, 'but your prayers are most welcome.' She took a seat across from him.

Michaelo asked whether Theo had found anyone in the chambers above the chapter house.

'It seems he frightened someone away,' said Adam. 'They knocked him over rushing from the chapter house. Theo had no time to move out of the way. Nor did he see who it was,

A Choir of Crows 39

though he had an impression of a large man. He is in some pain – a lump on his head and a sprained arm – but he will recover. I will send one of the clerks to your apothecary for anything you would recommend, Dame Lucie.'

She asked for more information about Theo's injuries.

While they were talking, Owen joined Hempe where he stood warming his backside at the hearth.

'Not a morning I want to be abroad in the city,' said Hempe. 'Why do murderers choose the most cursed weather?'

'With the archbishop's enthronement so near . . .' The precentor paused to ensure he was heard.

'Is this about the man who fell from the chapter-house roof and a murdered vicar?' asked Owen.

'You have heard of that?' Adam glanced at Michaelo, who had moved to a bench a little away from the fire. 'Yes, of course.' His nose quivered as he closed his eyes and began again. 'The fallen stranger is now removed to the shed behind the deanery. But the other soul – it has been a fell night for us, Captain – Ronan, one of my vicars . . .'

'May God have mercy on his soul.' Michaelo's voice broke as he lowered his head in prayer.

'A fell night indeed,' Owen said. 'And you believe he was murdered, Master Adam?'

'There is some blood, though we did not investigate. We have left him lying in the snow, awaiting your study,' said Adam. 'The coroner should be there by now, but I wanted all left as it was until you have seen him. Will you come?'

Only now did he ask for Owen's help, long after sending the young woman to him. 'If the mayor has agreed, of course,' said Owen, uninterested in forcing an apology fraught with righteous nonsense. With the woman sleeping in the solar and his suspicion about 'Master Ambrose' he would not rest until he knew the truth of the night's tragedy. 'I would see both bodies.' And then the chapter house. Owen regretted that his conversation with Magda must wait, but this was more urgent.

The precentor rose. 'I am most grateful, Captain Archer.' He paused, cleared his throat. 'As long as Prince Edward would not object.'

The relief that Owen had taken on the role of captain of the city's bailiffs had lasted only so long as it took for the news to spread that he was also now Prince Edward's man. His friends knew that he straddled both worlds as a means of keeping safe all he held dear, but some saw it differently, that he had divided loyalties. 'His Grace knows and approves of my position in the city. Though I should note that the minster liberty is not the city's responsibility.'

'Peace must be restored before the nobles and ranking churchmen arrive for the archbishop's enthronement. The mayor agrees.'

'Of course. When Prince Edward's representatives arrive I will convey to them your concerns.'

'The prince is sending . . . But of course. Yes. I— Yes, I pray you, express my thanks, and that of Dean John and all the chapter.'

Owen bent to kiss Lucie. 'I will send Alfred to you,' he whispered. Alfred had been his second in command when he was captain of Archbishop Thoresby's household guard. Owen now retained him and several others to serve him in his dual role.

'To guard our house?' she asked.

'As we know nothing of the woman, I think it best. If Ambrose should come here seeking shelter . . .'

He watched her consider. 'Of course.'

Master Adam had turned to Michaelo. 'You brought the youth? Where is he?'

Seeing a benefit in letting the precentor believe their guest was a male, Owen took the question. 'He is asleep up in the solar.'

'Ah. He did seem a delicate lad. Sick, was he?'

'No stomach for excitement,' said Michaelo with a sniff.

God be thanked Michaelo caught the omission. Not that Owen meant to keep the young woman a secret, but she was an unknown.

'Do you think him capable of murder, Captain?' Adam asked.

'He was in a faint by the time Brother Michaelo appeared at my door, so I could not say. We will know more when he wakes.'

'Ah. Of course.'

Sitting down to pull on his boots, Owen suggested the others do likewise. 'You will not want Ronan lying in the snow so long.'

Michaelo perched beside him, reaching for his own boots. 'I will accompany you.'

Quietly, for his ears only, Owen suggested Michaelo follow his lead in how much to share about what they already knew, or surmised. 'I must see the bodies, hear the stories, see how it all might fit together.'

'To begin with secrets seems a precarious foundation.'

'Even so.'

'I will do as you wish.' Michaelo bent to his boots.

Hempe was giving Owen a look that said: you will explain this over an ale in the York Tavern this evening. God grant Owen had something to share by then.

In the garden their boots punctuated the early morning hush, crunching and squeaking in the wet snow. Owen noted the slight warming of the air, not his ally in studying tracks in the snow, though better than a dry, frigid wind blowing what had fallen into drifts. Trees shed the weight of the night's storm, branches creaking overhead, showering them with snow as they passed beneath. Michaelo had fetched the sledge from the tavern yard and dragged it behind him. Before fastening the latch of his garden gate, Owen gazed back at the snow-laden linden, a grand old tree, the children's favorite. *God grant my children long, fruitful lives.*

Beyond St Helen's churchyard the men were able to walk four abreast, the street almost deserted with the snow, cold, and the early hour. The light was just enough now to distinguish colors, though not subtleties. Owen enjoyed the chill, refreshing after his sickroom vigil.

He asked Master Adam what he knew so far.

'Just before dawn a clerk stumbled over a body in the snow, in the shadow of the chapter house. As I was praying over him, a servant came upon Ronan lying in a drift by the gate of the chancellor's house.'

'Whose servant?' Hempe asked.

'The chancellor's. Master Thomas's kitchen help.'

'What else can you tell me about the body, besides some blood?' Owen asked.

'His face' – Adam paused in the street, eyes wide with the memory – 'such terror. Perhaps some bleeding at the nose? Some bruising?' He shivered and resumed his pace. 'I left two clerks to watch that no one disturbed the ground near Ronan, then went at once to the mayor to see about engaging you.'

'You woke the mayor?' Owen asked.

'He is as keen as we are to make a good impression on the Nevilles. All Alexander's kin will attend the enthronement, you can be sure. Neither the city nor the minster want them to hear rumors of a murderer loose in York.'

They would not be the only noble family descending on the city. This trouble might be but the first incident of many with a full complement of the powerful soon biding within the walls, a darksome prospect. He wondered which of the prince's emissaries would attend. Geoffrey Chaucer? Perhaps. More likely Owen's friend Dom Antony. Or Sir Lewis Clifford, a nobleman to deal with an ambitious clan.

'I need a list of all those who represented our new archbishop when he was a canon here, who worked for him,' said Owen.

'He was seldom in residence,' said Adam. 'But I see your point, Ronan was Neville's vicar. He would have had clerks advising him on matters that needed his attention. I will enquire.'

Owen debated whether or not it was time to divulge what he knew about Ronan's encounter with the white-haired stranger. He would not share his idea about the stranger's identity. If it was Ambrose Coates, he must know his purpose in returning to York from France before he could decide whether or not he was still someone who deserved his trust, whether or not he was a threat to the city or the realm. Ambrose's longtime lover Martin Wirthir shifted his allegiances with ease, and had powerful enemies in the realm, including at the royal court. King Edward's mistress Alice Perrers, for one. Owen must tread with care. 'When did you last see Ronan?'

'Master Thomas saw him last evening, in the minster nave, speaking with a stranger,' said Adam. 'French, from the style of his cloak, his long white hair. Ronan now wears that very cloak. Curious, is it not?'

'How do you know that about the cloak?' Owen asked.

'Thomas came out to see what was amiss. Saw Ronan lying there. He recognized the cloak.'

'What are we to make of that?' Hempe muttered. 'Chancellor sees him in the minster, then the man is murdered outside his gate in that cloak.'

What indeed. 'An odd twist,' said Owen. 'I did not know Ronan. What can you tell me about him?'

'Unlike most of our vicars, local men, many from St Peter's School, Ronan came to us from Oxford,' said the precentor. 'Recommended to us by Alexander Neville.' A shrug. 'He held himself above his fellows.'

'Resented?' Hempe asked.

'Not so much that his fellows would harm him, if that is what you are asking. But I did not often encounter him in the company of others.'

'Which is why the chancellor noted seeing him with the Frenchman in the minster last night?' asked Hempe.

'Now that you mention it, yes.'

'Did he live with the others in the Bedern?' Owen asked. The vicars choral had their own compound in a section of the minster liberty, now boasting a sheltered cloister and a fine refectory.

'He did. I can have someone escort you to his lodgings.'

Owen thanked him. 'And what of our jurisdiction? Are the city bailiffs free to go about the minster liberty?'

'As I sent for you I can hardly restrict you. Though if it is possible to limit the numbers, perhaps Hempe and whatever assistants you require, I would be grateful.' Master Adam rubbed his arms, as if comforting himself. 'Mourning our brother, preparing for Archbishop Neville's enthronement – we are in danger of forgetting our purpose, our prayers.'

Prayers. That was the least of Master Adam's problems in Owen's opinion, but he agreed to limit the number of men involved. As did Hempe.

At the minster gate, the guard reported seeing no strangers come through.

'What of other guards? None around the minster at night? Or near the homes?' Hempe asked.

'We've not seen the need to guard the minster at night,' said the precentor. 'Perhaps we have been unwise.'

'At such a time, with the preparations for the enthronement, valuables being placed in the building, vigilance is essential,' said Owen.

'Yes, I do see,' Adam murmured.

'I will loan you some men for the nonce,' Hempe offered. 'Until we know what happened.'

'More upheaval,' the precentor sighed.

'Not if we can prevent it,' said Owen.

Adam cleared his throat, nodded brusquely. 'Yes, of course. I would be grateful.'

As they passed the minster, morning prayers were in progress. Michaelo deposited the sledge where he had found it, at the door to the lady chapel.

'Once you have shown me the body, feel free go to your prayers,' said Owen. 'I know it is your office.'

'A kind offer, but no, I charged another with the task. I would see this through until Ronan can be removed to the Bedern.'

They cut behind the minster toward the chancellor's house as the first rays of sunlight shone between the buildings of the Bedern. Almost at once, a fog began to rise from the freshly fallen snow as the light met the cold.

The vicar's body had sunk into the bank of snow and was now only partially visible near the gate to the chancellor's house. Owen sent the pair standing guard to find a plank onto which the body might be moved. As he had anticipated, the earlier blowing snow had covered any clues as to whether Ronan had been attacked here or elsewhere, and, if the latter, whether he'd been carried or dragged. Master Adam could not recall seeing any footprints or signs of dragging when he had viewed the body earlier.

'I will have one of my men keep watch as the day warms,' said Owen. 'As the snow melts it might reveal lightly covered prints.'

'I see why you are valued,' said Adam.

Owen had learned that as a child in Wales, but he did not correct him. 'Did you reach the man fallen from the chapter house soon after he fell?' he asked.

'Yes. Even in this cold he was still warm,' said Adam.

'And you were summoned here shortly after that?'

'I had time to say but a few prayers over the fallen man. It could not have been long.'

'So Ronan might have been the first to die,' said Hempe. 'Was he still warm as well?'

'I removed my gloves to bless him and say prayers . . .' The precentor frowned down at his feet. 'Not so cold as to make me think he had been out in the snow for long, but not so warm as the other. I regret I cannot be more precise.'

'Anything you noticed is helpful,' Owen assured him.

When the men returned with a board Owen and Hempe helped them place Ronan's body on it. In the process the cloak fell open. Blood soaked the squirrel lining over the chest. Owen crouched to examine the corresponding wound. He had been stabbed through the heart.

Once the body was settled, those gathered stood with heads bowed, their breath rising like smoke about their heads, as Master Adam said a prayer. Owen was about to give the order to take Ronan to the deanery when someone approached from the chancellor's property.

It was Master Thomas himself, his long gown caught up in a belt so he might pick his way through the snow. The chancellor greeted all but the two clerks. 'You are welcome to bring him into the house while we send for a cart to carry him to the chapel in the Bedern.'

After Owen and the precentor agreed to the plan, the chancellor stepped over to the body and bowed his head, whispering a prayer.

'To look at him, one would guess he had lain down in the snow to sleep,' Master Adam said as the chancellor turned away.

Hardly, thought Owen. Adam had been right about the bloodied nose, the bruising.

'He would never be such a fool,' said Thomas.

Spoken with some emotion. Was he Ronan's friend, or more?
Owen glanced at Michaelo, who was studying the chancellor
with interest.

'Had he cause to come to your home this morning?' Owen
asked.

'At this hour?' Thomas looked at him askance. 'He would
not be so bold.'

'Unless he sought help,' Hempe suggested. 'Would he have
felt confident you would open the door to him in need?'

The chancellor blinked. 'I had not considered that. I would
turn away no one in such a circumstance. He would know
that. But your house is just beyond, Adam.'

Too eager to distance himself? Michaelo met Owen's eye,
raised a brow.

Hempe asked again whether he had been warm to the touch.

'Touch him? No. And in any case I was wearing gloves.'

So he had not rushed out the door unprepared. 'Were you
on your way out?' Owen asked.

'Why do you ask?'

'The gloves.'

'The cold is unkind to aging bones, Captain.' A stiff smile.
'Shall we move inside?'

The precentor had been shifting from foot to foot and
huddling deeper into his cloak. 'Bless you, Thomas, it is cold
out here.'

Little came of the talk in the chancellor's hall, where they
huddled round a brazier to warm themselves. The chancellor
and the precentor seemed most keen to lay the trouble at each
other's feet. Thomas did not seem to connect the 'Frenchman'
with anyone in particular, but Owen sensed the chancellor
knew who might want Ronan dead.

Taking his leave of him for now, Owen reviewed with
Michaelo all that he had noticed about the body so that the
monk might record it when he returned to his lodgings. The
stab wound, the injuries on the face suggesting a broken nose,
the ice on the front of the hat. As if he had been pushed face
down in the snow, then rolled over and stabbed. Whoever
stabbed him knew how to do it, and where.

'I cannot think of anyone in the minster liberty likely to be experienced with stabbing a man through the heart,' said Michaelo. 'Perhaps a guard?'

Owen approached the precentor, who was talking with Hempe. 'Any former soldiers among the vicars? Or in service here in the liberty?'

'One or two guards,' said the precentor. 'But I cannot think why any of them would attack Ronan.'

Master Adam led them to the deanery garden, where the other body had been laid out in a storage shed behind the kitchen. Looking at the damage to the head, Owen guessed the man's neck had snapped on impact, killing him at once. A blessing of a sort. The man was short but muscular, younger than Owen, mid- to late twenties. His hands were calloused and scarred, his nails jagged, dirty. Yet he seemed a tidy man, his thatch of brown hair trimmed with care, face shaved, his clothing well made, a leather jerkin beneath a padded jacket and heavy wool cloak, good boots, with wear from chafing caused by riding. No marks of livery, but when Owen pulled up the shirt, the scars on the torso were those of a soldier or guard. This was no traveling merchant. All this he shared with Michaelo, Hempe leaning close to catch it.

'I don't like the look of him,' said Hempe.

'Nor I,' said Owen. 'He would have had the strength to be Ronan's murderer. But the timing troubles me.' He handled the man's dagger, testing the balance, appreciating the quality. 'Well crafted. He fell with his weapon sheathed. No time to draw it,' he noted to Michaelo. It was not his dagger Michaelo had taken from the young woman. Glancing up at the precentor, who had been drawn aside by the servants guarding the body, 'Now the blood's washed off his face, do you know him?'

Adam sent his clerks off and returned his attention to Owen, his expression markedly less officious. 'Know him? No, Captain. Nor can I guess what business he had in the chapter house. Or how he gained access.'

'So the door would have been locked.'

'The clerk assigned to the evening rounds yesterday says he found the door unlocked and rectified that. We have warned the masons time and again to ensure that they have locked the door behind them.' The stonemasons at work on the lady chapel used some of the chambers above the chapter house to store tools and sketch plans.

'When would the evening check occur? Shortly after the sun set?' Which was about the time Michaelo recalled witnessing the exchange of cloaks.

'An hour or two after that. Sunset is so very early in Advent.'

'What about Theo? Had he locked the south door behind him when he came to investigate the singing?'

'Forgive me. I did not think to ask. But I will.'

Thanking him, Owen turned to Hempe. 'After I walk through their spaces up above, I would have some of them look to see if they find anything amiss. Care to join me?'

'Of course.'

Turning back to the body, Owen opened the man's mouth – gingerly, one side of the jaw crushed – and sniffed for any telltale scent of poison. Trouble breathing of a sudden, rushing up to the roof for air, becoming dizzy, falling . . . But he smelled nothing untoward.

'Services have begun for the day,' the precentor said at his back. 'You will not disturb them?'

Owen turned. 'You sent the lad to me, then went to the mayor to request my help. Have you changed your mind?'

With an apologetic shake of the head, Adam blessed them and asked God to guide them in their search.

'Remember the list of those who worked with Ronan,' said Owen. 'And whether Theo locked the door behind him.'

'Of course.'

As they left the dean's garden, Owen asked Michaelo for his impression of Master Adam.

'Risen above his capabilities, and therefore unbending in the rules as he understands them. Desperate for your help yet fearful lest you wrest control of his charges. He will do what he can, but with much complaint.'

Hempe chuckled.

'And the chancellor?' Owen asked.

'He fears what you will learn about him in regard to Ronan. I hesitate to say this—'

'I want to hear all that came to mind, Michaelo.'

'I sensed no surprise about Ronan meeting a violent death.'

'Do you think he might provide names?'

'I believe he knows far more than he is willing to share.'

Hempe grunted. 'Shall I collect him?'

'On what grounds?' asked Owen. 'That we sense there is much he is not telling us?'

Brother Michaelo bowed. 'I will deliver my report this evening, Captain.'

'Tomorrow. You need sleep.'

The monk bowed again and took his leave.

Watching him gliding away through the melting snow, Hempe said, 'I would never have believed you would accept his opinion on anything.'

'Nor would I.'

'So what changed your mind?'

'Realizing that what I took as Thoresby's insight benefited from his secretary's keen observation. Better to have it working for me.'

'Do you like him?'

'Does it matter?'

A chuckle. 'Not as long as he stays away from the York Tavern.'

'Agreed.' In truth, Owen could not imagine Michaelo having any interest in frequenting a common tavern.

They approached the masons' lodge, where Hempe had stationed a man to talk to the stoneworkers as they arrived for the day's work in the minster yard. At this time of year only the most skilled were retained, with a few apprentices to fetch and carry.

'Have any noticed strangers lurking about the past few days?' Hempe asked his man.

Blowing his hands, as if to remind his boss that he had been out in the cold all morning, the man shook his head. 'Most say they pay no heed to folk coming and going as long as they keep clear of the work in the lady chapel and stay out of the lodge. No one's bothered them of late.'

'Most say. Someone said otherwise?' Owen asked.

'Young one there says he felt someone watching him yesterday and early this morning when he came in.'

Owen walked over to the youth in the dusty hat who had been watching them.

'Hire me. I would be more help than that cotton-eared cur.'

'Where was the watcher?' Owen asked as Hempe joined them.

'More than one.' The lad pointed to a part of the minster roof, and on the ground behind the lady chapel.

'They were there this morning?' Hempe asked.

'Only one. On the ground.'

'You are happy here in the stoneyard?'

A sigh. 'I want to carve faces. But it takes years.'

Owen grinned. 'You sound like my son when he became apprentice to my wife. But his duties have quickly become far more to his liking.'

'If you decide that chasing down those who break the peace sounds better than helping to build this great minster, come and find me,' said Hempe. 'You have been helpful.'

The lad beamed as they headed toward the lady chapel. Beneath the overhang they found that the melting snow coming off the roof in icy chunks obliterated any sign of watchers.

Owen continued on round the corner and through the door. The activities of the day had begun in earnest within, the chapter at prayer in the choir, canon lawyers and their clerks at work in the transept, priests saying masses in the nave chantry chapels. Another one of Hempe's men guarded the door to the chapter house.

'Any activity?' Hempe asked.

'Clerks curious to hear more about the deaths, a mason wanting access to his tools, accused us of keeping them from their work. I told him to see you, Captain.'

'He had no key?'

'We were told not to let anyone past until you said so.'

'Welcome news,' said Hempe.

'Good man,' said Owen. 'Now if you will open the door.'

'No need, Captain.' He stepped aside. 'It's not locked while a guard is present.'

'I trust you will ensure that it is not left unattended, not even for the moment it might take to step outside and relieve yourself?'

A blush. God help them. 'Yes, Captain.'

Within, morning light flooded the circular room, though it was as cold as the rest of the vast interior of York Minster. Access to the upper reaches was by a small door to the left inside the main entrance, the stone steps narrow, unlit. 'We need your man's lantern.'

Hempe fetched the light. 'What are we looking for?'

'Other than a small chunk of wood out of the handle of a dagger, anything that might suggest a struggle, someone lurking a long while – candle wax, fresh piss.'

'Stonemasons piss elsewhere?'

'I said fresh.'

'Right. Whose dagger? The fallen man's had no chip.'

Owen told him of the dagger Michaelo had taken from their guest, moving off before he could ask more questions.

The steps opened onto a large area surrounding heavy wooden beams supporting the ceiling below. Colder here, his breath now smoking. Owen threw an end of his cloak over his shoulder and crouched to light the floor. Recently swept, and done well. Lighting a corner he saw that the sweeper had reached there. He doubted that last night's intruder would be so thorough. 'The masons are a tidy lot.'

'So whatever we find, it likely belongs to the lad or the man who fell.'

Owen said nothing as he moved farther and crouched again. He repeated that all the way to where the ladder led up to the roof. Almost at the bottom of the ladder, he found the piece of wood near the archway. Standing up, he searched the stone of the arch, and found a fresh scar – with a dark smudge that might be blood, at about the height he expected. The hand that drew the knife had been grabbed and slammed into the stone to release it. Owen recalled Lucie's description of the woman's right hand. So she had tried to defend herself?

'Found something?' Hempe asked. 'Connecting the lad to what happened up here?'

'About the lad,' said Owen. 'This is to be shared only with those who must know in order to assist in our search for the truth.'

Hempe stepped close, studying Owen's face in the lantern light. 'What is it?'

'A young woman, not a lad.'

A tired chuckle. 'They might pretend not to lie with women, but churchmen are not so innocent as to make such a mistake.'

'They are when the woman does all she can to appear a man.'

Hempe grunted. 'Such an effort speaks of trouble left behind.'

'It does.' Holding the lantern high over the ladder, Owen said, 'Ready for the cold?'

'I am already frozen, so it matters not a whit.'

As they began to climb, Hempe said, 'I did not want to say in front of Master Adam, but Ronan was called Neville's summoner. Some wondered whether he would still play that role now.'

'Sniffing out sin? But that was never Neville's duty, was it?'

'Which is why I find it of interest. Murder of an informer – not surprising.'

Having reached the top, Owen searched for something on which to hang the lantern, found it, then called down, 'Opening the hatch.'

Hempe looked away. Owen pushed with his left hand, turning his blind side to the rush of accumulated snow. There would have been far more last night. He hoisted himself up onto the walkway, staying in a crouch as he moved far enough for Hempe to join him. He was not at ease on precipitous ledges since losing half of his sight.

'Bloody—' Hempe caught his breath as he rose to full height. 'It would not take much to topple over.'

'No.'

'Even worse at night.'

'Can you see where Ronan lay from here?' Owen asked.

Hempe shielded his eyes from the pale sunlight and looked round, shook his head. 'Not from here. Maybe farther over.' He turned right, walking as if it were nothing to balance on the slippery edge of oblivion.

Owen cursed his own cowardice.

'No. Trees in the way.' Hempe turned back. 'You thought someone might have been watching, witnessed the attack?'

'It was a thought.'

'And just fell?'

'Or someone took care of the witness.'

'The woman?'

A possibility. But the woman's condition suggested she might simply have taken the opportunity to save herself from her attacker. 'Theo frightened someone out of the chapter house. Two men? Too early to say.'

'I will circle round,' said Hempe, moving on.

More snow, then melt. There was little he could tell from prints, but Owen crept over to the place where he guessed the body would have gone down and examined the stones for anything other than snow and ice. Blood would have been helpful. But he found nothing.

'Snow, slush, nothing else up here,' Hempe declared behind him.

Owen agreed, grateful to clamber down the ladder.

Back in the large space they explored the chambers opening off it. Mason's tools, several lanterns and oil lamps, pieces of candles, rope, neatly coiled – Owen noticed nothing helpful until a small room near the doorway to the steps to the ground revealed a pool of spilt lamp oil.

'Someone might have hidden here,' said Owen. Or was this where she had been placed while bound? And then what? Who had cut her bonds? Why? Was it to force her to scale the ladder on her own? The fallen man looked strong, but the woman was tall, and had she struggled . . . Indeed, if her captor had any sense he would not have attempted carrying her up the ladder. Two men? He stopped himself. How easily he made up a tale, with little proof.

'What is this?' Hempe dropped to his haunches and took out his dagger to poke at something where one of the wooden beams met the floor. Owen lowered the lantern.

'Beads.' Hempe dragged out a short strand. 'Bracelet?' He handed it to Owen.

Coral. A fine strand, the knots torn at the ends. The circle it formed seemed small for an adult wrist, the coral too fine for a child's. 'Or a piece of a paternoster,' said Owen. 'A woman's, I would think.'

'Our woman's? Or lost here long ago. Not a bad place to
bring a mistress. If one had a key.'

As he dropped the beads into his scrip, Owen asked
Hempe to arrange for one of his men to await the arrivals
of the masons at their lodge in the minster yard. 'Have him
take them through these spaces, find out whether they notice
anything amiss.'

'I will do it. While you're in the Bedern? No need for both
of us to go.'

'Right. Check the city gates for last night and this morning
as well. Find out what you can about strangers moving through,
in or out. Meet me at the York midday.'

'You are after something in particular?'

Nothing so clear. Vague feelings.

'After the bailiff's men have taken the masons through, keep
the chapter house locked and guarded,' said Owen.

'The masons will complain.'

'Let them. Pray God we will not need to guard it long.
I will have one of the precentor's men show me Ronan's
lodgings now.'

Taking his leave of Hempe, Owen moved back out into the
steadily warming morning. Thinking Brother Michaelo might
be of use in examining the vicar's rooms, he stopped at the
archdeacon's.

FIVE

The Riddle of the Cloak

B y now the Bedern was awake, the vicars choral and the canons already at morning prayer in the minster, lay folk moving about their chores, gossiping of the bodies in the minster yard. A tidy walkway had already been cleared throughout the area, allowing Owen, Michaelo, and the clerk leading the way to move quickly through the curious crowd to Ronan's lodgings near the center, close to the cloister and refectory. The clerk left them to a fellow clerk guarding the lodgings – Beck, who took offence at being introduced as Ronan's manservant.

'His clerk,' he corrected his fellow, who shrugged and departed.

With some reluctance, Beck stepped aside to allow Owen and Michaelo to enter, then followed them in.

'Spacious,' said Michaelo as he shone his lantern into the room.

'Master Ronan was held in high regard,' said Beck, setting his own lantern on a bench near the window to open the shutters. Facing north, they let in little light on a winter dawn. But the placement of his lantern revealed wet footprints on the floorboards. Snowy boots, Owen thought.

'I believe this is the cloak he had been wearing in the nave.' Michaelo held up a garment that had been draped on a stool beyond the bed. 'But how did it come to be here?' A chest stood open, clothes shoved to one side. 'Someone was in a hurry.'

'Not Ronan,' Owen noted. 'Those marks are recent.' He looked at Beck. 'Perhaps yours? Were you in here before we came?'

The clerk squirmed, shook his head.

'Do you know whether the tide has come in?' Owen asked.

'It has,' said Beck. 'I heard the bells on the river.' They
were set to be jostled by the rising tide, ringing out a warning.

'Is that relevant?' Michaelo asked.

Owen did not care to answer in the clerk's presence. 'We
have seen enough here. Bring the cloak.' As he strode out he
heard Michaelo advising Beck to watch the room.

'But I have others to serve,' the man whined.

'Then be sure to lock the door. Are you able to do that?'

'Yes. I will.'

When the monk caught up to Owen down on the street, he
gave a loud sigh, but said nothing.

'Are you certain that is the cloak he traded with Coates?'
Owen asked.

'If not, it is very like.'

Owen walked with him in silence for a time, then asked if
he could now direct him to Mary Garrett's bedside. 'Though
with the tide out, I may well have missed Dame Magda.'

'My impression is she comes and goes without a thought
to whether or not the tide is out,' said Michaelo. 'She has the
coracle. And the raggedy children who guard it.'

He knew more of Magda's situation than Owen would
have guessed. For Thoresby? 'If you will tell me how to
find her.'

Michaelo described where Mary Garrett's shack abutted
the north end of the minster. 'I had a thought as I began to
write out my account. Edwin, who clerked for Neville – he
might provide insight into Ronan. Though why I bother to
suggest such a thing . . .'

'I have offended you.'

'Your question about the tide. Why so secretive? Have I
not yet proved my usefulness?' Michaelo cursed as a clump
of snow slid from a roof onto his shoulder, slithering down
his cloak to land at his feet. He shook off the icy residue.

'You have proved yourself an excellent hound on the scent,
with a memory for detail of value to me. But the clerk stood
right there.'

'Ah.'

'Did you ever hear Ronan referred to as Neville's summoner?'

An eyebrow raised, a slight smile. 'That is it. A thought that kept slipping just out of reach. Yes. They also called him Neville's spy.'

'It is the summoner idea that interests me.' Owen thanked him. 'Bring the cloak and your notes to me at the end of the day.' It was clear Michaelo meant to complete them before he went to rest. 'And should you have the opportunity, a word with Edwin would be appreciated.'

'You trust me to do it myself?'

'I do.'

'I will do so.' With a satisfied sniff, Michaelo turned toward Archdeacon Jehannes's house in the minster close.

Owen trudged on. He had missed the prickly Michaelo.

A tattered blanket covered the elderly woman, including her face. 'When did Dame Magda depart?' Owen asked the man who had shown him into the draughty space.

'The Riverwoman's not long gone, Captain. With your long legs you might catch her at Bootham Bar. Have you heard there's a third body? Fished him up this morning.'

A third. God help them. 'Where?'

'Near Lendal Tower. Caught on a hook on the wall, bobbing in the tide.'

Ambrose? 'Anyone you know?' Folk who squatted round the minster were often the most knowledgeable inhabitants of the city when it came to misadventure, looking after their own, those the authorities preferred to ignore.

'A stranger. I've heard naught but he was a barrel of a man. And tall.'

No one would say that of Ambrose Coates. Relief washed over Owen, silencing him for a moment. He must still count Ambrose a friend.

But who was this third body? A coincidence? 'Who found him?'

'It was bailiff's men carried him to the deanery. To set beside one fell from the roof. A pair of them now, strong men, with soldiers' scars, though one tall, the other short, both broad in the chest.'

Owen gave the man a penny for his help and retraced his steps to the shed behind the deanery. One of Hempe's men stood guard outside.

'I heard there is a second body.'

'Another fighting man. Seen more fighting than the first by the look of him.'

'Has the coroner seen him?'

'He has, and not too happy about being called back. Says the city owes him a new pair of boots. Ruined his in the snow. Next he'll want a manservant sweeping the way for him.'

Owen stepped inside, opened a shutter on the lantern hanging on a hook within, and studied the newcomer. Poor sod. Boots heavy with river water, mouth agape. He had an oft-broken nose and a scar that pulled the left side of his mouth awry. Clothed well, his dagger missing. Someone in the city had a new weapon. Hempe would find it, unless it had sunk to the bottom of the Ouse. Even so, at low tide a shiny blade would not lie unclaimed for long. The clothing of both bodies suggested they were the unliveried retainers of powerful men, the sort one did not claim with badges, for they would see to the shadowy tasks – murder a rival, set fire to an enemy's barn, steal the cattle.

With less than a month before Alexander Neville's enthronement, at which time York would be crowded with representatives of all the powerful noble families in the North, such men were to be expected, ostensibly ensuring the safety of their masters. That several of them had converged on the minster in the early hours troubled him. Was Ambrose Coates the unwitting lure? It might explain this man's death, if he had been following Ambrose to the mudflats. But then he could not have been the one Theo scared off.

The river rushed over the makeshift causeway that afforded access to the stone island on which sat the home of Magda Digby, the Riverwoman. At low tide. Not at present.

'Penny to row you over, Captain.' The gangly lad was already dragging the coracle toward the dark waters of the Ouse.

'Penny to row me over and back?'

'Seeing as it's you . . .'

'Is the Riverwoman at home?'

'She is.' A grin revealed dark spaces between rotten teeth. He held out his gloved hand for his pay, bit the coin with what teeth he had, then motioned for Owen to climb aboard. 'Fine day for a crossing, Captain. A blessing the river ain't frozen over.'

Owen laughed. It was hardly a crossing. Had it been warmer, he would not have bothered with the coracle. Where had the lad learned of rivers freezing over? Tidal rivers rarely did so, and Owen could not recall it happening in his time in York. The lad was too young to have been alive before Owen arrived in the city. He hardly had time to entertain these thoughts before they arrived. As the coracle nudged the rock Owen felt the familiar shower of needle pricks over his blind eye. A warning. On Magda's island? He shook off the thought and stepped out, offered to help lift the boat out of the water.

But the lad declined, already pushing away as he glanced up at the dragon that hung upside down from the remnant of a Viking longboat that constituted the roof of Magda's weather-tight home. 'I will wait for you from the bank.'

Likely he did not care to sit beneath the dragon. Preferring the lad not overhear his conversation with Magda, Owen did not argue. 'Another penny to refuse transport to anyone else, and give me a full description of them when I am ready to return?'

A gappy grin. 'Agreed.'

Owen tossed him the coin, then turned to rap on the door. But it was already swinging open. Across the threshold stood the old healer, her strange garb of many colors making her seem to flutter in place.

'Has Hugh's fever broken?' she asked.

'In the night,' said Owen. 'Now they all rest.'

A brief smile. 'But there is no rest for thee, Bird-eye. Thy clear-seeing hast brought thee to roost precisely where Magda would have thee. An old friend awaits.' She beckoned him inside.

Bowing to clear the lintel, Owen breathed deep as he stepped into the warm, aromatic space. He had come to appreciate the bouquet of herbs and roots and the curious scent of Magda's hearth fire. She never divulged what woods fueled it, but he had never smelled a fire so subtle and rich.

A man rose from a low stool and took a step backward, as if uncertain of his welcome, his delicate hands crossed over his heart. Though the hair was no longer than Owen's, and dark, the cheeks less round than in memory, the eyes sunken, the hands gave him away. 'Ambrose.'

A slight nod. 'Owen.' More a worried whisper than a greeting.

'What is this?' Owen spread wide his arms. 'I rush here to see you, old friend, and you back away? You know me better than that.' He embraced Ambrose, who was taut with fear. Stepping back, Owen assured him that he came with no purpose but to hear his story.

'Forgive me. I should know from old that you seek ever to balance justice with mercy.'

'Have you need for mercy?'

'Dame Magda tells me I have left a trail of trouble, though how that has come to pass . . .' Ambrose spread his arms as if to show he carried no weapon.

Magda touched Owen's elbow. 'Thou hast not slept this night, Bird-eye. Wouldst thou accept a tonic in a cup of brandywine?'

'To help me think? I would, with thanks.'

He settled on a low bench by the fire, leaning forward to rub his hands, waiting for Ambrose to begin. But he merely stared back.

Magda handed Owen the cup. 'Thou art wasting time, Minstrel. Thou hast come a long way to save thy prince and thyself. Sit down and confide in thy friend.'

'Your prince?' Owen asked as Ambrose resumed his seat. 'French or English?'

'A fair question. Prince Edward, heir to the English throne and Duke of Aquitaine. I have spent years at the French court, it is true. Waiting for a lover who never returned. And while I waited I thought I might see for myself what so enticed Martin, why he could not set aside the life of a spy.'

'Did you discover its appeal?' Owen tasted the brandywine.

He could not tell what Magda had added, but after a few more sips he felt warm and far more alert.

'I found it foul. I can describe for you the bedchambers of the most powerful members of the French court, as well as their enemies. I have been feted, showered with luxuries, spit at, beaten, wooed back. It is more the life of a dog than a human with a soul.'

A grunt from where Magda bent over her worktable.

'And all the while I listened. A musician with no ambition to be more, no taste for the tournament lists – they considered me too unimportant and powerless to send me away while they drank wine and concocted their plots against all in their way. Especially "tiresome Aquitaine" – that is what they call Edward of Woodstock, and "Prince of Darkness". I know much that His Grace might use against them – desires, fears, appetites, weaknesses.'

A treasure. 'Then why come north to York?' Owen asked. 'You did not think Prince Edward would attend Neville's enthronement?'

'No. My plan was to retrieve the instruments I entrusted to Dame Magda, which I now understand to be in the workshop of your apothecary, so that I might ingratiate myself with someone in His Grace's circle and so find a sponsor to make my introduction. I have summarily failed in that so far. However, at Cawood Palace—'

'The archbishop's palace?'

'Yes. I . . . joined a company of players invited to provide entertainment for a gathering of Nevilles. Hoping to hear something that might be of help. That was where – have you any news of the lad with whom I was traveling?'

'The pale beauty? With the beautiful voice, according to Brother Michaelo. She sleeps in our solar at present.'

'Ah. So you know.'

'I know little else.'

'God be thanked she is safe,' Ambrose breathed.

Owen had forgotten how his entire face registered emotion, a gift for a performer, but a spy?

'How did you find her?' Ambrose asked. 'Dame Magda spoke of trouble. Is she safe?'

'She is safe for now. I would like a more detailed explanation of why you are here. And why you were at Cawood.'

'Will you not tell me what happened after I left the minster?'

'Last night you had long white hair.'

'You spoke to Ronan.'

He did not know? 'No. You were seen. We will speak of that. First I will hear your story.'

Ambrose glanced at Magda, who had busied herself with mortar and pestle. He returned his attention to Owen. 'You are more officious than I remember.'

'I was a long while in Thoresby's service.'

Ambrose drank down whatever Magda had put in his cup. A truth serum? Perhaps. For now he began to talk. 'To save which prince, you asked, England or France. And well you might. I arrived in Dover without a letter of safe passage. Who would have written such a thing for me? I prayed that God might show me the way – a repentant sinner, come to make amends, reparations. I heard in the taverns that Thoresby was dead, and you now in the prince's service. Even in the South they speak of you.'

'More likely they speak of Alexander Neville.'

'The prince's interest in York is the subject of much conjecture.'

'I see. Continue.'

'When I heard you now served Prince Edward I took it as the sign I had looked for and knew I was right to head north. I need you to speak in my favor, Owen, to assure His Grace that I am neither a spy nor an assassin. I want only to save his life.'

Not what Owen had expected. 'Why should you care so much as to risk everything?'

'Perhaps it is my penance for these wasted years. I might have— A conversation for another time.'

'The French plot to murder him? Or do you know of a cure for his lingering illness?'

'Both, in a fashion. I would warn him against his French physician, for his purpose is to sustain the illness that torments His Grace, that weakens him, and will in time kill him.'

'What is this?' Magda whispered, looking up from her work.

'The physicians who presented themselves to him in Bordeaux, including the one who returned in his household, they have betrayed him. Pierre de Manhi of Bordeaux brought four of them together in an effort to rid the realm of Aquitaine of the prince in a most humiliating manner. A pity, folk would say, this once feared warlord diminished by a flux that will not stop, a weakness that incapacitates him. When Edward was carried to Limoges on a litter they were amused. An image most gratifying.'

'Snakes,' Magda hissed.

'How did they do this?' asked Owen.

'Experiments with poisons – small amounts, imperceptible in otherwise ordinary physicks, taken over a long while. They were curious to learn whether the poisons would kill him or merely weaken him, whether they would prevent other physicks from working. The deadliest of them, mercury, is the particular curiosity of the viper who now resides in the prince's household, Monsieur Ricard.'

Magda left her worktable to join them by the fire.

She had spoken at length with Princess Joan about her husband's illness. 'Would the symptoms the princess described support these claims?' Owen asked.

'Quicksilver is an inconstant healer,' said Magda. 'It is possible Minstrel is right.' She held Owen's eye, looking deep. 'Trust him, Bird-eye. He has no cause to lie to thee. Nor would he come such a way to speak nonsense.'

'If this is true . . .' But what to do with Ambrose for now. With the children convalescing, and one stranger already installed in his home? 'Tell me about the young woman.'

Ambrose looked at him askance. 'Will you not say whether or not I might count on your help?'

'I need to think what I can do. But to the point, I need to know what danger sleeps near my children.'

'Of course. I had not considered . . .' Ambrose looked down at his hands, white, unlined, uncalloused but for the tips of his fingers. He spoke of noticing her amongst the players.

So she was not a Neville. 'How did you come upon them?' Owen asked.

'I overheard the leader at the tavern bragging that they were

to perform at Cawood Palace. I knew it to be one of the properties of the Archbishop of York. An opportunity to learn
something of use to you. A lure.'

'Found you a lure?'

'Sir John has placed Alexander on the archbishop's throne
to dominate the Northern lords, keep them in place.'

'Anyone with half a wit guessed that.'

'But I can attest to it. He sees Ravenser as a difficulty. And
you.'

Also not surprising. 'What does he propose to do about us?'

'That I cannot say.'

'Pity.'

'He wanted to know which merchants might be supportive.'

'Supportive of what?'

'My impression was that the prince's health emboldens them
to hope for the crown to go to Lancaster, the king's brother,
rather than Edward's son, Richard of Bordeaux. They spoke
of this in France, the powerful Lancaster ready to steal the
throne from the boy, who is much favored by the French.
Malleable. His mother fond of France.'

'This might be of use to the prince.' This and a warning
against the treacherous physician. 'Is there more?'

'Will you help me?'

Owen needed to know just how much trouble he was taking
on. 'First, the young woman. You heard this man boasting . . .'

'*Sacré Dieu*,' Ambrose muttered, but he nodded. 'I took
up my crwth and performed right there in the tavern, singing
a mournful ballad. They were impressed and invited me to
join them. I noticed the lad – as I thought him them – using
his fingers to mark out the notes of the song, as many are
trained in abbeys. He interested me. The leader noticed
and warned me away. But the lad, Matthew as he – as she
called herself, had a voice to complement mine, so I worked
with her. Noticed how she knew the modes – a way of
learning what notes belong together in sacred music.' He
hummed a tune that sounded vaguely familiar. 'You recognize it, yet it could be many hymns you have heard. Because
it is. My point being she is well trained. Convent-trained, I
would guess.'

Michaelo had been right. Again. 'She has not confided in you?'

'No. How did Brother Michaelo hear her? God help me, is she at the abbey? They will discover her.'

'No. Michaelo bides in the minster close. He was passing the minster before dawn and heard her singing in the chapter house.'

'Singing where?' Ambrose looked stunned. 'How did she come to be there?'

'I would guess she followed you to the minster last night. Perhaps witnessed your exchange of cloaks.'

'My— You know of that.' A muttered curse. 'I have not been so careful as I thought. No. I left her with the fiddler, Tucker. Why would she follow me there?'

'I know not. What did you do with Ronan's cloak?'

Ambrose gestured to a hook on the wall beside the door. 'It hangs there.'

From his seat, it looked to Owen very much like the one he had taken from Ronan's lodgings. He rose to examine it. The lining was not the same, but from a distance it would seem a match. 'Where did you go from the minster?'

'I came here. I wanted Dame Magda's advice about coming to you. And my meeting with Ronan troubled me. I'd sought his help, calling on our old acquaintance, favors I'd done for him. I asked him if he knew whether any Nevilles had arrived. I feared they'd followed me from Cawood. He said he would find out, and, if so, vouch for me – in exchange for my costly cloak.'

'I question the wisdom of offering yourself to the Nevilles.' Nor did he sense that Ambrose was telling him the full truth about the exchange. Something in his eyes, the smooth explication.

'How would you advise me?' asked Ambrose.

'I will think on it after you have told me all. It was not you who suggested the exchange?'

Ambrose looked surprised. 'To what purpose?'

'Disguise?'

A mirthless laugh. 'If they are Neville's trackers, they will not be so easily fooled.'

'You did not first go to Ronan's lodgings, switch to a different cloak?'

'Why would I? And how? It has been a long while. I've no idea where Ronan lives now. In any case, you see the cloak right there. Why are you asking this? Did Ronan come to you?' His voice broke on the last question. He was lying. Or holding something back.

But it seemed someone else had been in Ronan's room, and in the chest. Owen resumed his seat, more and more unsettled about what he might have missed. 'Ronan is dead. Murdered.'

'Dead? *Deus juva me.* But— How? When?'

Owen looked at Magda. 'You told him nothing about the deaths?'

'Magda spoke only of trouble,' she said. 'Better he heard of it from thee.'

'Deaths?' Ambrose whispered. 'More than Ronan?'

Owen told him of the other two.

Ambrose, already pale, turned ashen. '*Mon Dieu*, what did I do?' He looked away, breathing shallowly. 'Ronan. May God grant him peace.' He crossed himself with trembling hands. 'And the other two? Who were they? Oh God help me.'

Magda rose and went to him, gently guiding his head between his legs. 'Breathe slowly, three heartbeats in, three out.'

Hearing a shout from the riverbank, Owen went to the door, opening it just enough to see Hempe arguing with the river boy.

'Bailiff Hempe, is it? Wast thou followed?'

'I am as certain as I can be that I was not. Someone must have told George I'd asked about the tide, damn them.'

'Bailiff?' Ambrose stumbled up from his seat and caught Owen's arm. 'I've done nothing.'

'Three deaths in a matter of hours, Ambrose, and your exchange of cloaks with Ronan could be seen as connecting at least his murder to you. I need to talk to Hempe, hear why he has come.' Owen sensed Magda's eyes on him. 'I will do what I can.'

She nodded and gestured for him to go.

Once outside, Owen was relieved to see that Hempe appeared to have come alone. He considered whether it was better to have the lad bring him over, or to cross himself. He chose the latter, shouting for the lad, gesturing to him to come alone. Hempe made clear his frustration with a shouted curse, carried away by the rushing river. All but the tone, which was clear.

'I owe you an extra penny for this,' Owen told the lad as he stepped into the vessel. 'You have my gratitude for standing up to the bailiff.'

The gappy grin again. 'Tuppence extra.'

'Let us see just how many trips we will be making,' said Owen.

'I trust you, Captain.'

Owen hoped Hempe did as well. But when he heard what had sent his friend here, he was not at all sure how far the bailiff could go in protecting Ambrose.

'Whoever left the cloak stole a chest of coins and other valuable items the vicar had collected for the archbishop, calling in debts,' said Hempe.

Debts, or the takings of a summoner? 'Who told you this? Master Adam's clerk?'

'Ronan's clerk. Beck. He was determined I should know. To his mind you were not sufficiently concerned.'

'He mentioned nothing of valuables when I was there.'

'And the thief and murderer, so he calls him, had switched cloaks there.'

Owen detected a false tale spun from his interest in the cloak. A reminder to say nothing in the hearing of onlookers. Time to confide in Hempe. He needed his help. 'If you mean the man with whom Ronan exchanged cloaks in the minster last night, no. He came straight here.'

'In the night? The guards let him out Bootham Bar?'

'The other way, the river way.'

'So he's a river rat? And you have caught the culprit?'

'I will tell you all about him later. For now, I need you to trust me.'

'Words to chill the heart. What are you about, Owen?'

Glancing round to make sure the lad was too far away and close to the flood to overhear them, and no one else was about, Owen told Hempe of Ambrose's mission.

'God's blood, Owen. Does he – are they Neville's men we have behind the deanery?'

'The dead reveal little. But if someone was after the treasure Ronan had tucked in that chest in his lodgings, his death might have nothing to do with Ambrose.'

Hempe grunted. 'You might be right. But that cursed servant will have told all in the Bedern that Ambrose Coates is a thief and a murderer.'

'I know. I am curious why Beck told me nothing of this.'

'Had he just heard from you of Ronan's death?'

'No. The news had spread through the Bedern before we arrived. You say the valuables in Ronan's possession were payments for debts? Alexander Neville was in the business of loaning money?'

'Odd, isn't it? When he was a prebend, and never in the city himself. He spent most of his time at the papal court, at least that is what I recall.'

'He did.' Owen thought this tale very odd indeed. 'Was it Neville's practice, or had his vicar found a cunning scheme for profit?'

'I doubt you will find anyone willing to answer that.' Facing the river, Hempe nodded in that direction. 'Dame Magda is beckoning us to cross over.'

'Before we join her, I need to know how you will fall on this, George.'

'With the minster chapter, the mayor, council, and all the citizens desperate to keep the peace for the spectacle of Neville's enthronement, I must consider . . .' Hempe studied his muddy boots, muttering an oath. 'I had hoped we might be snowbound, delaying all the travelers, but with this melt . . .' He met Owen's gaze with a frustrated grimace. 'Am I bound to keep secret Ambrose's mission?'

'You know the answer to that, George. His Grace has set me to watch the powerful families here in the North. Were they to know what Ambrose knows . . .'

'We would have chaos as they all tried to catch the man so they might use him to gain influence with the prince.' Hempe cursed.

Feeling the weight of his new responsibilities, Owen realized what he must do. 'That is half of it. I am the prince's spy, but I am also captain of York with a duty to protect the city. To that end I must shield Ambrose from those who would condemn him so they might say all is well. Despite Magda's testimony that he was here. The murderer – or murderers – would still be free to kill again.'

'You order me to protect him?'

'I would prefer you agreed that we must protect him against those who would use him for their own ends. We might send him to safety on a barge, or look the other way while he crosses to the south bank, but with an escort, for the prince needs him. But who would escort him? And where?'

Hempe was shaking his head. 'I will not agree to send him away, not without knowing for certain he is innocent. You must keep him here in the city. Lock him away somewhere so that he is out of reach, but accessible to us should we discover he is guilty. If that is what you meant, I agree.'

Owen put his hand on his shoulder. 'Thank you.' He called to the lad to ferry them over to Magda.

Averting his eyes from the upside-down dragon – 'by the rood, I'd swear it's about to swoop down and toss me in the flood' – George Hempe tucked himself through Magda's doorway, greeting her with his thanks for the honor. Owen could not help but wonder whether the profuse thanks were for the benefit of the dragon more so than for Magda. But George was welcomed with warmth. Magda knew his worth.

He seemed confused by the slight, dark-haired man who softly greeted him. 'I was expecting Ambrose Coates.'

'I am he.'

'Your long white hair . . .'

'Who was it who saw me?' Ambrose asked.

'Brother Michaelo and the chancellor, Master Thomas,' said Owen.

'And the hair?' asked Hempe.

'Dame Magda thought it best to change his appearance.'

'Fooled me.' Hempe grinned. 'We have not met, Ambrose, though I remember your voice, and your playing.' He bobbed his head and took the seat Magda indicated. 'The captain has told me of your reasons for coming to York, and the tale you tell of your movements since meeting the vicar in the minster. Ronan's clerk tells a different story. He claims you returned to Ronan's room, switched cloaks, and stole money and jewels hidden in the same chest in which you found the replacement cloak.'

'He is wrong. The cloak you see there on the hook is the one Ronan traded with me. May he rest in God's grace.' Ambrose crossed himself, cleared his throat. 'This clerk – does he claim to have witnessed me entering the lodging?'

'No,' said Hempe. 'He concluded it from the cloak on the bed, the missing items.'

'So it might have been anyone,' said Owen. 'And it's possible that it was for the treasure that Ronan was murdered, rather than a mistaken attack on a man wearing Ambrose's magnificent cloak. You said earlier that you and Ronan were friends when you lived here?'

'Acquaintances. He knew someone who sold pieces of instruments I used to repair my own.'

'An honest source?' Hempe asked.

'For my sins, I did not care to ask,' said Ambrose. 'In exchange, I arranged his attendance at a few private performances. As my aide.'

'He enjoyed music?' asked Hempe.

'As I said, I did not ask.'

Owen and Hempe exchanged a look. Another curious detail about the dead man.

'You should know that I have been followed all along, at least since Calais,' said Ambrose. 'But until now, nothing happened. Whoever it was never took the opportunity to toss me into the sea or over a cliff. Yet so persistent. I could not lose him. Or perhaps them. And now, since Cawood – I am sure another man, or group of men, followed us from there. My companion was aware of them as well, asking me what sort of trouble I was in.'

'And this woman,' said Hempe, 'what do you know of her?'

'Very little.'

'Who are these men we found?' asked Hempe.

Ambrose lifted his arms as if to say, *Who, indeed?* But there was concern in his expression. 'Neville's perhaps? Or he who has followed me since France. It might be anyone, for anything. I do not know. I swear to you I do not.'

'But you sought Ronan's help with Neville's men,' said Owen.

Did he hesitate before saying yes? 'I thought I might have been caught spying at Cawood. And the family might think it best to silence me elsewhere. Ronan agreed it was likely, and, as I told you, Owen, he chose my cloak as a reasonable payment for his help. He would talk to them.'

'So they are in York?' Owen asked.

'He did not say, and I was in no position to question his intentions.' A deep breath. Ambrose wiped his eyes. 'God forgive me.'

'You know nothing of the woman's background? No one had shown interest?' asked Hempe.

'There was a man. At Cawood. He stared at her and no one else as we performed. Someone's retainer, far back in the shadows, but the eyes so keen I felt them as we stood together singing. I searched the crowd and found him. It was so at both performances.'

'Was she ever out of your sight?'

'While I arranged for a spy hole, and while I sat there listening, yes, of course. Are you thinking she might have met this man? That he— Perhaps I should see the bodies.'

'Why was this runaway in your company?' Hempe asked Ambrose.

'Someone had discovered the truth of her, and meant to take his pleasure,' said Ambrose.

'Vile,' Hempe growled.

'The question before us is how to protect you while we search for the murderer. Or murderers,' said Owen.

'More than one?' asked Ambrose.

'Possibly,' said Owen, not caring to elaborate.

'I could leave the city,' said Ambrose.

'No, that I cannot permit,' said Hempe. 'I propose the jail of the archbishop's palace. It is not in use at present.'

Owen began to point out that it was a Neville property, but Magda interrupted. 'Who will cook for him? Keep him in fuel for a fire?' It was the first time she had spoken.

'Do you have a better idea?' Hempe snapped, reddening as he remembered himself. A man so in awe of the Riverwoman treating her so . . . He made a conciliatory gesture.

Magda ignored it. 'Thou hast a room in thy house for a boarder. Empty since Old Nat died.'

'How do you know that?' Hempe frowned. 'Of course, Lotta told me that you had brought Old Nat a soothing tisane and a rub for his joints. But I am not a jailer.'

'Nor is Minstrel a murderer. He was with Magda when the men died. Wouldst thou mistreat an innocent man?'

'Dame Magda—' Hempe implored.

'Can you pay your way, Ambrose?' Owen asked.

'I would pay you well for the trouble, bailiff,' said Ambrose.

Hempe's expression softened. 'Pay. I had not thought— So we would consider you a boarder?'

'A boarder who does not venture forth except in the company of a few of our men, armed,' said Owen. 'It means he cannot buy his meals at the market stalls, nor take his wash to a laundress.'

'Lotta enjoys cooking for an appreciative eater,' said Hempe, considering. 'And she could arrange for the laundering. You must work out with my wife when you might make music so as not to disturb her.'

Ambrose gave a little bow. 'Of course.'

'My men Alfred and Stephen can take shifts watching the house,' said Owen.

Hempe looked from him to Magda. 'Had the two of you planned this?'

Owen assured him they had not.

'Bird-eye does not know Lotta as Magda does. She will welcome the challenge.'

'I believe you are right about my Lotta.' Slapping his thighs, Hempe suggested they depart at once.

SIX
Haunted Souls

The onset of winter brought a crush of folk to the apothecary seeking remedies for coughs, fever, earaches, headaches, stomach upsets, catarrh, as well as injuries from falls and frozen fingers and toes. Lucie and Jasper had no time for those who came for gossip about the deaths, requesting them to step aside so that those with ailing folk at home might come forward. The physicks contained any number of ingredients, and varied depending on the sufferer's age, a history of certain types of illnesses, weak lungs . . . Lucie and Jasper did not rush past the details, taking time with each customer. By mid-morning they had whittled down the line so that only one person still waited while another was served, affording Lucie the time to retreat into the workshop and mix more of the physicks most in demand – cough elixirs, headache powders, and aromatic oils to clear stuffy noses. Her hands were covered in oils and sap – bonewort, lichen, sneezewort, bugle, coltsfoot, feltwort, sweet marjoram, garlic, horehound, rosemary – always rosemary. To Lucie it was the mother of winter physicks. It was also a tonic for the voice. Something their guest might appreciate.

All morning Lucie half expected someone to rush into the shop demanding to see their guest. What would they call her? Or would they think her a lad? Who would she be to them? How long had they searched for her? To go about in such a guise, a wandering minstrel . . . From what or whom had she fled?

Lucie glanced up from her work and her runaway thoughts to find a pair of wise blue eyes observing her.

'Hast thou time for Magda?'

She had not noticed the healer's entrance, never felt the

draft as she opened the rear door. Yet Magda had already removed her boots, her bare, calloused feet curled round the supporting post at the bottom of the stool on which she perched. How long had she watched?

'Would you like to wait for me in the kitchen?' Lucie asked. 'I just need to tidy up and take these to Jasper in the shop.'

'A cup of ale and a moment by the kitchen fire would be most welcome.' The healer was wrapped in a cloak of skins – rabbit, squirrel, weasel, whatever she had found in the forest, or caught for food. Nothing went to waste. Her wrinkled face was rosy with the cold. Yet she had removed her boots. 'Do not be long. Magda has much to tell thee of her guest, now the guest of Lotta Hempe. Ambrose Coates.'

So it was the Ambrose Lucie knew. 'He came to you? He is safe? And now with the Hempes?'

Magda's wrinkles deepened with her teasing grin. 'Come along soon.' She slipped off the stool and tucked her feet in the fur-lined boots with a feline litheness. 'Do not tarry!' And she was gone.

Lucie made quick work of cleaning up and taking her preparations into the shop.

'Shut the shop for a while and join me in the kitchen. Magda has news.'

'The shop needs straightening and a good sweep,' said Jasper, though it was clear he wanted to hear what Magda had to say.

'Time enough for all that. Magda will be quick with the news. And you've seen to the daylight customers. The next influx will be those heading home from work as the light fades.'

He needed no more coaxing, rushing to tidy up and lock the shop door.

As the three sat by the fire, Magda told them what she knew of the night's events, then asked about the young woman. But Lucie had little to add but a summary of the woman's injuries.

'Who talked George Hempe into taking Ambrose as a lodger?' asked Jasper. 'Master George would not think of it. He would suggest one of the city jails. Was it Da's idea?'

'I would guess it was yours,' Lucie said, looking at Magda. A smile. 'Magda pointed the way.'

'George does not appreciate Lotta's talents,' said Lucie. 'He has been reluctant to involve her in his work for the city – she sees to the trade and the household. He is blind to her interest, how keen she is to hear about his day, nor does he give credit to her suggestions. She offered him a list of those who might bear watching after a string of burglaries: this one is wearing fine clothes of a sudden on a paltry income, that one's wife complains about the state of his clothing and how he's often home long past curfew, there is rumor of a stranger who walks the streets at night as if testing the night watch. George shook his head as if she'd just said something ridiculous. He might have found his man much sooner had he listened to her.'

'A man would be wise to respect Lotta's keen regard,' said Magda. As Kate brought a jug of ale to replenish the bowls on the table Magda asked her, 'Hast thou news of the children?'

'Mistress Alisoun says Hugh complains that Gwen is torturing him,' Kate laughed. 'She is pretending to teach Emma to sing, but the baby just squeals and shrieks with laughter and claps her hands. I offered to bring Gwen to the kitchen and give her some tasks.'

'That is just what my sly daughter hopes for,' said Lucie. 'She wearies of the nursery.' But she was glad Hugh was well enough to make moan about his sisters' noise.

Magda patted Lucie's hand. 'Thy daughter hast a strong will. Why resist it?'

'As you do with your apprentice?' Before Magda agreed to accept Alisoun as her apprentice the young woman served for a while as nursemaid to Gwen and Hugh. Quick to take offense, she had challenged every task Lucie set her. Time and again Magda had counseled Lucie to be firm, not give in.

'Not so often as before.' Magda smiled.

'It might be best to give in to Gwen's ploy else all will pay for it, Kate,' said Lucie. 'What news of our guest?'

'Mistress Alisoun says she has not stirred.'

Nothing unusual in that, but Lucie wanted to look in. Magda offered to accompany her.

The room had been created by walling off the long, narrow end of the children's bedchamber for Lucie's aunt, Philippa, who had come to live with them after suffering a palsy. A barred window allowed for some light and air, and the warmth from the nursery brazier was sufficient to heat it. But not to the point of causing the sheen of sweat on the sleeping woman. Her forehead was hot.

'She was not feverish when she arrived, but she is now.' Lucie lifted the woman's shift to examine her groin and armpits for boils. Nothing. God be thanked.

Settling across from Lucie, Magda bent to sniff the young woman's breath, pressed an ear to her chest, wiped the sweat from her neck and tasted it. 'Not all fevers point to illness. Long has she lived in the guise of a young man, unable to take her ease, alert to discovery, ready to take flight,' said Magda. 'Minstrel says she has been fasting and depriving herself of sleep as penances for he knows not what. Now that she is in a safe place, her body is taking her deep into a healing sleep. When thy mother first came to Freythorpe she had witnessed the slaughter of friends and kin, forced to hide, starving, cold.'

Lucie's late mother was Norman, from a noble family. A war prize bestowed on her father for his valor in the king's war for the crown of France.

'She had such a fever?'

Magda touched Lucie's hand, as if to comfort her. 'Amelie burned fierce while she slept such a deep sleep thine aunt worried she was dying. But Magda knew it to be a healing fire. When she woke, the memories were dimmed. A mercy. Come. Thou hast abundant stores in thine apothecary to assist her body in healing. Magda will guide thee.'

'Should someone stay with her?' Lucie asked, though she did not have anyone to spare.

'Nay. Though she may wake at any moment, she will be too weak to harm herself. Alisoun can see to her. Thy children will not need all her attention.'

'But Muriel Swann hopes to have Alisoun at her lying in.'

'Magda will see to that.'

'Alisoun might not wish to stay.'

'Magda will speak with her.'

'You have confidence Alisoun can care for this woman?'

A smile. 'The two young women will find much to share. Both have been tested, proved strong.'

'We know nothing of this woman. My children sleep in the next room.'

'Magda does sense an anger in her that she fights to drown with remorse. But she has no cause to point that anger at thee or thy family.'

'Remorse. Do you sense she harmed someone?'

'Who has not?'

If Magda had meant to reassure Lucie, she had failed.

As Owen had hoped, Lotta Hempe accepted the situation without argument, sitting Ambrose down by the kitchen fire while she set her maidservant to work airing out the bedchamber and lighting a fire in the brazier.

'Walking from Magda's rock to our home in such weather,' Lotta tsked. 'We must stoke the fire in your belly, Master Ambrose. Cook will see that you have something to eat and drink. Bring the strong claret,' she said to the woman standing over a cauldron of something aromatic, spicy.

'A good choice, mistress,' she said, wiping her hands on her apron and bustling to a locked cabinet in the corner.

Hempe paced in the hall, seeming eager to get back out into the city. Owen understood. They had stopped to show Ambrose the two corpses. He believed the fallen one to be the young woman's watcher at Cawood. He might have seen the drowned one there as well. All helpful. Taking him past had been worth the risk, but it had heightened Hempe's alarm. 'I would see what my men learned from the guards at the gates. Meet me at the York in early evening?'

Owen agreed.

Upon Hempe's departure Owen went in search of Lotta to thank her for taking on this task.

Standing in what would be Ambrose's bedchamber, a spacious room with good light and a door to the back garden, she responded to his thanks with a warm smile, her eyes alight. 'I am honored to have Dame Magda recommend me, and for your confidence. George is a fool about women. He wants to coddle and protect me. His trade has benefited from my part-nership, but he does not think of me as a partner. I ignore him and go about my work.' A widow, she had put much of her wealth in George's shipping interests when they wed.

'Marriage changes a man, but slowly,' said Owen. 'Lucie was patient with me.'

She touched Owen's scar, a surprising gesture of affection. Seeming to remember herself, she withdrew it, asking in a brusque tone, 'Should I expect trouble? Have our manservant accompany me on my rounds?'

He was glad she understood they did not yet know the danger. 'That would be wise. Would you note anything in Ambrose's conversation, or his requests, that might provide me with additional information? I am particularly keen to learn of anything he has to say about the dead man, Ronan.'

'I will stay alert and report anything I might learn, Captain.' She bobbed her head, all business. 'Is he a good musician?'

'Ask him to play and sing for you.' It reminded him of Lucie's request to return Ambrose's instruments to his care. 'We have kept his most treasured instruments for him all these years. Might I bring them? It would provide him occupation – tuning, polishing.'

She made a face. 'I pray he is not one of those who takes hours to find the pitch.' But she agreed. 'Bring them when you can. Now go, be about your work. Let him settle in.'

By now the streets were crowded despite the slush and the dripping eaves. With his height and his scarred face, the patch over his useless left eye, Owen was not a man who could disappear among those going about their day. Yet although folk stepped aside they did not fall silent at his passing, but rather plied him with questions, prayed for his speedy delivery of the murderer, named possible suspects – most likely unpleasant neighbors. As ever, the less they knew the more confident in their advice. A pity. Such eager assistants, but of no use to Owen at present. He kept his good eye focused on where to walk in the slush, doing his best to slough off the noise and arrive with some modicum of calm so that he did not frighten into silence the weasel who haunted his late employer's lodgings in the hope of gain.

With the crowd and all the curiosity it did Owen no good to watch the alleyways and shadows beneath the overhangs for someone too curious about him. Everyone was. But it gave him an idea. When he returned home he would ask Kate whether her siblings Rose and Rob might be willing to trail him about the city and make note of who watched him with too much interest. He knew he could rely on the twins' creative cunning and discretion – they had helped him before. Fifteen and unremarkable in their dress and demeanor, they would be ignored by the likes of those tracking Ambrose or his companion. The perfect spies.

His thoughts returned to the problem of Ronan's hiding place for the missing casket of valuables. The chest would be the obvious place to look. Had the vicar so trusted his fellows? Unlikely. Despite what Beck the weasel had said, Owen guessed that the missing casket held little of value, its purpose to foil a lazy thief. There had been no sign that someone had carried out a thorough search of the chamber. Had Beck been paid to make much of something of little value? Provide a diversion? For whom? It seemed to Owen the key to it all.

Climbing the outdoor stairs to Ronan's rooms he felt an energy that defied his sleepless state. He found the door ajar despite the biting cold, Beck huddled on a stool just inside watching with sullen countenance as a one-armed man searched the chamber. Owen had forgotten about Crispin Poole, who now served Archbishop Neville as Owen had Archbishop Thoresby – or at least in his former capacity of spy for the archbishop.

'Crispin.'

The searcher turned round. 'Owen. I have been expecting you. Any news?'

'Nothing yet. And you? Are you here on orders from Cawood Palace?'

A raised brow, in a face more suitable for a soldier than the

merchant he had returned to York to become. No noticeable
scars, but the life of a soldier was spent out in the elements,
weathering a man's skin. Crispin sank down onto the edge of
the bed. 'Is that where the Nevilles are?' A large man beginning to take on weight, he was sweating despite the chill draft
from the open door. 'I've received no orders.'

'Why are you here?' Owen asked.

'I might ask the same of you.'

'The precentor went to the mayor requesting my services.
I am charged with finding the men who broke the peace in
the close last night, killing a vicar and a stranger.'

'And drowning a third.'

'That could be an accident. The fall might also have been
unintended.'

'Do you think that?'

'That Ronan was murdered is not in question. And two
others are dead.' Crispin was Neville's man. Owen must have
a care.

Crispin pulled a cloth from his sleeve and mopped his brow.
'Too many guild dinners of late. I need activity. This cursed
snow.'

'You have not answered my question. Why are you here,
Crispin?'

'Ronan worked for His Grace the Archbishop of York, as
do I. His Grace will expect a full report of the incident.'

'I will have Brother Michaelo prepare one for you.'

'A generous offer. But His Grace will want my opinion.'

As would the archbishop's brother Sir John. 'So what have
you found?'

'Nothing. This one – Beck he calls himself – says a casket
of valuables has been removed from the chest.' Crispin
glanced at the man huddled by the door as he nudged said
chest with a walking stick. Owen had not seen him using
that before.

Deciding it was time to acknowledge the weasel's presence,
Owen turned to him. 'I hear you witnessed this theft.'

Beck looked up, startled. 'Me?'

'Why did you not stop him? Prevent his escape?'

'I never said I witnessed it.'

'You spoke with authority. We have taken a man into custody on your accusation. Are you now saying you saw nothing?'

'I—' A cringe, as if expecting a blow. 'Not as such.'

Owen gave the man his fiercest one-eyed glare. 'If I've allowed the murderer to escape while I rounded up an innocent man on your word, you will pay.'

'You— But he was wearing that cloak, was he not?' Beck gestured toward the bed, where it had lain. 'The cloak Master Ronan wore yesterday. You have it. And he left a trail of melted snow on the floor – you saw it.'

'The trail might have been made by anyone. Even you.'

'Me? No!'

'Why are you so certain Ronan wore that particular cloak last night? Did you watch him dress?'

'No.'

'I have seen one very like it elsewhere, also Ronan's cloak. Can you tell me how you tell the difference?'

'Two? But . . .'

'Are you lying about serving as his clerk?'

'No! I came to him midsummer.'

'Yet you did not know of his second cloak?'

'I did not dress him. I serve several in the Bedern.'

'Tell me. What were your duties here?'

'Errands, tidied the place – it needed little of that, fetched meals for him, received deliveries when he could not be here . . .' His voice grew softer and softer.

'What sort of deliveries?'

'All sorts.'

'The sorts of things you say were stolen?'

'It was not my place to pry.'

'Last night. Did you see someone come into the lodgings?'

'I – I wasn't here as such.'

So Ronan himself might have removed the casket. Owen walked toward the weasel, slowly. 'Where were *you* last evening?'

'I—' Eyes locked on Owen's good one, Beck rose and stumbled backwards, flattening himself against the wall.

'You have wasted our time spewing false accusations.' Owen

continued to advance. 'Why else but to permit the true murderer to escape? Unless you murdered Ronan.' He caught the man by the shoulder and shook him once.

'Is that necessary?' Crispin asked.

Owen turned to him. 'Can you explain why he would make up such a lie?'

'The casket *is* missing,' Beck whispered.

Crispin nodded. 'It is curious you know that, but not that Ronan had two cloaks so alike.'

Owen turned back to the weasel. 'Well?'

'I forgot about the other cloak,' he whispered.

'You forgot? You realize that the bailiff might have injured the accused had he tried to run, and all on your false witness?' Owen tightened his grip on the man's shoulder. 'What else is hidden in this room?'

'Naught that I know of. I swear!'

Owen shook him again and released him, turning back to Crispin as the weasel slumped to the floor. 'Tell me about the casket.'

'I know little more than that Ronan had been assigned the task of calling in promised tributes for the archbishop,' said Crispin. 'Merchants and churchmen who had pledged support.'

Not debts? 'Such as Thoresby did with donations for his lady chapel?'

'Yes, though he was vague as to what project.'

'You would be a more likely one to receive such items.'

'I agree. But Ronan argued that it was not seemly, the merchants might resent me.'

It was true that Crispin's acceptance into the society of York merchants was crucial to his effectiveness as the new archbishop's spy. 'I heard they were perhaps not so much support as payments for debts.'

Crispin cleared his throat. 'I have heard such rumors as well.'

'Who gave Ronan the role of debt collector?'

'His Grace, I presume.'

'But you don't know?'

Still sitting on the bed, Crispin looked down at his booted feet, thinking. A slow shake of the head. 'As I said, I heard a rumor. I asked Ronan about it.' A moment of thought, and then looked up with a nod. 'I see. You are thinking Ronan wished to keep the task to himself. For profit?'

Or he had taken it upon himself to devise a way to rob his former master. Not something Owen cared to share with Crispin at present. 'I know too little to judge whether he has kept anything for himself.' He sensed the weasel slinking out the door behind him. Good. 'Are you finished here?' he asked Crispin.

'I have a duty to the archbishop.'

'I will wait.' Owen leaned against the wall, crossed his arms.

Crispin narrowed his eyes. 'Do you count me a suspect?'

The thought had not occurred to Owen until he found Crispin in the room. He considered it unlikely. Crispin was desperate to wed the widow Muriel Swann and help raise the child that might be born any day now. A man might commit such a crime in his circumstances, but not for the benefit of a master he distrusted, which was the case with Crispin and the archbishop. 'I prefer to be alone when I search,' said Owen. 'I will tell you all you need to know in good time.'

'In good time. I expect His Grace to arrive within the week. And you did not answer my question.'

'A week? Then I must get to work.'

Crispin plucked his hat from the bed, picked up his walking stick.

'An injury?' Owen asked.

'Reached out with the hand no longer attached to my arm. Though it pains me as if still there, it proved useless in preventing a fall on snowy cobbles.'

'Has Magda looked at it?'

'Not yet.'

'With her skill you might soon discard the cane.'

Crispin lifted it and swung it round, stabbing out. He grinned. 'I might just keep it with me. Not a bad thing, to pretend I cannot protect myself, and then strike.'

Owen chuckled despite himself.

'How are the children?' Crispin asked.

'They have come through the worst of it. Lucie says they are out of danger.'

'God be praised.' Crispin pressed Owen's shoulder as he limped past him and out the door. He moved with the weariness of a man with a burdened soul, reminding Owen of Crispin's distaste for his lord, Alexander Neville.

'It is too early to say you are above suspicion,' Owen called out, 'but I do not think you would be so inept.'

'A compliment?' Crispin grinned. 'I will expect that report.'

'You will have it.'

Once alone, Owen studied the room, then began testing the floorboards, knocking on the paneled walls. On the last wall the sound changed. He'd left it to last because to access it would require moving the bed, which appeared to be built into the wall. But he found he could move it. With his dagger he tested the edges of the wall panels until one gave way, revealing a square opening in which he found a pouch filled with jewels, small gold and silver objects, and silver coins, all representing a considerable fortune.

Two treasures in the vicar's lodgings, one undiscovered, the other either stolen after his murder or removed by Ronan. And stolen by his murderer? Beck had known of the casket in the chest, of course, but Owen did not think him the murderer. He was a noisemaker, a complainer, not a man who took action. But someone may have come for the casket expecting far more, then confronted Ronan, demanding the rest. Or perhaps they killed Ronan first, then came to the room. If so, the murderer might return to search once he found the takings so disappointing. Owen would set a watch on the lodgings.

He considered Ronan's remarkable cache. With such treasure, Owen could not be certain that Ambrose's cloak had anything to do with the vicar choral's murder. Though the confluence of events— If it had nothing to do with whoever had chased Ambrose, and drowned— No, somehow they were connected.

The sack of jewels and coins must be stored in a safer place. To whom might he entrust it? Neither the precentor nor the acting dean had much power. Nor did they seem men of great courage. The chancellor of the chapter – no, Master Thomas must remain under suspicion. And, in truth, Owen should not entrust it to any in the chapter or Ronan's fellows in the Bedern until he knew more. Those with any authority were all scrambling for donations to the minster fabric so that they might make a good impression on the Nevilles. Such a windfall might prove irresistible to any of them.

He decided to take it to his friend Dom Jehannes, Archdeacon of York. There were few men Owen trusted so completely. Closing up the hole, he moved the bed back into place, then tucked the heavy bag into his padded jacket. His cloak would disguise the extra bulk.

'You are clanking,' Brother Michaelo noted as Owen stomped his boots on the stone outside Jehannes's door.

'So I am. I thought you would be resting.'

'I have.'

'Hardly enough to make up for missing a night's sleep.' Owen settled on the bench inside the door to remove his boots.

'Sufficient for the moment. I wished to write up all that I heard this morning before I confuse details with what I hear out in the city. Three deaths in one night. The story will be unrecognizable to us by evening.'

Jehannes hurried out of his parlor to greet Owen, calling to his cook for wine. 'Or will you break bread with me? I've not yet broken my fast.'

'Some bread and cheese would be welcome,' said Owen. 'But first . . .' He opened his jacket and pulled out the treasure, taking it to a small table near the fire where he opened it, revealing the marvels within.

'By the rood, what is this?' asked Jehannes.

'Ronan's hoard,' said Owen.

Jehannes looked up at Owen. 'A vicar choral?'

'Might I trouble you to safeguard this until Archbishop Neville arrives?'

'He stole this from the archbishop?'

'Perhaps.'

Michaelo coughed. Both men turned to him. 'If I might suggest the hiding place beneath the buttery. Access is through a loose stone in the floor that I did not notice until I encountered Cook opening it.'

Jehannes's moon-shaped face lit up with gratitude. 'The very place. Yes, yes, of course you might entrust it to us.' A nod. 'Is it not a blessing Brother Michaelo did not choose to return to Normandy?'

'Unexpected talents,' Owen murmured.

The archdeacon was moving toward the kitchen when he halted, turning back with a pained expression. 'You are certain this hoard belongs to Alexander Neville?'

'At present I believe so. When I unravel the knot of last night's murders I might revise that theory. And I will take full responsibility for it. You need not engage with him on the matter.'

'Good.' With a nod, Jehannes continued on to the kitchen to order breakfast.

Michaelo had been fingering the items in the hoard. Straightening, he brushed off his hands as if to rid himself of temptation. 'He dreads the arrival of the new archbishop.'

'As do we all.'

'We might have had a man of noble character.'

'Ravenser?' Thoresby's nephew had promised to keep Michaelo as his secretary should he win the seat. But the Nevilles had prevailed.

'He above all, but there were others who would have been far more appropriate to the second highest ecclesiastical seat in England.'

Easing himself down onto a settle near the fire, Owen rested his head against the back and closed his eye. 'What might have been is not a game I care to play. I am far too busy with what was, and is.'

'To that end, I will leave you and complete my account of your investigations.'

'Our investigations, Michaelo. Did you speak with Edwin?'

'Not yet.'

'I count on it.'

'You are determined to dominate my hours,' Michaelo said, his words a complaint but his tone more of someone deeply satisfied.

SEVEN

A Deepening Mystery

'Ronan was calling in pledges for His Grace the archbishop? Or debts?' Master Thomas turned to gaze out the window of his parlor. A bird pecked at the bright berries on a holly bush. 'I had heard nothing of this.' Though the chancellor's posture hinted otherwise.

Owen pursued it. 'If you were to surmise about the manner of such loans or donations, what might they be? What favors might His Grace offer to extend to citizens of York? Or what cause? Building project?'

Master Thomas glanced at Michaelo, who was making notes of the conversation. 'Is his scratching necessary?'

Michaelo knew many of the clerics and their clerks, so his insight might prove useful. To have him taking notes suggested he was merely assisting, not listening closely. 'I can more fully listen to you when I do not need to worry about remembering everything. We were speaking of the type of pledges Alexander Neville might have received in the city.'

'Do you mean as a prebend? Before his enthronement?' Thomas shook his head. 'I cannot think what it might be. He was rarely here. You might ask his secretary. Or the clerk Edwin. Are you certain this Beck is to be trusted?'

'I doubt that he is. But Crispin Poole spoke to Ronan about this collection, so I am not depending solely on Beck's charge.'

A sigh. 'There is the matter of the Italian archdeacons. However, I should think it would be my fellows in the chapter who cared about that, not the lay citizens of York.'

'Not necessarily. I should like to hear what you are thinking, what he might offer.'

Thomas continued to present his back to Owen. Perhaps he meant to imply that this questioning was beneath him. He might not realize it as a behavior often used by the guilty. In either case, and whether or not he was guilty of more than pride, the chancellor interested Owen more and more. Now he glanced back with a cold look. 'Except for your friend Dom Jehannes, the current archdeacons under the archbishop of York are all Italian clerics.' He returned his gaze to the winter garden. 'Absentee heads of their jurisdictions, they are leeches draining the resources of the diocese. With his connections in the papal court, Neville was the obvious solution, the man who might argue at the papal court for more appropriate archdeacons. But Neville, too, was seldom here, so I had thought the idea abandoned. Perhaps someone pursued this.'

'That is helpful. Thank you. Can you suggest any reason why laymen might care about the Italian archdeacons?'

'Not the archdeacons. But they might have other concerns. Issues of marriage and inheritance can involve the pope. Perhaps Neville offered to intercede. Or to carry documents. Recommend lawyers.'

'A man might grow wealthy offering such services to those with deep purses,' said Owen.

A shrug.

'How well did you know Ronan?'

'Not well.'

'But you had met with him yesterday?'

A slight shiver. 'We are, or rather were, all consulting him on the archbishop's preferences, Captain Archer. You will find few in the close who have not met with him frequently in the past fortnight. So much to be done. We must make a good impression.'

'If you do not?'

At last the chancellor turned from the window, frowning. 'I fear His Grace and his ambitious brother will make trouble for the dean and chapter. They count this as a great step up for the family. The second most powerful man in the English church is now a Neville. They expect us to make a great show of welcoming him, giving him the honor they believe he deserves. Or, perhaps, desires. One wonders . . . Alexander is so young. Were he not the brother of Sir John Neville – Admiral of the North, Steward of the King's Household – would he have been considered for the post? Has he the maturity and breadth of experience to wield the power of this position with the proper mix of compassion and authority?' A slight shake of the head, making clear Thomas's impression.

Owen stepped into the opening the chancellor had provided. 'I understand the family took an active role in convincing the chapter to choose Alexander as archbishop.'

A misstep. Thomas's smile was anything but friendly. 'Of course you'd hoped Ravenser would be chosen. A smooth transition for you, a malleable archbishop.'

'An honorable man trusted by King Edward and his late beloved queen. Yes, I prefer him by far as a shepherd of the Church.' Owen smiled. 'But I did not serve John Thoresby without learning what is needed in the role.'

'So you see the benefit of a Neville in the position.'

'I do. That was not my question. Is it possible that the new archbishop made loans as promises of support to come?'

'Acting as a money-lender? Captain, you know that is forbidden.'

'And yet such agreements are often made.'

A shrug. 'As I have no knowledge of any such loans, I could not presume to speak to that. Nor have I any knowledge of his seeking contributions to the funds for the lady chapel or other building projects. He did not consult me about anything of the sort.'

A careful man, the chancellor. Owen learned little more, and left before his impatience became obvious. His lack of sleep threatened to impair his tact. He rose so abruptly that Michaelo looked up from his work, startled. He had almost forgotten the monk's presence, he had been so quiet. He wondered whether it was an art Michaelo had perfected as a child, his ability to disappear in full sight, or come upon one with no warning, or whether it was something he had learned in Thoresby's service.

Before continuing on to the shops of the gold- and silversmiths whose work had been included in Ronan's hoard, Owen told Michaelo he wished to stop at home to make his request to Kate regarding her twin siblings.

'If you do not require my services for this, I will withdraw to Jehannes's house for an hour of prayer,' said Michaelo.

'Of course.'

At the bottom of Stonegate, Owen noticed that a line had formed in front of the apothecary, common at this time of year in the morning and early evening, but not so soon after midday. He avoided notice by using the garden gate off Davygate and hurried to the workroom behind the shop to see whether anything had happened, a fresh outbreak of the pestilence or some other illness rushing through the city.

Jasper bent over the long worktable in the middle, crushing precious stones.

'Your favorite task,' Owen noted.

A dramatic groan. Jasper displayed reddened hands. 'I do it only to spare Mother's hands and arms.'

Owen flicked at a gray powder on the hank of fair hair falling over Jasper's eyes. 'Why such a long line at this time of day?'

'I closed for a while, to hear what Dame Magda had to say. When I opened up to sweep the entrance, folk poured in. They come for the gossip.'

'And the stones?' Owen had never known them to be in such immediate demand to warrant attention at a busy time.

'Red Timothy asked me whether it was true that precious stones were good protection from fever. I should have said nothing, but it was something I know about and I started talking about the protective properties of some jewels, pearls, other stones . . .' Jasper screwed up his face. 'And then everyone wanted stone powder in their physicks. Now I pay for it.'

'As do they. Raises the price.'

Jasper grinned. 'That it does.'

'Have you overheard any helpful rumors?'

'No. Except that Tucker's been injured. That's a fact, not a rumor. We made up a salve for him, and Dame Magda went to see to him.'

'Tucker the fiddler?'

Jasper nodded. 'He lodged Ambrose, didn't he? And the woman.'

'He did,' said Owen. 'Who came to the shop for the salve? What sort of injury?'

'His wife, Dame Judith. Says when she returned from market the door was swinging open and Tucker lying on the floor groaning, pressing a cut on his forehead to stop the bleeding. But it's his back that's bad. He fell backward over a bench. Now he cannot straighten to walk.'

'Can he talk?'

'Sounds like it.'

'And Magda is with him now?'

Jasper nodded. 'It seems a lot of trouble for two minstrels.'

'Ah. Magda told you how Ambrose came to be here.'

'She did. But – how much trouble could he cause the king of France with his story?'

'Quite a lot if the prince's brothers decide to blame King Charles's men for his long illness and the loss of so much of the Aquitaine.'

'But without Prince Edward to lead them in battle . . .'

'Even so, son. I will talk to Tucker.' Owen began to head into the shop to see how Lucie fared.

'I would not go out there if I were you,' said Jasper. 'They will fall upon you with their questions.'

Which would do nothing to help Lucie and Jasper manage the crowd. 'What do you hear of our guest?'

'Deep in a fever sleep. Not pestilence.' A shrug. 'I've yet to meet her.'

'Do not let Alisoun know you are so eager,' Owen teased.

Jasper rolled his eyes.

Owen thanked his son and left. Out in the garden he paused. This morning's serene blanket of snow now dripped and puddled, revealing leafless stalks and muddy paths. As he stood there the kitchen door opened.

'Da! I'm baking!' Gwen's dark curls were dusted with flour.

'That you are, my beauty,' said Owen, picking her up and twirling her around. She might be eight years old, but she was still his baby and his darling, and he felt his heart might burst with the joy of seeing her well. She giggled and screeched until he reminded her of her brother and sister in the nursery, and their guest. As he lowered her to the threshold he put a finger to her lips, and was rewarded with a peck on his cheek and a throaty giggle.

Kate took his cloak and hung it near the fire. 'Have you taken time for dinner, Captain? Most everyone's already eaten, but there is plenty.'

'I am hungry.' Despite the bread and cheese with Jehannes. 'Would you join me? I would have a word with you about the twins.' He glanced at Gwen, considering how she might react to what he had to say, but she had returned to work, standing on a stool to reach the bowl of dough she appeared to be kneading to death, and humming as she did so.

Over a savory pie washed down with Tom Merchet's ale, Owen explained what he needed of Kate's siblings, Rose and Rob.

'Of course they will agree,' Kate said. 'They itch to work for you again.'

'Will your mother permit it?'

'She will be glad to have them out of the house. Too wild to be of much use to her, except when she needs strong arms and backs.'

'Should I speak with your mother, or would a message from you suffice?'

'You have work to do. I will pass the word, and they will find you, never worry.'

As Owen rose to leave, Kate mentioned that Magda had arranged for Alisoun to continue to bide with them to look after the children and their guest.

'She is not to attend Muriel Swann's lying in?' Owen knew Alisoun to be proud of the widow's confidence in her skills.

'Dame Muriel will not be neglected. Dame Magda will be there in Alisoun's stead.'

That was not the issue. Alisoun could make the family's life a penance if she resented the arrangement. Owen prayed she had chosen to stay of her own free will.

Gwen ran over to him as he sat to pull on his boots. 'The angel sings like the sisters at St Clement's,' she said. 'Is she a nun?'

'She is awake?'

'Mistress Alisoun said not to peek, but I heard her singing.'

'What do you mean she sings like the sisters?' Owen asked. Lucie had been educated at St Clement's, and occasionally provided physics their infirmarian needed. She had on occasion taken Gwen with her to see the gardens.

'*Deus in* something *intende*,' she chanted. 'Then *Domine* . . .' She gave a solemn bow.

'Well done, Gwen. Sing that for your mother. She might know what it is,' he said. Convent-trained indeed.

'Shall I spy on her?'

'No, my love. She is a guest in our home and deserves our respect.'

Gwen rose on her toes and spun around. 'I could dance for her and she might talk to me to keep me with her.'

Fighting a smile, Owen pretended to frown as he considered. 'You might ask Alisoun whether in her opinion such a dance would be soothing for our guest when she wakes.' He believed he knew what Alisoun would say to that. He kissed her. 'And now I must be away.' He thanked Kate for the food, and for giving Gwen a task.

Kate glanced up from her work. 'She lifts my— Brother Michaelo! I did not see you step in.'

The monk stood in the doorway with a thoughtful expression. 'I believe she was singing the beginning of the hours, Captain.' He chanted the entire phrase. 'I know how difficult it is to complete one's daily prayers when not in community.'

'And while deep in a fever sleep,' said Owen, plucking his cloak from the hook.

Michaelo touched his arm. 'Fever? Not—'

'No. Not pestilence.'

Michaelo crossed himself.

In the garden, Owen turned toward the gate that led into the York Tavern yard. 'Before Stonegate, Tucker's home. I will explain why as we walk.'

'I was correct about the woman,' Michaelo said softly.

'It would appear so.'

'I become indispensable.'

'Insufferable.'

Michaelo sniffed.

After Gwen danced down the steps, Alisoun stood in the doorway of the nursery listening to the stranger's singing.

The child was right, this was music one heard in church, not out on the streets or in taverns. A voice so strong, so clear . . . Peering back into the nursery to make sure both Hugh and Emma slept, she filled a cup from a jug of water and knocked on the shut door.

'Mistress, are you awake? Would you care for some water?'

The singing paused. A whispered exclamation Alisoun could not make out. Then silence.

Alisoun knocked once more. 'Do not be afraid. You are in a safe place.'

'There are bars on the window.'

'Protection for a beloved elder who grew confused before her death.'

Movement, then a rustling at the door. 'I am locked in?'

Alisoun moved the wood stop installed for Dame Philippa. 'Try again.' She stepped aside as the door swung outward.

'Oh.' Pale eyes peered out from a damp tumble of curls fairer than Jasper's. The only color on the woman's ivory skin was two spots of red on her cheeks. Her borrowed smock hung limp with sweat over a skinny frame, stopping above knobby ankles. 'I am thirsty.'

The fiddler lived in a small cottage behind a more substantial home, across a garden that received so little light it was still blanketed in snow except for the pathway to the door, which was melting around icy footprints that would take more time to soften. Footprints circled the cottage as well. Owen took a moment to study the multiple tracks ringing the building, one set going out to a woodpile behind the house, the others staying close. A widening in the track suggested that someone had stood for a while at the shuttered window beside the door. He was able to make out the prints of at last two different pairs of boots, one longer and wider than the other. Fewer prints than the smaller man. The front door hung on one hinge. When Owen knocked, Magda called out that he should lift the right corner of the door in order to enter.

He stepped into a warm room with fresh rushes on the floor, well-scrubbed stones surrounding the central fire, a pair of box beds in opposite corners, a ladder rising up into the rafters.

Spare but inviting. After Brother Michaelo had passed through, Owen closed the door.

Tucker lay face down on a trestle table near the fire. Owen thought of his daughter's kneading as Judith, a woman of some strength, pressed and pummeled her husband's back under Magda's watchful eyes.

'Might I interrupt?'

'Help him turn and sit up,' said Magda, nodding with satisfaction as the man was able to walk to a chair with Owen's assistance.

Out of breath, but grateful, Tucker thanked Magda. 'Bless you.'

Judith wiped her eyes with her apron and greeted Owen and Michaelo. 'There was no need to bring a priest, Captain. Tucker is not in danger of death.'

'I am the captain's secretary, not a priest,' said Brother Michaelo, taking a seat.

With a curt nod, she turned her attention to the pot over the fire.

Magda drew a blanket round Tucker's bare torso. 'Not too long,' she warned Owen. She held his eye for a moment and whispered, 'Much not said.'

He gave a little nod. 'I am grateful you were able to come to him so soon, so that he is able to answer my questions while the ordeal is fresh to him.' He turned to Tucker. 'Who attacked you?'

'I don't know him, Captain, but I have seen him before, watching the house. One of several who've been sniffing around. But they have never trespassed farther than the garden.'

'None tried to talk to Ambrose?'

'Not that I saw.'

'Your old friend brought this trouble,' Judith muttered.

'He did,' said Tucker. 'But he warned me there might be someone following him.'

Judith hit the pot with her spoon. 'That is the first I have heard of it, husband.'

'How could I refuse him shelter? A friend is a friend in all ways for all days.'

'That is a child's song, you dunderhead.' Judith wiped her eyes and stabbed at the stew.

Magda crossed the room and put an arm round Judith, spoke in her ear. The woman seemed to calm.

'She will not soon forgive me,' said Tucker.

Owen thought it likely Judith's anger masked her fear for her husband, but he said nothing of that, pulling up a stool so he and the injured man might talk quietly. 'Tell me all you can about your intruder.'

'I found him tossing stuff about and challenged him. He turned on me and cursed me as he struck.'

'You had gone out?'

A nod that caused him to wince and touch his back. 'Carrying in wood for the fire. So quick he'd come in, gone straight to the bed over there.' He began to nod, then said, 'One to my right, where Ambrose slept. He stank of horses and sweat, but his clothes were well made. Wore a hat covering his hair, if he had aught.'

'Was your attacker alone?'

'Yes, God be thanked.' He began to move his hand, perhaps to cross himself, but stopped. Noticing how Tucker trembled, Owen hurried on with his questions.

'Could you tell anything of him by his speech?'

'From across the sea. I know a Frenchman when I hear one.'

Impossible to know whether either of the corpses were French. Owen thought he might take a closer look at their clothing. 'He was searching through Ambrose's things?'

'That I could not say, for Judith had put what Ambrose and the lad had left in that bed, so we might use the other again.'

'Do you know what was in those packs? Have you looked?'

'Ambrose promised to pay us, but left without doing so, and once the rumor spread that he'd murdered the cleric and stolen his treasure, well—'

'What did you find?'

'Naught but their traveling kits – wooden spoons and cups, combs, bits of clothing, nothing worth stealing. Broken paternoster beads, coral and jet. A few pence in coin, no more.' Tucker's voice trembled – the pain? Or a lie?

'No letters of passage?'

'Nothing like that.'

'They both left their packs?' A nod. 'Did you expect them to return?'

'Ambrose said he might be called away with little warning and asked if I would send his pack on to Dame Magda if he did not return in a day. But he meant for the youth to stay. He'd send the money, he said, and word of where to take the youth.'

Owen glanced over at Magda, who raised a brow at that. So Tucker had known Ambrose meant to go to Magda, or at least entrusted his things to her. Had he informed the one who'd drowned?

'Yet his companion left as well,' said Owen.

'Matthew went out to the midden after Ambrose left and didn't return. I hear he spent the night in the chapter house. And now he's with you?' He glanced over at his wife. 'Or she. Judith said—'

'Hush, husband!'

'Yes. Our guest now. Have either of you told anyone about Matthew and your suspicion?' Owen asked.

Bowing his head, Tucker shook it. 'No.'

'Nor I,' said Judith. 'The youth had a reason for so hiding.'

'Good. Say nothing to anyone for now,' he said, looking first at Tucker, then Judith. They both swore they would keep the secret. The truth would be out in time, but it might help to keep people guessing for now. 'Nothing in the pack to suggest this? That the intruder might have seen? Or taken? Did he take anything?'

'No,' said Judith. 'I checked. The prayer beads might be more a woman's style, but many men like a jeweled trinket.'

'Did your intruder ask after either of them?'

Tucker snorted. 'He was not so polite as that.'

'You could understand him sufficiently to be certain?'

'A curse is clear in any tongue, Captain. He said no more.'

'Might he have been a Fleming?' Michaelo asked.

'Nay, I know the weavers. They don't speak as he did.'

Michaelo was thinking of Ambrose's former lover, Martin Wirthir, spy, assassin, pirate. 'Did you injure him?' Owen asked.

'Never had the chance.'

'Did he seem hampered in his movement in any way? A previous injury?' Owen asked. 'Did he use both arms?' Martin was missing a hand.

'He came on me so fast I couldn't say, Captain.'

Owen thanked Tucker and wished him swift healing. 'I will take their packs,' he said as he rose. Magda went to fetch them while Owen helped Tucker move back to the table.

'Good riddance to the both of them,' Judith muttered as she wiped her sweaty forehead with her apron and returned to the table, assisting Owen in easing her husband down and rolling him back onto his stomach.

Magda resumed her instructions as Owen lifted the door to swing it open.

The twins stood just outside, stamping their feet and hugging themselves to keep warm.

'How might we serve you, Captain?' asked Rose.

He gave them the packs to leave at his home. 'I will be on Stonegate, in and out of the shops. Catch me there, stay without, observe who is too curious.'

'Our pleasure!' said Rob as he snatched the packs and headed off.

'Can he still fiddle?' Rose asked, nodding back toward Tucker's house.

'Dame Magda will see that he is able.'

'Good,' said the girl. 'Dame Judith counts on that money to keep them in food.'

'He makes so little at the stable?'

'He's working off a debt there.'

'How do you know this?'

'I listen.'

So Tucker needed money. 'Glad to have you and Rob on my side.'

Rose grinned and ran off after her twin, stopping once as her right foot stepped out of its boot, jamming it back on, hurrying on. Owen would see that the city paid them well so they might have boots to fit.

*   *   *

Owen stepped out of the goldsmith's shop on the corner of Stonegate and Petergate. It was late afternoon, growing colder as the light faded, but it would be a still night, no icy wind. Melting snow puddled on the street and dripped from the eaves. Time to let the tradespeople go home for the evening. He pulled his cloak round him and glanced back toward his own home. No, not yet.

'I want a closer look at the dead men's clothing,' he told Michaelo. 'You are free to go about your evening work in the minster yard.'

'I will complete the day with you, Captain.'

'As you wish.'

They made their way to the shed behind the deanery. In the fading light Owen could just pick out a well-worn path circling the small building, the snow long gone. It was impossible to know how many had been lurking.

'Who goes there?' Alfred called from within in his most threatening voice.

'Archer, with Brother Michaelo.'

The door opened, and Alfred bowed them in. 'Bloody cold in here.' Of course a brazier was out of the question. The corpses were best kept cold.

'All the tracks outside – have you met any of the visitors?'

'A few vicars and their clerks who thought Ronan was here. Others are gone before I can identify them. The clerk Edwin thought he might have seen this one before.' He nodded to the one who'd drowned. 'He didn't want to say, but I caught his look.'

'That is helpful. Did he say more?'

'No. Could not think where or when, or name companions.'

Edwin having worked for Alexander Neville, it might be significant.

'And you? What have you learned, Captain?'

Owen told him of Tucker's intruder, and his visits to the gold- and silversmiths, as well as the pewterers along Stonegate. Only one had made himself unavailable, Will Farfield. He heard from the others that Will had sent his family away to avoid the pestilence in the city. Foolish man, sending them south to his wife's parents where the sickness took one of his daughters. None had any dealing with Ronan, a few had with Neville, but they all expressed disgust at the thought of paying him to move anything along in the papal court. Difficult to judge how many were lying, but most seemed eager to prove to Owen they had nothing to hide, keen to see the items and identify the owners. None had noticed a Frenchman being a particular nuisance, though there were many strangers about, organizing lodgings for the enthronement celebration. From all the great Northern houses, and a few farther afield.

The chill already penetrated Owen's cloak. Alfred blew on his gloved hands and wiggled one foot at a time, as if testing for feeling. His usually pale face was red and chapped with the cold.

'Go home,' said Owen. 'Rest. Another guard should be here soon. For the nonce, I have much to think about and the quiet will serve me.'

'No, Captain, I am fine. It was just last night you watched over your son Hugh. You need the rest.'

But when Owen insisted, Alfred shrugged and moved toward the door. Where he stopped, listening.

Owen heard it as well. A shout and a curse, the latter a young woman's voice.

Throwing open the door, Alfred stood back in amazement as young Rob and Rose escorted a man into the shed.

'He's been too curious for my taste,' said Rose.

'We thought it best to introduce you, Captain,' said Rob.

Bald and barrel-chested, the man was dressed much like the unknown corpses lying on the slab, especially the drowned one. 'Cursed street rats. Who do they think they are?'

'My watchers,' said Owen. He nodded to the twins. 'Well done. You can release him now.'

The man staggered a moment as the two let go, but caught his balance and made a show of brushing off his cloak and straightening the padded jacket beneath.

'You must be Captain Owen Archer,' he said, struggling to regain his dignity. 'I have heard much about you.'

'And you are?'

'I'm called Pit.'

'Not a Christian name.'

'It's what I'm called.'

'A stranger in York?'

'I am. I came here—' He glanced at Alfred, Michaelo, and the twins.

'Wait outside,' Owen told Alfred and the twins. 'We will not be long. Brother Michaelo stays.'

Alfred bobbed his head and exited with Rob and Rose.

'You carry yourself like a lordling,' said Pit. 'Or a commander.'

Owen ignored him. 'You were explaining what brought you to the city.'

'I was ordered to follow two minstrels who performed for my master and then slipped away.'

A surprising admission. But then Pit did not know how much Owen knew. 'I see. Is your master Sir John Neville or His Grace Alexander Neville, Archbishop of York?'

He liked the man's discomfited surprise, how he hesitated before responding. 'I prefer not to say.'

'Perhaps after a night in the castle jail you will feel otherwise.'

Pit glanced round as if sizing up his chance of escape. Owen grabbed his arm and twisted it behind his back.

'God's blood!' Pit cried. 'I've done nothing to warrant this. Or your threat.'

'You would not tell me if you had,' said Owen. 'Whom do you serve?' A yank.

Pit cursed. 'Sir John Neville.'

'Why is he interested in the minstrels?'

'He thinks them spies.'

'And your orders?'

'What do you think?'

Yet he was confessing to Owen. 'Why are you here now? Did you suspect the men lying on those slabs were the minstrels?'

'No. I come to claim my friend.'

'Which one might he be?' Owen released him.

Nursing his arm, Pit moved to the drowned man, the one Edwin might have recognized. One of Neville's men. That made sense.

'Gareth was following one of the minstrels, the older man. We were fools to move about without lanterns in the winter dark.'

'You say he was following one of the minstrels. Where were you?'

'We'd argued about which one to follow. I tracked one to the chancellor's house. As he entered and took off his hat I saw he might be wearing the cloak, but he was balding.' A deepening frown. 'Gareth chose the other for the way he walked.' His voice had gone gruff.

'What did you do then?'

'Went looking for the other minstrel, the younger one. He'd gone into the minster, but I thought by then he might have returned to his lodgings. No sign of him. Downed a few tankards at an alehouse and stumbled to my bed. Gareth still wasn't back when I woke. Thought he might be waiting for me in the minster yard. Didn't really think he'd be so daft but I had to do something. Someone was pacing back and forth in front of the chancellor's house.'

'Could you identify him?'

'No. Still dark. And snowing.'

'How did you know it wasn't Gareth?'

'Didn't move like him. So I gave up. Reached the hovels on the north side when I heard a cry. Ran back.'

'What did you see?'

'I heard a shout up above, on the chapter-house roof, I thought. Sounded like a scuffle. Then a sound nearer to hand, where the one had paced. Moved toward it and a body hit the ground. Just missed me. God help him.' A pause. Cleared his throat. 'Thought I'd best disappear or I'd be caught up in it.'

'Would you recognize the voice calling from the roof?'

'Shouts are shouts. I could see nothing but shadowy shapes. Even the man who fell, could not really see him. Just the snow darkening.' He glanced over at the corpse and crossed himself. 'Is that him?'

'It is. Have you seen him before?'

A nervous swallow, a shake of the head.

'Take a close look.'

He did so, lingering on the ruined face. 'No.'

Owen sensed a lie. 'You were to follow the two minstrels and then what?'

'See who they met.'

'Why?'

'My lord did not say. Only to return to report where they are, who took them in.'

'Not kill them?'

The man crossed his arms over his chest and averted his eyes.

'They lodged with Tucker for several days,' said Owen. 'Yet you stayed.'

'An old friend who would take him in for some coin. But he was not what drew them to York. I reckoned the old one, his clothing so fine, he would have important friends. I waited for him to go to them. Find out who might have sent him spying on my lord.'

'That was why you followed him last night.'

'Lost him at the minster. Did someone else make my mistake? Was the murdered vicar the one wearing the fine cloak? It's what I thought I saw. A glimmer of the white lining when he turned.'

'He was.'

'Someone meant to kill the old minstrel and killed a vicar?'

'It would seem,' said Owen, seeing no need to provide more information.

'Poor fool. I hear the old minstrel went to the Riverwoman, so Gareth must have been on the right path when the river took him.' Cleared his throat again. 'They say the Riverwoman has power. Did she know Gareth was coming and bade the river stop him?' He crossed himself.

Magda would enjoy that tale. 'And if the old minstrel did meet with someone of importance to your lord, what then?'

'I would tell Sir John.'

'No more.'

Silence.

As Owen had thought. 'Have a moment with Gareth, but he stays in my custody until we know what happened here.'

'My lord will not like that.'

'What would you do with him? Drag him back to Cawood? Pay for his burial?'

'Don't know. I'd not thought so far.'

He pretended to be far simpler than he was. Owen stepped away while he considered what to do with Pit. He'd been sent to silence a pair of spies. And he'd failed. Sir John would not take that kindly. Seemed to Owen that Pit had two choices – either go to his lord, confess his failure, and accept whatever insult his lord felt appropriate, or disappear. Yet now that he was in Owen's hands he confessed his mission – a third option? Submit to Owen, seek his protection? Perhaps, but he was clearly lying about much, or at least holding back information. He either underestimated Owen or – what? He thought to hold onto something with which he might bargain?

When Pit turned from his orisons Owen kicked the door and called out to Alfred to come within, he had a man to escort to the castle.

'I told you what I know!' Pit protested as Alfred stepped in, placing a hand on his shoulder and standing in the way of his escape.

'Do you count me such a fool as to set you free to finish your work?' Owen told Rose and Rob to wait there until someone relieved them.

'Shall I come?' Michaelo asked.

'I have no time to spend with this liar this evening. If you would send a messenger to Hempe's home in case he's there, tell him to meet us at the castle. Then go about your other business.'

Michaelo bowed and folded up his wax tablet. Rising, he whispered, 'May God watch over you.'

EIGHT

Sandrine

Lighting a second lamp to brighten the entrance of the apothecary, Lucie asked again whether Jasper would like her to stay. Such a long day. He moved slowly, and his hands were not as steady as usual. 'Grinding stones,' he said when she noted it. 'You need the rest, Ma. I will close the shop during the next lull.'

Lucie doubted he would turn anyone away who caught him shutting the door, but she thanked him, kissed his cheek, and withdrew to the workroom. Though she was eager to cross the garden and check that all was well with the children, she took the time to tidy the workspace. Her legs ached from hours of standing, and her arms complained as she lifted a heavy jar to a shelf above her head. But it was the satisfying weariness at the end of a busy day, not the strained, frightened, agonized weariness of the fortnight past, as she sat vigil with her feverish babies. She bowed her head at the memory, feeling again the terror, seeing the haunted look in Owen's eye as she relieved him, having tossed and turned and pretended to believe she might sleep. She depended on her husband's quiet strength. It anchored her. But even that eluded her when their children were threatened by disease, the invisible enemy he could not vanquish.

Lucie removed her apron and blew out all but one lamp. Stepping out into the garden she braced herself against a damp wind that shook the remaining snow from the branches above and created a second snowfall, brightening the twilight, stinging her skin. Glancing up at the heavens she watched tendrils of cloud and mist dance beneath the early evening star field. The moment of peace seemed a benediction. She glanced up as someone entered the garden through the gate from the York Tavern yard.

'Dame Lucie.'

'Alisoun?' Lucie caught herself before asking who was with the children. Alisoun was sensitive to any suggestion of irresponsibility.

'I went to the Swann home. I thought I should be the one to ask Dame Muriel whether Magda might take my place at her lying-in.' The crackle in Alisoun's voice suggested the conversation had been challenging.

'She protested?'

'At first. But when I spoke of your guest, the fever . . .'

Lucie's heart sank. Had Alisoun revealed their guest's sex? 'Did you mention that the he is a she?'

'No. I thought that unwise, with Crispin Poole always about. Neville's man.' Alisoun spoke with quiet assurance, no bristling at a perceived slight. Maturing by leaps and bounds of late, which gladdened Lucie's heart. She had believed in the young woman, but at times she had worried about her reactive nature.

Which deepened Lucie's remorse for doubting Alisoun's discretion. 'Crispin is there often?' she asked.

'According to the cook he dines there daily, and often returns in the evening.'

'A complaint?'

'No. He boasted of it. A household needs a man, especially a household with an infant. And all say Crispin makes no secret of hoping to wed Dame Muriel as soon as she agrees to put aside her mourning.'

'Does she seem ready for Magda?'

'No. The child is strong, punching and kicking, but not ready to greet the world.' A soft laugh. 'Dame Muriel believes it is a girl, for what boy would put such effort in movement that will not be seen and praised.'

Lucie laughed. 'What a miracle that she has such joy.' Muriel had suffered the triple loss of her husband, his father, and her own brother less than two months earlier. Violent deaths. At the time, all had feared Muriel, who had waited years to conceive, would lose the child. 'Truly a miracle.'

'She says some find offense in her joy.'

'Her family?'

'Her brother's widow.'

'One can forgive her.' Lucie shivered. 'Shall we go in? I enjoyed the first moments out here, but now I am chilled to the bone.'

Alisoun looped her hand through Lucie's arm as they hurried to the house. 'I spoke to our guest,' she said. 'Gave her water. She asked for cloth, thread, needle to add some length to the gown you left for her. She sewed for a while, but when Magda went in to speak with her she had fallen asleep.'

'Did she tell you anything about herself? Her name?'

'She calls herself Sandrine, but when I called out to her she did not respond at once. And something about the way she gave it up – it is not her name. She asked after Ambrose, said he has been good to her. Oh, and she is fasting for her sins.'

'Do you think she has run away from a nunnery?'

'I would not know how to tell.' Alisoun reached out and opened the kitchen door.

Five pairs of eyes watched them enter. Magda, holding Emma on her lap, was telling a tale of a hawk riding the wind over the moors to Gwen and Hugh, who sat bundled in blankets on the settle by the fire. Kate left the pot she had been tending to offer help with their cloaks and boots.

'What is this?' Lucie asked.

'Mistress Sandrine cried out in her sleep, frightening the little ones,' said Kate. 'So Dame Magda brought them down here. A warm, welcoming kitchen with hot drinks and a few tales soon calmed them.'

'Did you hear her cry out?'

'No. Too far away, I think. But Gwen asked me if her Da knew that woman killed a man.'

Killed a man. Poor Gwen. A house of healing was no place for such fears to arise. Lucie closed her eyes and whispered a Hail Mary, then joined Magda and the children.

'Dame Magda nursed a fox cub,' Hugh lisped through the space where a baby tooth had recently fallen out.

'And a wounded eagle,' said Gwen. 'Come. Sit and hear her stories.'

'I cannot at the moment, my love,' said Lucie. She kissed each child in turn, then signaled to Alisoun to take over while she talked to Magda.

Lifting Emma from Magda's arms, Alisoun began to sing a silly tune the children loved. As Lucie led Magda out into the hall Gwen and Hugh joined in.

'So our guest is disruptive despite the medicine?'

'She refuses all food and drink,' said Magda. 'To appease her god, or so she says. Penance.'

'Penance for what?'

'She cried to her god for forgiveness, she had not meant to kill him.' Magda held Lucie in her keen gaze. 'A confession? Or an overwrought sense of remorse for an injury to the heart? That is for thee to discover.'

'I will go to her. If she wishes to stay, she must accept our healing drafts.'

Magda pressed Lucie's shoulder. 'Thou canst see that thy children are out of danger. Since morning Hugh has gained strength.'

He did look and sound so much more himself. 'I do see it. Yet too much excitement . . .'

'Magda agrees. Whether or not she has taken a life, thy family needs rest. Peace. If she will not abide by thy rules, she cannot stay.'

But where to send her? In a city soon to be crowded with visitors, and Owen doubtless wanting to keep watch on her, where might Sandrine go? Perhaps she might trade places with Ambrose. Or – as Lucie reached the landing she thought of the appropriate lodging for Sandrine. Though she would need to convince the prioress to allow guards access.

Knocking on the door of the guest chamber, Lucie waited for a moment, then went in. Sandrine sat on the edge of the bed, hugging herself, pulling the covers round her when Lucie stepped in as if embarrassed to be seen in but a shift.

'*Benedicite*, Dame Lucie,' she whispered. 'Mistress Alisoun said that is what I should call you.'

Lucie touched her forehead. Cool now. 'You frightened my children when you cried out in your sleep. Dame Magda took them down to the kitchen to calm them.' She lifted the young woman's chin so that she might meet Lucie's gaze.

'I regret frightening them. I will endeavor—'

'You will agree to consume all that Dame Magda and I

prepare so that you stay calm and recover your health. If you refuse, you cannot remain in my home. My children are recovering from illness and must not be excited.'

The jaw tightened. 'I cannot. I must do penance.'

'I am convent-raised,' said Lucie. 'I know the power, and the challenge, of obedience. To humble yourself before God, surrendering to the path on which He has set you – that can be a powerful penance.'

Silence.

'But if you refuse, I will find another place for you. I—'

Sandrine suddenly straightened, staring past Lucie toward the door. 'Oh!'

Lucie turned to discover Owen in the doorway. 'This is my husband, Owen. Captain Archer, as he is known.'

A deep blush as Sandrine clutched the covers higher. '*Benedicite*, Captain Archer.'

'Owen, this is Sandrine.'

He nodded, but said nothing as Lucie joined him at the door. He carried the scent of snow and cold though he'd removed his cloak, boots, hat. His curly hair was wild as if he'd run his hands through it.

'I must speak with our guest.' His tone was sharp. 'If you would stay with us?' Leaning close so that only Lucie could hear, Owen warned her that he must be harsh with the young woman. He must know what she knew, whether she was a danger to the household. 'I will tell you everything when we leave her.'

'Of course.'

He plucked up the stool that Lucie had used and moved it closer to Sandrine.

'Tell me what happened in the chapter house last night.'

Pressing her lips together, the young woman shook her head. 'I know nothing. I was so frightened I – I prayed for sleep and God granted it. When I woke, I was so cold. I thought if I sang, someone would hear. Help would come. And it did.'

'You were up in the masons' chambers.'

She glanced at Lucie, back to Owen, shaking her head. 'Where?'

'The masons' chambers are up above the ceiling of the main chamber in the chapter house,' said Owen.

Lucie watched the woman's eyes as she devised a response.

'Why do you say that?'

From his scrip Owen drew out two strands of beads – a short strand of coral beads and a much longer strand of coral and jet, the jets at ten-bead intervals, suggesting a broken set of paternoster beads. Lucie noticed that the smaller strand had ten beads and extra knots at one end as if it had become a bracelet, albeit for the slender wrist of a child. Or their guest's, she realized, noticing her unusually narrow wrists. It was the same coral as the longer strand.

Sandrine recoiled, her pale skin flushed, eyes filling with tears.

'I have spoken to a man who witnessed the man's fall from the chapter-house roof,' said Owen. 'He says there was at least one shout from the roof, and a scuffle. You must have heard something. If it was a chase, they would have passed through the upper floor, where I found your beads.'

'How do you know they are my beads?'

'The larger strand was in the pack you left in Tucker's home.'

'You have my pack?'

Owen nodded. 'Someone must have carried a lantern. You would have seen a light.'

'I told you, I fell asleep.'

'I do not believe you slept through that. Especially as you lost your beads up above. Brother Michaelo tells me your clothing was wet when he found you. I noted your stockings were wet, inside your boots. And here is the knife Brother Michaelo took from your hand.' He drew it out of the scrip.

She stared at it.

'See how the handle is chipped? Here is the missing piece, which I found at the foot of the ladder to the roof.'

Eyes flickering here, there, anywhere but Owen's face.

'You waste my time.' Owen rose with an impatient sigh. 'We cannot shelter a possible murderer. I will take you to the castle at first light.'

Taking up her part, Lucie expressed alarm. 'You cannot mean it.'

Owen turned aside to her, still perched at the threshold. 'No doubt you have a gentle alternative, perhaps the poor sisters on Castlegate.'

'Or St Clement's. I might coax Prioress Isabel into accepting her as a charity case. You think me too compassionate?'

'For all we know she murdered the man. Gwen heard her cry out that she did. I cannot risk her harming anyone else.'

'What is the castle?' Sandrine asked in small voice.

Owen turned back to her. 'York Castle. For you, it will be a prison.'

'Master Ambrose said I might trust you.'

'When did he say this?' Lucie asked.

'Yesterday, before he left for the minster. He told me if anything were to happen to him I should seek Lucie Wilton, the apothecary, and her husband Captain Archer. That you would protect me.'

'How did you come to be traveling with him?' Owen asked.

After a moment's hesitation, Sandrine gave an account of an elegant minstrel who joined the company of musicians and players, how he taught her a song he had composed. Then rescued her. Her story matched what Ambrose had told Owen.

'I am most grateful to him,' said Sandrine. 'But when he said we were being followed, and it was not likely to be the players, I feared I had been mistaken to trust him. Yet I could not stay with them, not after what happened.' Tears started again, her face flushing crimson. Genuine emotion.

'Your attacker was one of your fellow players?'

She crossed herself and murmured a yes.

'What did you know of the players when you joined them?' Owen asked.

'Simple folk. Not so grand as Master Ambrose, with his trained voice, his beautiful crwth, his Parisian speech, his costly cloak.'

'The cloak,' said Lucie. 'Did you witness the exchange in the minster?'

A slight nod.

'Why did you go into the chapter house?' asked Lucie.

'I was afraid,' Sandrine whispered, still looking away. 'I am guilty. I did not push him, but I could not stand. He tripped over me and . . . I am guilty.' She covered her face and wept.

Owen knelt to her, gently took her hands in his. She tried to turn away.

'Why?' he asked. 'What had he done?'

'Not him,' she sobbed. 'What I did.' She shook her head and began to whisper the words of the *Kyrie*.

'I pray you. Tell me what happened.'

'I must make my confession. I will bare my soul to a priest, no other.' She bowed her head and returned to the prayer of contrition.

'Tell me at least this. Was there another man in the chapter house with you?'

'I was not aware of another.'

'Can you tell me anything else?'

Sandrine shook her head. 'I want a priest.'

With a frustrated sigh Owen rose, drawing Lucie out the door. 'If Jehannes hears her confession, I will still know nothing.'

'We cannot deny her.' She saw how he fought anger and pity.

He returned to the room. 'Forgive me, but I must know. Had this anything to do with the murder of the vicar down below?'

Sandrine shook her head and lay down on the bed, turning her back to them.

'I will send for a priest I trust, an archdeacon. Should you disturb the children tonight, we will move you to the kitchen. And tomorrow—' He shrugged and strode out.

Lucie shut the door behind them. She prayed that gentle Jehannes would coax the woman to care for her body as well as her soul.

Once down the stairs, Owen drew Lucie over to the hearth. 'Before I go to Jehannes, I must tell you what I've learned.' At the corner of his good eye, he spied Magda slipping out the kitchen door. 'Come. Sit with us. I have much to tell.'

Moving quietly, Magda chose a spot near the garden window, far from the heat of the fire. 'Thy guest refuses to confide in thee?'

'She admits to being the cause of the man's fall. And claims it had nothing to do with Ronan's murder. Nor was there a second man in the chapter house.'

'That she was aware of,' Lucie added.

Owen settled on a bench, stretching his feet to the fire. 'I am uneasy about her being here. If a man had made such a confession I would take him to the castle until I knew whether he was dangerous.'

'I trust you agree that the castle dungeons are no place for a woman,' said Lucie. 'You will find a safer arrangement. Unless you believe she is for hanging— But think, my love. She is a beautiful young woman, you cannot entrust her to the jailers. Or do you know of several strong, trustworthy women who might both guard and protect her?'

Lucie knew him so well. Of course he hoped for a safer solution. Some – perhaps most – of the guards were no better than they needed to be with criminals, and Sandrine might prove too tempting, damn them. The bailiffs would curse him for the extra men – or women – necessary to protect her at a time when the city was about to be filled with strangers for the enthronement.

'Perhaps Jehannes will guide me,' he said, then turned so that he could watch Magda's reactions as well as Lucie's as he recounted his interview with Tucker, much of what Magda had no doubt overheard, and Rose's insight. Magda nodded. He asked what else she had noticed.

'Judith distrusts what her husband is about. Mayhap Tucker took in his old friend only to profit from betraying him.'

'Might he have gone to the minster last night?'

'Magda will ask Judith.'

He continued with his encounter with Pit, which brought an impatient hiss from Lucie, a shrug from Magda. He mentioned Crispin Poole's injury.

'I expected he would have come to you when he was injured, Magda.'

'He may not wish his new master to know he consults a

healer who does not share his faith,' she said. 'Magda may see him at Dame Muriel's.'

'That is settled?' Owen asked. 'Alisoun is willing to stay?'

Lucie told him of her conversation with Alisoun in the garden. He was relieved she took it well.

Pit and his mate Gareth interested Lucie, who found it peculiar that he would be so forthcoming about being John Neville's man.

'He may welcome my interference as a way to delay reporting his failure to Sir John. His lord will turn his anger on me, let Pit quietly withdraw amongst his fellows. But from what I know of John Neville, Pit is doomed either way.'

'You believe Pit recognized the other man?' Lucie asked.

'I do. Made him ill at ease. The bailiffs' men are moving the bodies to the castle this evening, once the nightwatchmen are out on their rounds, extra eyes to notice anyone taking more than an idle interest.' Owen nodded toward the steps and said, 'Perhaps one of you might inform our guest of the additional deaths.'

'Where will the children sleep tonight?' Lucie wondered aloud.

'Just for tonight, we might let them enjoy sleeping in the kitchen, with Kate and Alisoun to fuss over them,' he suggested. 'A change from that room in which they spent a fortnight.' He watched Lucie consider, saw her accept the idea. God be thanked. 'I will not be long,' he said.

Magda drew an arm round Lucie. 'While Bird-eye fetches the crow, Magda will take thy guest a bowl of watery broth with a pinch of something to calm her. Once he departs, take her the jug of honey water Magda will prepare with a touch of sleep. If Gwen and Hugh fret about sleeping in the kitchen, thou canst assure them that the stranger sleeps.'

'She will not drink either preparation.'

'Dost thou doubt Magda?'

Though he was curious how this exchange would resolve, Owen considered his mission urgent. With a bow to the two healers, he withdrew.

In the kitchen Hugh and Gwen snuggled together as they listened to Alisoun rocking Emma to sleep with lullabies.

Booted and cloaked, Owen plucked a lantern from a hook near the door, lit it, and departed, heading toward Stonegate.

Rising from prayers, Jehannes listened to Owen's request with a deepening frown creasing his pleasant features. 'Are you certain you wish me to do this, my friend? I have not the right to reveal what she tells me in confession. Will it be a wedge between us?'

Michaelo, garbed in his penitential robes, hovered in the background, clearly curious. Owen assured both of them he was well aware what this meant, yet he could think of no one else he would so trust.

'I ask you to consider the forces that might bear down on you should someone discover that she confessed to you,' said Owen. 'Nevilles in particular, though so far they have not claimed the fallen man.'

Jehannes smiled. 'I pride myself in my stubbornness. And who in your household would betray us?'

'You might be seen arriving or departing my home.'

'Then we must think of a clever explanation.'

Michaelo handed the archdeacon his cloak, followed him to the bench by the door to assist him with his boots. Jehannes waved him away.

'I pray you are not hoping to accompany me to take notes,' he teased.

'A tempting thought,' Michaelo said, 'but I am better occupied assisting the poor in the minster yard. For my sins.' With a bow, he departed.

'The cutting Michaelo returns,' Jehannes remarked when he stood, booted and cloaked. 'He had come to me broken, humbled. I worried. But now . . . I am unsure whether or not to rejoice.'

Owen shared a companionable laugh with him as they walked out into a misty night.

'By the way,' said Jehannes, 'Michaelo spoke with the clerk Edwin. He distrusted Ronan, preferred to work directly with Neville. Engaged as little as possible with Ronan when Neville was away. He mentioned Ronan being called Neville's summoner, doubted Neville would overstep his position when a prebend.'

'Loyal to Neville.'

'A most careful man, I think. As to who might want him dead, he said most in the Bedern resented Ronan, but he knew of no one who would go to the extent of killing him.'

Disliked but not so much as to inspire violence. Always the safe answers.

Staring out of the garden windows into the swirling mist, Lucie imagined herself the pale, ethereal Sandrine, kneeling before Dom Jehannes and, at long last, making her confession. Imagining how it would feel to be assured this priest would keep her secrets, would not betray her sex, or her identity, would neither judge nor push away in horror. She could not think of a better confessor for a woman who had feared revealing anything about herself for so long. Tears stung her eyes, wet her cheeks.

Owen took her hand. 'What is it?'

'I am imagining her suffering. How much she has borne with no one in whom she might confide. You will not send her to the castle?'

'No matter her crime, I would not subject her to that. I cannot know what a woman suffers regarding men. I will do as you and Magda advise.'

She kissed his hand.

He nodded toward the steps. 'Jehannes.'

Wiping her eyes, Lucie watched Jehannes pause at the foot of the steps, cross himself, and set aside his prayer book before continuing toward them. She sensed Owen tense.

'Your guest did not tell me who she is. But I advise you take her to St Clement's. If you agree, I will accompany you and speak with the prioress.'

'So she is a nun?' said Lucie.

Jehannes crossed himself, but would say no more.

'Are the children safe with her in our home?' Lucie asked.

'I would say you need not fear her. But I do not know enough to say whether her presence will draw trouble your way. The fallen man was not alone in the city. You might encounter his companion. But I doubt she knows anything about Ronan's death.'

Expressing his gratitude, Owen invited Jehannes to share some wine, but he declined.

'Another time, my friends. May God watch over this house.'

Lucie walked him to the door. 'Bless you for shriving her.'

'Your home is just the shelter she needed to begin healing.'

'But you believe she will be more at ease at St Clement's?'

'It is where she belongs.'

Hearing Jehannes take his leave out in the hall, Magda rose from her seat by the kitchen fire and collected the tray she had prepared, broth with herbs to heal voice and spirit as well as ensure a restful sleep, and warm, honeyed water. In addition, she carried a pouch containing willow, madder, mallow, chamomile, rosemary, sage, and a few other blood-strengthening roots and herbs to encourage her womb to renew itself. Ordeals such as Sandrine's often choked the womb, preventing the monthly courses. Alisoun's insight into the young woman's strongest emotions, fear and a deep sorrow, suggested to both of them that this might be so, and that she feared she might be with child.

'Will you come back to tell more stories?' Hugh asked, tugging at Magda's skirt as she passed, though his eyes were closing.

Bending to kiss his forehead, Magda whispered, 'Beseech Alisoun to tell thee of the fox cub she nursed back to health.'

He did just that as Magda withdrew.

In the hall, she set aside the tray for a moment to hear the news. Most significant for her was that Sandrine was likely a nun. Helpful. Owen had more to tell, but Magda suggested they talk after she had seen to the young woman. Lucie offered to carry the tray, but Magda preferred that she led the way, opening the door.

Owen felt the need to explain why he did not offer. 'I was harsh with her. She might not welcome my presence.'

'No need to apologize for respecting her, Bird-eye.'

Up in Philippa's chamber, the young woman knelt with her back to the door, fingering the broken paternoster beads. Her fingers fumbled with the next bead. Of more concern was how her slight body swayed as she knelt, an uneven movement

Sandrine checked with every breath. Now and then, her head also nodded forward, as if her body yearned for rest.

'How she fights to stay awake,' whispered Lucie.

'Tonight Magda will turn this child toward healing. On the morrow, she becomes thy work, and Alisoun's. Magda must see to Muriel Swann.'

Stepping into the room, Magda nodded to Lucie to shut the door behind her. She busied herself placing the items on a squat table, then settled on a stool beneath the shuttered window to wait. 'Pay Magda no heed until thou art finished with thy prayers,' she said when Sandrine glanced up. She hoped it would not be too long, or both the broth and the water would grow cold, the ingredients settle. But healing could not be rushed.

Her head level with the kneeling woman, who remained bowed, Magda noticed her pallor, even to the long lashes resting on her cheeks. Lack of food and rest, perhaps. But she would be curious to see the woman's eyes, whether they were pale. And weak.

She waited. In a short while, the woman raised her head. Pale eyes. She blinked, then focused on Magda with ease, saw her. Still, her lack of color was more than depletion.

'You were with Dame Lucie and Captain Archer,' said Sandrine, 'but they did not say who you are.' A resonant voice. Strong.

'Magda Digby, midwife, healer, friend to Ambrose, thy minstrel companion. He asked me to watch over thee, see that thou art in good hands.'

'You are the one they call the Riverwoman?'

'He told you of Magda?'

'I heard him asking about you, whether you still lived on your island in the river. He asked you to watch over me?'

'He did.'

Magda lifted the jug. 'Warm water with just enough honey to ease thy voice.'

'I am fasting.'

'Thou hast been entrusted by thy god with this body, yet thou hast tested it almost beyond repair.'

'Penance,' Sandrine whispered.

Magda sensed her wavering. 'A harsh penance. Dost thou take it upon thyself to make amends for others' sins against thee?'

'You sound like Dom Jehannes. He said I have been sinned against, and that is no sin.'

'A wise man. It is not for thee to decide whether or not to end thy life.'

'That was not my intention.'

'Intention is the key, but all acts are best undertaken with compassion and a willingness to accept help. Magda understands thou hast dedicated thy voice to prayers to thy god. Is that so?'

'You speak as if you are not a Christian.'

'Magda honors all creation, and lives to serve. Such a voice as Ambrose describes is not to be neglected. Thou must care for such a gift.'

The pale eyes lowered. Good teeth bit back the full lower lip. The woman would quickly regain her health if she wished it. But her spirit was caught in confusion and weighted by a darksome fear that the confession had failed to calm. Magda stirred the honey water and poured a little into the bowl, held it out.

'Wilt thou drink?'

Sandrine took the offering, tasted, then drank deep, emptying the bowl, handing it back with thanks.

Magda bowed to the young woman. Setting aside the bowl she took Sandrine's hand, holding it for a moment while looking into her eyes. Yearning, sorrow, fear. Yet also strength. Remarkable strength from which arose a deep, simmering anger. After a time Magda released the hand, her gaze. She sat in silence, eyes closed, until the young woman chose to speak.

'I lived to serve as well. I meant to dedicate my voice to God.'

'Heal and return to thy work.'

'I do not think I can.'

Magda waited.

'I have not bled for a long while. Since I was—' Once again Sandrine bowed her head.

Here was the source of her fear. 'Might Magda touch thy stomach?'

'No spells!'

'Magda wishes to examine thee, no more.'

A nod.

Kneeling to the woman, Magda placed her hands on her stomach, closed her eyes. Tightness, anger, fear, sorrow, but no extra heartbeat, no sign of life. Opening her eyes she touched Sandrine's cheek.

'No child swims in thy womb. Thou hast suffered much, but not that.'

A gasp that became a sob.

Rising to sit beside the troubled young woman, Magda put a warming arm round her, took her hand. 'Have men forced themselves on thee?'

'The first one never touched me. Others have tried. I fought them off, always I thought in time. But when I did not bleed . . . I feared that in my ignorance I had not been quick enough.'

She pressed Magda's hand, the heat of her anger flushing both of them.

'Canst thou feel thy strength?' Magda smiled.

'You have given me hope. If I could prove to the sisters I am chaste, perhaps I might do as Dom Jehannes advised, seek sanctuary at the priory, with the sisters.'

'Dost thou desire that?'

'More than anything.'

'Thy voice will delight them. But to prove to the sisters thou art untouched – what dost thou seek for this?'

'To bleed. And the witness of someone whose word they would accept. Dame Lucie?'

Out of the bag hanging from her girdle Magda pulled the pouch of blood-strengthening roots and herbs she had prepared.

'If Magda adds herbs to thy honeyed water to encourage thy womb to renew, to flush out the old blood, wilt thou drink?'

'It will not sicken me? You swear there is no child? You are not killing it?'

'Magda spoke truth about there being no child. Her purpose is to heal, only to heal.'

Sandrine looked into Magda's eyes. 'I will drink.'

Magda invited the young woman to watch as she mixed a few pinches of the powder with the water in the jug. 'Thrice daily, until thy womb responds.' She poured the fresh mixture into the bowl.

Sandrine took it with thanks, sniffed, sipped, drank it down. 'Bless you. It slips down my throat with ease.'

'More?'

A nod.

When she set the bowl aside, Sandrine blinked. 'My eyelids feel heavy. You swore no spells.'

'Magda uses the earth's bounty to heal. No more, no less. We are of earth.'

'Our bodies, yes. But not our souls. They are of God.' A frown.

This touched her fear. Magda did not argue. 'A bit of broth now? To nourish thy body.' She held out the bowl.

Sandrine sipped it.

'Sandrine is not thy given name, is it?'

A searching look. 'How—?'

'Magda listens, as do all in this house caring for thee.'

'My name is Marian,' she said, softly.

'So many Marys. Thy name will not betray thee.'

Marian fought to remain upright as she drank the broth. 'Why is the captain angry?'

'He has taken on the burden of keeping safe all he loves, and his heart encompasses much. Now he has three deaths to resolve before the powerful Nevilles arrive. The city is grateful, though not so grateful as before they learned he also serves the king's heir, the fair Joan's husband, Prince Edward. To whom is the captain loyal, they wonder? They fear. And they are silent when he only wishes to help. Benighted creatures.'

'Dame Agnes says we are clumsy babes always tripping over our own feet because we will not look into each other's eyes, where truth resides.'

'A wise woman.'

Marian swiped at tears. 'Is Ambrose a good man?'

'He is, despite himself. A tale for another day. Tomorrow Magda must see to the lying-in of a widow bearing her only child. But Alisoun will know all that Magda has mixed for thee. She, too, is a healer, and gifted with a voice that softens her sharp wit. She is nursing thine hosts' children. A fever threatened the lives of all three. Only last night did the last break, Hugh with the fiery hair. That, too, has shortened the captain's temper, and Dame Lucie's as well. She is an apothecary, but she cannot work miracles, even for her beloved children. She has of late lost an aunt. There has been much heaviness in this household. Be patient with them, tell them what they need to know, and they will be valuable allies.' As Magda spoke, she helped Marian ease down onto the bed. 'Sleep now.'

With a little smile, Marian closed her eyes, the anger that had simmered atop her fear abated for the moment.

Watching Lucie return from the landing, Owen invited her to the settle near the fire. He had much to tell her, about Tucker, Pit, but he touched her chin, gently turned her toward him, and began to kiss her. Forehead, cheeks, eyelids, mouth, neck.

With a soft laugh she pulled away. 'My love, what is it?'

'I have missed you. All the days and nights watching in the sickroom, I yearned for you. And now, when we might at last have peace, all this.'

Putting her arms round him, she kissed him back. 'You have a good heart, my love. You were right to give her shelter. My anger was the residue of days and nights of worry.'

'No need to explain. I knew. I felt the same.'

Holding each other close they shared now all the thoughts they dare not voice while the fever raged in the nursery. Owen felt Lucie's heart racing, realized his beat just as wildly. He fell to kissing her to save them both from the darkness.

NINE

A Night Watch

A soft tread on the steps. Owen eased his arms from round Lucie, sat back. She straightened her gown. Magda drew a stool near to them and settled, reaching her hands toward the fire with a sigh of ease. Lucie asked about Sandrine.

'Magda must come back to herself.' She watched the flames for a moment, then nodded and turned to them. 'And now to the child above.'

Owen bowed his head as he learned more of Marian's ordeal, how she had defended herself against men's predations, her fear of defilement, being turned away by the sisters. He could feel Lucie's distress.

'I regret being harsh with her,' he said.

'She is safe here. Thou hast been good to her.'

'I pray she knows she is safe with us,' said Lucie.

'She does. And for now she sleeps,' said Magda.

'Marian,' Lucie whispered. Wiping her eyes, she rose. 'I will tell Alisoun. And see how it goes with the children.' Thanking Magda for her help, she excused herself.

'Might we talk of Ambrose?' asked Owen.

'Thou hast no need for such formality, Bird-eye. What troubles thee?'

'Ambrose survived a dangerous journey without mishap despite his admitted lack of skill as a spy. I believe he had a protector. Have you any sense of Martin Wirthir's presence?'

'Thou art thinking of Tucker's attacker? Perhaps. The Minstrel left much unspoken. Thou art the one who gathers the threads and weaves the tapestry. Not Magda. Open thine eyes, Bird-eye.' She pressed a point between his scarred and his good eye. 'Magda has told thee what she knows, but she is a healer, not the one to seek out the answers. That is for thee to discover.'

'No advice?'

'Have a care moving Dame Marian. Magda advises patience. Choose the right moment, for the safety of all.'

She left him then, joining Alisoun and Lucie in the kitchen. Owen followed, discovered the children asleep on their pallet by the fire, the three women moving off to the side to talk. Kate kneaded bread while Jasper stood beside her chopping roots.

'I am going to the tavern. I agreed to meet George Hempe there,' Owen told the three women. 'Then Jasper and I will accompany him home with Ambrose's instruments.'

It was clear Jasper had heard, his face alight with anticipation as Owen turned to him.

'Could you ready Ambrose's instruments so we might deliver them to him at Hempe's home?'

'Gladly, Da.'

Donning boots and cloak, slipping a sheathed dagger onto his belt, Owen stepped out into the damp evening.

Tucked into the farthest corner of the tavern room, Hempe lifted a hand in greeting. All eyes were on Owen as he wound his way toward the bailiff, pausing at a table to ask after a man's dying wife, for whom Lucie had prepared a special mixture for her pain. Tobin clutched Owen's hand, red-rimmed eyes brimming with tears. 'God beckons her heavenward. Soon, now. Bless Dame Lucie for easing her last days with me.' Humbled, Owen slumped into his seat.

'Lucie is the hero of the people of York, not me.'

'She is a treasure,' said Hempe. 'But you do your part. As do I. Not everyone has her skill. Or the Riverwoman's. Or Mistress Alisoun's.' He drank down his ale and signaled to Tom Merchet, who hastened over with a jug.

'Where is the queen of York, Tom?' asked Hempe.

'Training a cook. You can talk in peace tonight.' Tom grinned as he bustled off.

'Most fortunate man,' said Hempe. 'This tavern would be nothing without our Bess.' He leaned forward, tapping Owen's tankard. 'Now to work. Household officials representing the great Northern families are entering the city as the snow recedes. Earlier than expected. Amidst all that it is impossible to ferret out anyone related to the deaths at the gates this morning. Hard to believe it was only this morning.'

More than disappointing, the news was worrying. 'The Neville household?' Owen asked.

'I passed the palace in the minster yard and saw servants opening shutters, shaking out cushions, clearing the steps. They expect Sir John and Archbishop Alexander soon. Not good.'

'And we know so little.' Owen told him what little he'd gleaned.

Hempe liked Jehannes's proposal regarding the young woman. 'But escorting her to St Clement's. If Neville's men recognize her before she is safe within.' He groaned. 'We will need guards there, but it is so far from all else we cannot use them for other duties, walking a watch. If we could wait to move her until after we have Ronan's murderer?'

Another urging Owen to be patient. 'I will think about it. If the prince's representatives arrive soon they might bring extra men.'

'That would be a blessing.' Hempe drank down his ale. 'I should see to my own household.'

'Jasper and I thought to accompany you with Ambrose's instruments.'

'You mean him to play?'

'A little while. See who is attracted.'

'You're expecting someone? Not Wirthir? God help us, Owen, I know that look. If he is in the city . . . You think he was Tucker's French attacker?' He squeezed his eyes shut and muttered a curse.

'Someone followed Ambrose from the French court, protected him, I am sure of it. One short test to see whether we snare a shadow.'

'Come along then. Let's be done with it.'

Owen, Jasper, and Hempe bobbed their heads to Harry Green, a nightwatchman, who paused as they passed.

'Quiet night?' Owen asked.

A nod. 'Pray God it ends so, Captain. Heard your children were ill.'

'On the mend.'

'God be thanked.'

'You should know that Gemma's twins are working for me.'

'So they tell me.' A grin.

'Tonight?'

'Came past a while ago. Slipping in and out between the houses and shops. My duty to inquire.'

'Did they appear to be following someone?'

'Not as I could see, Captain. Not many folk about.'

'No one unfamiliar?' asked Hempe.

'Nay. Crispin Poole was by, and I recall thinking he was headed wrongways. At this time of the evening he calls on the widow Swann.'

'But not tonight?' said Owen.

Harry shook his head. 'Heading toward Petergate, not away. Limping and glowering, he was. I wouldn't care to be the one who called him away from a pleasant evening. But I've seen nothing to worry me.'

'If you see Poole again this evening, let me know,' said Owen. 'I will be at Hempe's, then with the bodies at the dean's house.'

The man peered at Owen with interest. 'I will, Captain. God watch over you.'

'And over you,' Owen said, moving on with Jasper and Hempe.

So Crispin had been called away from Muriel. Interesting. A sign that the Nevilles were about to appear?

As they turned into Low Petergate, Owen noticed movement to his right. Gone. The twins?

A servant opened the Hempes' door on the first knock, beaming a welcome to all three. From the guest room Owen could hear Ambrose playing the crwth. It had been a long time since he had heard those sweet sounds. He need not request that Ambrose play.

Hempe took Lotta aside, quietly explaining Owen's mission.

She looked up at Owen. 'You mean to lure someone with his music?' Her expression was accusing.

'I do. I will join Stephen in watching.'

'Do you need me?' asked Hempe.

'I need you in here,' said Owen. 'In case Stephen and I are both fooled.'

'And me?' Jasper asked, setting down the fiddle case and rubbing his hands together. As usual, he had forgotten his gloves.

'Take the instruments to him and stay a while. You might ask him to play one of the other instruments. If he traveled with only the crwth, Neville's men might be listening for it. It is not them I hope to attract.'

Pressing Jasper's shoulder, Owen thanked him, thanked all of them, shuttered his lantern, and departed.

Out on Petergate, he stood at the mouth of the alleyway beside Hempe's house, watching for movement on the street. After a time, he heard someone behind him and turned.

'Are ye lost?' Stephen asked, his voice, though quiet, threatening. Owen knew he would have his hand on his dagger.

'Glad it is you who has tonight's watch, Stephen,' said Owen, keeping his voice low.

'Captain! Hempe asked me to take the first night, thinking if trouble is coming it might well be tonight.'

'Anyone yet?'

'Not to see, but I feel eyes. Knew you weren't that one.'

'But no movement.'

'I've not seen any. A dog, a few cats. But someone's watching.'

'Can you point to where you sense it?'

'Come round back.'

'Before we do that – we must not speak back there – once you have shown me, go to Crispin Poole's house, walk round it, then watch it for a while. Report to me anything you notice.'

'What am I looking for?'

'A reason why he is not with the widow Swann this evening. He may not be at home, but his mother will be. So there should be lights – not for her, she's blind, but for the servants.'

'How long?'

'I trust you to know when you are satisfied.'

A grunt, and then they moved through the alleyway. Owen kept his ears pricked for sounds beyond their cautious footsteps. It was warm enough that the snow continued to melt after dark. Dripping eaves obscured his ability to hear. He would move away from the house for his watch.

Once past the main building, Stephen used the light spilling out from Ambrose's shuttered window to point to his left, then motion away from the house. Owen patted his shoulder and withdrew into the shadow of the alleyway. He would stay here for a while after Stephen left. Then he would wind his way back into the shadows behind the garden shed. His watch began.

Owen had moved from the alleyway to a shed a few steps away from the shuttered window of Ambrose's room. No music. He pricked his ears as he heard voices. Jasper and Ambrose. Now a bow scraped over a fiddle. Again. Tuning. Owen settled back to wait. A tune began. A flat string. A halt for more tuning.

Owen sensed a presence.

'Step forward and show yourself,' he growled.

A drunken lad teetered through the light, leaving a trail of piss in his wake, just missing Owen's boots. Using the house for support he inched his way along the back to the alley, stumbled down it, one hand on the wall. Stepping out into the street he fell flat on his face, just as Harry Green appeared, shining his lantern to see what it was.

'Crab, is it you again?' The watchman glanced up at Owen. 'Lad's been at the ale all week. Lass broke his spirit, he says, robbed him of his soul.'

'As long as you know him . . .' said Owen.

'I do. Too well. Come on, you young fool.' Harry crouched and tugged the lad's arm, then lifted him up as if he were no heavier than a pup. 'I will take you home.'

Owen watched them move off in the direction of Christchurch. Satisfied that no one lurked behind them, he slipped down to the rear garden and took up position to wait for Stephen. A long wait. All the while Owen sensed a presence, yet no matter how stealthily he crept about he found no one. He began to doubt his own senses.

Ambrose had just begun a melancholy ballad when Stephen appeared, peering about, sniffing. And then he was beside Owen.

'Anything?' Owen asked.

'Found Crispin in his kitchen talking to that pair of armed men he wants us to believe are his menservants. Shouting at them, more like. Angry. Slapped one who'd grinned. Barked orders at him. "See to it." That one came slinking out the door with a curse. When I saw that Crispin and the other were still sitting about drinking ale, I chose to follow the one on the errand. Long walk. Stables across the Ouse. Arranged for three horses in the morning. I would love the chance to ride out on the morrow.'

'Not without sleep. The bailiffs can provide a few men. Good choice, following that one.'

'And you?'

'Nothing except a heartsick lad who had too much ale, pissing himself. Harry Green escorted him home.'

'I will keep an eye out.'

Knocking on the Hempe door, Owen stepped in to report what Stephen learned. 'Crispin might be riding out to meet Neville. You know to deny knowing anything about the white-haired minstrel, nor a youth companion.'

'White-haired? Seen no such man.' Hempe's grin twisted with a bit of worry. 'You will have someone here?'

'Two. Ned and Alfred. But that means your men must follow Crispin.'

'I will see to it. And is he here? Ambrose's friend?'

'If he is, he outwitted me.'

'Give it up?'

'There's the matter of Tucker's attacker,' Owen said.

'Martin Wirthir is not the only one who might have followed Ambrose across the water. We will find him.'

In the kitchen, the children slept on pallets by the fire into which Magda Digby sat staring as she sipped ale. He had not expected her to be here. She nodded to Owen, but her eyes were far away. Kate handed Owen and Jasper cups of hot spiced wine. Owen paused by the children, grateful to see their peaceful faces. Hugh still wheezed slightly, but he seemed comfortable. Tonight, Owen would sleep with Lucie in his arms.

In the hall, Lucie sat near the fire with Alisoun, who was spinning, a skill she had once avoided with disdain, but lately taken up, something to do with her hands as she watched her patients. Both glanced up when they approached.

'Did Ambrose play for you?' Lucie asked Jasper as he went to stand near Alisoun, watching her work.

'He did. And he was as good as ever. But the hair. That color.' Jasper wrinkled his nose.

'I should like to hear him play,' said Alisoun, looking up at Jasper with a shy smile.

'Once it's safe for him, I hope he will come play for all of us.' Jasper smiled down at her. 'I am glad you are staying with the little ones.'

'Did you see who you'd thought to see?' Lucie asked Owen as he settled beside her.

'Not tonight. I begin to think I am chasing my own shadow.'

That caught Jasper's interest. 'Are you watching for Martin Wirthir?'

'Am I so predictable?'

'When I heard about Tucker's attacker, I wondered.' Jasper drank down his cup, wished them all a good night.

Alisoun rose. 'I should see to the children, then go up to Dame Marian.' She followed Jasper into the kitchen.

Owen slipped an arm round Lucie.

'Will we take Marian to the priory tomorrow?' she asked.

'Not yet.' He repeated the warnings from Magda and Hempe.

'She will be disappointed. When I took her a fresh lamp she wanted to hear about St Clement's.'

'Did she tell you anything more?'

'Only that it meant something to her that it is a Benedictine priory.' Lucie rested her head on Owen's shoulder. 'Why would she lie about her name once we knew she was not a he?' she asked sleepily.

'Because someone is searching for her, I would guess. Someone she fears. Neville's men? They would not know her as Marian.' He drank down his wine and kissed the top of

Lucie's head. 'Tomorrow will be another long day. I need sleep. As do you.'

They were halfway up the steps when Alisoun returned. 'Magda said she will stay the night, watching over the children. Shall I sit with Marian? Magda encouraged me to talk to her if she is wakeful, share my story, gain her trust.'

Owen looked to Lucie. She touched his arm and whispered, 'I welcome the rest.'

'We would be grateful,' said Owen, thanking her for the generous offer.

Lucie slumped down on the edge of the bed, pressing a hand to her forehead. 'If Martin Wirthir had been there, and Jasper had seen him—'

Owen had been waiting for that. 'Martin once saved our son's life. He would never harm him.'

'But what of Jasper's pain? If Martin were the murderer . . . No. I give our son too little credit. He is a strong young man.'

'He is.' Owen sat down beside her, took her hand, kissed her cheek. 'Danger is everywhere. I want only to protect all whom I love.'

Smoothing his hair from his forehead, she frowned at him, but he saw no anger in her blue-gray eyes. 'I know. And I would never ask you to change.' She took a deep breath. 'And Jasper is so proud tonight.' She pressed her hand to her heart. 'So I will say no more about that.'

'Come to bed, my love.'

TEN

Visitors and Intruders

Uncertain what woke him, Owen rubbed his scarred eye and sat up, belatedly noticing the shower of needle pricks. He rose, alarmed. Not by the sensation, but the portent – trouble was near. Moving to the window overlooking Davygate, he peered out at what he could see in the pale light of a winter dawn. More color in the sky, promising sunlight. A draught chilled him, but gentler than a few days earlier. Not much cooler than yesterday midday. More thawing, which meant the roads, though muddy, would be passable. The Nevilles might arrive at any time.

A sharp reminder of the portent set him in motion. He was dressed by the time Lucie woke to ask what was wrong.

'Sleep, my love. I woke restless.' He bent to kiss her forehead.

With a contented sigh she rolled over and snuggled beneath the covers.

Retrieving his leather patch from the shelf near the door, he positioned it over his ruined eye, ran his fingers through his hair, and stepped out onto the landing. Habit sent him to the next room. Empty. As he began to worry his mind caught up. The children had slept in the kitchen. He listened at the last door, heard voices, soft, two of them, Alisoun and Marian. Uncertain whether to interrupt, he decided as all appeared peaceful he would first go below, check the garden, the shop.

A fire already burned in the hall hearth, though the room was deserted. He crossed to the long garden window. A cacophony of drips masked all other sound, but he saw nothing obvious. He would make a slow circuit on his way to the apothecary.

A peal of laughter rang out from the kitchen. Hugh was awake and laughing. Loudly. God be thanked. Pushing open the door, he was greeted by a cheery scene, Gwen and Hugh in a tickling match, his youngest watching in wonder from Magda's lap. Emma squealed to see Owen, lifting up her arms to be picked up. He was happy to oblige, spinning her round and hugging her close as her giggle turned to hiccups.

'Didst thou sleep?' Magda asked, rising to stretch her back.

'I did.' Kissing Emma, he handed her back to Magda, crouched down to tickle Gwen and Hugh, raising the noise to a startling level, and, laughing, crossed over to the boot bench.

'Ale?' Kate asked from the hearth.

'In a moment. I need the garden.' Best she thought he was focused solely on emptying his bladder.

Gently rocking Emma, Magda perched beside him as he pulled on his boots.

'Thou'rt worried, Bird-eye?' she asked in a quiet voice, not easily overheard.

He met her gaze. 'Trouble is nigh.' His whisper became laughter as Emma grabbed at his hair.

'Da!'

Magda tickled Emma's chin as she said, 'Thou hast a shower in thine eye?'

'I do.'

A nod, and she rose to rejoin the children, Emma squealing her farewell.

Owen's love for all he held so dear propelled him forward into the day. Booted, he threw on a cloak and stepped out into the muddy aftermath of the first snow and thaw. His boots squelched on the pathway that wound beneath the bare-limbed linden and through the tall rosemary shrubs shimmering with a film of ice. A startled bird darted up and away, another flew to the top of the wall, watching him with one eye. The needle pricks were fading out here. Perhaps whatever had threatened moved on. Not necessarily a good sign. A watcher was unwelcome. He should have thought to have one of his men walking a circuit round the house and shop. One of the bailiffs' men. He supposed they, too, were his now. At the midden he relieved himself, then turned back, pausing to search for movement, his ears pricked. Nothing. But as he moved down the path leading to the shop, the shower of needle pricks intensified. Crossing with as little noise as possible by stepping on rotten vegetation at the side of the path rather than the bare mud that sucked at his boots he approached the back door opening onto the workshop. Stepping inside, he felt the prickling intensify and rushed through to the shop just as the door closed. Slamming it open he almost knocked Jasper over.

'Da?' Jasper had lifted his broom as if to use it as a pike. Now he lowered it with a sheepish grin. 'You saw him, too?'

'Who?'

'A man standing among the graves, watching the shop and the house. Cloaked. Must have sensed me coming out. He's gone now.'

Owen crossed over and climbed up the short wall into the graveyard, checking with Jasper until his son motioned he was on the spot. Muddy indentation. Poor prints, difficult to follow out. Across the way he hailed a lad pushing a cart toward the river. But the boy had seen nothing. Slogging back across the cemetery, Owen shook his head at Jasper's questioning frown.

'I lost him.' Seeing how his son's shoulders sagged with defeat, Owen put an arm round him. 'You did well. I will arrange a watch, not just in the garden but out on the street.' Noticing the lad had come out without a cloak, he turned him round. 'Come and break your fast with me.'

Alisoun's body ached from sleeping all night slumped on a hard bench against the cold wall of Marian's bedchamber, made worse by her reluctance to stretch while Marian knelt at the bedside, hands folded in prayer. When at last the woman rose, Alisoun escorted her out to the midden. As they'd passed through the kitchen, Lucie and Magda were herding the children into the hall with bowls of bread and cheese and something steaming in a jug. Alisoun shook her head at Lucie's curious glance – no, she had learned no more. A futile vigil.

'We will be taking the children up to the nursery after they eat,' said Lucie. 'Kate will be grateful for some space.'

Kate made a face as she held the door open for the procession. 'They are no trouble.'

Lucie kissed Kate's cheek as she passed and called back to Alisoun and Marian to take their ease in the warm kitchen.

'Dame Lucie treats the kitchen maid as if she were family,' Marian noted with puzzlement once out in the garden.

'It is their way. Kate's elder sister worked here for a long while and is now wed to the steward at Dame Lucie's manor – I should say young Hugh's manor, when he comes of age,' said Alisoun as they stepped out into the mild but damp winter morning.

'Manor?'

'Come along. My teeth will start chattering if we are not quick,' Alisoun urged, picking up the pace to the end of the garden. She hugged herself and moved about as she waited for Marian. Just as she turned away to start back she caught a movement behind the wall. Holding up her hand to silence Marian, she listened. Nothing now. But it reminded her to be vigilant.

In the kitchen, Magda placed a jug of honeyed water and a bowl of bread and cheese on the edge of the bench Alisoun shared with Marian. 'Thy fast is over,' she said, gazing into the young woman's eyes. Marian promised to eat.

'Will you go to Muriel Swann today?' Alisoun asked her teacher.

'When Magda shepherds the little ones up to their chamber, she hands them into thy care.' She bade them eat hearty and withdrew to the hall.

'Dame Magda has a strong presence, a power,' said Marian.

Long ago Alisoun tried hard to resist that power. She smiled to think of it. Stubborn child.

'You disagree?'

'No. I am glad for you. That you have felt it.' Breaking off a chunk of bread, Alisoun was just reaching for a piece of cheese when the door from the hall opened.

'The precentor from the minster is here,' said Lucie. She kept her voice low, but the tone was urgent. 'He must not see Marian.' She reached for a basket on the boot bench. Kate helped her place the food in the basket. 'Go to Jasper's rooms above the shop.'

Remembering her fleeting impression, Alisoun handed Marian one of Lucie's cloaks. 'Cover your hair,' she told her.

Within moments they were outside, almost colliding with the captain and Jasper.

'Where are you going?' Owen demanded.

'The precentor is in the hall,' said Alisoun. 'Dame Lucie thinks it safer that we come to the shop. Up above. To break our fast.'

'Escort them,' the captain told Jasper. 'I will see to Master Adam.'

Alisoun touched the captain's arm. 'I sensed a watcher when we were at the midden. Hiding behind the wall.'

He glanced toward the end of the garden. Nodded. 'Jasper saw one standing in the cemetery. Keep Dame Marian away from the windows.'

In the workshop, Marian stopped at one of the work tables, bending to smell the roots being cleaned, picking up a jar and sniffing the contents. 'It is like Dame Justina's corner in the infirmary.'

Jasper, who seemed unable to stop staring at Marian once she had pushed back her hood, stepped up to explain each item, going into detail about the ingredients, and which were from the garden. Embarrassed for him, Alisoun pushed past them and carried the basket of food and the jug of Magda's honey water up to the guest room toward the front of the house, setting it all up on a small table. She had just stepped back into the workshop when a man's voice called out from the shop, 'Are you open?'

'I must have forgotten to latch it,' Jasper said softly. 'Leave your boots down here and be as quiet as you can as you go up the steps.'

Alisoun drew Marian out of sight as Jasper stepped through the beaded curtain. 'How might I help you?'

'I need a salve for my horse. A new bit is chafing him.'

'I have just the thing.'

The sound of Jasper moving the stool to climb to one of the higher shelves. Alisoun realized she was holding her breath. She reached for Marian as the woman began to wander and put a finger to her lips. Marian stood still.

'Heard Captain Archer took in the minstrel's lad,' said a

second voice. 'Tossed a man off the minster roof, they say, then sang like an angel. A queer tale. True?'

'I am an apprentice here in the apothecary. I know nothing of such things.'

'Oh, but you're Jasper de Melton, I think. The minstrel's lover saved your life when you were just a slip of a boy, so they say.'

'Be careful what you believe,' said Jasper. 'Here we are.' A thud as he set the heavy jar down on the counter with more force than was his wont. He was angry. 'A penny's worth should be plenty.'

'You're a tight-lipped lad,' said the first.

'You will find that so for most of us in the city when strangers stick their noses where they don't belong. You do have a penny?'

A muttered curse, the sound of a coin bouncing off the jar. And the door slammed shut.

Alisoun peered through the curtain. Jasper locked the door and hurried toward them. She stepped away just in time.

'I heard.' She touched his arm. 'Who were they?'

'Don't know. I've not seen them before.' He frowned. 'You smile?'

'You amazed me, Jasper de Melton.' She kissed his cheek.

He grinned, pulled her close for a moment, kissing her back.

'They are away,' Marian called down.

'Keep her from the window,' said Jasper. 'I need to tell the captain, describe their dress. Break your fasts up above – but do it in my bedchamber. It's over this room not the shop. I must open the shop when I return.' He kissed Alisoun's hand. 'Be safe,' he whispered.

'You, too.' This odd life suited Jasper. And her.

After moving the table across the landing to the larger room, placing it near but not too near the window overlooking the garden, Alisoun and Marian eased down onto a bench, side by side, and stared out at the dreary winter drizzle for a moment.

'You must be bursting with questions,' said Alisoun.

It won her an unexpected smile as Marian turned toward her, straddling the bench.

'That must have been easier in men's clothing,' Alisoun said.

A laugh. 'I confess there were times I enjoyed it.' Her smile transformed her face, her eyes dipping up at the corners, pale eyes twinkling, not unlike Magda's. 'But yes, I do have questions.'

'While we break bread, I will tell you what I can.'

Marian nodded and bowed her head, whispering a prayer of thanks for the food. She glanced up at Alisoun's *Amen.* 'You are not a pagan, like your teacher.'

'No.' Alisoun helped herself to bread and cheese.

Marian poured some of Magda's preparation into two bowls. Knowing what Magda had added, Alisoun set hers aside, wanting no unexpected bleeding while the captain and Dame Lucie needed her.

After a few bites of bread and cheese and more than a few sips of the honeyed water, Marian said, 'I can tell that Jasper is worried I have brought trouble to your doorstep.'

'Not you alone. Ambrose as well. But he knows that Captain Archer and Dame Lucie accepted the charge to hold you here.'

'Jasper knows Master Ambrose.'

'He knew his friend, who saved his life. I am not sure he knew Ambrose well.'

'How did the monk know to bring me here? Master Ambrose meant to introduce me to the captain and Dame Lucie. Had he told the monk? Did he know I was in the chapter house?'

'Ambrose had nothing to do with that. Brother Michaelo brought you here on the order of the precentor at the minster.' She saw the woman's doubt and could not blame her. 'I can understand why you might wonder. But once you know more about this family you will see why both men had the same thought for your safety.'

'And it is the precentor who is now at the house?'

'Yes.'

'Did he guess my sex?'

'No. But Brother Michaelo did, and judged it best to follow the order though he knew we had been nursing the children. Your secret is safe with all in this household, and the monk.'

'Bless you.' Again, that radiant smile. She had a delicate

beauty, the fair hair and ivory skin, the slender wrists. But her voice had a strong resonance, throaty, much like Gwen's, a reminder that a delicate appearance did not mean a weak mind.

'You seem a devout woman,' said Alisoun. 'Companies of minstrels and players are not known for their piety. Did you travel with them for long?'

'No. Not long.' Marian drank down the honeyed water, took another bite of bread and cheese, swinging one leg as she chewed. She seemed at ease. Magda's miracle potions. 'And you? Have you always been Dame Magda's apprentice?'

The thought made Alisoun smile. 'No. And I count it one of God's mysterious gifts that he convinced her to take me on – though Dame Magda would reject His part in it. And she did test me for a long while before fully trusting me. To see whether my desire to heal was sincere.'

'How did she test you?'

Alisoun poured more of the drink for Marian while she considered what might encourage an equal sharing, as Magda had instructed her. *Thou art close to her age. She might confide in thee as a friend.* She had thought it would feel false, but Alisoun did feel a bond of some sort. Perhaps enumerating the tasks she had endured – companion to wealthy, much-spoiled young widows; runner of errands for a number of demanding elderly people; guard of Magda's donkey when visiting patients outside the city; nursemaid to Gwenllian and Hugh, and later Emma as well from time to time. 'But I admit I do love the three of them. And Dame Lucie and the captain have been good to me. Far kinder than I deserved.'

'None of these seem unreasonable tasks for an apprentice. Why did you resent them? Because Dame Magda is a heathen?'

'What she believes is of no concern to me. She encourages me to honor my beliefs. But I wanted to be a healer. I wanted her to teach me what she knows. I wanted to stay with her, follow her and learn by watching, and she pushed me away. Or so it seemed.'

'You had a fierce knowing that this was your calling.'

'I like how you phrased that. I did. I do. And you? Is your calling the convent or music?'

'The convent? What did Dame Magda tell you?'

'She said you liked Dom Jehannes's suggestion that you would be most at ease at St Clement's Priory. And you might have slept until I woke. Instead you knelt by your bed to pray before dawn. I thought perhaps you would choose a life of prayer if you could, closed off from the world.' There was also the slip about Dame Justina's infirmary.

Marian dropped her gaze to her bowl. 'I am called to both music and a life dedicated to God,' she said in a choked whisper.

Alisoun almost dare not breathe. Magda would say, *Continue with them as thou hast begun. Do not stop at the fact that thou didst hope to hear. A deeper truth may follow. Listen as long as thou canst.*

'I have been inside only one nunnery, to help Dame Lucie deliver some of her physicks to the infirmarian at St Clement's,' said Alisoun, 'so I have little experience with nuns. But traveling in a company of players does not seem a way to win their welcome.'

Marian met her gaze, her face a mask of grief. No sign of the smile now. 'I did not choose to go wayfaring. I had chosen—' She abruptly set the bowl aside. 'I was ripped from a life that was my heart's desire and left without hope.'

'I see why you would like to go to St Clement's.'

'They will not accept me as one of them. I will be a guest, no more.'

'But you are not with child. If you are called to the veil, how can they refuse you? On what grounds? If you did not choose . . .' A misstep. Marian looked ready to take flight. 'Forgive me. What else would you know?'

In a voice now brisk with a need to change the topic, Marian said that Ambrose held the captain and the apothecary in high esteem, yet he'd seemed uncertain the captain would trust him. 'Was it Dame Lucie who was his friend?'

'I have never met this minstrel. He left before I came to the city.'

'He is no ordinary minstrel. He was long at the court of the French king, and I could see why he was so honored – the song he composed for the pleasure of the Neville gathering – it was clever, yet he could not help but make sure it was also beautiful. I have not heard him play anything but his crwth and Tucker's fiddle, but I can tell he has more talent than any of the sisters at—' She stopped and picked up her empty bowl, set it down. 'And his voice, such range – he shaped it to mine with such ease. A most accomplished musician and performer.'

Alisoun was far more interested in how Marian's dream was taken from her, but she must have a care. 'I should like to hear him perform. Jasper took him several more instruments last night. They had been stored in the apothecary workroom. I've been curious about them.' A little laugh. 'Mostly because I was warned not to touch them.'

'Perhaps we might ask?' A smile, and then Marian fell to her food, finishing it.

'I am glad to see you eating. Dame Magda says you have long been denying yourself, and your spirit is weakened.'

'She heals souls as well as bodies?'

'She would not call it that.'

'Dame Lucie. You mentioned her father's manor. Is she of noble birth?'

'She is. But when her mother died . . . It is a long story.'

Lucie cut short her greeting when she noticed the mud on Owen's boots. 'Is the garden such a mire?'

'I will explain,' he said under his breath. 'Master Adam?'

'In the hall.'

Owen asked Kate to bring them refreshments. 'Where are the children?'

'We took them up before Magda left,' said Lucie.

Owen kissed her cheek. 'Forgive me.'

'Go!'

Adam had been gazing out of the garden window. 'Most comfortable, this home of yours. Your wife's father's, was it not? Sir Robert D'Arby?'

'Yes.'

'And you were a soldier. Captain of Archers. Served Henry of Grosmont, Duke of Lancaster. Then Thoresby, now the prince.'

It seemed an odd way to begin. Owen offered him a cup of ale, which he accepted with thanks.

'You must wonder why I am recounting your history.' A mirthless smile. 'I am reminding myself that great men have trusted you. Why should I not trust you, trust that you are searching for Ronan's murderer? Yet so far . . .'

'I've had but a day, a day riddled with three corpses before noon. I might ask you why no one from the chapter has come forward with helpful information.'

'Was I to ask them?' Adam lifted the cup to his lips. Drank a little.

'You are in the best position to do so.' The precentor scowled. 'If no one steps forward, I intend to speak to all in the chapter,' said Owen. 'I welcome your advice in choosing the order.'

'You think it is one of us.'

'I did not say that. Chapter members might know something of use to me – perhaps without realizing it. A passing remark, a memory of someone missing prayers or neglecting their responsibilities, angry words overheard, a certain cooling between Ronan and another.'

'I see. We were his companions. We would notice a changed pattern. I do see.' The precentor drank down his ale and set the bowl aside.

'Did he have particular friends?'

Adam wrinkled his brow as he stroked his chin with swollen fingers. Gout? 'No one comes to mind.'

'Were you friends with him?'

'I preferred to keep my distance. His air of disdain, you see. Most vexing. I found him most vexing. As did many in the chapter. Not to the extent that they would wish him harm. We all prayed that he would learn humility. Unfortunately, with Alexander Neville's elevation, and his previous preference for Ronan's services over others, his arrogance only grew. I wondered what drew them together.' A shrug. 'But our feelings for the man are of no importance in this matter. What was done was wrong. Criminal. And with the archbishop expected at any time, Ronan's murderer must be found and brought to justice.'

'As Ronan was struck down in the minster liberty it will fall to the archbishop himself to mete out punishment,' said Owen. 'If his murderer proves to be a member of the chapter that is doubly true.'

'Then you must find irrefutable proof, Captain.'

'You do not trust a Neville investigation?'

Adam cleared his throat. 'I meant exactly what I said, Captain.'

'How do you propose I proceed?'

'I might mention it at the chapter meeting this morning, that they should come to me if they know anything, if they have noticed anything that might help you find his murderer. In private, if they prefer.'

'A good beginning.'

Adam rose. 'And I shall prepare an ordered list of those with whom I am aware Ronan had cause to speak.' Bristly. He had come to task Owen, not be tasked.

'That would be most helpful. Would you like Brother Michaelo's assistance?'

A sniff. 'My clerks write a good hand. And know the names. Though I dare say Brother Michaelo has made a point of learning them. He seems keen to be of use in the city.'

Archdeacon Jehannes had put out the word that Brother Michaelo was available after the death of his patron, the late archbishop. The plan had been for Michaelo to return to Normandy, live out his days in a monastery near his home. But he had balked at the prospect, a man who had tasted the life of an archbishop's aide, traveling, mixing with an array of worthies both religious and secular. For the most part the religious communities in the city shunned his services, though a few pastors and a sprinkling of Dominicans and, oddly, the prioress of St Clement's requested his services from time to time. The communities knew the rumors about why the abbot of St Mary's refused to take him back upon Thoresby's death, a failed attempt on the life of the late infirmarian Brother Wulfstan, a beloved figure. Though the incident was years in the past, and, for the most part, Brother Michaelo's behavior since had been above reproach, his reputation as both a poisoner and sodomite condemned him. An unfortunate incident the previous year had sealed Michaelo's fate with many. It had done the opposite with Owen. Michaelo's remorse had convinced Owen he was a changed man.

'I have come to value Brother Michaelo's talents,' said Owen. 'His Grace the archbishop trained him well, tested his skills, and expanded his assignments to his advantage. And now mine.' He watched the precentor consider this revelation.

'Perhaps I should reconsider. Dean John *is* challenged by the duties he is forced to shoulder as acting dean. With Brother Michaelo's knowledge acquired in the archbishop's service . . .' He stroked his chin again, an odd gesture for a beardless man. 'I will suggest he engage the monk, see whether he is of use to us. For now, God go with you, Captain. I will send word when the list is ready.'

Owen showed him out the front door.

As soon as the precentor left, Lucie ushered Jasper into the hall, watching Owen's face as he listened to his son's report. She was proud of Jasper's calm, his detailed description of the men and their clothing. So was Owen.

'You have a keen eye,' he said. 'Neither looked like the one you saw earlier?'

'No. Different clothing, thicker limbs.'

'From the garb I would guess them to be more of Neville's men,' said Owen. 'Did Alisoun and Marian hear them?'

'They did. I cautioned them to stay in my room, over the workroom, not the shop, and away from the windows.'

'Good,' said Owen. 'I will see to that watch on the house and shop I spoke of. And we need to move both of them tonight, Marian to the priory and Ambrose – I need to—'

Someone pounded on the hall door. Owen thanked Jasper. 'Best to open the shop before folk wonder.'

With a nod, Jasper left.

Lucie reluctantly climbed the steps to the nursery.

Muttering a curse, Owen went to answer. He was relieved to see Rose and Rob, interested by their report: trouble in Ronan's chamber.

'His neighbor heard unholy bumping and sliding above, and feared it was poor Master Ronan's confused spirit,' said Rose. 'Something about how the murdered do not know they are dead until their murderer is found.'

'Fool,' Rob muttered.

'How did you hear of it?' Owen asked.

'From our landlord,' said Rose. 'Ma provides his meals for part of the rent. He's Ronan's landlord as well. While he broke his fast he spoke of the trouble. He found the furniture all flung about. A gaping hole in one wall. And Beck, Master Ronan's clerk, lying on the floor face down, the back of his head bloody.'

Beck. The weasel haunting Ronan's lodging the previous day.

'He said he righted the bed and laid him on it, then went to Master Adam, the precentor. It is to him they go if the residents of the Bedern cause trouble. But they told him Master Adam had called on you, so he sent us to fetch you.'

'Did Beck wake? Did he know him?'

'He opened his eyes. Said nothing. Will you come, Captain?'

'I will be there as soon as possible.'

Their mission accomplished, the two were off before Owen closed the door.

Lucie stepped out onto the landing when Owen knocked, closing the door so the children would not hear, listening to the news with growing concern. 'What of Marian and Alisoun?'

'I will escort them back here. Neville's men are less likely to walk into our home. If you are able to learn any more about Marian, I would be grateful.'

'Of course.'

Once Owen escorted Alisoun and Marian back to the house, Lucie stood for a moment staring out of her bedroom window saying a silent prayer for the injured clerk. Owen had seemed relieved that something had happened, as if he had been holding his breath, waiting for it. But how he might cut through the maze of incidents . . .

Lucie crossed herself. God protect her family.

Three men dead – a cleric who had been Archbishop Alexander Neville's vicar, murdered; one of Sir John Neville's men, drowned; a man whose clothes suggested he, too, was a lord's retainer fallen from a roof. The Nevilles had become one of the most powerful Northern families, whom Owen was to watch for the prince. Ambrose Coates had spied on the Nevilles while on a mission to alert Prince Edward that his French physician meant him harm, that he and his cohort had already weakened the prince with illness. He had come from the Neville gathering with Marian, who had been hiding as a boy in a traveling company of musicians and players. One of the dead men had watched Marian at Cawood. The man who had fallen from the roof. For whose death she claimed guilt. What had she done before? Why was she running? Why had she hidden her name even here? Surely if she were hiding from the Nevilles she would not have risked performing at Cawood. Yet someone knew her. So many questions.

Even so, there was no question in Lucie's heart – she would do her best to help the young woman.

A voice drifted down from above, soft, conversational. Alisoun had seemed hopeful, whispering as she passed Lucie on the landing that Marian had eaten, and was more at ease, talking more. Lucie had suggested that with Magda gone to the Swann home Marian might help with some darning while in the company of Alisoun and the children. She would fetch the sewing basket from the kitchen, and then speak with Marian before she joined Alisoun and the children. It was time she did that.

When Lucie entered the guest chamber she found Marian standing at the window, her hair aglow in the morning light.

'With Dame Magda gone, Alisoun must attend her duties with the children,' said Lucie. 'I thought you might like to join them while you work.'

She smiled to see what Lucie carried. 'I would like to be of use. You will trust me?'

'Mark me, the vicar's murderer is still abroad,' said Lucie. She recounted what had happened at Ronan's lodging. 'And you heard the men in the shop. You must keep yourself hidden.'

Marian hugged the sewing basket and nodded. Lucie opened the door and motioned to her to join Alisoun in the nursery.

'May God bless you for your kindness, Dame Lucie.'

'May He watch over us and keep us safe,' said Lucie.

*　　*　　*

At the minster gate Owen was hailed by Brother Michaelo.

'Well met! I am on my way to Ronan's lodgings. There has been trouble. I would welcome your company.'

'I will attend you, of course,' said Michaelo.

While they walked, Owen told him all he had missed.

'Dame Marian,' he whispered to himself. 'It sounds as if she has suffered much.'

Owen did not reply, his attention drawn to the men lounging in front of Ronan's lodgings, men dressed much like Pit. Yet familiar. One of them turned to grin crookedly, a scar puckering one side of his mouth. Crispin Poole's men, the retainers he had brought with him to York, now dressed as part of the Neville pack. Not the pair who visited the shop earlier, but bad news all the same.

'What is your business here?' Owen asked.

'You will need to ask Master Crispin,' said crooked grin. 'He is up above, in the dead man's chamber.'

Owen was already halfway up the steps, Michaelo following. He reached the landing as Crispin stepped out of Ronan's room.

'And so we meet here again, Owen.'

'Why are you here?'

'A rumor of trouble here. It's Beck, the clerk. Wounded.'

'You brought your men to guard you? Is Beck so dangerous even when wounded?'

Crispin looked pained. 'One of His Grace the archbishop's men arrived this morning with livery for my men and orders that they now serve His Grace. They seem to have interpreted that as being promoted, now my peers. Insisted on accompanying me, though they could not be bothered to climb the steps.'

'I trust you will correct them.'

'I am tempted to refuse them food and board. Let His Grace see to their needs. Though I believe they are in truth Sir John Neville's creatures.'

Owen had never understood why Crispin had felt the need to keep armed retainers when he put aside his military past to become a merchant in York. It had not occurred to him that someone else had assigned the men to him. 'Is Beck alive?'

'As far as I can tell.' Crispin stepped aside, gesturing that Owen was welcome to enter. 'It is anyone's guess what he was doing here before he scuffled with someone, whether he was searching or they were. Have a care where you step.' He leaned heavily on his cane, his face drawn as if he'd had little sleep.

'Who was here first? Him? Or the attackers?'

'I do not know. As I said, watch where you walk.'

The furnishings had indeed been tossed about, bits and pieces of the bedding, the legs of a broken stool, all ready to trip one up. The searcher had found the hiding place behind the wall boards, though of course it was empty. Beck lay on a bare mattress on the bed, a bloody cloth wrapped round his head. Owen sat down beside him.

'Beck, can you hear me?'

The yes was more of an outbreath.

'It's Captain Archer. We met yesterday. Who did this to you?'

'Did not see.' He reached up to clutch Owen's arm, opening his eyes wide, closing them, opening them and forcing them wider with his fingers. 'I cannot see, Captain.' A pitiful keen.

Owen understood the terror of that realization, the frantic testing, the disbelief. Lifting the man's hands from his eyes, Owen held them firmly. 'I will send for the Riverwoman, Beck. Were you here when they came, or did you walk in on them?'

'Walked in. Swearing and tossing stuff about, they were. Why can't I see?' He tugged at his captive hands.

'You suffered a blow to the head. That can cause such a loss. Dame Magda will be able to tell you more. I mean to find who did this to you. Did you see anything at all? Smell? Hear?'

'Both wore hoods. Scarves over faces. Something about salt. Salt!' A moan.

'Salt or psalter?' Brother Michaelo asked in a soft voice.

'Psalter.' Beck licked his lips as if tasting the word. 'Mayhap. I had not thought—' He moaned and closed his eyes.

'You will soon have something to ease the pain,' Owen assured him. A psalter? There were no books in the bag he had taken to the archdeacon for safekeeping.

'Bless you,' the injured man whimpered.

'How many men?'

'Two? All I saw before I saw no more.'

'Shall we remove him to a safe place?' Michaelo whispered. 'The archdeacon's?'

Owen agreed. Finding Rose and Rob hovering on the landing, he sent them to fetch Magda Digby from the Swann residence. 'If she can be spared, ask her to come to Archdeacon Jehannes's house. If not, fetch Mistress Alisoun from my house.'

They nodded and skipped down the steps.

'Might I be of help?' asked Crispin.

It was tempting to use his men to carry Beck, but Owen did not trust them. Or Crispin, at present. Finding him in Ronan's lodgings once might be accident, but not twice.

'How did you hear of Beck's beating?'

'Folk talking of it in the street.'

'Have your men been with you all morning?'

Crispin checked Owen's expression. 'No. They were off on a task for His Grace.'

Searching for a psalter? 'Do not follow me,' said Owen.

'Owen—'

'Good day to you and your men.'

Back in the room, he fashioned a bandage out of a piece of clothing in the pile of things flung about, then hoisted Beck up and slung him over his shoulder.

'Lead the way, Michaelo.'

Jehannes's cook stood with hands on hips, shaking her head as Owen laid Beck down on the pallet the archdeacon's clerk had dragged near the hearth.

'What now? I thought we were safe in the shadow of the great minster. The folk have lost their way. They are wandering in the wilderness, led by the devil himself.'

'Be so good as to set aside the sermon and bring the captain a basin of warm water and some cloths, goodwife,' said Michaelo. He crouched down beside Owen. 'What might I do to assist?'

'I am trying to settle him on his stomach, with his head to

one side so that he is not pressing on the injury. But our patient wishes to lie on his back.' Beck wriggled about, clearly trying to flip himself.

'Perhaps something warm on his back,' said the cook, standing over them with a bowl of water. 'If this is placed right, he will find it soothing to his back and lie still. My ma taught me the trick. My da would come in from a day of plowing swearing he'd broken his back.'

'Preacher and nurse. You are a marvel, Goodwife Anna,' Michaelo murmured as he moved away to allow her access.

Once the bowl was balanced Owen wet a cloth and began to clean the blood from the parts of Beck's face and neck that he could see. As he worked he felt Beck relax beneath him. While holding the bowl so that Beck could turn his head to expose the other cheek Owen sensed Magda standing over him. He resettled the bowl and rose to allow her to take over.

'Jehannes wishes to speak with thee, Bird-eye. Magda can manage from here.'

Quietly Owen told her how Beck had been found, and that what most frightened him was that he could not see.

'Thou knowest the dread,' she said. 'Magda will do what she can. Now go. Put an end to these troubles so that Muriel Swann can birth her babe in peace.'

Out in the hall, Owen sat for a moment to speak with Jehannes.

'My summoner advises you to talk to Franz of Antwerp, one of Ronan's fellow vicars,' said Jehannes. 'According to Colin, though Master Adam will tell you that all in the liberty sought Ronan's advice regarding the new archbishop, in truth few trusted the man. Franz was the one in whose company he saw him most often of late.'

Jehannes's summoner, Colin, was a trustworthy man. 'Were they friends?'

'I've noticed Franz cowering from Ronan, but Colin says he did his bidding. It would be in Ronan's character to threaten to bring him before the chapter to be chastised for living with the mother of his five children.'

'Is that not your summoner's duty?'

'His duty is to obey my bidding. I prefer to make examples of those who take no responsibility for their weaknesses. The children and their mother depend on Franz's income. And he is in all other ways a pious man who goes about his duties with nary a complaint.'

Time and again Jehannes restored Owen's faith that there were amongst the clergy dedicated shepherds of men's souls.

'And what of Ronan's relationship with the chancellor? What might connect them?'

'Ah. Last evening's meeting. The Nevilles, I should think. They might be generous benefactors for Thomas's work for the minster. He is keen to raise sufficient funds to complete Thoresby's lady chapel.'

'Is he?' That was news to Owen. 'Did Ronan still have such influence with the new archbishop?'

'That remained to be seen. It was said that Ronan had expected to become the archbishop's confessor or personal secretary, his Brother Michaelo. He was said to have been angry about being passed over by two men who had never set foot in York Minster.'

So Ronan might have been the one hoping to gain by a friendship with members of the chapter. Owen tucked that away.

'What of Beck, Ronan's clerk?'

'According to Colin, Beck admired Ronan for all the wrong reasons. He had heard whispers about Beck threatening to reveal secrets – limiting himself to servants, avoiding being squashed by one with some influence.'

'I thought him a weasel.'

'You are a good judge of men. But then you need to be in your work.'

'Any others like him?'

'He did say Ronan spent a curious amount of time on Stonegate. Offering his services as an intermediary between the archbishop and the merchants?'

'Did you ever see Ronan with a psalter?'

'A psalter? No. But then, a vicar owning something of such value might raise eyebrows amongst his betters, and envy amongst his peers. Hence he might reserve such items for private prayer. How long will Beck be here?' Before Owen could respond, Jehannes held up a hand. 'As long as you judge him safest here, here he will stay. Now go, see Franz.' He told Owen how to find the man.

Heading toward the Bedern, Owen moved against a tide of clerks hastening toward the minster. Sext, he thought, midday prayer. Franz might not be at his lodgings. But his mistress might afford Owen some insight into her sense of Ronan. He pushed along toward the address at the edge of the Bedern. The house as described was down an alleyway, narrower than most in this part of the city, not one of the lodgings refurbished for the vicars. Owen almost passed it in the shadow of the jutting stories. Before he could knock the door was opened from within by a man dressed to depart. He started at Owen's presence, took a step backward. Franz, Owen guessed. How now to proceed? Their proposed conversation was one he did not care to conduct where others might hear. He needed to lure the man back inside.

How better than to trespass? Pushing his way into the room, Owen kept moving, his sight adjusting to the dimness as he reached a second, inner room. Deserted. No further door affording an escape out the back.

Franz had followed, now blocking the doorway to the outer room. 'Who are you to force your way into my home? I am expected at midday prayers in the minster. State your business.' The last word was little more than a squeak.

Owen felt a twinge of guilt. And also interest. The man's speech had a hint of Flemish. So the Antwerp was not a legacy from parents, but based on his own origins.

'I pray you, forgive me. I am Owen Archer, captain of the city. In my concern for your safety I overstepped.'

'Concern for my safety?' The man opened the shutter wider on the lantern near the door. He had thrown back one side of his short cloak to reveal that his right hand, childlike in its dimpled softness, rested on a small dagger.

'I pray you, allow me to explain myself,' said Owen. 'I am searching for the murderer of the vicar Ronan. You were recommended to me as one of his closest friends. Until I understand someone's motive for murdering him, I cannot be certain that his friends are safe. I did not know whether a vicar would think to protect himself. I see that I was wrong about you.' He gestured toward the dagger.

'You were ensuring that no one lurked in my house? That was your purpose in calling on me?' Franz did not relax his hand.

'There is more. I hoped you might be able to help me find the man who attacked Ronan. As his friend, you might know who might wish him harm.'

'Who sent you here?'

'Forgive me, but people are less willing to help me if I divulge names. I will share nothing of what you share with me. No one you name will hear of our meeting.'

As Owen spoke he caught whiffs of scents peculiar to a home with infants. Milky, soured by the baby's excretions from mouth and nether regions. Stale now, not fresh. And all sign of such children had been cleared from the room. Indeed, except for a narrow pallet near the door and some men's clothes hanging from hooks the room was empty. Blind in one eye, Owen was obvious when looking round a room. Noticing, Franz cast furtive glances round his lodgings as well.

'Someone has led you astray, Captain Archer. I knew Ronan, worked for him on occasion. But a friend? No one who knew either of us would call us friends.'

'You were seen with him of late. Frequently.'

'That would be true. But we were not friends.'

'He abused you?'

A step backward. 'What do you mean?'

'Cheated you. Took credit for your work. I pray you, I need to know who he was, why someone would cut him down.'

'You will be hard pressed to find anyone in the Bedern who called him friend, I can tell you that.'

'Why? What do they have against him?'

A slight shift of posture, less alert. 'His behavior toward all of us. He was of the opinion that his university training set him above us, made him our superior. He pretended to do us favors by offering to pay us to do his work, but we received no credit and a pittance of his earnings, while he moved about the city selling himself to prospective patrons, free as a bird, wealthier by the day.'

As Owen had suspected, it was likely that not all the treasure Ronan hoarded was meant for Alexander Neville.

'I understand these are reasons to shun him. But murder? Did he commit more serious, even less forgivable transgressions? I ask because – you must understand, the anger I sense in you as you speak would seem an inordinate response to what you describe, a greedy partner. Though I suppose with a family to feed . . .'

'You know about my family?'

Owen took a gamble. 'Your mistress is known to my wife, the apothecary.'

'Ah. I should realize that all the women of the city will be aware of my circumstance. But I am not the only one.'

'I am well aware of that. I am curious, though.' Owen gestured round the room. 'I see no sign of your family. Have you sent them away?'

'I have. The new archbishop – I fear him. Archbishop Thoresby could be harsh, but I knew him to be fair. As is Archdeacon Jehannes. But Alexander Neville – I fear what he would do to my family were he to learn of it. Ronan was his source of gossip about his fellow vicars.'

'I see. So Ronan was a threat to you.'

'If you are asking whether I would murder him to silence him, no. I have no such courage. I have thought of leaving, but how would I support my family?'

'I understand.'

'I realize it might be too late. Ronan might have already reported me to His Grace. If that is so, I will join my family. Until then, I support them by fulfilling my duties in the chapter. Which I must be about . . .'

Owen bowed to Franz. 'I will not keep you. Forgive my intrusion.'

Franz stepped aside to let Owen pass, then followed with the lantern. The outer room had a small table, a few benches, and hooks on the wall by the door, empty at present. One of the benches had a solid base, as if used for storage. Owen resisted opening it.

Turning just as he was stepping out, he said, 'I could not help but notice that your speech carries a memory of Flanders.' The lantern light wavered. 'Have you by any chance noticed a fellow Fleming in the city, one who might be mistaken for me – at a distance, though I have both hands, and wear this patch?'

Franz peered more closely at Owen, shook his head. 'I have seen no such man, Captain.'

'You are certain?'

'I have no reason to lie about it. I thank you for your concern. Good day to you.'

Owen believed him. Hempe was right, he risked being blinded by his unproven theory that Martin Wirthir was Ambrose's protector. But then who was the Frenchman?

Owen followed Franz at a discreet distance until he was confident the man was heading straight to the minster. Along the way Stephen joined Owen, who set him the task of arranging a watch on Franz's house.

'He might be our murderer?'

'No. But add Franz to someone's circuit.'

'I will arrange it.'

'And my home, the shop.'

'Jasper told me about the watchers and visitors. I went straight to the bailiff. He's sent someone for the day. Ned.'

Trustworthy. 'I can't thank you enough.'

'No need, Captain.' Stephen turned and headed back toward the castle.

As Owen turned toward Jehannes's, he glimpsed two figures making haste from the chancellor's door, slipping round the side of the house, one of them glancing back as if checking that no one followed. A hood kept his face in shadow, but Owen thought he glimpsed the twisted grin of Crispin's man. He gave chase, but by the time he reached the back garden the men were gone. Already he doubted his impression of the man's face. Yet at the moment the impression had been strong.

A servant leaned against the kitchen doorway, spitting blood on a mound of melting snow and cradling one arm.

Owen identified himself as he approached. 'What happened? You look badly injured.'

'They shoved me aside so hard I fell on my shoulder. God's blood, I think it is broken.'

Owen guessed it was pulled out of joint. He knew the pain of that. The blood came from a split lip. 'Who were they?'

'Don't know.'

'Come into the house. I will look at the arm while you tell me what happened.'

As Owen felt round the shoulder the man told him how he'd returned from market to discover two men searching the hall, turning things over, looking behind hangings.

'You came through the front door?'

'No, round to the kitchen with the baskets.'

'Was that still locked?'

'In the minster yard we don't lock doors unless going away for a long while. We've never had trouble.'

Until Ronan was murdered just outside the gate. 'How did you discover them?'

'I was unpacking when I heard what sounded like someone shoving the furnishings about. The chancellor is a quiet man, as are his clerks. All wrong, and none of us feeling at ease since the vicar was murdered right outside the gate.' He crossed himself with his good hand. 'From the doorway I saw two men doing just that, moving things about, heavy items even, peering under and round and behind. I thought to run to the archdeacon's house. I looked again to make certain I did not recognize them. I'd seen only their backs. Waited until I saw their faces – but they covered them with cloths from nose to chin. One of them picked up something from a stack of books and document rolls. Not large, stuffed it in a pack. It was then he saw me. Came rushing at me, dragged me in there, shoved me down hard and held me there with his foot on my back. *No killing*, the other said. Made his voice gruff, like he did not want me to know it. And they ran out.' He crossed himself again.

'You have been fortunate. Now I need you to sit up and look away.'

'Look away?' The man straightened and glanced away just

as Owen pressed the shoulder with one hand and yanked the arm with the other.

The servant screamed.

'It will begin to feel much better in a while,' said Owen. 'I am going to bind it close to you and send someone from my wife's apothecary with a salve you need to put on it twice a day while it aches. Do you understand? Is there someone who can help you?'

'Cook should be back soon.'

'Good.' Owen examined the man's lip. 'I'll send something for that as well. For now, this will stop the bleeding.' He plucked a cloth from a shelf and filled it with snow outside the door. 'What do you drink to ease pain?'

The man glanced toward a small barrel on a shelf as he began to rise. Owen patted his arm, then found a cup and poured some wine.

'Bless you, Captain.' The wounded man took a long drink. 'They are not the first strangers I have seen about since the vicar was murdered, but the first who came in. There are rumors that the dead man handed something over to Master Thomas before he was killed. But we would have known if he had come back that morning. We would have known.'

'And he did not?'

'No. I tend the fires early. By the time I heard the shouts I had stoked them and fetched wood for the hall.'

On departing, Owen passed a man he presumed was the cook rounding the corner of the house. A lad followed him, stumbling beneath the weight of a fat goose.

The chancellor expected guests.

Of course, the city would soon be filled with potential patrons for the minster. And Owen much feared that this morning's rash of intruders meant that whoever was behind Ronan's murder was becoming desperate. Crispin? Was it him? Or was he hoping to restore calm and order before the archbishop and his family arrived? Owen stopped outside the chancellor's gate, considering where they might try next. His home? He trusted Ned, but he would check there on his way to the castle to talk to Pit.

ELEVEN
A Maid's Tale

On Davygate a cluster of neighbors argued with Bess Merchet, who stood so that she blocked their view into Owen's garden. Over the din of their fuss he heard the twins shouting something about a man unable to breathe with his face in the mud. Owen pushed his way through the crowd mouthing apologies.

Bess opened the gate and motioned him into the yard. 'Heaven protect us from the fair Alisoun's suitors,' she muttered behind him.

Fair Alisoun? She stood toward the rear wall of the garden training an arrow on Ned where he sat astride a man lying face forward in the slush, head twisted to one side. It was the fallen man who gasped for air. He did not look like either of Crispin's men. A relief. But Ned's behavior sounded an alarm. He was not one to panic.

'Let him stand, Ned, or you won't sit for a long while,' said Alisoun with a menacing calm.

Rose and Rob looked on in horror.

'He attacked a man in the king's service,' said Ned in a cold, equally menacing voice.

'Who is on the ground?' Owen asked Bess.

'A trespasser. From what I've heard he shut Ned in the garden shed and took over his watch on the house. I leave you to deal with them while I drag a pallet near the kitchen fire so the victim might lie down while you tend his wound. I would not be so kind to him, but you are a household of healers. Though I must say, at present Mistress Alisoun seems more a warrior.'

Owen called to Rose and Rob to watch the gates, and headed toward the drama. If it was true Ned had been humbled in front of Alisoun, he understood the temptation to lash out, but past experience would have suggested the young man would hold his discipline, remember his responsibilities. Grasping a handful of Ned's clothing, Owen yanked him up and tossed him aside. The man lying in the mud made choking sounds as he attempted to prop himself up to breathe, his effort stymied by an arrow in his right arm just above the elbow. Owen grasped him around the chest and lifted him high enough that he could use his legs to turn and sit while he gulped air.

Releasing her stance, Alisoun slung her bow over her shoulder and tucked the unspent arrow in the quiver. 'He was watching the house. When Rob and Rose approached him he dashed for the wall, tried to scale it. I stopped him with the arrow while the twins let Ned out of the shack.' Stepping closer, she added in a low voice, 'His name is Gabriel. According to Marian he's Sir Thomas Percy's man.'

Percy. God in heaven. 'How does she know?'

'He was the partner of the one who fell from the roof. They were following her. I did not stay for more.'

Marian's story involved the Percys as well as the Nevilles, the two most powerful families in the North. Owen cursed under his breath. 'Did he give Ned any trouble after you'd shot him?'

'How could he?'

Owen offered Gabriel a hand. 'Let us see to that arm.'

Ned scrambled to his feet. 'Captain—'

'I will deal with you later. Come along, Gabriel,' said Owen.

Injured and dizzy from lack of air the man stumbled against Owen as he struggled to his feet, causing his hat to fly off. Owen steadied him, ordering Ned to fetch the man's hat and bring it with him to the kitchen. It was no wonder Gabriel's first impulse was to reclaim his disguise – his bright red hair, like Owen's son Hugh's, was a liability for a spy or a tracker, so easily picked out in a crowd.

'Rob and Rose, make the rounds of the houses in the minster yard. Let me know if you come upon any trouble,' Owen called to the twins.

With a nod, the two ran off.

As Owen supported Gabriel down the path to the kitchen door he noticed how the man cradled his injured arm, saw the muscles in his neck bulge as he limped. Either he'd injured his leg or foot in the fall after the arrow hit him or Ned's fury had caused further damage. Gabriel would find his work challenging for a while, which might make Owen's work easier, but would only antagonize the Percy family.

As promised, Bess Merchet had moved the pallet on which the children had spent the night closer to the fire and was now removing the bedding. 'Put him here,' she said. 'I will see whether I'm needed with the children.' She bustled off to the hall.

Owen ordered Ned to remove Gabriel's boots, warning him to have a care with the left one. 'If you cause any further injury I will lock you in the garden shed overnight.'

'Captain,' Ned grumbled as he tossed off his remaining boot and then knelt before Percy's man.

Owen took Alisoun aside to learn more about Gabriel, but she had little more information.

'I am glad you at least took care not to cause him more harm than necessary.'

'I hunt only what I intend to eat.'

Ned glanced over with a startled expression.

Owen drew Alisoun farther from the bench. 'If this morning is an example of what is to come, Marian may be trouble for us. Is she a Percy?'

'She did not say how she knew his name. But I do not believe this trouble is of her doing, Captain. As it seems likely she is convent-educated, I think she was removed from a convent against her will. When Rose came to tell us there was a watcher in the garden we asked Marian to look. That's when she told us his name and fealty, and that he traveled with the other, the one who fell yesterday morning.'

'Both Percy's men?'

'Yes.'

They both glanced up as Lucie entered the kitchen and joined them.

'How might I help?'

Owen knew how he wanted to proceed, but it would contradict all Lucie held sacred about a healer's behavior. 'My need to learn all that he knows will make me seem cruel. I promise you I will then remove the arrow and allow the two of you to see to him. Will you support me in this?'

'I will,' said Alisoun.

Lucie touched Owen's cheek. 'I trust you.' She looked toward the two young men as Ned, who had placed himself on Gabriel's wounded side, roughly pushed him toward the pallet by the fire. 'You might keep Ned away before he does more injury. He will not soon forgive the humbling.'

'Did you attempt to reason with Ned?' Owen asked Alisoun.

'He burst from the shed in a fury. There was no stopping him.'

'Bloody fool.' Owen pushed Ned out of the way and took charge of Gabriel, helping him ease down onto the pallet and find a comfortable position on his uninjured side.

'It is easier to talk when sitting up,' Lucie said. 'We will prop him up on cushions so that he is half sitting.' She disappeared into the hall to collect what she needed, Alisoun following.

Owen fetched a bowl of water, the basket of potions, instruments, and bandages that Lucie kept near the door, additional rags, a flagon of wine and a bowl, and a low stool to sit on while he questioned the man. Ned retreated to the bench near the door.

Once the patient was settled, Lucie and Alisoun withdrew to seats sufficiently close that they might hear all that was said, but out of Gabriel's sight so as not to distract him.

Resting elbows on knees Owen studied Gabriel, his guarded expression, the stubborn set of the jaw. 'Are you comfortable?'

'No I'm not comfortable, I have an arrow in my arm, or did you not notice?'

'I am well aware of it, and have every intention of seeing to it. But first you will tell me what you know of our houseguest.'

'I saw her at the midden this morning. Did she tell you who I am?'

'Gabriel. Now what can you tell us of Marian?'

'No longer Matthew?' A little laugh. 'She must feel safe here.' A shrug that caused a wince.

Owen slipped out his dagger, touched it to the wound. 'I prefer to play the healer with you, but unless you tell me all you know of the woman and what she has endured . . .' He twirled the dagger. 'Your choice.'

Gabriel pressed back against the cushions. 'I am Sir Thomas Percy's man. If you dare harm me—'

'Sir Thomas, is it? We are acquainted.' Long ago, on a battlefield, and Percy had no reason to remember Owen, but this ginger pup would not know that. 'He is an honorable man and will take the word of Prince Edward's man in York. Besides, the harm has been done, eh?' He kept his one-eyed gaze steady on the man who stank with fear and blood and a long while on the road. 'You would do well to talk to me.'

Gabriel attempted to cross his arms, another ill-advised gesture.

'Best wait until I remove the arrow to do that,' Owen said. 'You've only to tell me what you know and I will get to work.'

Silence.

'As you wish.' Owen rose and strolled over toward the fire. 'I should fetch more firewood.'

Lucie took his cue and headed for the door. 'I will check on the shop.'

Gabriel wrenched himself round to see the two of them. 'You would leave me here?'

'Alisoun will call us back when you are ready to talk.'

'But the children,' Alisoun protested.

'What of my arm?' cried Gabriel. Yet when Alisoun approached he shrank from her.

Assuring him that she meant him no harm, she knelt beside him, gently resting one hand above and one below his injury. 'I do not like the feel of the flesh around the wound. I would advise you speak up, and quickly.'

'You did this.'

'You might have knocked and stated your purpose. Instead you accosted the bailiff's man and trapped him in the garden shed.' She rose and started for the door to the hall.

'Come back,' Gabriel whimpered, 'I cannot lose my arm. I will tell you what you want to know if you help me.'

Owen was back on his stool in a few breaths. The flushed face might be emotion, might be fever. 'Tell me.'

'She is Dame Marian, a sister of Wherwell Abbey. Sir Thomas Percy's ward.'

Owen knew of Wherwell, a fine abbey between Salisbury and Winchester. Bishop Wykeham's territory. 'The abbey is far from Percy lands.'

'But near one of Sir Thomas's manors. A royal gift in token of his services. His widowed sister Lady Edwina manages it for him.'

'How came Dame Marian to stray so far from the abbey?'

'She went missing the night of a fire at the abbey in the week after Pentecost.'

Late May. 'She escaped a fire?' Owen asked.

A deep breath. 'The fire began around the window in the library that holds the nuns' music. Dame Marian's pallet was right there. When she was not among the sisters helping pass buckets of water or carrying manuscripts out of harm's way they feared they would find her bones in the ashes. But when the laborers searched the ashes the next morning they found no bones. The fire had not burned so long that a body would leave no trace. Her nun's garb was found in a gardener's shed in the outer part of the abbey enclosure. The reverend mother and Dame Eloise, the cantrice who taught her, both insisted someone had taken her, that she would not have set the fire, she would not have run on her own accord.'

'Unless she feared she would be blamed for the fire,' said Owen.

'You would not be the first to suggest that. Sir Thomas and his sister, Lady Edwina, thought that likely and expected her to come to them. But we searched the countryside between the abbey and both their houses and found no sign of her. Then one of my fellows learned that his brother Phillip, Dame Marian's music teacher in Lady Edwina's household, had disappeared a few days before the fire. His family was frightened. He'd seemed obsessed with his former student, enraged when she went to the abbey, saying they had been meant for each other and he would find a way to rescue her.' Gabriel had been speaking so quickly he needed to pause for breath. His voice had grown raspy. 'Might I have some of that wine?'

Keen to keep him talking, Owen poured a cup, handed it to him. 'And so you were sent to find Phillip and Marian?'

'Four pairs of us, plotting our paths with information Rupert gave us about his brother's rambling, where he had served, where he studied. We were to track the two of them, take them both, return them to Sir Thomas. Whether we returned with Phillip alive or dead mattered not a whit to my lord. But Dame Marian was to be treated with respect.'

'Was this Rupert of the party?'

'He was my comrade on the road.'

The brother of the man suspected of abducting Dame Marian had been trusted as part of the search party? 'Just the two of you?'

'Yes.'

Unwise. Owen wondered how Sir Thomas justified that. 'Have you found Phillip?'

'What we found were rumors of his death. That villagers burned him as a pestilence-carrier, but she escaped. She might have betrayed him to them. Or so the story went.'

'Did you send word to your lord?'

'We were in pursuit. That would have taken time.'

'So then your mark was only Dame Marian, the betrayer of your partner's brother?'

Gabriel looked away. 'I was caught up in the chase. I did not think.'

'Go on. You were now searching for her.'

'We lost all track of her for a good long while and wondered whether the villagers had not wished to admit they had burned her as well. If they'd learned she had been a bride of Christ they would fear God's punishment. We were about to turn back north of Bath when we heard of a company of minstrels and players with a comely lad, voice of an angel, fair hair, pale eyes— We kept going.'

'And once you found her Rupert leaped off the roof of the chapter house?'

'I don't know what happened between them. I was waiting outside the minster. I did not see them disappear into the chapter house.' Gabriel was panting with fear. 'I pray you, save my arm!'

'You rode together, drank together, but you have no idea why Rupert would take her somewhere without informing you? I don't believe you. I think you knew he meant to punish her for his brother's death and something went wrong.'

'I knew of no such intention, I swear. We were following the French spy, Ambrose Coates. We thought he would be a fine addition to our catch. I waited without that evening, Rupert went in to watch the meeting. Ambrose had told her he was meeting someone about her stolen prayer book. I don't think she believed him. I had told her Ambrose was a French spy.'

A stolen prayer book? The psalter? 'How did you know Ambrose, and the rumors about him?'

'He is not a man one forgets.'

'Where had you seen him?'

'At the French court. A few years past. I offered Dame Marian a trade – information about the French spy for a message to Sir Thomas telling him where I'd found her and that we would travel south as soon as the snow melted.'

'As was your duty.'

'She did not know that.'

'Did you send the message?'

'I did. As was my duty.' He drained his cup, set it aside with a clatter, closing his eyes. 'I would speak with her. Find out what happened that night. I followed the clerk who unlocked the south transept, but he returned while I was searching the chapter house, before I found anything. She had been in there with him?'

'It was you who accosted the clerk when he returned to lock the door?'

'I am sorry for that. Was she with him?'

'Was there anyone else in the chapter house when you searched?'

'I found no one.'

'That was not long after Rupert fell. How did you learn of it? Were you still at the minster?'

'I'd returned, hoping to sneak in with someone. That's when I heard a man had fallen.'

'Did you see him?'

'I joined the clerks crowding round him. I could see enough in the lantern light.'

'Did you see the vicar's body near the chancellor's house?'

'No. Though I saw men there as well. I swear I had nothing to do with that. I did not know the man. Ambrose did. Ask him.' His voice broke and he closed his eyes for a moment, his breath shallow.

'What did you intend to do with Ambrose?'

Licking his lips, Gabriel rasped, 'The enthronement. All the Northern families would be coming. Keep watch, deliver him up to the Percys. Deliver both.'

Owen took out the shears, began to cut away the sleeve around the arrow. 'Where did you plan to keep Marian until then?'

'With Tucker the fiddler. Gave the goodwife coin to take good care of her.'

Alisoun brought the kettle to add hot water to the bowl.

'Take good care?' Owen said. 'Why not St Clement's Priory, where she need not pretend to be a lad, where she would be safe?'

Gabriel opened his eyes wide. 'You are angry. How can I trust—' Noticing Alisoun's hands on him he tried to wrench away his arm.

'Do not be such a fool,' she said in an even tone. 'I am cleaning the wound.'

He watched her closely for a moment.

'St Clement's,' Owen prompted.

'We did not think of the nuns.'

Good at tracking, too inexperienced to plan the rest. Not surprising. The wound clean, Owen summoned Ned to hold Gabriel's legs, asked Alisoun to hold his shoulders while he pulled the cushions away. Once the man was lying flat, Owen cut the shaft as close to the arm as he dared, then, while holding down the arm with his knee, pulled out the rest. Painful, but quick. Gabriel shrieked and kicked Ned in the mouth.

'Now you see why I had you remove his boots,' said Owen.

Ned muttered a curse as he sat back to nurse his jaw. Gabriel moaned and thrashed.

'Be still while Alisoun cleans it and wraps it in a poultice,' Owen said.

'You cannot keep me here.'

'I do not intend to. Where are you lodging?'

Closed eyes, tightened mouth.

'Then I will take you to the castle.'

'Holy Trinity Priory.'

'Good. I will deliver you to the infirmarian at the priory.'

'Might I see her? I need to know why he jumped. If she pushed him. What happened.'

'When the infirmarian judges you fit, you may return. I suggest that you knock on the door and make your request with courtesy. Until then, she is under my protection.'

'You will take the credit.'

Owen chuckled. 'No, young Gabriel, I assure you that the tale is yours to tell to her family. You have much to explain.'

'We found her!'

'And I would guess by the welts on her wrists and ankles that Rupert had no intention of delivering her safe to her family. I would guess he meant to throw her off the roof. Had you two been in the chapter house before?'

'I was never there.'

'But he?'

'I don't know.'

'You each went your own way in the city?'

'At times.' Gabriel caught Owen's arm as he began to rise. 'Will I heal?'

'Be still and receive our ministrations with good grace. The more patient you are, the better the outcome. Tell me about the prayer book.'

'A small thing, but Lady Edwina claims it has value. She commissioned it for Dame Marian, a gift when she took her vows. My lord Percy called it "a choir of crows." The illustrations. Said it was his sister's jape, the sisters being crows cawing around Dame Marian, the nightingale.'

'When was it lost?'

'At Tucker's. According to Dame Marian, Ambrose believed their host stole it, claims he followed him to Ronan's lodgings. He believed that the vicar either bought it from Tucker or advised him as to its value.'

'Did you retrieve it?'

'No. We might ask Dame Marian. She might have overheard Ambrose meeting with that vicar.'

A choir of crows. Magda had called Thoresby the Old Crow. By extension all clerics were crows to her. And nuns? Lady Edwina shared her humor. 'Did you see the prayer book?'

'How would I?'

Gabriel looked up as Alisoun knelt to his wounded side. 'How can she do that? Shoot me, then tend me?'

'Ask her.' Owen rose. 'I will return for you in a little while.'

He went over to talk to Ned, giving him a simple task. Once they had deposited Gabriel in the infirmary, Ned was to find Hempe and tell him what they'd learned about Dame Marian and the Percys, and ask him to speak with Tucker's wife, Judith, about Gabriel's claim he gave her money to care for Marian. If true, she was not dependent on Tucker's work for a while. He might become informative after a night in the castle. When Ned had accomplished the task, he was to return to the infirmary.

'I count on you to return to your senses. I understand how you feel, but I cannot condone it. Consider what you have just heard, all that the young woman suffered at the hands of an unwanted suitor.'

Ned bowed his head.

'Alisoun is her own woman. Show her your best self. Respect her right to her own choice.'

'I have been a fool.'

Owen did not argue that. 'Return to your watch on the house and shop. I will come for you when Gabriel is ready to be moved.'

Lucie had heard much of their conversation. Now she smiled as Owen approached.

'Might we leave Alisoun with Gabriel and go to Marian?' he asked.

She hesitated, searching his face for a sign of what he hoped to accomplish. Her own anger at the presumption of men sounded a warning in her head that Marian had suffered enough of men's company for a long while. Yet, hearing his talk with Ned she knew that Owen had been much moved by Marian's story. Still . . . Lucie drew him out to the hall where they might speak in private, settled on a bench near the window.

'Why now?' she asked gently. 'Why you?'

'I understand your hesitance. I mean to recount Gabriel's story. Whether or not she chooses to correct, add, that is for her to decide. She deserves to hear what he said of her.'

That seemed fair. Lucie agreed, beginning to rise, but Owen stayed her.

'Ned is not the only one with much to learn from the story of Phillip's and his brother's transgressions against Marian. Watching how Ned watches Alisoun reminds me how I watched you, how I yearned to possess you. I was fortunate. Somehow I earned your love. But I see how it poisons love to think of possession. What she suffered. What right had he to pluck her away? To decide for her?'

Lucie had never loved Owen more than she did at this moment. She studied him as she thought what to say.

'If I—' he began.

She pressed a finger to his mouth. Shook her head. 'If you express this to her, I believe she might be inspired to trust us. To trust you.' She took his hand. 'Come. Let us meet with Dame Marian.'

Setting aside the basket of needlework she had carried from the nursery, their guest sat with hands folded in her lap, head bowed, listening to Owen's account, occasionally nodding. Lucie had chosen a seat to the side, allowing him to have his say. She was there if Marian wanted her, but she wished the woman to hear how a man might respond to the story.

Arriving at the end of Gabriel's account, Owen said, 'We wanted you to know what he said of you, what he might tell your aunt and uncle. And I wished to say . . .' He paused. 'As a man I recognized myself in Phillip's and Rupert's behavior, and I am ashamed for us all. Forgive me for threatening you last night.'

Marian looked up, startled. 'No, Captain. You are nothing like them. Nothing. But . . .' She caught her breath, tears welling in her eyes. 'Bless you,' she whispered.

Lucie moved to sit beside her, gathering her into her arms, holding her as she wept. 'Perhaps we should leave now,' she whispered when the storm passed.

'No. I pray you, stay.' Marian sat up, wiping her eyes. 'Gabriel and Rupert did find me in Cawood. They had heard about me at a tavern there, and that the company I was with were to perform at the palace. All the village were talking about it. At the palace they recognized Master Ambrose as well.'

'Did Gabriel tell you this?' Lucie asked.

'Later, yes. They had been watching Tucker's house. Gabriel caught me out at the midden one night. He told me that Master Ambrose had long lived at the court of King Charles and was known to be a spy for the French. As he said, he promised to take me to Sir Thomas if I told him whatever I might glean about Master Ambrose's movements in the city. Anything useful I might overhear.'

'Is it true what Gabriel said about Ambrose and your stolen prayer book?' asked Lucie.

'Yes. All this trouble is my fault.' Marian's voice broke.

'No,' Owen said. 'You are not to blame. You have been ill used.'

'I have trusted the wrong people. I believed Gabriel. Master Ambrose had spoken French, told the leader of the company of his fame among the nobles there. Gabriel said he must have guessed who I was and pretended to help me, thinking to use me in some way, spy that he was, and Sir Thomas being trusted by the king and his son Prince Edward.' As she spoke her voice grew hoarse. 'Might I have some water?'

Lucie began to rise but Owen insisted on going.

'I would prefer honey water to wine, with some of Dame Magda's physick. Alisoun will know,' said Marian.

When Owen had left the room Marian said, 'You are most fortunate in your husband.'

'I am.' Lucie smiled. 'While we wait for him, tell me about Wherwell Abbey. Were you happy there?'

'How could I not be? Dedicating my life to God, using my one gift to sing His praises. It is all I ever wanted.'

Lucie recalled many a girl silenced by the nuns at St Clement's when she boarded there. 'You were encouraged to sing?'

'My voice was the reason they welcomed me to Wherwell. The cantrice herself, Dame Eloise, undertook my training. I worked hard, learned all that she set before me, devoted myself to my lessons. She is aged, her health failing. She said she was at peace knowing that I would be there in the abbey to lead the sisters in song when she was gone.' Again, Marian's voice broke. 'It hurts to speak of this when I have had no word about her, whether she survived the fire.'

'I pray some of your kin coming for the archbishop's enthronement will have news for you.'

A knock. Owen entered with a tray of cups and flagons of water and wine. Lucie offered to pour.

'How is Gabriel?' Marian asked.

'Resting,' said Owen. 'Alisoun is satisfied that his forehead is cool.'

'I would not have expected her to be skilled with a bow,' said Marian.

'We were speaking of how Dame Marian came to Wherwell Abbey,' said Lucie. 'She studied under the cantrice.' She handed Marian a cup of honeyed water. 'Gabriel believed that your former music tutor had set that fire. Tell me how you met him.'

'Would that I never had.' Marian drank some honeyed water, closed her eyes as she swallowed, thanked Owen. 'After the death of my father, my mother asked Sir Thomas, my god-father, to be my guardian. I was to live away from home, in one of Sir Thomas's manor houses, supervised by his sister, Lady Edwina. Her first act was to hire a tutor for me, to teach me all I needed to know so that I might be welcome at one of the great abbeys as an asset with my voice and knowledge of music – Sir Thomas had always encouraged me to sing at the Christmas and harvest feasts on the manor. The tutor,

Phillip, was the brother of one of Sir Thomas's retainers. Lady Edwina and my mother considered him a good choice because his father had once been a musician in the court of the King of Bohemia. And he was studying for the Church. Neither of them knew anything more of him. They had heard him play. One of his own compositions. I was happy. Music was all I cared about. That must be how he came to his grievous misunderstanding.'

'Phillip? Your music-master?' Lucie asked.

'Yes. I often smile when I sing. Did he think I meant the smiles for him? All I thought about was the music. I looked forward to the day when I would devote my life to God.'

Seeing the pain and doubt in her eyes, hearing it in her voice, Lucie gently asked about that day, when she finally went to the abbey.

'Mistress Edwina and Sir Thomas accompanied me to Wherwell. Everything depended on that meeting. I was so in awe I could not breathe when the abbess commanded me to sing for her. But with Mistress Edwina smiling and encouraging me I found my breath and began to sing *Benedicamus Domino*.' Lucie knew that to be part of the daily office, a piece every sister would know. 'The abbess interrupted to summon Dame Eloise, the cantrice. Once I saw Dame Eloise I found the courage and the breath to sing my best. She had such kind eyes.'

Marian broke off and rose to sing a *Benedicamus Domino* unlike any Lucie had ever heard, notes climbing, then curling back. Soul-lifting. When she paused, the silence in the room felt alive, resonant with prayer. Owen looked on in awe.

As if unaware of the effect she had Marian resumed her seat and continued. 'After I sang Dame Eloise clapped her hands, tears streaming from her eyes. She enfolded me in her arms. She said that God had answered her prayers. She would train me to be her sub-cantrice. I felt so welcome.'

'God answered your prayers as well,' said Lucie. 'Tell me more about Dame Eloise.'

'I loved her the moment I met her, such a gentle, sweet face, her pale eyes a little clouded with age yet somehow still keen. And so kind. Her hands were soft, cushioned as if she had no sharp bones.' Marian gave a little laugh. A lovely, throaty laugh.

'How long were you there?' Lucie asked.

'Seven years. I thought I would live there until God claimed me.' Marian pressed her hand to her forehead, her sleeve falling away from the slender wrist that seemed far too frail to support her long-fingered hands. 'But everything fell apart in the spring. I have prayed and prayed and I cannot think what the sin might be for which I am so punished. Pride?' She glanced up at Lucie, tears shimmering in her eyes, spots of color on her cheeks. 'Was I too proud of my voice? I thought it God's gift.' There was an edge to her voice. 'I thought I was meant to use it to praise Him. Dame Eloise said it was so. I cannot think why God so punished me.'

Reaching out to take Marian's hand, Lucie held it firmly as she asked whether she needed some wine.

Marian shook her head. 'To be among women again. You cannot know how good it has been to be with you, Dame Lucie. And Alisoun and Dame Magda, Dame Bess. You as well, Captain Archer. What you said – I have not felt so safe since that terrible night. And now I would – Gabriel promised to find out whether Dame Eloise survived the fire. But I cannot expect him to do so now. Rupert was his friend. I am sure he blames me for the deaths of both him and his brother.' Her voice rose, her eyes flashing, but as suddenly as the anger flashed, she quelled it, paused to drink water, wipe her eyes. 'I pray that the prioress of St Clement's might find out for me. Or, as you said, Dame Lucie, perhaps someone coming for the enthronement will have news.'

'Did Ambrose tell you who he was meeting at the minster?' Owen asked.

'No. He had mentioned only a few people in my hearing – the Riverwoman, you, Dame Lucie. I could not think it would be either Dame Lucie or Dame Magda, but I did mention you. I have betrayed you. And Master Ambrose. I do not deny it. I have been such a fool.'

'You survived. That is no small accomplishment,' said Owen.

Marian dismissed it with a shake of her head.

'What else did you tell them about Ambrose?' asked Owen.

'I knew little else. He sometimes mutters to himself over his instrument, thinking perhaps that no one will be able to understand him. That is how I learned of the Riverwoman.' A pause. 'There was a time when I would have shunned a woman like Dame Magda. But I would have been wrong. God clearly works through her.'

'She would smile to hear that,' said Lucie.

'That is what Alisoun said.' Another pause, suddenly not meeting Lucie's gaze. 'Alisoun told me she lost her family to pestilence. It returned to the south in summer.'

'Here as well,' said Lucie. 'Our nursemaid left us to nurse her mother, but lost her, and when she returned and our children fell ill . . . I could not convince her it was not pestilence. She fled. That is when Magda sent Alisoun to help us.'

Marian crossed herself, but did not speak, her pale eyes watching something far beyond the room. A sob escaped her and she turned away, wiping her eyes.

'I let him die. I refused to help him.'

'Phillip? But he took you from the abbey,' said Lucie. The young woman was trembling so hard. Lucie took her hand.

'I wanted him to pay for what he did. He took me away from all that I loved.'

'Yes. He hurt you,' said Lucie.

'I did nothing for him. Nothing,' Marian sobbed.

Lucie touched her hot cheeks, shushing her as she would one of the children. 'Sip your water. Rest a moment.'

'I will never rest. I am damned.'

'No one is beyond redemption.'

'And now I've brought trouble on your house. And the city.'

'You are helping by telling your story so that we might know whether there are others besides Gabriel who might be a threat to us,' said Owen.

'How can I know whether or not there are more?'

'How did you come to leave Wherwell?' Lucie asked. 'Did Phillip take you away? How did he gain access?' She was guessing, connecting bits and pieces of information and in-tuited pain. 'Did he tell you?'

'Lady Edwina had visited me earlier in the year. I wanted to show her one of the manuscripts. The illustrations reminded me of those in a book she had shown me when I first came to stay with her. Dame Eloise permitted me to bring her to my cell off the room where the musical manuscripts were stored. Phillip said she told him about it, answering all his questions, so helpful, he said. From her he learned where I slept, where the music library was. How could she be so—' Marian stopped herself.

In that moment, watching her fight the anger, push it down – again smoothing the brow, relaxing the mouth, softening the eyes, taking a deep breath, Lucie understood the enigma the young woman presented. She, too, had been shaped by the sisters. *Anger is a grievous sin, Lucia. A girl must follow the Blessed Mother's model – humble, obedient, ever cheerful.*

'How did he use what she had told him?' Lucie asked.

'On the Feast of Pentecost he attended a service at the abbey, and afterward hid himself in a garden shed. He bragged of his cleverness to me. At nightfall, he crept out and set a fire beneath the window of the music library. I slept beneath that window. I woke coughing. At first I did not understand, and then I smelled it, felt the smoke in my eyes. A fire! I called out to warn everyone as I ran to assist Dame Eloise, but another sister was already leading her out. And then all was confusion. So many rushing about. I was trying to move the most precious manuscripts out of harm's way. The smoke made me dizzy. I fell against a burning timber. Someone carried me to a window and tossed me out, shouting at me to roll myself through the dew in the grass. He was waiting there. He picked me up, saying he would take me to a safe place. I thought at first he was the gardener, but the voice. I recognized the voice.' She stopped, staring down at her hands. 'I was fighting him, kicking and screaming and I managed to get free. I remember running and seeing that the gates were open so that carts could come with water . . . I doubled back, ashamed to be running instead of helping. And then – what happened then I know not. I woke up in a barn, dressed in clothes that were not mine, my hair uncovered . . .' Her voice broke.

'You must have been so frightened. And angry.'

Marian met Lucie's gaze. 'Angry,' she whispered. 'Yes. I

have done penance for my anger. And for Dame Eloise and all the sisters, and the manuscripts. I have ached to know how much damage I caused.'

'*You* caused?' Lucie found it difficult to control her own outrage. '*He* started the fire. You rushed to help.'

'I do not know how, but I inspired in Phillip a belief that God meant us to be together, that I had taken vows in ignorance— He called my vows a mistake.'

'Arrogant cur,' Owen muttered. He clenched his hands, holding himself still to listen.

'You were seven years in the convent,' said Lucie. 'I presume he had no contact with you in all that time. He spun a tale that he began to believe. It had nothing to do with you. Did he ask you how you felt? What you wanted?'

'He believed—'

'He believed what he wanted to believe,' Lucie snapped.

'I want to believe that.' Marian reached for Lucie's hand, held it for a moment, whispering her thanks. 'Shall I go on?'

'Yes, I pray you, what happened then? Where were you when the pestilence struck him down?'

'A shed at the edge of a marsh. With a hole for a window, another for a door. He called it a house. A fog of foul vapors surrounded it morning and night. At first I blamed them on his labored breathing, but when the first pustule burst, I knew. Down a track I'd found a village. I had managed to barter for a young woman to come out and cook for us. But when he sickened she disappeared. I searched his bags, hoping to find money for food, and I found my prayer book, the one Dame Edwina had copied for me, and my paternoster beads. He had stolen my prayer book and beads. He had taken me from all that I loved, starved me, dragged me to such a cursed place – was that not enough? He would rob me of these as well?' She paused. 'Yes, I admit to my anger, I do. I finally saw what he was and I knew then that if he recovered he would take my virginity, my last blessing. I had begged him not to touch me, and he had agreed, for the nonce, he said, he would be patient. Patient.' She spit the word. 'I saw what a child I was to believe anything he said. No wonder God so punished him. I felt it a sign that I was right not to nurse him. God had condemned him with the pestilence. And I was untouched. I must flee while that was still true. I took his clothes, washed them well, and turned myself into Matthew. I collected anything that might be of value, and I left.'

'He was still alive?' Lucie asked.

'He was weak, the fever had stolen his wits, but he yet lived.'

All that she described took time – the maidservant deserting, her preparations for leaving. Most died quickly after the pustules broke. In Lucie's experience those who lingered were rare, and they were the ones who survived. She wondered whether Marian knew that.

'Have you had any news of him?' Lucie asked. 'Was he buried?'

'I heard a tale of villagers burning a pestilence-carrier in a hut near a marsh and I wondered if it might be him. I was not far from there when I heard it from men in the fields. They were warning me away. Strangers were not welcome when Death walked the land.' Tears fell down her cheeks. She brushed them away with her hands. 'You cannot know how I have agonized over all I did. And did not do.'

Lucie poured water, gave it to her to drink.

'How did you find food?' she asked.

'I traded my prayer beads one or two at a time for food. I believed the Blessed Mother and her Son would understand.'

'Folk shared their food?'

'They refused me shelter but they were not lacking charity. Some sold me food, not wishing me to starve.'

'Where did you encounter the company of musicians?'

'In a tavern along the road out of Bath. I hoped to find work at the stables there, but I was shooed away like a stray cat. One of the musicians – Wojon, he called himself, he saw what happened and offered to buy me some food and drink. We sat at a table with some of the others. After more ale they began to tease about how I looked a lad who could be cleaned up and become their lady. They asked me to sing. I sang a carol my mother taught me as a child and one of them hurried inside to fetch their leader. He was happy to take me along.' Marian closed her eyes.

Lucie gently touched her hand. 'You have stirred up much

pain in the telling. But it is helpful. Now, tell us of that night in the chapter house. Why did you go in there?'

'I thought I saw the player who attacked me at Cawood. The drummer, Paul. He'd finally guessed I was no lad. And after drinking the good ale at the palace—' A ragged breath. 'He is big, and strong. I do not know how Master Ambrose had the strength to pull him off, but he did.'

'You sought to hide from him in the chapter house?' Lucie asked.

'Yes,' Marian breathed. 'I thought to slip out in a while. I meant only to lose him.'

'Had he seen you?' Owen asked.

'I don't know. I don't even know if it was him.'

'But you stayed,' said Lucie.

'Someone locked the door.' Marian shuddered and licked her lips. 'I told myself I would be safe, I would curl up in my cloak and sleep, and in the morning I would be discovered. I did not know at first I was not alone.'

'What happened?' asked Lucie.

'Once I calmed I stumbled around in the dark searching for the door. Maybe it was shut, not locked. Maybe I could open it from within. He waited there. I heard his breath as I touched the door. He caught me up and threw me to the floor. I bit and kicked and he kept hissing in my ear that he meant to avenge his brother. I escaped from him once. In the dark I thought he might not see me. I heard something that sounded as if it came from the other side of the door. I went toward it, pulled, pushed, rattled, shouted. He laughed all the while.' Tears now streamed down Marian's face as her words tumbled out, an outpouring of horror. 'How could they not hear?'

'Did you know that Gabriel's partner was Phillip's brother?' Owen asked in his gentlest voice.

'Not until Rupert told me that night.' A sob. 'I stopped thinking, just waited for death. He tied my hands and feet, slung me over his shoulder, and carried me up narrow stairs, tossed me down on a wood floor, sat on me, and opened the shutter on a lantern. I thought then he meant to enjoy me before he killed me. But he just kept whispering about his dear brother, saintly Phillip. I had burned him alive. The villagers said they could hear him screaming.'

So he *had* survived the pestilence. Weak, but alive. And then burned. 'He kept you there all night?' Lucie asked.

'Yes.' A whisper.

'Did he take you?'

'No. He said I disgusted him.'

God be thanked.

'How did you get to the roof?' asked Owen.

'Rupert had left me, taken the lantern and gone away. I heard him moving up above. Hunting for the worst way to kill me, I thought. I heard from afar the night office being sung. I kicked the floor. Again. Again. Could they not hear?' A pause for breath. 'Rupert came clattering down from above. I rolled away so he would not find me at once, but I caught against something and he was there, yanking me up, cutting my bonds, telling me to walk. He held a knife at my back. I could not feel my legs or my arms but somehow I moved. I drew my knife and he knocked it out of my hands, shoved me against a ladder, shouted for me to climb. I felt something wet and cold. Snow. I started to climb. He was behind me, so close, I pulled myself up and over. So cold, so cold and wet. But the air – if I could find the edge I would be free. A sin, I know, to take my life. But I was so wretched.'

'A night of such fear,' said Lucie.

'I walked to the edge. He came up behind me and shouted at me to take one more step. I wanted to fly but my legs gave out from under me. He must have reached to push as I fell and tripped over me. He went off the edge. I am doubly damned. I killed both brothers.' She stared at nothing.

Lucie crossed herself. Not for the brothers, but for Marian. 'And your prayer book?' she asked.

'I never saw it.'

'Paul the drummer?' asked Owen.

'I don't know whether it was him, or my fear manifest.' She gave Owen a questioning look.

'I will ask about players and musicians at the taverns,' he said.

'That morning in the chapter house, how were you able to sing after such a night?' asked Lucie.

Marian turned to her. Tears wet her cheeks, but in her eyes Lucie saw the spark of anger as she swiped at the tears, an impatient gesture. 'I was certain I would never again sing in a sacred space, not after— They would say I lured Phillip, and then Rupert. The woman is ever blamed. We are Eve's children, the temptresses.'

'The wrong was done to you,' said Lucie

'You are not the one who will stand in judgment.'

'I will make Prioress Isabel understand.'

'Will you?'

Would she?

'I know this was difficult for you,' said Owen, 'and I am grateful, Dame Marian. I see now that what happened in the chapter house likely has nothing to do with Ronan's murderer.' He rose to leave. At the door he turned to assure her that she was safe with them, and he would find a way to take her to St Clement's.

Thanking him, Marian took up the basket of needlework and said she would return to Bess and the children.

TWELVE
Complications

In a grim mood, Owen led Gabriel and Ned down Stonegate, away from the route to the priory on Micklegate.

'You said you would take me to the priory,' said Gabriel.

Lucie had suggested St Mary's – it was closer, and the abbot and infirmarian more likely to cooperate with Owen's request to alert him at once if anyone came seeking Gabriel or he tried to leave. 'I prefer St Mary's Abbey. I trust their infirmarian.'

'My things—' Gabriel tried to turn back.

Owen gripped his upper arm, yanking him around. 'You will not need them today.'

At the corner of Stonegate and Petergate, Owen's old friend Robert Dale stood in the doorway of his goldsmith's shop as if welcoming a breath of fresh air. When Owen raised his hand in greeting Robert bowed his head and withdrew, shutting the door. Something was very wrong.

The incident troubling him, Owen made use of Ned's and Gabriel's silences to think. Today's revelations brought him no closer to solving Ronan's murder. Crispin Poole was questioning folk about Ronan. Perhaps Robert Dale felt the bite of that and wanted to avoid any further questions. How many of the merchants had Crispin antagonized? It might have been Crispin's men who attacked Beck when he discovered them searching the vicar's room. He did not like to think that. Had Crispin not worked for Alexander Neville, Owen might have been his friend. Crispin understood what it meant to try to start again after a debilitating injury ended a life of soldiering – Owen with the loss of his left eye, Crispin with his loss of half his arm. They had shared stories in the York Tavern, a comfortable camaraderie. But since learning that Crispin served the new archbishop, Owen had avoided him. Even before he had learned that his retainers were actually Neville's men. How had Crispin injured his leg? Slipped on a snowy morning while attacking Ronan? Owen was so absorbed in thought that he barely noticed passing through Bootham Bar and turning toward St Mary's gates.

As they entered the abbey grounds Owen felt Gabriel's tension subside.

'Much finer than Holy Trinity,' he said.

'Wealthier,' said Ned.

Brother Henry welcomed Owen to his infirmary, calling for his assistant Peter to escort Gabriel to a bed in an area screened off from those of the infirm monks and make him comfortable. Ned took his leave, promising to return as soon as he had completed his mission. Owen explained to the infirmarian who Gabriel was, what had happened, why he must be watched.

A raised brow. 'You would have him relaxed, sleepy?' asked Brother Henry.

'Brother Wulfstan taught you well.'

They both crossed themselves in memory of Henry's predecessor as infirmarian, a wise, gentle monk who had been both Lucie's and Jasper's good friend.

'My thoughts were filled with him as the pestilence struck this summer,' said Henry. Wulfstan had died assisting victims of the pestilence. 'We lost two members of the community this time.'

'You have a new assistant.'

'Yes. I blamed myself – my tales of Wulfstan's self-sacrifice inspired him. Yet how could I forbid him? He was doing God's work.' A shuddering sigh. 'You might wish to speak with Abbot William. One of Sir John Neville's retainers called on him, wanting to know who had arranged to lodge at the abbey for the enthronement.' He nodded at Owen's thanks. 'And now to work.' Henry poured a cup of wine from a pitcher and emptied a small vial into it. 'I will administer this after I tend to his injuries. I need him awake to tell me what he feels. Once he drinks this, he will soon find it difficult to rise from his bed.'

'A little something first, to make him drowsy?'

Henry agreed. 'A drop.'

'If he should speak of a guest in my home, a woman, I ask you and Peter to say nothing of it to anyone. Can Peter be trusted?'

'He believes God calls him to work by my side, and he is keen, quick to help. If I order him to silence, he will obey. He would not risk my ire. This young man, Ned. He said he would be returning. Do you trust him to watch over Gabriel?'

'I need him elsewhere. Is there anyone at the abbey you might trust to guard your infirmary for the nonce? Until I make another arrangement?'

Henry walked over to a window opening onto the apothecary garden. A lay brother knelt on the path, moving with studied patience as he clipped wilting plants, plucked up weeds. 'Malkin!' the infirmarian called out. The gardener turned, raising a large, meaty hand in greeting. His face was scarred, his nose flattened by repeated breaks. 'I need you in the infirmary for a while.'

With a wistful glance back at his work the man rose, unfurling a muscle-bound body, and lumbered slowly up the path.

'Former soldier,' Owen said. 'Good choice.' Even if the man now shunned his old life as a soldier his presence should be an effective deterrent to violence.

The abbot's house was near the infirmary, nestled in well-tended gardens. A novice answered Owen's knock, bowing him in and motioning him to a seat in the anteroom screened off from the modest hall, all without making eye contact. Cowed by Abbot William, Owen guessed. The abbot was not well loved. Not as high born as his predecessor Campian and anxious to appease his superiors, he took out his frustrations on his subordinates. The novice quickly returned to escort Owen to the abbot's study.

'My dear Captain Archer.' The abbot bowed to Owen and motioned him to a comfortable chair by a window opening onto the garden. 'Wine?' Owen's connection to Prince Edward made him a favored visitor.

'I would welcome a cup,' said Owen, taking his seat. 'I

have installed a member of Sir Thomas Percy's household in
your infirmary. A hunting accident.'

'Sir Thomas Percy. Ah.' An obsequious smile.

'It is important that I hear at once of anyone seeking to
speak with him or of any attempt on his part to leave the abbey
grounds.'

'He is not free to move about?'

'A young man with an unfortunate penchant for trouble.
With His Grace the archbishop's enthronement about to
commence, I would have peace in the city.'

'He is not involved in the vicar's death? Or the man fallen
from the chapter-house roof?'

'I cannot say that I am satisfied with his explanations of
where he was that morning, however, as he is Percy's man . . .'

A worried frown, quickly smoothed away. 'I see.'

'Brother Henry has arranged for a lay brother to guard him
until I can send one of the city's men to take his place.'

'Good. Good. I understand the chapter house was graced
by an angelic voice that night.' Unlike his predecessor, William
relished gossip.

'So they say.'

'The singer is not lodging with you?'

'The youth is ill. I cannot attest to an angelic voice,' said
Owen. 'I understand Sir John Neville has asked for a list of
those who will lodge here for his brother's enthronement.'

'You heard?' An indignant shiver. 'The gall. The arrogance.
But I could hardly deny his request.'

'Might you share the list with me? For His Grace the prince?
He will be sending representatives . . .'

'Yes, the pair will lodge here, I am pleased to say, with
their servants.'

'Did you hear whether Dom Antony is in the party? He had
been uncertain . . .'

'He is indeed. I am honored to welcome him back. His
companion is a knight, though the message did not stipulate
which knight.'

Sir Lewis Clifford, Owen prayed, a reasonable man. 'You
will understand, then, that His Grace will want to know who
else will be here.'

'Of course. Several knights in the service of the Percy family, all those not lodging in townhouses outside the minster liberty.' Most of the prominent families of the North owned property in the city, leased to townsfolk or visiting clergy, but with insufficient room for all their attendants and retainers. 'The remaining space here will be filled by clerics displaced by the influx of nobles and their own superiors. We will be quite full. One prays that few linger beyond the festivities.'

Percys at the Abbey was good news. They could take charge of Gabriel once they arrived. 'No Nevilles here?'

'No. They will of course bide in the archbishop's palace here and at Bishopthorpe.'

'Does Brother Henry know the Percys will be here?'

'It is no secret. I have met with all the obedientiaries to discuss how we shall cope with so many guests. It will strain discipline, draw our attention from prayer.'

Owen had learned what he needed. Taking his leave of the abbot, he found Ned awaiting him near the door. He had found Hempe, delivered the messages, and reported that the bailiff was off to speak with Judith, Tucker's wife.

Once Lucie and Alisoun had removed all trace of the injured man from the kitchen, they relieved Bess Merchet of the children.

'Where is Marian? I thought she was to sit with you,' said Alisoun.

'She returned for a while, then retired to her chamber to rest,' said Bess. Tickling Emma, hugging Gwen and Hugh, she bustled out onto the landing. 'And now I must see how the tavern has fared without me.'

Lucie walked her out, apologizing for keeping her so long from her work.

Bess squeezed her shoulder. 'It is good to see the bloom of health on the three of them – even Hugh. I feared for him. He took so long to recover. Forgive me for mentioning it.'

'As if it were far from my mind? Not yet. You love them as if they were yours, I know, Bess.'

'In truth I miss having little ones underfoot. My petty complaints fade away listening to their prattle. You should know that Gwen is much troubled about Marian's presence in the house.'

'Is she?' Lucie had worried. Emma was of course too young to make anything of the addition to the household. But Gwen listened with keen ears to all that was said in the household, and Hugh followed her lead in everything. 'Is Hugh also worried?'

'He seems yet too sleepy to care about aught but snuggling, stories, and comforting food and drink. And your Gwen took care to appear sunny and full of song until her brother began to snore and Marian withdrew. Then she whispered a tale of a boy turned woman appearing in the minster as two men died without, in the snow. Her eyes grew huge in the telling, how Brother Michaelo brought the shape-shifter here and she transformed once more, this time into an angel, and now this morning the Angel Gabriel had come for her, but Alisoun did not understand and shot him so that he could not fly.'

Such an elaborate tale. How had her daughter heard so much? When Rose burst into the street door to warn them of a man standing in the garden, Lucie had drawn her out of the kitchen so that the children would not hear. Had Gwen listened at the door? Crestfallen, Lucie hesitated at the door to the apothecary workroom. 'Should I go back to her?'

'You should, but with this.' Bess bustled past her through the door, then halted, looking around with dismay. 'Where— I set her in here when I heard Alisoun challenging the intruder. Did I shut the door? Dear heaven.' She hurried through the workroom into the shop, where she stopped and sighed, hand to heart. 'There she is.'

'The butcher's daughter?' Lucie asked, confused.

Jasper was crouched down to little Mair, who giggled as a kitten she cradled in her arms twisted her head to see who had entered the room, stretching out a paw to Lucie as if in greeting.

'I turned around and she was in the workroom doorway, batting at the beads,' said Jasper. Instead of a door, the rooms were separated by strings of beads.

'I set her back there and forgot.' Bess bent to scoop her up.

'Tut now, Mair,' she said as the little girl screwed up her face and began to cry. 'She is a gift for the apothecary's children.'

'You brought us a kitten?' Lucie asked. 'Why?' In faith, her heart was already melting at the way the kitten touched Jasper's face and purred. She reminded her of Melisende, the cat who had comforted her during her first husband's long illness. Gray, brown, white, she was a little beauty.

'She rushed into the kitchen this morning when I opened the door and would not be shooed away. I cannot have animals underfoot in our busy kitchen, and certainly not in the bedchambers. Men in their cups are not to be trusted with anything. I thought your little ones would like her. She seems a gentle thing, talkative and silly. She will make Gwen laugh.' Bess searched Lucie's face.

'She will. Bless you, Bess.' Lucie hugged her friend. 'Come with me to present her to the children?'

'I have been out too long as it is.' Bess hugged her back and whispered, 'Find a new situation for Marian, I pray you.'

'We mean to take her to St Clement's. I will explain another time.'

'Good.' Bess hurried out through the workshop.

'You will keep her, Ma?' Jasper asked.

'Do you approve?'

'We've needed a cat ever since Crowder died.' Ambrose and Martin had entrusted the ginger cat to Jasper when they fled York years earlier. Jasper had been devastated to wake one morning to find the cat lifeless beside him, old age having claimed him after a long, pampered life. He stood with shoulders slumped, remembering.

'Shall I see to the shop and you can take her to them?' Lucie asked.

'Could I?'

'Be off with you. Eat something as well. You might ask Alisoun to invite Marian to see the kitten. She has had a difficult day.'

'I heard a ruckus in the garden.'

Telling him briefly what had happened, Lucie smiled to see the admiration in Jasper's eyes. 'There is much more to tell. About Marian. We know her story. She can be trusted.'

'I am glad of that.'

'Now go!' Lucie turned to greet a customer.

Four customers served, and she was helping the last in line, Cass, a young midwife, explaining the differences between two powders for soothing toothaches, when the woman glanced up and said, 'Your apprentice needs to speak with you. See to him. I am in no hurry.' The woman's eyes were on Jasper, not Lucie, as she smiled.

He *was* a handsome young man. 'I will be but a moment,' said Lucie, slipping through the beaded curtain, her amusement turning to alarm as she saw Jasper's distress. 'What is it? One of the children?'

'Marian is gone.'

'What?'

He explained that while he was introducing the children to the kitten, whom Gwen immediately named Ariel, Alisoun had gone to invite Marian, as Lucie had suggested. She was not there. Nor were her cloak and boots.

Lucie closed her eyes, trying to think where to search. Her tale told, why would Marian flee? What did she fear now? 'I must talk to Bess. She might have noticed something.'

'I will see to Mistress Cass.'

'I am sorry you had so little time. Did you eat?'

'Go!'

She found Bess plumping cushions in the single guest room. 'I see to them myself for lodgers with fat purses. Cannot be— What is it? Did the kitten escape?'

'No, our houseguest. Can you recall anything about the moment she chose to leave you alone with the children?'

'She had completed the stitchwork you had given her, and I thought that was why she wished to lie down. I did not think to attend her. And the children . . .'

'You could not know, Bess.'

'What were we about? Ah, it was Hugh. He talked about a drum George Hempe permitted him to beat at his house. How he hoped to go again. Marian asked where the bailiff lived and Hugh was so proud to know. *A few houses afore Christchurch*, he said. Before that, we were speaking of Brother Michaelo. Gwen said that he wrote a most beautiful script, and Marian said that he would have learned that at the abbey. Your daughter informed her that as long as she has been alive he has not lived in an abbey, that he was secretary to archbishops and archdeacons, and that is where he learned to write.'

'Bless you, Bess.' Lucie hugged her friend and hurried off. George Hempe's home seemed most likely. Marian sought to speak with Ambrose. As with her daughter, Lucie needed to be warier about speaking anywhere near Marian. Returning to the house for her cloak, she told Kate where she was headed, in case Owen returned before she did.

On Stonegate she responded to greetings and called out a few of her own so as not to call attention to herself by seeming preoccupied or in a hurry. On Low Petergate she muttered a curse as the ever-ailing pastor of Christchurch approached. If he delayed her with his usual litany of complaints she feared she might snap at him. But he merely bobbed his head with a short greeting and an apology for being in a rush. God be thanked. And there was the door to the Hempe home. Her knock was quickly answered by a flustered Lotta.

'Are you here after that woman? Your guest?'

A moment of relief. 'Yes. Is she here?'

Lotta drew Lucie in, shut the door. 'No. But I believe I know where she has gone, the foolish child. I passed her at the crossing on Stonegate heading toward the minster gate. I thought her a peddler at first, or beggar, with the torn and stained cloak too short to cover her gown. But there was something about her. I watched her pass through the gate and hurried home to ask Ambrose why she might be about.'

Lucie had not noticed Ambrose sitting by the fire. He joined them now, his face folded in concern.

'Perhaps the minster? She might have lost something there?' he said.

'Owen already searched and confronted her with what she had lost there,' said Lucie. Archbishops and archdeacons, Gwen had said. 'I think she might be seeking Dom Jehannes.'

Lotta sighed. 'You should know, Sir John Neville's party has arrived in the city. They will be occupying the palace in the minster yard. It is dangerous for her there.'

'So soon?' Lucie felt her heart racing.

'Let me accompany you,' said Ambrose. Lucie and Lotta both protested the idea, but he argued that he was responsible for bringing Marian to York. 'If she is causing trouble, I want to help.'

'You have no need to make amends,' said Lucie. She told them a little of what they had learned about the evening in the minster, enough to explain why Marian had been there, and that she had betrayed him.

Ambrose shrugged it off. 'I care not whether she betrayed me. You are the ones I want to help. With my hair shorn and colored, who will recognize me?'

'And how would you help?' Lucie asked, though a possibility occurred to her. 'Is Martin Wirthir in the city?'

Ambrose looked pained. 'Well you might wonder. I have as well, ever since safely crossing from Calais. My sudden decision to leave the court and return to the country I had seemingly abandoned . . . Those who had spoken so freely in my presence, would they not be alarmed? I felt almost certain I would be followed, at least for a time. Or worse. That I would not reach Dover. One hears tales. To drown on the crossing is a common way to eliminate the inconvenient.'

'Yet you left,' said Lotta.

'No one deserves to suffer as Prince Edward is suffering. He is at the mercy of treacherous physicians and godless nobles who laugh at his pain, who applaud his humiliation. I want to believe that my empty years in that court will benefit the realm. That God meant me to be there to learn this.' Ambrose seemed alight, as when he performed. This appeared no artifice, but a passion that arose from deep within him.

'I pray Owen may convince the prince's envoys to hear you out and help you carry out your mission,' she said. 'But what of Martin Wirthir?'

'Martin.' A whisper. 'I felt his protection throughout my journey. It gave me the courage to continue. But he has not revealed himself to me.'

'Someone else?'

'It is possible. Denis, a friend from court. A close friend. A man much like Martin, but until now loyal to King Charles. He divined my reason for leaving and encouraged me.'

Ambrose shrugged at Lucie's frown. 'I fail in subtlety, I know. He might have betrayed me. But I think not. And if he is here in the city he might have gathered information for me while I have been off the streets.'

'Do you believe he would help us?' asked Lotta.

'If he sees that I walk freely with Dame Lucie, I believe so.'

'Your hair? Will he know you looking like that?' asked Lucie.

'If he is here, he doubtless followed the captain and your husband from the riverbank yesterday.'

So many ifs. It was a risk, either way. But with the Nevilles so close, Owen would be pressed to resolve the murder quickly to avert the risk that they, or others, would falsely name someone convenient to them, whose death would serve as a warning. An innocent would suffer. And the murderer would still be free.

'No gloves, no singing,' Lucie warned.

Ambrose hurried to fetch his cloak, but Lotta stopped him, offering one of her husband's cloaks. 'You must not walk out in clothes they will know.'

Glancing up from his work, Brother Michaelo discovered goodwife Anna hovering in the doorway of his chamber. He must remember to close the door while he worked. When the archdeacon was out the cook seemed unable to pass an hour without a question for Michaelo.

'A woman to see you,' said Anna. 'I think she is the one you rescued in the minster. Pale hair and eyes, tall, skinny. She calls herself Dame Marian.'

'Alone?'

A nod.

Had she run away? Michaelo took a deep breath.

'May God watch over us,' said Anna. 'The Nevilles are at the palace in the minster yard. All the yard is talking about it. So many servants and armed men. Trouble will come of it.'

Two pieces of unwelcome news. 'I know you are a busy woman, goodwife Anna. But might you ask your husband to watch for Captain Archer, tell him who is here, and what you've told me about the Nevilles?' Her husband was a stone-mason working on the minster.

'Now?'

'I would be most grateful.'

A momentary twinkle in her eye. 'I might take him some of the pork pie, still warm.'

'Bless you.'

'What about the woman?'

'Invite her to sit by the fire. Tell her I will join her there.'

'Wine?'

'Yes.'

With a sniff, the goodwife flounced away. A woman as changeable as a Yorkshire sky, glowering one moment, shining brightly the next. He never understood how he had offended or pleased. At times he felt his mere presence in this house irritated her, though she told him often that he was good for the archdeacon. In what way, he could not imagine. He sanded the letter he had been copying and covered his work against prying eyes. With a prayer for patience, he set off for the hall.

Dame Marian glanced up and then stood, asking Michaelo when Dom Jehannes might return, she had a favor to ask.

'Does Captain Archer know you are here?' Michaelo asked.

'No.'

'Dame Lucie?'

'No.'

He'd thought not. Pray God the captain passed near the stonemasons' lodge, and soon.

Already hatted and cloaked, the goodwife bustled in with a flagon of wine and two cups, set them down with a nod, and hastened out the door.

'Have I offended her?' asked Marian.

'More to the point, I have no doubt you have offended the captain and Dame Lucie, who mean only to protect you.'

'I know how much I owe them,' said Marian. 'My purpose is to protect them. Twice today they suffered intruders because of me. I hope to convince Dom Jehannes to escort me to St Clement's himself, without endangering Dame Lucie.'

'Without her, I am not certain the prioress will take you in. Dame Lucie knows Prioress Isabel, and how to persuade her to take such a risk. But come, have some wine while you tell me about these intruders. Then I must think what to do.'

As she walked with Ambrose, Lucie related what had happened with Gabriel, his tale, and Marian's.

'*Deus juva me*,' Ambrose said, crossing himself. 'I shudder to think how, but for her crying out, I might have abandoned her.'

'But you did not,' said Lucie.

'No. I brought the trouble to your door. I am sorry.'

She paused inside the minster gate, drew him toward a quiet spot where she might watch those passing yet not be overheard. 'Why did you not tell Owen about the prayer book?'

Ambrose looked aggrieved. 'Forgive me. But I felt it was for her to tell you, if she trusted you to know of it.'

Misplaced courtesy. 'Tell me about it.'

'I had noticed a pack that Tucker took with him on occasion, careful to hide it beneath his cloak. For a man whose wife complained of their ability to feed two more mouths I wondered what he shielded with such care. When the prayer book disappeared I feared I had lodged us with a thief. When next he left with the pack I followed him – to Ronan the vicar's lodging. I cannot be certain the bag was empty when he left Ronan's, but I heard rumors about the vicar collecting tribute for the new archbishop that included fines for transgressions that should be the concern of a summoner. And as Tucker went there . . .' He made a face as if uncertain that his reasoning made sense, now that he heard himself speak it aloud. 'I thought it worth asking Ronan. Putting it as a request to advise me who in the Bedern might be receiving such items.'

'That is why you met him in the minster?'

'Yes. I sent word asking him to meet me there. I found him little changed in face – older, but still the long nose, deep-set eyes, yet far less trustful in manner. Tucker had warned me that there had been much gossip about my sudden disappearance years ago. If Ronan knew where I had been, he might also

think me a spy for King Charles. But he heard me out, and
offered to make inquiries. I was to call on him in the morning.
It was he who suggested we exchange cloaks, for I might not
wish to call attention to myself. I sensed it a false charity, that
he recognized its value and intended it as payment. I was not
unaware that he might be mistaken for me, yet I did not warn
him. I am responsible for his death.'

'How can you be certain?' Lucie asked.

'Why else would he have been attacked that night? I know
from George Hempe that he was wearing my cloak and that
my hat was found beside his body. Swathed in my clothes,
with just the snow to illuminate the night, he would have been
mistaken for me. Can you suggest how that would not be so?'

The attacker knew of the exchange? She did not think it
likely.

'I pray you forgive me for not speaking of this earlier,' said
Ambrose.

'You risked your mission, pursuing Ronan,' Lucie said.

'I felt responsible for trusting Tucker.'

She had learned what she needed from him. 'Come. I need
to know if Marian is with Jehannes.'

'Dame Lucie—' Ambrose touched her arm they resumed
walking. 'I believe I just saw Carl, who led the company of
players. You said Marian thought one of them might be in the
minster. Something about how he kept to the shadows close
to the buildings. Why would he behave so?'

'I will tell Owen,' she said. They had reached the archdeacon's house. 'Did you sense your protector?'

'No.'

She touched his shoulder, assuring him she appreciated his
intention.

Brother Michaelo answered the knock. 'Dame Lucie!' She
read his relief in voice and odd smile. 'I can guess what brings
you here.' He eyed her dark-haired companion. 'And this man?'

'He is with me,' said Lucie. 'Might we come in?'

Michaelo stepped back and shut the door as soon as they
both passed through.

With a mixture of relief and anger Lucie watched Marian
rise from a chair by the fire and touch her heart.

As he took Lucie's cloak Michaelo must have noticed the heat in her eyes. 'Before you say anything you might permit her to explain herself. She thought to protect you and your family,' he said quietly.

Marian was staring at the dark-haired newcomer. 'Master Ambrose?'

'Of course,' Michaelo murmured, 'his hands. The musician.' He bowed to Lucie. 'I will bring wine.'

Lucie thanked him and approached Marian. 'I hoped you knew you could trust us.'

'I do. You have been so kind to me I want to protect you,' said Marian. 'The intruders today, the two at the shop, and Gabriel. I hoped to convince Dom Jehannes to take me to St Clement's Priory today. So that I might no longer attract danger to you and the children. I could not bear it if any of you suffered for my transgressions.'

Whether or not she had committed any transgressions seemed beside the point at present. 'With Neville's men searching the city for you and Ambrose how were we to know you had walked out of your own accord?' asked Lucie.

'They would not know me. They thought me a young man.'

'We speak of the Nevilles. Sir John arrived this very day, the one who sent men to silence you and Ambrose, believing the two of you to be spies. His men have been scouring the city for information. By now he will know full well you are not what you seemed. And all who have sheltered you are in danger.'

A flicker of uncertainty in Marian's eyes. Ambrose understood well enough, glancing toward the window with unease.

'Would it not be safer for everyone if I went at once to the priory?' asked Marian.

'My husband advised us to wait until he has a plan in place for your protection. Our protection. It is a long way, and there are strangers abroad in the city. Possibly even the players with whom you traveled. You may indeed have seen Paul in the minster. Ambrose believes he just saw Carl.'

That unsettled her. 'You see? I must leave, I—'

She was interrupted by goodwife Anna flinging open the door and rushing into the hall. 'Oh dear heaven, armed retainers approach, in the company of the archbishop's secretary.'

'Ah, my cousin.' Michaelo gave a mirthless chuckle as he set down the wine. 'His corpulence will slow them.'

Lucie was already in motion. 'Servants. You are servants,' she said as she took Marian by the hand and looked to the goodwife.

'Yes. She can wrap her hair and scrub my table in the kitchen.'

'And Ambrose?' Lucie asked.

'He can take the shovel just outside the kitchen door and work up a sweat. I will fetch my husband's hat and gloves,' said Anna.

Ambrose and Marian hurried away with her.

Lucie was surprised her hand was so steady as she poured herself some wine and turned to Brother Michaelo. 'Now, what is the purpose of my visit?'

THIRTEEN
Two Days

Alfred leaned against the abbey gate as Owen and Ned approached. 'I have news.'

'As do I.' Ned stood watch as Owen took Alfred aside. 'Tell me.'

Alfred reported that Sir John Neville's party had arrived betimes, pausing for the midday meal at Holy Trinity Priory, Micklegate, messengers sent on to the staff preparing the archbishop's palace in the minster yard. God be thanked Owen had taken Gabriel to St Mary's. Owen gave him a brief account of his day's gleanings, including a little of Ned's part.

Alfred laughed. 'Poor sod. We've all been in that painful place.'

'I have a mission for him at present. Then I would have him report to you. Keep him busy. And set a watch on Master Thomas's house. I want to know who visits him, who might be watching him. Ronan called on the chancellor the evening before he was murdered in front of that very house. I do not think his return to that house was accidental. Now that we know how Rupert fell and Gareth drowned, our attention is on finding Ronan's murderer.'

'We have only Pit's idea of how Gareth drowned, Captain.'

'Have you heard anything to contradict it?'

'No.'

'Nor I. Ronan. Just him. I will be at the archbishop's palace. I prefer to deprive Sir John of the pleasure of summoning me when he learns that his man Pit is in the castle. From there I will go to Jehannes while Ned goes to the castle to warn the bailiff on duty to prepare for Sir John sending men to demand Pit's release.'

'I will be at the castle arranging the watches. I could meet him there.'

'Good. He will be tasked to tell you what transpired at the palace. Warn the bailiff on duty to keep a close watch on Pit. Tell him that I've said on no account should he be released to Sir John Neville.'

'It will be done, Captain.'

Memories haunted Owen as he approached the archbishop's palace in the minster yard. In the past he would have been stewing about why Thoresby had summoned him, or ordering his thoughts to report progress. He had resented his obligation to Thoresby, disliked the man's priorities, how he favored the powerful. To Owen's mind Thoresby transgressed his role as a spiritual shepherd guiding souls to God, though he had come to see that the late archbishop struggled with his conflicting responsibilities as a servant of God, of the pope, and of the king, especially the latter. For many years Thoresby had served as King Edward's lord chancellor and close advisor, and the king had expected him to continue giving more weight to his interests than he did to either the pope or his spiritual duties. When that conflict had grown too much for Thoresby's conscience, he had given up the lord chancellor's chain. In retrospect, Owen admired him. And missed him.

He was startled out of his thoughts as the guards on the steps to the great hall ordered him to halt and state his name, status, and mission. Proof that the Neville principals had arrived. Owen wondered whether Alexander would retain such a martial presence when it was only him in residence. A sure way to antagonize the citizens of York, and the minster chapter. When the guards stepped aside to let him pass, Owen told Ned to follow him. Not to speak.

Beyond the heavy oak doors, the great hall was in chaos. Servants rushed about as Neville retainers shouted conflicting orders. A far cry from the serene elegance of Thoresby's household under the direction of Brother Michaelo. Owen searched the hall for an oasis of calm and found it surrounding a man of imposing stature standing beneath one of the opened casements, his back to the noise. Owen made his way toward him. When he was within hailing distance, his way was blocked by an armed retainer bristling with self-importance.

'Who are you? What is your business here?'

'Owen Archer, captain of the city, here to see Sir John Neville.'

'Wait there.' Rudely pushing aside a servant as he turned, the man headed straight for the figure at the window.

Neville continued to face out as the man delivered his message. Only when the man had backed away did Neville turn slightly and gesture for Owen to be brought to him.

Without waiting, Owen joined him at the window, standing facing the same direction. Ned followed at a slight distance.

'My lord Neville,' said Owen.

'Captain Archer. You hold two of my men at York Castle. On what charges?' A low, resonant voice that required no volume to be heard despite the noise in the hall.

'One is dead, drowned, ready to be claimed. That would be Gareth. Pit is held until his name is cleared of murder.'

'Whose murder?'

'That of Ronan, former vicar to His Grace the archbishop.'

Now Sir John turned to study Owen. 'A Neville retainer murdering a Neville servant?'

'A vicar of York Minster, not a Neville servant, once answering to your brother, but no longer. There might be reasons to find him an embarrassment to your family.'

'I am intrigued, Captain.' Cool grey eyes studied Owen for a moment. 'Have you proof of Pit's guilt?'

'Not yet.'

'Then I question your right to imprison him.'

'I understand. But as the city fills with the worthies attending your brother's enthronement you can appreciate that we are taking precautions against violence. Your safety and that of His Grace the archbishop are our first concern.'

'You claim to protect me from my own man? Amusing.'

Owen did not flinch at the threatening grin. Though he knew his argument sounded weak, better that than admit that he expected Alexander Neville to draw many enemies down on the city.

'I know you are Prince Edward's man, Archer.' Neville slowly shook his head. 'I wonder that he can stomach you. He cannot have missed what his fair wife sees when she looks at you – her beloved Holland resurrected.' Princess Joan's late husband. 'She forsook her rightful first husband the Duke of Salisbury for one-eyed Holland, and now . . . *I* would wonder. You must be good indeed for the prince to overlook the resemblance.'

'Many lose eyes in battle.'

'Of course. I give you two days to solve your puzzle, and then you will hand over my man, the French spy, and the young woman disguised as a lad, or I will drag you out of Micklegate Bar and all the way to Windsor to deliver what's left of you to the Christmas court.'

Owen had known Sir John would be a challenging adversary. There was nothing for the arrogance of the man but to nod and wish him good day, measuring his steps with care so that he did not falter, not for a breath, as he strode out through the chaotic hall, Ned scuttling to keep up. Out in the minster yard Owen continued for a while, letting the rising wind cool him.

'Will he do that?' Ned asked, breathing hard as he kept up with Owen.

'No doubt it would give him pleasure, but no, he would not dare cross the prince. He might be arrogant, but he did not rise to such a height at court by reckless acts. I stood up to him with a reasonable argument. He saw need to strut boldly before his men, making threats dripping with blood-lust, the howl of a savage beast. They will drink to him tonight, and brag of him in the taverns.' Meanwhile, Owen had two days before the man did all he could to distract him from his work.

And was there something in the way he described Marian suggesting he knew who she was? Lucie had reminded him as he went out the door that Sir John Neville's wife, Maud Percy, was sister to Sir Thomas and Lady Edwina, the aunt who had commissioned the lost prayer book. If Neville's men had found that book Sir John would be all the more keen to reclaim his wife's kinswoman.

Ned pulled him from his thoughts. 'Where now, Captain?'

'Alfred awaits you at the castle. Tell him all that you heard, then follow his orders. You will be working under him. No punishment. I need you.'

Ned searched Owen's face, nodded. 'Thank you, Captain. I will not disappoint you again.'

'I count on that.'

They parted ways, Owen heading for the archdeacon's.

As he passed the west entrance to the minster Owen heard someone calling him, but so softly he had almost missed it. Glancing round, he saw the lad with whom he had talked the previous day standing in the corner where the south transept jutted out from the nave. The lad removed his dusty hat and looked round, as if checking that they were not observed.

'You are worried about talking to me?'

'There are eyes.'

'From the roof?'

'No. The stone workers. They've warned me to stay out of the troubles in the chapter and liberty.'

'But—?'

'I thought you might like to know that Sir John Neville's men followed Dom Jehannes's cook back to the archdeacon's house. The fat secretary walks slowly, but they might be there by now.'

'Do you have reason to think they mean trouble?'

'Dame Lucie is there. And I think the minstrel's lad, dressed as a lass.'

God help them. 'Bless you, lad.'

'Simon.'

Owen nodded. 'Simon, beware of His Grace the archbishop, and his kin. This is a dangerous time, as nobles and others seek advancement with a new regime. Do you understand?'

'I do, Captain.'

'Do you know where I live?' When the lad nodded, Owen suggested he come to his home next time he had a report. His fellows would be less likely to notice. 'Come through the garden gate, knock at the kitchen door. If I'm not there, Kate will be sure to feed you while you wait.'

With a grave, 'Yes, Captain,' the lad picked up the handle of a sled and trundled off toward the lady chapel.

Owen hastened toward Jehannes's house.

* * *

A discreet knock. Brother Michaelo rose, assuring Lucie that he was the appropriate one to welcome his cousin. She settled back, sipping the wine, willing herself to calm. They had chosen the purpose of her visit as her concern for the clerk Beck, still recovering in the kitchen from his beating. At present he was asleep, and Marian, her hair wrapped in a clean white cloth, her sleeves protected by white cuffs, was scrubbing the table on which goodwife Anna would be kneading the dough rising on a counter by the garden window. Outside, Ambrose, wearing work gloves and a hat encrusted with stone dust, shoveled and tidied the path through the melting snow to the movable hut over the household midden.

'Cousin. Are you come to invite me to dine at the archbishop's palace?'

'No, cousin.' Dom Leufrid's voice was hoarse, as if he were short of breath. 'I would speak with Dom Jehannes, the archdeacon.'

Still standing in the doorway, Michaelo explained that Jehannes was at the deanery. 'I will tell him you called.'

Too curious to sit back, Lucie rose. Dom Leufrid's wide body almost filled the doorway. Over his shoulders she could just make out two men with grim countenances. One of them appeared to nudge the cleric, who jerked, then chided Michaelo for his discourtesy.

'I propose to sit by the fire and await his return,' Leufrid wheezed.

Congested lungs, weak heart, Lucie thought as Michaelo stepped aside to let Leufrid pass. A limp added gout to her list of his ailments.

Three armed men followed, taking a stance just inside the door, as if guarding the inhabitants from departing. She recognized the one who had nudged Leufrid forward as one of the men Crispin Poole had brought with him when he'd arrived in York in summer. She knew him by a scar that twisted his mouth to one side. Had he been Neville's man all the time? Curious. The archbishop's household was doing little to earn him a welcome in York.

Leufrid looked inquiringly at Lucie.

'Dame Lucie, this is my cousin Dom Leufrid, personal

secretary to His Grace, Archbishop Neville.' Michaelo's blank face gave no hint of his clear insult, giving her the higher rank in the order of introduction.

Leufrid sniffed and raised a thin brow in response to his cousin, turning to Lucie with a chilly smile. 'Should I know your name, Dame Lucie?'

Before Lucie could answer, Michaelo said, 'If you have need of an apothecary while in York, I would advise remembering the name of Dame Lucie Wilton.'

'I enjoy good health,' said Leufrid, glaring at his cousin as if to challenge his thinking otherwise. 'Is there illness in this household?'

'An injured clerk,' said Lucie. 'I came to consult with Brother Michaelo on his care.' As she spoke, a voice wafted out from the kitchen, a woman singing a few lines of a rhythmic song. *Listen, lordings, what I shall say / A great marvel tell I may* . . . Quickly hushed.

Both thin brows raised. 'A beautiful voice.' Dom Leufrid's three chins jiggled as he spoke, a comic accent on a tense moment.

'A gift to one in pain,' said Michaelo.

'You are fortunate in your servants.'

'Dom Jehannes inspires harmony in his household.'

'I shall say a prayer over the injured clerk.' Leufrid moved toward the kitchen, accompanied by twisted mouth.

'We pray with him throughout the day, cousin,' said Michaelo, following close behind.

As they reached the kitchen doorway, Owen stepped through. 'Ah, Brother Michaelo, forgive me. I did not see that you had company.' He glanced from Leufrid to the retainers and rested a hand on his dagger. 'What is the trouble, Dom Leufrid?'

'Of course, you have met.' Michaelo's voice was tight.

Lucie watched with interest as Owen waited for the cleric to explain.

'Hearing that two men have been murdered in the minster yard, His Grace thought it best we move about with protection at all times.'

'I see.' Owen stepped forward, forcing Dom Leufrid to either step aside or retreat.

The secretary chose the latter, backing toward Lucie, lowering himself down with effort into the chair farthest from her.

Owen came to stand by Lucie, a hand on her shoulder. 'I see my wife has already met you. Seeing to Beck?' he asked her.

'Judging whether it is time for a milder plaster for his head.'

'I noticed as I came through the kitchen that he improves.'

'We were interrupted before I could examine Beck,' said Lucie. 'Brother Michaelo tells me he has not yet regained his sight.'

'The clerk was blinded?' asked Leufrid. 'Both eyes?'

'Yes,' said Owen. 'Not a direct wounding, like mine, but caused by a hard blow to the head. He surprised someone ransacking the chamber of the murdered vicar.'

'I pray you caught them,' said Leufrid.

'Not yet,' said Owen. Lucie noticed him watching the one with the twisted mouth, who averted his eyes.

'A pity, the one witness blinded,' said Leufrid.

'Would you care for some wine?' Michaelo was rising to play host when Jehannes opened the door, starting at the sight of the armed guards in his hall.

'Am I to be arrested?'

Dom Leufrid rose, with some difficulty. 'Dom Jehannes, I am Dom Leufrid, personal secretary to His Grace, Archbishop Neville.'

'Do you always move about with armed companions?' asked Jehannes. 'Is that what we should come to expect from the archbishop's household?'

Leufrid opened his mouth to respond.

Owen preempted him. 'Might I remind you, Dom Leufrid, that Prince Edward is keen to hear how the Nevilles treat the city. Hostile behavior toward members of the clergy will concern him. Nor will such tactics win His Grace support here.'

'Indeed,' said Jehannes, settling beside Lucie.

Leufrid repeated his explanation about the recent murders, his voice querulous.

During the ensuing discussion Lucie slipped away to the kitchen to silence Marian before another outburst of song.

Goodwife Anna now stood at the table Marian had been washing, kneading dough and shaking her head at the young woman now sitting beside Beck and holding his hand as she softly sang a hymn to the Virgin Mary.

'You would be wise to remember not to sing when in disguise,' Lucie said. 'And that you are a kitchen maid, not a healer.'

'He was moaning,' said Marian. 'What would you have me do?'

'Send goodwife Anna out to fetch me.'

Marian rose. Picking up the pail and rag she had been using she turned toward the table.

Anna shooed her off. 'I am using it now. You are welcome to scrub the floor.'

'Will they soon be gone?' Marian asked.

'I cannot tell,' said Lucie. 'My husband prevented the archbishop's secretary from coming into the kitchen, but if he insists we dare not refuse him. It would only convince him we have something to hide. Where is the one who arrived with me?' She preferred not to speak Ambrose's name aloud.

'Still without, knocking snow off the bushes and the roof over the midden,' said the cook. 'He is a hard worker. As is this young woman.'

With a glum sigh, Marian moved to the far corner of the room and dropped to her knees.

She had just begun to scrub when the kitchen door opened, and Jehannes led Leufrid and the guard with twisted mouth to Beck's bedside. Lucie wondered whether the large cleric would attempt to kneel beside the pallet, which sat on the stone floor. Even the stool was low and possibly too fragile to hold his weight. Goodwife Anna rushed to fetch a sturdy bench by the door. But Leufrid ignored her, choosing merely to stand over the injured man.

Beck turned his head toward him and reached out a hand. 'I cannot see. Who are you?'

'Best not touch him, Dom Leufrid,' said the guard.

Lucie noted how Beck drew into himself at the sound of the man's odd speech.

It was Jehannes who perched on the bench and took Beck's hand. 'This is Dom Leufrid, the archbishop's secretary,' he said in his most soothing voice. 'He wishes to say a prayer over you.'

'I pray that my sight might be restored,' Beck whimpered. 'Even a warm kitchen is a fearful place in this darkness.'

Making the sign of the cross over Beck, Leufrid whispered a prayer of no particular pertinence, then stepped away, gazing for a moment at Marian, who dutifully scrubbed the flagstones.

'So many servants,' he said, shaking his head as he turned and made his way in a slow shuffle back out to the hall, the guard following.

Jehannes nodded to Lucie as he followed, gesturing that he would see the intruders out.

Taking Jehannes's place on the bench, Lucie identified herself to Beck and assured him that the secretary and his armed escort were back in the hall where they could not hear. 'Did you recognize the voice of the guard?'

'It was him and another I came upon in Master Ronan's lodging. The ones who blinded me.'

'I will tell my husband. He will know what to do.'

'You will not send me away?'

Lucie squeezed his hand and assured him that he would be cared for.

Moments after Leufrid and his guards departed, Hempe arrived, curious about armed guards escorting the archbishop's secretary from Jehannes's home. He laughed when he realized his mistake, a brief moment of jollity dampened by Owen's account of his meeting with Sir John Neville.

'Two days,' Hempe growled. 'Who does he think he is, arriving in the city and ordering us about?' He slumped down in a chair, joining Jehannes, Owen, Lucie, Michaelo, and Ambrose, a dour group.

'We've no time to waste on complaints.' Owen removed his hat and raked a hand through his hair. 'We can only hope that they believed Ambrose and Marian to be household servants, but we cannot depend on that. Leufrid and the guards may have decided to withdraw and consider how to proceed. We need to move her to St Clement's tonight.'

'What of Ambrose?' asked Jehannes.

'They may not have seen him,' said Owen. 'Were you able to speak with Tucker's wife?'

'I was. Dame Judith says Percy's men did pay her to care for the young woman. She seemed not as worried about Tucker as she was about losing the money. I permitted her to keep it, as Tucker will be bringing nothing home for a while. The fiddler complained loudly all the way to the castle, but being closed in a damp room silenced him. After a night in there I believe he will talk.'

'Pray God he does,' said Owen. 'And that he knows something of use. We have another concern.' He told them how Carl, the leader of the company with whom Marian had traveled, had been watching Ambrose out near the midden, but ran off when he noticed Owen observing him with interest. Hempe would tell his men to watch out for Carl, follow him, find out whether the company was in the city to perform, or the man had followed alone. And then they fell to planning how they would escort Marian to the priory outside the city walls.

A knock on the door interrupted their tense debate.

Lucie touched Owen arm as he rose to answer, his hand on the dagger beneath his jacket. 'Should I withdraw to Jehannes's parlor with Ambrose and Marian?'

Jehannes rose to help but Owen motioned him down. 'Only Ambrose and Marian in the parlor. Then return to us.'

With a nod, Lucie went to fetch them.

Owen crossed to the door. A lad bowed to him, the movement releasing a puff of sparkling powder. Dust from a goldsmith's workshop.

'You've been sent by Robert Dale?' Owen guessed.

Startled, the lad stuttered, 'Y-yes, Captain. I am glad to find you here. My master begs to speak with you. At his shop, sir. As soon as you might, sir.'

'Is he in danger?'

'I am to say no more, but to implore you to come quickly.'

'I will come.'

Closing the door Owen was barraged with questions he could not answer.

'Robert Dale is not one to waste my time. I will return as soon as I may. Ambrose will accompany me. If there are other members of Carl's company about, he can point them out.'

Lucie rose to follow him to the parlor, asking why the musicians were important to him.

'I am not sure. Marian thought she saw the drummer Paul in the minster that night. Carl is watching Ambrose. I want to know why.'

'Your eye warns you of them?'

She knew him well. 'It does.'

'Will we take her to St Clement's tonight?' she asked.

'I think it best. I hope you need not come.' He kissed her and called to Ambrose.

Outside, the shadows were already lengthening, a chill dampness rising. They must hurry.

FOURTEEN

An Unlikely Ally

R obert Dale led Owen and Ambrose to his office behind
the bustling shop. Even here, Owen felt the heat from
the fire over which the gold was softened.

Crispin Poole rose from a seat, leaning heavily on his cane
as he greeted Owen and glanced with interest at Ambrose.

'What is this?' said Owen, looking to Robert.

'You have Poole to thank for this meeting,' said Robert.
'Hear him out. He has convinced me that I have information
you need. As does he.'

A lad brought in a flagon of wine and three cups, then
apologized, noticing there were four to serve. After he delivered
a fourth, Robert told him to close the door as he left.

'We can speak freely?' asked Crispin indicating Ambrose.

'That depends,' said Owen. 'Are you here as Neville's man?'

'No. As your friend, and a concerned citizen.'

'I just encountered one of your men escorting Dom Leufrid.
The one with the scarred cheek.'

'Diggs. You met him at the archdeacon's house?'

'You knew of the visit?'

'Diggs says the woman who fled Cawood with the French
spy is there. They planned to search the house.'

It was as Owen had feared.

'The Nevilles want her,' said Crispin. 'They believe her to
be someone of value to them. Their interest should concern
you.'

'It does.'

'Good. We have little time. It might help me to know who
she is.'

'We? How do I know your men—'

'I have told you, they are not my men. Never were. For a
while I thought they might be useful, but they have

become my bane, my curse. I sent them off to lodge with their fellows, my excuse my mother's failing health.'

'You serve Archbishop Neville.'

'No longer, though he does not yet know. I thought it best to do what I could for you before speaking with him. So that I might still receive reports. I know Sir John has given you two days to find Ronan's murderer. He's keen to put the blame on the French spy.'

'French spy?'

'You know of whom I speak. The musician Ambrose Coates.'

'He is no spy for the French,' said Owen. 'But you are right about Sir John's threat.'

'Who is she?'

Owen glanced at Robert. 'What was it you wished to tell me?'

Fine, close work had ruined Robert's eyesight, his habitual squint giving him the air of a man whose worries weighed him down. Yet Owen knew him to be blessed with a successful business and a happy family life. He peered at Owen, then Crispin, who, with a sigh of frustration, resumed his seat, plucking a cloth from his sleeve and wiping his brow.

'It is about Ronan's book,' said Robert, 'what he called his psalter.'

'A prayer book?'

'No. His distasteful humor.'

Owen sat down as well and poured himself some wine. 'Go on.'

'A few days before his death Ronan swooped into my shop with a nasty glint in his eyes, trailed by that clerk of his, Beck. He dared accuse me of being late to deliver a gold cross the new archbishop had ordered from me. I questioned his authority to represent His Grace, for he had taken no part in the original transaction, it was all done by messenger through His Grace's secretary Leufrid, the usual empty flattery, currying favor with local merchants. Months ago Leufrid had sent a message, all apologies, His Grace had changed his mind and was cancelling the order. I do not like to speak ill of the dead, but my questioning Ronan's authority set him to spewing vile things. Vile.

He accused my beloved wife Julia—' Robert paused a moment to breathe and calm himself. 'I left the room to fetch the message and the two halves of the tally from the desk of one of my clerks who was working with the accounts in the shop. When I returned Ronan did not at first notice me. He had brought out the little book in which he jotted down items – parchment sewn together with a leather cover, costly for keeping accounts, but that was the man, vainglorious, delighting in show. He called it his psalter, and indeed the outward appearance would fool one.'

'So you had seen it before,' said Owen.

'Oh yes, as have my fellow goldsmiths and many other merchants. Since his death I have prayed that Ronan had not pushed one of my friends to his limit, fearing his ruin. He was devious, greedy, cruel, lacking all compassion. The sort of churchman that causes a crisis of faith in the most pious of worshippers.'

Owen looked to Crispin. 'Did Ronan still represent Neville in such transactions?'

'Ronan certainly believed so, though Leufrid disagrees. In truth, he said that the archbishop had never considered Ronan to be in his service.'

'I was told that he recommended Ronan as a vicar for the chapter.'

'I did not know that,' Crispin admitted.

'When I asked you about his hoard the other day you mentioned nothing of this.'

'That was before my conversation with the secretary.'

Robert looked from one to the other. 'But Ronan has plagued me and my fellow merchants in the city and collected fees, valuable items . . . You say he was not authorized? Have we been robbed?' He hissed a curse.

Crispin rubbed what was left of his right arm. 'I have no proof, but considering Neville's behavior before becoming archbishop I would guess Ronan *had* been engaged by him, but that now, under the watchful eyes of his powerful brother, he has abandoned his partners in crime.'

'I smell a cunning squirrel hiding away a winter's worth of feasts before the first snow,' Robert growled.

Owen had ample evidence of that in the cache he'd hidden at Jehannes's home. 'How did he behave when shown proof the order was cancelled?'

'He seemed confused, but tried to hide it with fresh accusations. I ordered him out and warned him not to return or I would have a word with Master Adam, his precentor. He warned me that a goldsmith depended on a good reputation and he could ruin me. But I waved the proof before him and opened the shop door, loudly ordering him out. When he insulted my wife, he went too far.' Clenched fists, a red face, the man's passion was clear. Yet not for a moment did Owen consider Robert as Ronan's murderer. He had known him too long,

'Did you know of this psalter?' Owen asked Crispin.

'I guessed he kept some record of the accounts he claimed to be monitoring, but no, I'd never heard of the book.'

'I believe it is what your men were after when Beck surprised them at Ronan's lodging.'

'Porter and Diggs? You are certain it was them?' Poole's tone held no surprise.

'As of this afternoon, yes. Beck recognized Diggs's voice when he escorted Leufrid into Jehannes's kitchen to pray over the injured man. The way his twisted mouth shapes his words. Diggs had no cause to speak. He meant to frighten Beck, but his arrogance betrayed him.'

Crispin merely nodded. 'I have no trouble believing it, and the account book would be something Neville would wish to retrieve. But it is not the only book they want. They believe Ronan had in his possession something belonging to the woman you have sheltered. A prayer book illustrated with crows. Sir John's wife, Lady Maud, a Percy by birth, says her sister gave it to her ward, Marian Percy, when she took vows at Wherwell Abbey. They want the book, and they want the nun, who has been missing since Pentecost. Your fair singer, if I am not mistaken, now hiding in the archdeacon's house. Hence their interest.'

So they had recognized her. Owen cursed under his breath. They knew. And Crispin had already heard.

'They believe Ambrose Coates means to use her to bargain

with Sir Thomas Percy, her guardian, Lady Maud's brother. I want to help.'

'Help?' Owen asked.

'I understand your wariness. But I am sincere. Call it atonement for my past sins, proof to the citizens of York that I am a man they can trust, a man worthy of Muriel Swann and the child she carries.'

'The Nevilles are the new power in the city,' said Owen. 'Why would you cross them?'

'They have yet to earn the trust of the citizens,' said Robert. 'My tale should make that clear.'

This would be the time for the shower of needle pricks to warn him away, but Owen felt nothing, nothing but the importance of moving fast. He regarded Crispin, noticed how much more at ease he seemed than the last few times they met. A man at peace with himself. 'I intend to move Dame Marian to St Clement's Priory tonight.'

'I had much the same idea, except that I think tonight might be too late,' said Crispin. 'I intended to escort my mother there in a few days. I propose that I escort her there as soon as possible, with the Percy woman attending her.'

'It might work,' said Owen. 'No one would expect the woman to be entrusted to you. Might I suggest the addition of Alisoun Ffulford? Your mother trusts her as a healer, and knows she is an excellent, fearless shot. In the event you are set upon.'

'The young woman who saved my mother's life? I welcome her,' said Crispin.

'How will you move the young woman from the archdeacon's?' asked Robert.

'In the guise of a man,' said Ambrose, the first words he had spoken since arriving. 'She is accustomed to playing the part. Once she reaches your home, she transforms into a serving maid.'

'Are you—' Crispin leaned over to Ambrose, touched his temple, held up his fingers to show a dark smudge. The heat in the room had caused the dye to bleed. 'You are the white-haired musician, Ambrose Coates.'

'And if I am?'

'The captain says you are not spying for the French. What, then, did you want with the Nevilles at Cawood?'

'I learned of the captain's new connection to Prince Edward, so I headed north. Hearing of a gathering of Nevilles at Cawood, I thought I might glean something of use to the captain to offer in exchange for an introduction to the prince.'

'York seems an odd destination for a mission to Prince Edward,' said Crispin. 'You wish an introduction to him? Why? I should think he has his choice of musicians. Why not stay at the French court?'

'A tale for another time,' said Owen as he rose. 'Your offer is generous, Crispin.'

'I would rather not include Ambrose in the scheme.'

'I have no intention of further endangering Dame Marian,' said Ambrose.

'Then why are you here?'

'It seems the company of musicians and players with whom Dame Marian traveled is in the city,' said Owen. 'Ambrose knows them well enough to help me track them to their lodgings.'

'You think they mean trouble?' Crispin asked. 'Why?'

'Too curious about Marian and Ambrose. I want to know why,' said Owen. 'Do you have any more to share, Robert? Have you any sense of who Ronan might have pushed to the point of desperation? A man fearing the loss of all he has worked for, whose family is in danger of destitution? The most pious man might break beneath such a fear.'

'Any number of us, to be honest, and yet I have sensed nothing among those with whom I have spoken. Beecham detested the man, but he has just returned from London. The snow had trapped him south of York.'

'What of Will Farfield?' The silversmith whose apprentices had seemed frightened when Owen had called, saying their master was ill. Yet Lucie and Jasper had seen no one from his household in the shop despite the Farfields being regular customers. And there was something— 'Did he not lose his wife or one of his daughters to pestilence?' Owen asked.

Robert flinched.

'I am a fair man, Robert, you know that.'

'I do, Owen, I do.' He pressed the bridge of his nose, nodded to himself. 'Will sent his wife and children off to her parents in Shelby this past summer.'

'Why?'

'He claimed for fear of the pestilence. And then . . . When my wife called to see whether there was anything she might do she was sent away with such dispatch she worried about the welfare of his apprentices. I dislike accusing a fellow merchant . . .'

'Is his business prospering?'

'He has always struggled. A surly man at the best of times. Lacks his father's eye for quality, has no patience with apprentices. No, his business is not prospering.'

Owen thanked him. 'If you think of anyone else, encounter anyone . . .'

'I will come to you,' said Robert. 'I swear.'

One of the apprentices knocked, and as Robert consulted with him regarding an order, Owen rose, nodded his thanks, and withdrew with Ambrose.

Crispin followed. Outside, they agreed on a plan.

'I thank you for this,' Owen said as they were parting.

'You have my betrothed to thank for the idea. Muriel is my conscience, my guide. I seek her advice in everything. She encouraged me to distance myself from the archbishop, a connection that she believes will make it difficult for me among my fellow merchants.'

Owen had not guessed Muriel Swann to be someone so attuned to the temper of her late husband's colleagues. 'May God watch over her and the child in her womb,' he said.

Returning to Jehannes's house Owen explained Crispin's plan. After some initial hesitation, Hempe, Jehannes, Michaelo, Lucie, and Marian admitted they could think of no timely alternative.

Michaelo offered to accompany the party, lending Marian the robe of a Benedictine monk for the walk to Crispin's home.

'A monk would not serve as an attendant for a widow,' said Marian.

'Carry your clothes with you,' said Lucie. 'Once you reach

Crispin's home you will shed the disguise. I will help you
dress before I leave. You must look believable as a monk. We
must hasten, for I must also prepare Alisoun and send her on
her way.'

Michaelo went to fetch one of his habits and a hooded cape.
Lucie asked Anna the cook for a comb and something to tie
back Marian's hair. When all was assembled, including a plain
cloth sack for the change of clothing, Lucie led Marian into
Jehannes's parlor.

'I cannot believe I will be back among sisters of my order
so soon,' Marian said, her eyes alight. She burst into the
Benedicamus Domino she had sung earlier, lowered her
voice and sang more, cutting herself off with laughter. In that
same low voice she asked, 'Will I do as a monk?'

Lucie smiled to see her come alive. 'You will.' But as she
lifted Marian's gown over her head, she groaned. 'Your shift.
You are bleeding.'

'My courses?'

'I believe so.'

Marian spun round and caught Lucie up in a hug. 'That is
good! Bless Dame Magda.' She released Lucie and twisted
the shift round to see. 'But we have no time to wash out my
shift.'

Lucie began to undress.

'What are you doing?'

'You will wear my shift beneath the monk's robes.' Lucie
held it up for Marian. 'Too short, but it matters not. Dame
Euphemia's maidservant is tall and slender. Borrow something
from her. I will be back with cloths. You must inform the
sisters of your needs tonight.'

'Yes!'

Lucie silently echoed Marian, *Bless Dame Magda.*

When at last Marian stepped into the hall in Michaelo's
robes her stride was longer, her expression pinched, her voice,
when she spoke, huskier than her normal tone but not as
exaggerated as the voice that had set her laughing. A hood
covered her hair.

'You are transformed,' said Michaelo, his smile expressing
approval. 'Shall we depart?'

Owen took Lucie aside. 'How is she?'

'Excited. Happy. I pray this works.'

A curt nod, signaling his concern. 'I have checked round the house. It looks safe for them to depart. We have done all we can.'

'I need to prepare Alisoun. *Then* we will have done all we can.'

Once the monks and Lucie had taken their leave, Owen turned his attention to Beck. Clearly the man knew far more than he had admitted.

Jehannes suggested the blinded man be questioned in his parlor, and that he attend. 'I would know what I am sheltering in my home.'

Owen could hardly object, and Beck was sufficiently improved that he could walk with support. As Jehannes guided Beck into the parlor, describing where he was, adding cushions to the chair in which he was seated, asking whether he might need a lap rug, Anna followed with a bowl of ale to calm him, for the man behaved as if he were being summoned to his execution despite Owen's assurance that he had nothing to fear as long as he told the truth. When Jehannes withdrew to his seat, and Beck appeared able to reach for the bowl beside him, Owen settled across from him, reaching out to touch his hand, let him know where he was.

He began by talking a little of his own experience in losing sight, some of the things he had found helpful, such as all that they had been doing to make him comfortable. With a shaky voice, Beck thanked him and the archdeacon.

'But why am I here?' he asked.

'You have not told us all you know,' said Owen. 'So we are giving you the opportunity to do so.'

'You call me a liar?'

'I have learned from a trusted and well-respected citizen of York that you accompanied the vicar Ronan on his visits to merchants, that you witnessed him consulting his account book, which he called his psalter, and know much about his threats to merchants and how often they rebuked him for exaggerating and making false claims. Tell me about this account book of his. Where did he keep it? Where else did he hide the items and money he collected, besides what you say was stolen from the chest? He was a careful man, Beck, he would not have hidden everything in plain sight.'

The man was sweating as he shakily reached for the bowl of ale. Owen leaned forward and assisted him.

'I do not know his hiding places. He trusted no one with that, I think.'

'And the account book, his so-called psalter. Why did you pretend you did not know what the men were searching for in his lodgings?'

'He made me swear I would never speak of it. Never. He said he would curse me.'

'And you believe he is capable of that?'

'He is not yet buried, is he?'

That made a difference? Owen glanced up at Jehannes.

'It is not uncommon to fear that a soul does not rest until the body be buried in blessed ground,' said Jehannes. 'But the vicar has been placed in a temporary sarcophagus in the Bedern chapel, Beck. A sacred space equal to burial in blessed ground. He can no longer carry out such a threat, if he ever could. Churchmen are not trained to curse their fellow man.'

Beck frowned, as if taking this in.

'If you refuse to speak truth to Captain Archer, you must leave my house,' said Jehannes.

'You would throw me out?'

'I would hand you over to Master Adam, the precentor.'

'Does Diggs frighten you?' asked Owen. 'Crispin Poole's man?'

Beck squirmed in his chair.

'If you tell me the tale, from the beginning, I will protect you from him,' said Owen.

'You can do that?'

'He can,' said Jehannes. 'Tell him what he needs to know.'

'Were you with Ronan when he left for the minster that evening?' Owen asked.

Once again, Beck reached for the ale and Owen assisted him, giving him a moment, then took possession of the now empty bowl.

'I grow impatient,' said Jehannes.

Beck nodded as best he could. 'I was there. I came after my pay. He had not paid me for a long while. He said he must meet someone, must not keep them waiting. I said but my pay and he said he would pay me the next day, ordered me to lock the door when I left, and hurried out. He knew I knew of the box of coins and jewels in the chest. Why would he trust me—?' He bowed his head.

'You stole it,' said Owen.

'God forgive me, I did,' Beck said.

'Did you return to his lodging that night?'

'Passed it. Much later. Saw a light in his window and him watching the street. I thought he watched for me.'

'Was anyone else on the street?'

'One man. He stood beneath the eaves of the house across the way and growled at me when I passed, like an animal.'

'Did you stay?' asked Owen.

'Would you? I went home and all night I feared every noise. When I heard of the vicar's murder— Someone had been after his treasure, I guessed, and now I had it. Would they come for me? I could not rest until I put it back. I went to check if his door was locked or guarded. But you came, with the monk.'

'Were you putting it back when Porter and Diggs found you?'

'I was. I told them they could have it. But they beat me anyway. They wanted the account book. I did not know where it was.'

Is that what they later took from the chancellor's hall? Or was it Marian's prayer book? Or neither?

'Did the vicar take anything with him when he left for the minster that afternoon? His account book?'

'Don't know.'

'Did he say who he was meeting?'

'No.'

A knock on the door. 'Yes, Anna, come in,' said Jehannes.

'The chancellor is here to speak with you and Captain Archer,' the cook announced. 'Shall I show him in?'

Owen rose. 'No, Anna. We will speak with him out in the hall after we help Beck back to his bed in the kitchen.'

Jehannes signaled his agreement. 'More ale for the fellow, Anna.'

'May I stay in your home?' Beck asked.

'For now,' said Jehannes, as he and Owen led the man by the arm.

'Bless you, Father.'

Meaning to ask Ambrose if he had noticed whether Ronan had worn a scrip beneath his cloak, Owen looked for him in the kitchen. 'Where is he, Anna?'

'He stood in the doorway a long while, watching evening fall, and then he was gone.'

Damn the man. Bloody fool. 'Did you see anyone else with him? Was he following someone?'

'I did not know to look,' she said with a sniff.

Inspired by Owen's concern for his serving man, how he had tended to his shoulder after the burglars injured him, the chancellor wished at last to speak of his conversation with Ronan in the early evening before the vicar's murder. Master Thomas had summoned Ronan to learn more of Sir John Neville's tastes, what he might enjoy when he came to dine.

'He had boasted of his connection to the family, so you can imagine my surprise – indeed my disappointment – when he confessed he had never met either Sir John or his wife. His only advice was that as Lady Maud was a Percy she might appreciate some of her kinsmen being included in a dinner.'

'Lady Maud will be in attendance?' This was news to Owen.

'Unless he was still pretending knowledge he did not have. But he seemed certain of that.'

Good news? Sister to Sir Thomas Percy, Maud might be willing to vouch for Marian at St Clement's, which would be helpful if the prioress was hesitant to accept the young woman back in the fold. It was also possible that the family considered Marian wayward, partly to blame. 'Will Lady Maud lodge with her husband at the palace?'

Thomas presumed so. But he seemed far more interested in complaining about Ronan's deception, enumerating the many people who had sought his advice – all the resident canons, the heads of the religious houses, prominent merchants and officers of the city. 'Many of those noted in the account book he carried.'

God's blood, the imbecile. Owen checked his temper. 'He showed it to you?'

'Pushed it at me. I refused it, but he stuffed it into a pile of books and fled. He said someone was following him. He feared for his safety. No one would know—'

Fighting a desire to grab the man and shake him, Owen quietly asked where the book was now.

'I am sorry to say it is gone. Stolen by the intruders who injured my serving man.' Apparently sensing Owen's growing anger, Thomas held up a hand as if to ward him off. 'I know I should have told you of this when you first asked. I know. But I thought— To my shame I thought I might make a good impression with Sir John were I to deliver it up to him.'

'Sir John? Not His Grace?'

A frown. 'You do not for a moment believe Alexander is suddenly the power in the family? Everything he has he owes to his eldest brother. No, I meant to give it to Sir John.'

By now Owen was only half listening to the chancellor. He had learned what he needed, that the account book was now in Sir John's possession – unless Porter and Diggs were fools. Now it was Ambrose's disappearance that distracted him. It weighed on his conscience. His duty to the prince was clear. He must protect Ambrose, which meant finding him. When it was plain he would learn no more of immediate use from Thomas, he excused himself.

'Call on me at any hour, Captain. I wish to help in any way I can. I pray you forgive me—'

But Owen was at the door, off in search of Hempe, hoping one of his men might have seen or heard something of Ambrose.

FIFTEEN
Ouse Bridge, the Cross Keys

I n the course of his long service to the late Archbishop Thoresby, Brother Michaelo had become far more than a personal secretary, eventually running the household. He'd prided himself on his efficiency, and organized many a journey for His Grace. He was no stranger to all that such preparations entailed, and he had doubted that Crispin Poole would fulfill his promise to move his elderly mother and her belongings in a matter of a few hours. Yet by the early December dusk Michaelo found himself walking down Petergate behind a cart carrying Dame Euphemia and her belongings, as well as her companion Dame Marian. Crispin had recruited a strong young man, Drake, who worked in his warehouse near the staithes, to guide the donkey that pulled the covered cart. Alisoun Ffulford had chosen to walk with Drake, keeping an eye out for trouble as they made idle conversation. Crispin, walking alongside Michaelo, spoke only when passers-by curious about the procession called out to him. *My mother's health is failing and she has chosen to retire to St Clement's Priory.* When asked the purpose of a covered wagon Crispin gestured upward, indicating the soft drizzle.

Michaelo stayed close to the cart so that he might listen to the conversation between the blind widow and the nun, for Euphemia seemed fascinated by her companion.

As soon as Marian had stepped into the elderly woman's room she had been ordered to approach so that Euphemia might stroke her face and feel her hands, which she pronounced too rough to be those of a Percy. Marian had explained that all the sisters in the abbey worked with their hands, and as she had been traveling through the summer . . . Euphemia had interrupted her to ask whether it was true she was an obedientiary at the esteemed Wherwell Abbey. Marian said that she had been training as sub-cantrice. *And what is that, precisely?*

And so it had gone, and continued for a time until Crispin had announced their departure.

'At last. Difficult to arrange for a covered cart with such little notice, but one of my guild members came to my aid, bless him.' Crispin had not wished Marian to be visible as they moved through the city. Although Euphemia's maidservant provided an appropriate gown and a hat that covered the young woman's hair, Marian's pale brows were distinctive. 'Few people have seen her, yet the ones most keen to find her will know of her pallor.'

Indeed, Michaelo had felt his heart in his stomach as he and Marian, dressed as a humble monk, had walked through the Bedern, choosing the less-traveled alleyways, taking advantage of a loud argument over a spilled cart to rush across St Andrewgate and into the rear garden of Crispin Poole's home. Whisked inside by Crispin himself, Michaelo had crumpled onto a bench as the maidservant led Marian away to change clothing.

'Were you followed?' Crispin had asked, no doubt alarmed by Michaelo's behavior.

'I pray God we were not. No one seemed unduly interested in our passage. But one skilled in stealth would not permit himself to be seen.'

Crispin seemed satisfied.

As her belongings were carried out to the cart, Dame Euphemia had taken Marian's hand and declared, 'We travel under the protection of my son, a citizen of York and a member of the archbishop's household. Be assured that you are safe in our care.'

And Alisoun's, Michaelo thought, her strung bow and quiver of arrows concealed beneath her cloak.

Now, as they approached the ever-crowded bridge over the Ouse, Michaelo sensed Crispin tensed for trouble. He said a silent prayer for protection.

When Owen found Hempe at the castle, the bailiff's face was creased with worry. 'I hoped to warn them. Lady Neville is

expected at St Clement's, to stay at the priory until the ceremo-
nies begin, when she will move to the palace. But by the time
my messenger arrived at Crispin's house they were gone, and
I thought it dangerous to call attention by chasing after them,
make public your reconciliation.'

'I agree that would not serve. All may be well.' Owen shared
his hope about Lady Maud's support for Marian.

'It is in God's hands.' Hempe gestured to a man passing
by, told him to find a partner and follow Crispin Poole
and the cart at a discreet distance, assist them if necessary.
The man looked to Owen for his agreement before hurrying
off. Hempe grunted. 'Already they see you as their captain.
If they behave so with my fellow bailiff it will chafe.
Compton sees the change as a sign the mayor has no
confidence in us.'

'No time to appease him now, but I should invite him to the
York Tavern once the city is quiet again.'

'Might help, might not. When will you talk to Beck?'

'I already did.' Owen related the man's confession. And
the chancellor's.

'God help us. The weasel is also a thief. And now that part
of the treasure is in Neville's hands.'

'If Porter and Diggs are honest.'

Hempe grunted. 'If so, will that satisfy Neville, that is the
question.'

'Might provide evidence that there should be more than
what Beck stole.'

'If the two did not keep the goods.'

A lad came to a sliding halt before them.

'What news?' Owen asked.

'I heard about a company of musicians lodging at the
Cross Keys atop Micklegate hill. And the one you set us to
watch for, Captain, I might have seen him on Micklegate. Ran
as fast as I could to tell you.'

Owen looked to Hempe. 'Shall we chase?'

'I am aching for a good fight. Are you armed?'

'I am. You?'

'Always.'

* * *

As Dame Marian enumerated the responsibilities of the cantrice – she must know the Church calendar and the appropriate liturgy for each day, choose the music from the library over which she presided, adding music where necessary, devising original music, always keeping in mind the abilities of the sisters in residence, share the training with the novice-mistress – Dame Euphemia grew increasingly loud in her assurances that all would be well, Prioress Isabel would be made aware of Dame Marian's importance, how her presence would benefit the priory. Michaelo was shaking his head over the widow's blatant worship of noble blood and prestige when the cart came to an abrupt halt.

Crispin had limped forward, calling out in a loud voice, 'Let us through!'

Dame Euphemia opened the curtain on Michaelo's side. 'Monk! What is happening?'

'I am unsure. Your son is investigating.'

'Find out.'

Biting back a retort, Michaelo approached Alisoun, who stood quite still, watching the liveried men speaking to Crispin.

'Who are they?' he asked.

'Neville retainers on horses,' said Alisoun. 'The fools. One loud noise or child dashing across their paths and the horses will rear up or bolt. In such a crowd . . .'

'They lead their horses.'

'Now. They were still mounted when they ordered us to clear the way. How is a cart to do so with no room to turn?'

Though the buildings on the bridge complied with the restrictions meant to allow passage for carts, vendors encroached on the roadway and folk loitered around them. Crispin had known the cart to be a risk. He had meant to transport his mother by barge, but with the change of plans there had not been sufficient time to arrange that.

'Help me down, monk,' Dame Euphemia called.

Alisoun joined Michaelo, speaking softly to the blind woman as they guided her to stand beside her son.

Euphemia lost no time. 'My son is a citizen of York, an important merchant as well as an advisor to Archbishop Neville. He is escorting me to the priory of St Clement's. I am old, blind, and ailing.' She hardly seemed the latter at present. 'Who are you to demand us to make way for you?'

'Advisor to the archbishop?' said one of the men, looking more closely at Crispin, who gave a little bow. 'Forgive us, sir. We make haste to his brother Sir John Neville to advise him of the arrival of his lady at that very priory.'

Crispin said nothing, just leaned on his cane and waited for them to make way. When they did, he took his time helping his mother back into the cart, with Michaelo's assistance, Dame Euphemia moving with unhurried dignity.

Their ensuing halting progress across the bridge did nothing to ease Michaelo's tension, but he now had more respect for mother and son, and the risk they were taking for Marian's sake. He was grateful to reach the slope down to the riverbank, where the fishmongers sold their wares. They were long gone for the day, but the stench of rotting fish lingered and Michaelo slowed to pull a lavender-scented cloth from his sleeve. It was then he noticed a crook-backed figure slinking past, circling round the back of the cart, and decided to follow him. As the man began to lift a corner of the covering Michaelo put a hand on his shoulder. Whence came the courage? He would later wonder whether Dame Euphemia inspired him.

'Fitch the Snoop, they call you in the minster yard.' Michaelo spoke loud and sharp, startling the wizened man. 'Have you no respect for a blind widow?'

By now Crispin had heard, ordered Drake to halt, and joined him. 'Who is paying you, Snoop?'

'Master Crispin, is it? A flock of nobles perching all about the city are surely curious about their rivals' minions, sir.'

'You dare to insult both my reverend mother and me, you crook-backed worm?' Crispin poked at the man's scrip with his cane, making the contents jingle. 'I see you already have takings. You've no need of more from me. What I can promise is not to tell the mayor that you piss on his doorstep and spit on his children.'

Michaelo stifled a laugh as Euphemia called out, 'Shame on you, Fitch. And to think I gave you alms when you begged on the corner.'

'You are a nasty man, Crispin Poole.'

'As a raven knows a crow,' said Crispin with a laugh. 'Now off with you, and remember. I have more I could tell the Nevilles. And the Graa brothers.'

The crook-back scuttled off. Crispin thanked Michaelo for his keen eye. The cart rumbled off the bridge.

As Owen and Hempe hurried toward Micklegate they met Ned, who told a tale of conflict and victory at the bridgehead involving Crispin and his dam, how they had humbled Neville retainers and continued on their way. Ned was most impressed by Alisoun, who remained quiet and unmoved during the altercation, though anyone knowing her as he did would be aware of how she stood ready to throw back her cloak and draw out her bow should the men not yield.

Glancing at Owen, Hempe made a sympathetic face.

God be thanked she contained herself, thought Owen. He invited Ned to join them, filling him in as they walked.

Several others had joined them by the time they climbed Micklegate hill, and Owen divided them, Ned and one other coming with him to the Cross Keys, the others assisting Hempe in searching the alleys along the way. The three broke off and continued up Micklegate, pushing through the crowds of folk hurrying to their lodgings as evening took hold, a good many of them strangers, here for the enthronement.

Reaching the well-lit tavern tucked back in an alley, Owen ordered Ned to watch the rear, the other to hang about outside the entrance. 'Both of you come in only if you see Neville's men arriving. You are to take a seat away from me. I will notice you.'

Once inside, Owen greeted the taverner, quietly inquiring whether the players lodging there were at the tables this evening. The taverner, an old friend of Tom Merchet's, described the table where he might find them.

'Is their leader, Carl, with them? Possibly bandaged hands?'

'Not here. Might be up in the long room they share.' He told Owen how to find it. 'Will there be trouble?'

'My aim is to keep the peace. But I want Carl.'

The taverner sighed, but poured Owen a tankard and refused his coin. 'You're the captain.'

Taking a sip, Owen turned to gaze round the room, passing over the table of players as if they did not interest him. He noted that one was drunkenly cradling a damaged lute, two pegs dangling. In a while he moved toward a small table just beyond the players that had no room, then turned round as if just noticing that and perched at the edge of the players' long table as if still considering his options.

The one with the broken lute looked over, middling age, bald, bleary-eyed. 'Soldier, are you?' He waved his hand toward Owen's eye.

'And what if I am?' Owen growled.

'Roland means naught by the question,' said one with a wild thicket of fair hair. 'Considers himself a deep thinker because he notices folk. Begging your pardon, sir.'

'Did the snow blow you into town?' Owen said with a mirthless chuckle.

'We come to entertain the nobles descending on this fair city for the crowning of the archbishop,' said another, youthful, with a carefully cut beard, cleaner than the others.

The bald one cuffed the youth's ear. 'Crowning? Ye're daft, boy.'

'Musicians?' Owen asked.

'And players.' The youth put hand to heart and bowed, earning himself another cuff which he tried to return but was met with a volley of strikes.

'He would please the ladies,' said Owen.

'He *is* our lady. Only one now,' said a muscular man with a dour expression who had been drumming his fingers on the table. Owen wondered whether this was Paul, the one who had attacked Marian and was in the minster when Ambrose met with Ronan.

'Where will you be performing?' Owen lifted his tankard to the taverner who was serving the next table. 'A round for these fine musicians.'

'Fine musicians?' asked the taverner as he filled the proffered tankards. 'I would welcome a good fiddler late in the day.'

'We had the finest fiddler in the land, we did,' said one who had been staring into his lap the while Owen had been seated there. He'd thought him asleep.

'Carl?' The bald one snorted up ale, wiped his nose on his sleeve. 'Not the finest. Not him.'

'Died, did he? This Carl?' Owen asked in an offhand way, as if tolerating the men who had turned their stools to include him.

'Carl? Hardly dead, is he, soaring to the heights of bliss a few nights past. But the archbishop's mighty brother broke his fingers, he did,' said the youth.

The mop top took his turn cuffing the youth's ears. 'You talk too much.'

'So you've no place to perform?' asked Owen.

Shrugs all round. 'Carl's seeing to it,' said the bald one.

'We thought to set up in the field near Micklegate Bar, lure folk in as they come to town. They chased us off. It's for pavilions for the lords' armies,' said the mop top.

'You're not one of them, are you?' asked the one Owen thought to be Paul.

Owen laughed. 'I kiss no lord's arse.' That won hoots and laughter. 'But I know some as do. And any soldier will welcome a bit of music after a long march, some bawdy tales. Where would they find your man with the broken fingers?'

'Here, when his woman kicks him out for being greedy,' said the bald one.

'Out all night, is he?'

'Dusk till dawn,' said the youth with a wink.

'Most fortunate of men, eh?' Owen said as he rose, flipping the taverner a coin as he left, walking out into the street, shaking his head at his man so he did not follow. He walked on toward Micklegate Bar.

A fiddler with broken fingers might never regain mastery of his instrument. Owen knew about that with his blinding. He still bested most at the butts, but he would never be as confident as he had been before his injury. Since his youth he had depended on his left eye for judging the trajectory. Losing the sight in that eye led him to doubt that he knew precisely where the target stood or moved, and how far away, and thinking it through only slowed him down. Hesitation was the enemy of rhythm. As with music. Owen knew from his experience playing the lute that a musician depended on knowing

that his fingers would perform without effort, without thought.
Carl's injury was as devastating to a fiddler as Owen's was to
an archer. He remembered his own fury. Fury came before
despair.

Neville would have done the deed while questioning Carl
about Ambrose and Marian. The musician had good reason to
hate Neville, but his anger, his hunger for vengeance, was
more easily satisfied by attacking the musician and the singer
whose escape had brought Carl to the attention of Sir John.
Had Paul meant to help in some way?

When sure he had not been followed, Owen doubled back,
whispered to his man out front to stay put, and moved down
the alley to the rear, to the steps leading up to the lodgings
above the tavern. For a moment he wondered whether Ned
had wandered off.

'Here, Captain.' Ned seemed to materialize out of the
shadows.

'Anyone pass by? Hear anything?'

'Maidservant cleaning a pot, a drunk puking. Heard what
sounded like a pair mating, then two men came past adjusting
their cocks and heading back in for more drink.'

'I am going up to the bedchambers. If someone comes
running down, stop them. If anyone approaches, make noise.'

With a nod, Ned slipped back into the shadows.

Pricking up his ears, Owen listened for signs of life as he
crept up the steps. Quiet. Too quiet? He caught the murmur
of voices as he reached the landing, but afar off, not the
chamber the taverner had indicated, which was the first on his
left. Pausing to listen at the door, he eased it open, stepped
in. Someone had left an oil lamp burning. Intending to return?
Owen moved quickly, searching packs, bedclothes, instruments. He found a stash of jewels beneath the mattress.
Interesting, but not his business. And then a slit in the mattress
with something small, stiff within. A small book with a supple
leather cover. Costly, not something one of them would likely
own. He was stuffing it into his scrip when Ned shouted a
drunken curse down below.

A step creaked, then a board on the landing. Drawing his
dagger, Owen waited behind the door, watched the man step

into the room. Paul. Catching him from behind, Owen silenced him with a knife to his throat.

'What were you doing in the minster the night before the vicar's murder?' Owen asked softly, drawing Paul back into the shadows, turning him around and pushing him against the wall.

'You. I knew you were spying on us.' Paul reached for a knife.

Owen kicked it out of his hand, yanked the man toward him, and slammed him back into the wall. A blow for Marian. 'Now talk.'

'I never touched the dead man.'

'What of the girl? You touched her. She ran off because of you. Is that how Carl forced you to do his bidding? To repay him?'

'How do you know so much, one-eye?' Owen began to pull him up, ready to beat him senseless for assaulting a woman. But before he could slam him against the wall the man cried out, begging for mercy. 'I will tell you! Carl wanted to know about the minstrel. I stayed just long enough to be sure it was him. Saw the girl run away. I didn't follow her!'

From below, Ned sent up a string of curses.

Someone stumbled up the stairs, breathing hard.

'If you say a word you will be as crippled as Carl,' Owen warned.

A man came rushing into the room, throwing himself on the mattress. Owen smelled blood, saw it smeared on the man's gloves as he fumbled with them.

'Not Carl! Not Carl!' he shouted as two young men stormed into the room, one of them roughly grabbing him just as the second glove fell.

No bandages.

'You fools,' Owen growled, dragging Paul out and tossing him on the bed. 'Remove the gloves next time.' He turned to Paul, who was eyeing his comrade's bloody hands. 'Where is Carl?'

'I don't know. I swear.'

Owen ordered the two fools to come with him, leading them out and down, nodding to Ned as he passed. 'Keep watch.'

'Captain, we thought—' one of the young men began.

'Thinking had nothing to do with it,' Owen growled. But he was glad. He knew now that Carl had been waiting for Ambrose at the minster. He thought it likely the exchange of cloaks led Carl to murder the wrong man.

Down Skeldergate the cart rumbled unchecked, but the two incidents on the bridge had clearly added to the tensions of the party. As the afternoon light faded away Alisoun and Drake looked round at every step and the conversation in the cart grew hesitant, more anxious. Crispin walked along in silence, no longer obliged to greet his peers. At this hour in winter the waterfront warehouses were deserted, the merchants back in their well-lit homes or shops. Now the streets along the south bank of the river were the domain of the poor and the criminal. Crispin's only comment to Michaelo was a request to continue to be on alert for anyone who seemed too curious, apologizing that the need for a humble procession had meant no guards. Michaelo had reminded him of Alisoun's prowess with the bow. Though as dusk fell and the river mist rose an attacker would appear at too close range for a bow to be effective.

In the cart, Euphemia expressed her unease with questions about Marian's aunt, Maud Neville. The simple answer that she knew her far less well than she did Lady Edwina or Sir Thomas did not satisfy.

'Will she support you, that is my question.'

'I cannot say how she will see my disappearance. A woman is oft blamed for luring a man no matter how hard she fought him, how fiercely she defended her purity. The one man who could attest to never having touched me is dead.'

'What of the musicians?'

'Until that night at Cawood, none of them had dared approach me in that way. I had thought it because my disguise convinced them. But I have come to think that Carl, their leader, had forbidden them to touch me, and they dared not disobey.'

'God be thanked,' said Euphemia.

Michaelo had been unable to make out Marian's quiet response.

'Have you any hope your Percy kin will believe you?' asked Euphemia.

The woman lacked all courtesy and compassion.

'I believe my guardian and Lady Edwina will if I am able to speak to them myself. They know me well. I cannot say whether Lady Maud will.'

'What of your mother? Surely she will believe you.'

'My mother defers to her betters in all things regarding me.' Sadness tinged the words. Michaelo crossed himself and said a prayer for the young nun.

Conversation died with that. Michaelo was relieved for Dame Marian's sake, but he regretted the loss of a diversion. Now he was too aware of Crispin's unease, and the enveloping darkness. It was with relief that he spied up ahead a pool of light spilling out from a building, and noticed the sound of a hammer on steel.

'Two men ahead,' Alisoun called out as she flipped back her cloak and shrugged the bow from her shoulder, testing the string, plucking an arrow from her quiver.

Following the line of her arrow, Michaelo caught the movements just beyond the pool of light. They were drawing weapons.

Crispin limped forward. 'Do not shoot until we see who they are.'

Dame Euphemia peered out. 'What is happening?'

'Someone standing in our path,' said Michaelo. 'Weapons drawn. Mistress Alisoun has readied an arrow.'

'God help us.'

'Come, let us pray, Dame Euphemia,' Marian said. She began to recite a hail Mary.

Euphemia withdrew and joined in the prayer.

Michaelo's heart pounded.

As the cart moved into the light Crispin put a hand on Drake's arm and quietly ordered him to halt. He stepped forward, leaning on his cane.

'Porter and Diggs. Have you come to assist us?'

One of the men wagged his dagger at Crispin. 'Who do you serve, Poole?'

'At present, my blind, elderly dam.'

'You expect us to believe she is in there?'

Euphemia poked her head out. 'Who are you to question my son?'

'Now step aside, Diggs.' Crispin shifted the cane to the other hand and began to turn back.

But Diggs, dagger poised, came forward.

Alisoun let her arrow fly, catching Diggs above the elbow on his dagger arm. With a shout of pain he dropped the weapon and stumbled to the side of the track as the other moved toward Alisoun. Michaelo stepped forward, but there was no need. Before he could draw his weapon Drake stuck out a leg and the man tripped and fell.

'Bastard!' Porter shouted.

Drake kicked him hard, then rolled him over to the side of the track and, with a nod from Crispin, resumed his hold on the donkey, guiding the cart past the trouble-makers.

'What will Sir John say when he learns you attacked a man escorting his elderly mother to the good sisters?' Crispin called out as he passed.

'What need has he of a cripple like you?' growled Porter.

Stinging words, and Michaelo felt for Crispin, whose limp had become more pronounced the farther they walked. But he made no complaint.

As they moved back into darkness the women in the cart resumed their prayers, Michaelo accompanying them in silence. He strained to hear anything moving in the darkness, difficult over the clomping of the donkey's hooves, the creak of the wheels, the flutter of the cart covering, the pounding of his own heart. He peered into the darkness, seeking unnatural movement. Even so, he was startled when Alisoun plucked up a lantern from the cart and opened a shutter, revealing a covey of children preparing to jump on the cart from a porch roof. He had never heard them.

'Jump and the men within will skewer you on their swords, little ones,' Alisoun warned.

They crept back into the darkness.

Well done, thought Michaelo. How she had detected their presence on the roof he could not guess, but he was grateful for her keen senses, far better than his, and her courage.

They rolled on a little longer, Marian's murmured prayers now accompanied by Euphemia's snore. As the ground rose above Michaelo to his right, seeming to press them all the closer to the mist-shrouded river, the cart slowed.

'The Old Baile,' said Crispin. 'We must move with care.'

'May God watch over us,' Michaelo whispered.

Euphemia ceased snoring and rejoined Marian in prayer.

At a small gate affording access beyond the walls they came to a complete halt. Drake fetched a second small lantern that had been hanging on the side of the cart, opening the shutters and handing it to Crispin. Alisoun passed hers to Drake.

'I will walk on ahead,' said Crispin, 'check that the track beyond the gate is cart-worthy.'

Michaelo had wondered. Beyond the gate had once been a moat. Debris had been piled up to create a pathway. Planks were kept in a shed by the gateway for use when floods or storms washed it out. When Crispin returned with the good news that it was passable Michaelo said a prayer of thanks. They moved on, slowly, the cart bumping over the uneven ground.

As they gained the smoother path on the other side Michaelo heard horses approaching, then spied the flickering light of a torch. Two riders.

'Who approaches the priory of St Clement's at this late hour?' one of them called.

Crispin limped forward, identifying himself. The men dismounted. One of them engaged Crispin while the one holding the torch approached the cart. Michaelo narrated for Euphemia as the man studied Alisoun and her companion. He moved past them to shine his light on Michaelo, forcing him to shield his eyes.

'Who is in the cart, Father?'

'Master Crispin's widowed mother, who seeks the care of the good sisters,' said Michaelo.

At that moment the man's companion called him back. 'Come. We will escort them on to the priory.'

God be thanked.

More retainers flanked the gateway to the modest priory. Beyond, the yard was bright with lanterns and torches. A groom came forth to watch the donkey while Crispin and the young man opened the curtains and lowered the gate on the back, Marian handing Crispin the wooden steps for disembarking. As Euphemia was eased to the ground by her son, two sisters hurried toward them.

Michaelo greeted the prioress and precentrice, Dames Isabel and Veronica, both of whom had recently employed him as a scribe for confidential matters. He introduced the party, referring to the young woman as Mistress Marian, Dame Euphemia's companion. It would be the young woman's choice when to reveal her identity. He ended with an entreaty that at the very least they receive the two women, explaining that the others were her escort and might return to the city. Though in his heart he dreaded the thought of returning in the dark.

'If we might leave the cart here until morning, I would be grateful,' said Crispin.

Euphemia began to protest, but her son kissed her hand and assured her that his only concern was for her comfort.

'Where might we place my mother's chests?' he asked.

The prioress was all aflutter. 'Master Crispin, we expected your mother in a week's time. It is most unfortunate you have come betimes, and without warning.' Michaelo was taken aback by her discourtesy. 'Lady Maud Neville and her women arrived this day. You must understand our priory is small, poor, we are hard pressed—'

'I will double the donation to your building works,' said Crispin. 'Will that suffice?'

It was Dame Veronica who took Euphemia's hands and welcomed her warmly, and then Marian. 'I pray you, do not take offense. Mother Isabel frets about the great lady's expectations. But a house of women is what Lady Maud chose over the palace, and that we are without a doubt. Mother Isabel will soon see her worries were unfounded. Lady Maud seems most gracious.' She touched the prioress's arm. 'Where shall they set the chests?'

With a sigh, the prioress directed the party to follow her into a screens passage in the hall of the guest house, where she indicated they might deposit Euphemia's belongings.

From beyond the screen came a low hum of women's voices, punctuated by laughter, shouted questions, bursts of singing that dissolved into giggles or whispers. Michaelo noticed Marian's eyes aglow, and he prayed she might be truly welcomed back into the order, restored to the life among pious women that she had chosen.

While the two sisters stepped aside, no doubt arguing about where to put the two women, Marian turned to gaze at a wall hanging. Though it was tattered and darkened by smoke or mold from the river damp it was a radiant depiction of the Virgin and Child. Michaelo, too, found it a soothing point of focus after the tense journey.

'Have we company?' A richly garbed woman came round the screens, followed by two much younger women in only slightly less elegant travel attire.

Marian turned, and with a slight inhale of breath took a step backward.

'Marian, is it you? Can it be you?' the woman whispered.

'Lady Maud,' Marian said, hand to heart, bowing.

'God is merciful!' Maud cried as she rushed forward and gathered Marian in her arms. 'You are found in a nunnery! Oh, my dear, dear girl, we have been so frightened for you.' She stepped back, holding Marian at arm's length. 'But why did you not send word? And why are you in such clothing?'

The prioress, witnessing the happy reunion, approached with a furrowed brow. 'My lady, you know this woman?'

'May I present my niece, Dame Marian, sub-cantrice of Wherwell Abbey.'

'Is this so?' Dame Isabel looked to Marian.

'I was—'

Lady Maud cut in, 'She was seven years at Wherwell when a godless madman set fire to the abbey so that he might take her away. My brother Sir Thomas has been searching for her since Pentecost. All this time I have prayed . . .' She took Marian's hand in both her own. 'Pray assure me, Mother Prioress, that you were notified to provide her shelter should she seek it here?'

'I did not know she was anywhere near, my lady. She has just this moment arrived. Brother Michaelo introduced her as Dame Euphemia's companion.' Isabel gestured toward Michaelo.

A burst of rose scent as Lady Maud turned to him. 'Brother Michaelo. You are the monk who discovered my niece in the minster and carried her to safety, are you not?'

He was confused. She had just implied she'd not known where Marian might be, yet she knew of her night in the chapter house? 'My lady, it was my honor,' said Michaelo with a bow. 'Her heavenly voice led me to her. But how did you hear of this?'

'Is this true?' asked the prioress, glancing at Dame Euphemia, who had pushed forward to stand beside Marian, placing a hand on her arm.

'Perhaps we should continue this discussion where we might provide Dame Euphemia with a place to sit,' said Alisoun, who had been watching over the blind widow.

The prioress nodded. 'Lady Maud, Dame Marian, shall we—'

'We must include Brother Michaelo in any discussion,' said Marian. 'I have him to thank for guiding me to Captain Archer and Dame Lucie Wilton, who have healed, sheltered, and defended me. They deserve a full report of my reception here, and my reconciliation with my family.'

The smile she bestowed on Michaelo, the warmth in her pale eyes – he found himself bowing his head in humble gratitude. Rarely did others judge him for his present actions with no thought for his past. Perhaps she had not heard of his sins.

'We are well aware of the virtues of Brother Michaelo,' said Dame Veronica. 'He has come to our aid of late. A man of many talents. He was long the personal secretary of our late archbishop, John Thoresby.'

Lady Maud gestured toward the prioress. 'Might I suggest your parlor, Mother Prioress, where the fire has warmed the stones and you have a suitable chair for Dame Euphemia?' Whom she studied with interest.

SIXTEEN
Ruined

The children abed, Kate, Lucie, and Jasper sat by the kitchen fire taking turns keeping Ariel the kitten engaged and away from the flame with string play and cuddles and the remnants of a meat pie. Their talk was aimless for they were all anxious to hear that Marian had safely arrived at St Clement's and that Owen had found Ambrose before the Nevilles did.

Still apprehensive about the children's recoveries, Lucie went to the nursery, listening to their breathing. Quiet, deep. God be thanked. Here was her heart, here in this home, her family. As with Owen, all she did in the larger world was to protect her loved ones, to do what she could to create a safe community that would embrace and support them. Amidst the drama of Marian and Ambrose, it felt important to remember this.

Making her way down to the hall she discovered Owen, his face twisted in frustration as he paced back and forth by the garden window. She waited until he turned toward her and then opened her arms to him.

'Oh, my love,' he sighed as he embraced her, clutching her to him as if she were his lifeline.

The sound of his strong, steady heartbeat reassured her, eased the worry that had become habit whenever he chased a criminal. She smiled at the contrary evidence of that heartbeat – frustrated he might be, but deep down he was confident. Kissing him on the cheek she wriggled out of his arms. 'What is it?'

'An evening wasted on a false report. We scoured the city south of the river all the way to Micklegate Bar and found no sign of Carl. But I know now what he's suffered, why he might be out for revenge. And that he waited for Ambrose outside the minster.' He described Paul's confession, the conversation in the tavern, Neville's cruelty. Despite Owen's sense of Carl's violent potential, Lucie understood the musician's anger. As would Ambrose. 'We will have no joy of the Nevilles,' she said.

A bitter chuckle. 'And I've had no word of Ambrose. None of our men have seen him.'

'He knows the danger,' said Lucie. 'Perhaps he has found his protector.'

She saw the idea was no comfort to Owen. And understood. His heart's desire was to help Ambrose fulfill his mission to save Prince Edward's life, or at the very least reveal to the prince the source of his long, increasingly debilitating illness. She kissed Owen's hand, touched his cheek. 'Food and drink?'

He drew her back into his arms, kissed her hard, and, with a growl, scooped her up. Threading her arms round him she laughed softly as he carried her up the steps. In their chamber he eased her down onto the bed and flopped down, pulling her atop him.

'I have wanted to do this for so long,' he whispered, kissing her. 'I mean to wait no longer.'

Jasper and Kate glanced up with concern that softened to curiosity when Lucie and Owen appeared in the kitchen smiling and arm in arm.

'Now I am ready for your wonderful stew, Kate,' said Owen, easing down onto a chair by the fire.

Lucie poured ale for both of them and settled near him. She had teased Owen about his lust, that his rough treatment of Paul had heated his blood, but he insisted it was the building frustration of the weeks sleeping in shifts, so that one of them could always be with the children, never together in bed. Afterward he'd conceded that the release in finally catching a suspect had stirred his blood, woken his appetites. She said a silent *mea culpa* for her gratitude. Such wantonness.

'What of this treasure?' she asked, impatient for the unveiling of something precious he had promised to show them all.

Jasper had been drowsing by the fire, but perked up at the question, keeping an eye on Owen while he finished the meal

Kate had put out for him. When at last Owen sat back with a satisfied sigh Jasper cried, 'Da! What did you find?'

'Fetch me my scrip. On the peg beneath my cloak.'

Quick on his feet, Jasper delivered it with a bow, then hovered near.

Owen drew a small book out of his scrip. 'Dame Marian's prayer book.'

'A Choir of Crows,' Lucie murmured, receiving it into her hands, turning it round to admire the cover, the intricate design etched into the supple leather. Opening it, she was impressed by the elegant, most regular hand in which the prayers were written, and delighted by the illustrations, some inspiring, many comical.

Kate peered over her shoulder. 'Fat crows,' she remarked. 'They feed well.'

Jasper joined her. 'They look more like brothers than sisters,' he said. 'All the canons and vicars crowding in the minster choir cawing their praise of Archbishop Neville.'

'Notice me! Notice me!' Kate sang.

The humorous images – crows in the habits of Benedictine nuns standing in a choir, heads lifted up, beaks open in song, perched at refectory tables nibbling as one stood at a lectern, flapping down corridors, sitting in a circle pecking at embroideries – were interspersed with drawings of the Madonna and Child, Christ on the cross with the Marys weeping below, angels, and several of a human sister going about her chores, singing, kneeling in prayer, her pale face aglow. A compilation planned with humor, piety, and deep affection for a niece.

They were poring over the little book when the door opened, letting in a chilly breeze.

'All will be well, I think,' Alisoun said in greeting. And though she settled on the bench by the door with a weary sigh, she smiled at some thought while removing her boots, laughing as Ariel pawed at her skirt, scooping the kitten up to carry her to a seat beside Jasper, settling her on her lap. 'What's the fun?'

'Dame Marian's prayer book,' said Lucie, passing it to her. Jasper showed Alisoun what he thought the funniest illustrations, repeated his description of the minster chapter's behavior. They laughed together.

Poor Ned. He did not have a chance with Alisoun, not with the mutual affection she saw as their eyes met.

She gave them a moment before asking Alisoun to tell them about her journey, and Marian's reception.

Rarely did Alisoun have such a rapt audience, and she drank up the attention, giving a dramatic account of the altercation at the bridge, Fitch the Snoop's humbling, the deepening darkness as they moved along the far bank, the encounter with Porter and Diggs, the children on the roof, the unease when the Neville retainers surrounded them out beyond the Old Baile.

'Porter and Diggs again.' Lucie looked at Owen. 'Will they do more?'

'I am certain they will try.'

'They will not appreciate being humbled by a woman,' said Alisoun. 'Or Drake, a warehouse worker.'

'Who's Drake?' Jasper asked. Alisoun had mentioned him by name several times.

'I set his arm once when he broke it in a brawl. He works in Crispin's warehouse, came along to guide the donkey. I walked with him.'

Jasper frowned. 'Young and handsome, I'd wager.'

'And strong!' Alisoun said with a teasing grin, elbowing Jasper and touching his hand. She continued her account with their reception at St Clement's, the prioress's clear reluctance to receive them. 'All that changed when Lady Maud came forward to embrace Marian and questioned why she was not garbed in the habit of the order. The prioress whined, Brother Michaelo smoothed feathers, they all retired to Prioress Isabel's parlor, and Crispin, Drake, and I headed home.'

'Any trouble on your return?' Owen asked.

'We were ready for real trouble, but found no sign of Porter and Diggs. Now and then some fool began to follow, but we frightened them off. Nothing more.'

'Brother Michaelo will spend the night?' asked Jasper.

'Yes. Sharing the priest's chamber. Marian insisted. The precentrice Dame Veronica was very welcoming. I think with

Lady Maud's support Marian will soon take her place among her sisters at Wherwell.'

'That is for the archbishop to decide.' Lucie saw how that news erased all the smiles. 'You remember with Dame Joanna . . .' A nun who had run away from St Clement's some time ago.

'But she was nothing like Dame Marian,' Jasper protested. 'She had brought on her troubles with crime and sin.'

'She was mad, as her mother before her,' said Owen. 'I, for one, could not bring myself to judge her in the end.'

Jasper flushed at the implied criticism, ducking his head.

'But all you heard were my curses and complaints,' Owen admitted, winning a cautious grin.

He was a good father. When the prayer book had been put away, Owen spoke of the confessions of Beck and the chancellor. A pair of greedy cowards, Lucie declared them. But she was relieved. Marian was safe, and Owen was surely closer to solving Ronan's murder. Soon they might all sleep more peacefully.

'Tell me more about this Drake,' said Jasper, poking his face close to Alisoun's.

Lucie leaned to Owen, whispered a request to return to their earlier discussion up in their bedchamber. He needed no further prompting. She asked Alisoun to damp the fire in the hall. 'Jasper can help you. Let Kate get a good night's sleep.'

As they climbed to the solar Owen asked whether it was wise to leave them unchaperoned.

'I choose to trust them.'

On the landing Lucie turned to watch Alisoun and Jasper slip into the hall, hand in hand.

Owen woke in the night to a soft knock on the door. Expecting Gwen, who often came to them with bad dreams, he groped on the floor for his shirt before sticking his head out the door. But it was Kate, who apologized for waking him before dawn but a man had brought Ambrose, who was injured.

'I will dress and come down,' he whispered, hoping not to wake Lucie. 'Bring out the pallet we used for Gabriel.'

Owen was fumbling with the rest of his clothes in the dark when Lucie startled him by opening the shutter on the lantern they kept by the door, for the children. 'I did not hear you rise,' he said.

She laughed. 'How could you with all the noise you're making stumbling about? What has happened?'

'Ambrose is here. Injured.'

'I will come.'

'But—'

'No arguments.'

As he stepped out onto the landing Owen saw Alisoun peering round the nursery door. 'Is there trouble?' she whispered.

'Ambrose is here.'

Lucie joined Owen, motioning to Alisoun to go back to sleep, and the two crept down the steps.

In the kitchen, Kate was stoking the fire. Owen did not know the gray-haired man who bent over Ambrose, who lay on the pallet near the fire, but he guessed by the French endearments that this was the one who had followed him from France, protecting him. He looked the part of a soldier, puckered scar on his neck, weathered face, now drawn down in concern for his friend. Owen greeted him, identified himself. The man offered his name, Denis, pronounced as the French would.

Joining him to kneel beside Ambrose, Owen opened the cloak. A cloth wrapped round Ambrose's chest was so blood-soaked he could not tell the precise location of the wound. Denis indicated a space just below the heart. As Ambrose's breathing was shallow, but quiet, and he was not gasping, it seemed the lung was spared. God be thanked.

'What happened, Denis?' Owen asked. 'Would you prefer we speak French?'

'*Merci*, but no, I had much practice speaking your tongue when Ambrose was first at court. I was walking down the alley to the home of the vicar where I have sheltered – Franz – when I heard Ambrose cry out behind me. I was not aware that he had followed me, but I knew his voice and rushed back to help. The musician Carl had fallen on him, wounding him as you see, but Ambrose fought back before falling to the ground, slicing open the man's knife arm. When I turned round

Carl was running away. Ambrose told me to follow him. He ran to Stonegate, disappearing down an alleyway. I did not care. My concern was Ambrose. I carried him to Franz's house. We bandaged him, but we could not stop the bleeding. Is Dame Lucie—?'

'I am here,' said Lucie, kneeling to Ambrose, taking his hand, whispering his name. When Owen showed her where the knife had entered, she agreed he was most fortunate.

'But he lost so much blood,' said Denis.

'He will be weak,' she said, 'but I feel no fever. That is good.' Kate handed her the basket in which she kept her medicines and bandages, offered all four ale.

The day had begun.

Shortly before dawn, Stephen and Alfred called to report quiet nights on the watches set around Hempe's and the chancellor's houses. Both men were relieved to see Ambrose. One search to call off. They offered to help search for Carl.

Denis said he had disappeared on the opposite side of Stonegate from Robert Dale's shop, past Swinegate. The description fit the home and shop of the silversmith Will Farfield.

First Owen wanted to move Ambrose to the safety of St Mary's infirmary. Lucie agreed to the idea, though of course he could not walk there. Not bothering to don a cloak, Owen crossed to the York Tavern, already well lit, the staff bustling about the morning chores.

His eyes still puffy with sleep, Tom Merchet listened to Owen's proposal, scratching his chin, yawning. 'You are in luck, my friend. I've a few barrels I might spare. The lay brother at the postern gate has the abbot's blessing to give me access in the early hours.'

'What about Bootham Bar? Will they let you through?'

'For free tankards for an evening they will.' Tom tapped the side of his nose and winked. 'Carry him over and we will tuck him in with your message.'

'Bless you.'

'Now hurry before my Bess wastes your time with more questions.'

* * *

Once Ambrose was safely delivered to Tom, the four set out, watching the street and the alleys as they approached Will Farfield's. Most of the shops showed signs of life, lamps flickering, smoke rising from chimneys and snaking down the alleys, a few apprentices sweeping the doorsteps. But Will Farfield's shop was dark. An apprentice at the entrance next door leaned on his broom and watched Owen and the others circling the building.

'Sent his apprentices off a few days ago. One of them staying with us,' he said when Owen greeted him.

'Do you think the apprentice would talk to me?'

'Still sleeping. I have the early shift. If you want to talk to him later . . .'

'I will come by if I still need information. He's a fortunate lad.'

'The master will work him hard, but he's kind and we eat well.' A grin. 'Will you be dragging Master Will away for his debts?'

'I am not a debt collector, lad. Keeping the peace, that is what we're about.'

The lad glanced at the hulking shape of Stephen, the wiry edginess of Denis, but he was most interested in Alfred, who was working the lock on Will's shop door. Grinning, the apprentice bid Owen good luck and hurried into his shop, no doubt to share what he had learned.

'Best take Carl now, before we collect an audience,' said Owen. He directed Denis and Alfred to slip inside the shop and hold there, ready to catch anyone trying to escape. He and Stephen would go in through the rear door.

At the back Stephen chose to kick in the door rather than fiddle with a lock and risk being heard, stepping aside to allow Owen to enter first. In the dim light a man cowered in a corner moaning, 'I am ruined, ruined. God help me, I am ruined.' Stephen lit a lamp from the embers of the kitchen fire, revealing the speaker to be Will Farfield.

'You are injured?' Owen asked the silversmith, touching his blood-stained shirt.

'Not mine. His.' Will started shivering.

'We'll stoke the fire when we have him,' said Owen. 'Is he here?'

A nod. 'He heard you and ran toward the shop.'

Gesturing to Stephen to stay with Will, Owen picked up the lamp and stepped into the next room. Quiet, dark, but gradually he detected rough breathing, soft, muffled. Setting down the lamp, Owen crept toward the sound. It paused. He paused.

'We know you are here, Carl. We surround you. You have nowhere to run.'

With a hiss the man reared up and lunged at Owen with a knife in his fist ready to stab. But Owen had halted where he had space to step aside and let the man crash to the floor. By the time Stephen rushed in Owen knelt on Carl's back, holding down the man's bandaged arm.

'I cannot breathe,' Carl cried, proving the lie.

'If I let you up and you charge me, you're a dead man. Understand?' A feeble attempt to nod. Owen plucked Carl up by the shoulders and dragged him out to the kitchen before he could regain his footing.

'I have them!' he shouted. He heard Denis and Alfred fumbling their way toward them through the shop.

Stephen moved Will Farfield to a bench and turned to help Owen with Carl, who had begun to struggle.

'I will see to him,' Denis called and lunged toward the man in Owen's grasp.

Jerking Carl to the side Owen kicked over a stool to trip Denis. He fell and rolled away.

Denis picked himself up, muttering French curses.

'I want the story while he has his teeth and can still be understood,' said Owen.

Owen pushed Carl down onto the bench. 'I will tie you down if you try to move.'

'The folk talk of you as the guardian angel of the city. What will they think when they learn you're protecting a pair of spies for King Charles?'

'By the time you are able to speak in any public space they will know the truth about Ambrose, you fool.'

Carl cradled his bandaged arm. 'I'm bleeding again,' he whimpered.

'Be quiet,' Stephen growled.

Owen dragged chairs and stools into a circle.

Alfred stoked the fire, adding bricks of peat. 'No wood or coal?' he asked Will.

The silversmith sank onto a stool and leaned his head back against the wall. 'No.'

Once seated, Owen leaned forward, elbows on his knees, and looked long at Carl, then Will, curious about their partnership. Time to question them, while they were humbled, cold, no doubt hungry. He saw no evidence of a recent meal.

'I want to know what led up to Ronan's murder,' he said.

Will sat up, glaring at Carl. 'You've told him?'

'I've said nothing, you dalcop.'

'I want to hear all of it,' said Owen. 'Who would like to begin? Will? I took you for the honest sort.'

'I am! But that monster—'

'Honest, are you?' Carl spit on the floor. 'I came upon you trying to rob the vicar of his scrip.' He looked to Owen and the others. 'Found him wrestling the man to the ground and kicking him as he lay in the snow.'

'Then you fell upon him and stabbed him,' Will cried. 'You're the murderer. Only you murdered the wrong man. I heard you curse when Ronan's hat rolled away. You cursed at him and came at me.' Will looked at Owen. 'Mistook the vicar for the musician in that costly cloak and velvet hat. The man he murdered last night.'

'So Will knocked Ronan to the ground, and Carl made certain he was dead.' Alfred looked from Will to Carl. 'Both guilty.'

'I murdered no one,' Will whined. 'I just wanted his scrip. I've been mad with grief, out of my senses, but I never meant to kill him. I wanted the account book. Thought it was in his scrip. Always was when he came here. It would have been my salvation. I meant to prove he tried to ruin us all to fill his purse, and the archbishop's.'

Carl laughed. 'But that isn't what the vicar had in his scrip that morning, was it? Had the whore's beloved prayer book is what he had.'

'And now this monster has murdered two men,' said Will. 'Last night. That's how he was wounded.'

Denis shook his head. 'Ambrose Coates lives.'

'The cur lives?' Carl let out a string of curses as he held up his hands, the bandages on his fingers as bloody and soiled as the one on his arm. 'His work, the traitor. He lied to us, used us to spy on the Nevilles. How does he thank us? Takes off with the Percy girl. And there we are, looking like we helped the traitor spy on the Nevilles and run off with the prize.'

'I heard it was Sir John Neville who broke your fingers, not Ambrose Coates,' said Owen.

'Because of him! Sir John's men dragged me to their lord. *Who was the white-haired musician? For whom was he spying? Where has he taken the lass?* His men held down my hands, splayed my fingers. Neville had a wooden mallet. Every *I don't know* rewarded with a thwack.' He stomped his foot. 'Thwack. Thwack.' Tears of anger turned to despair and pain at the memory. 'Took the lass I protected with my life for months. My treasure. I knew who she was. The missing Percy, the nun who abandoned her lover, let the villagers burn him. I meant to turn south after Cawood, deliver her up to Sir Thomas Percy. But he stole her. And ruined me. I will never play again. Never. A musician with crushed fingers?' He stabbed a hand at Denis. 'Your comrade destroyed me.'

'You did it to yourself, you greedy cur,' Stephen growled.

'You failed her that night at Cawood,' said Denis. 'Took off to the fields with the cook while one of your men crawled onto her pallet. How could Ambrose leave her?'

'Time enough for that after you finish the tale,' said Owen. 'Tell me all that happened the night of Ronan's death.'

As they bickered through the telling, Carl cursing, Will moaning, Owen pieced together a picture of the moments leading up to and past Ronan's murder. Will's excuse – cajoled into investing in a shipment of goods, promised riches, celebrating with his partner's maidservant, and then the terrible news, pirates, complete loss, a loss of his daughters' dowries, the business partner threatening to expose him for getting his maidservant with child, the cost of caring for her. An endless trap. His wife's disbelief when he obeyed his confessor and told her everything. Her flight south to her parents with the children, where the pestilence of summer took one of his daughters.

'I wanted the account book. God forgive me, that is all I wanted. I meant to take it to Dom Jehannes. He's a kind man. He would listen. He would convince my Mary that I had been one of many Ronan ruined. That I meant to restore the dowries.' Will groaned. 'But that wasn't what Ronan carried. I am cursed. It was not the book.'

'How could you tell in the dark?' Owen asked.

'What he carried was too big. The account book is smaller. Thinner.'

'What did you do with the book he carried?'

'Tossed it away. No use to me.'

'And you took it up.' Owen nodded to Carl. 'How did you come to this house?'

'I followed him home that morning. I wanted a place I could slip in and out while watching for Ambrose Coates.'

Will groaned again. 'I ran from the minster yard. Never looked back.'

'Course not,' said Carl. 'A whipped pup running to hide in his den, lick his wounds. I followed him. Watched. Saw he had troubles, no sign of a wife, family, his apprentices cursing him for cold food and little of it.'

'Who was the partner who ruined you, Will?' Owen asked. It might be useful to have that name.

'No!' Will shook his head with a vehemence. 'I could never again show my face in the city. And with Neville now the archbishop. No.'

It stank of Gisburne. Was that why Owen found himself devising a way to keep Will's name out of this, to spare him? An ally when needed against the man he intended to ruin someday, somehow? Needle pricks across his ruined eye. He had pushed that resolve far back in his mind, only to have it surface now. A curse.

He needed to inform Sir John Neville of his findings. But the precentor and dean deserved to be the first to receive word.

'Denis, Stephen, watch them.' Motioning to Alfred to follow him, Owen went out to the shop.

'Can I trust Denis to guard Will here for the day, to spare him public humiliation?' Owen asked.

'As long as he's not responsible for Carl as well, I would trust him,' said Alfred. 'But why ask me?'

'I've no time to think it through. I need to move quickly, before Sir John hears that Ambrose is recovering in my home.'

'But he's at the abbey.'

'I pray his spies followed them to our door and then went back to make their report. No eyes left watching to see Tom Merchet take delivery.' When he saw that Alfred understood, Owen set out his plan. Alfred and Stephen were to deliver Carl to the castle. Denis would guard Will at the house. By nightfall Owen would know whether or not Will Farfield was to be freed to follow his despair, or whether he, too, was for the castle.

'Where are you going?' asked Alfred.

'To Jehannes. I'll collect Beck and Ronan's hoard, and take them to the dean and precentor.' Beck would do his best to be seen assisting the investigation if he hoped to remain a clerk in the service of the minster chapter. 'From there to Neville.'

'A day's work before you reach the palace? Tell the others and be on your way, Captain.'

For the moment the apothecary was quiet, the sole customer a young servant wide-eyed with the importance of the mission entrusted to him, fetching a headache powder for his master. As Jasper finished wrapping the physick he heard the squeak of the gate from the tavern yard. He had left the rear door ajar so he might listen for that very sound, or for Alisoun calling for him. Neither doubted someone would try to retrieve Ambrose. Handing the lad the small package, Jasper saw him out, and was about to shut the street door when George Hempe rushed through, finger to mouth, gesturing toward the back.

Jasper closed the street door, locked it.

'Two men in the garden,' said Hempe. 'Seen dumping Pit's body in the Ouse this morning. One of my men is waiting in the tavern yard. We'll take them.'

'They will be here for Ambrose,' said Jasper, picking up a

dagger and cudgel as he followed Hempe's silent passage through the workroom. A few steps out the door, Hempe stopped. Was he grinning? Jasper peered round him to see.

Alisoun stood in front of the long window next door, an arrow aimed at a pair on the garden path halfway between the shop and the house, their backs to Jasper and Hempe. One of the men was injured, an arm in a sling. The other leaned heavily on one leg. Porter and Diggs, Jasper guessed, wanting vengeance and the reward of delivering Ambrose.

'Put that away, girl,' Diggs drawled. 'Luck served you last night. It won't today. We want the minstrel. Hand him over and there will be no trouble.'

Alisoun aimed at Diggs's uninjured arm. 'Are you certain you want to test me?'

Diggs wobbled as if finding it difficult to stay upright, but Porter lunged. Jasper was there before Hempe could reach him, delivering a blow to the head sufficient to fell him. Hempe called to the men waiting at either gate.

'They'll be coming with me to the castle,' said Hempe. He nodded to one of the men to pick up Porter, who lay limp on the ground. The other had already secured Diggs, with Alisoun's help.

'Get your hands off me, you filthy cow,' Diggs growled, and caught Jasper's cudgel in his gut.

'Send for a healer for this one,' Alisoun told Hempe. 'His sleeve reeks of low-tide mud and muck and he grows weak.'

Hempe thanked Alisoun and Jasper. 'With you two guarding him, Ambrose can rest easy.'

Alisoun grinned. 'He went to the abbey hours ago.'

Hempe chuckled. 'Of course Owen would think of that.' He nodded and was off, pushing past Rose and Rob, who were crestfallen to have missed the excitement.

The twins hailed Owen just as he reached the minster gate with a tale of Alisoun's and Jasper's bravery, Pit's demise. As Owen had guessed, Pit's mission failed, Sir John had condemned him. Or Porter and Diggs had taken it upon themselves, hoping to redeem themselves after last night's foolishness. They had triply failed.

He set the twins the task of taking food and ale to Denis, then briefly told them enough about what he had learned of Ronan's murder to satisfy Lucie and give her the background she needed in case Sir John Neville sent more men to the house.

SEVENTEEN
The Archbishop's Choice

Jehannes need say nothing, his expression made clear the weakness of Owen's argument on Will Farfield's behalf.

'It is for the dean to decide whether or not Will was culpable in this.'

'I fear he will defer to the archbishop.'

'I've little doubt he will do just that,' said Jehannes. 'But you do not want to cross His Grace at a time when he is most keen to impress us with the strength of the family supporting him. Is that not the very purpose of the Nevilles' strong presence in the city? If you should embarrass him before them . . .' Jehannes placed a hand on Owen's shoulder. 'You carry a double burden – the honor of the city and the heir to the throne. You do not need the Nevilles as enemies.'

Dean John and Master Adam grew anxious of the time. They had arranged for the chapter to meet after morning prayers and the hour approached when they must appear. Yet here they were, waiting at the palace.

'Do they mean to insult us?' the dean snapped, looking to Owen as if he knew the answer.

On arrival at the palace they had been told Archbishop Neville was celebrating Mass for his family in the chapel. Sir John was there, but would be informed of their presence. And then the long wait. Did Sir John mean to keep them there until he had heard from all the men out scouring the city for Ambrose? Or was he not in the chapel but out on other business? Excusing himself, Owen hastened to the stonemasons' lodge where young Simon was laying out tools for the day's work.

'No, Captain, I've not seen the great lord this morning, and I've been here since first light.'

It was the best he could do. Heading back, Owen was gratified to see Sir John entering the hall, followed closely by the archbishop. The contrast between the two was sharp – Sir John tall, lean, handsome, with an air of cordiality – false, but to the untrained eye welcoming; Alexander a bloated man with a small mouth frozen in a scowl, jowls that trembled as he walked, and hands too tiny to wear well the ring of office. He looked far older than his brother, though he was the younger by a decade. As they were drawn aside by a man standing too far in the shadows to identify, a woman appeared, pausing to study the crowd. Catching sight of Owen, she approached his group, people scattering from her path. Brother Michaelo followed in her wake, arms folded, hands tucked into the opposite sleeves, head bowed. The woman's gown flowed round her as she moved, a mark of costly fabric, though the cut, design, and color were simple to the point of austere, the only jewels the rubies and emeralds studding the crispinette encasing her dark hair. As she drew close Owen saw the family resemblance in the shape of her face, though in Marian the colors were faded almost to white whereas this lady's eyes were dark, her color high, the brows and lashes as dark as her hair.

Brother Michaelo introduced Lady Maud Neville to Owen, Dean John, and Master Adam.

She repeated their names as she welcomed them to the palace. Turning to Owen she held out a slender, long-fingered hand graced with a gold ring of intricate design holding one ruby, one emerald. 'Captain Archer, I am grateful for the chance to thank you for all you did for my niece Marian.'

Owen's response was cut short by the arrival of the lady's husband, who nodded to the three and demanded to know why Ambrose Coates was not with them.

'He is recovering from a grievous injury inflicted by the murderer of the vicar, Ronan,' said Owen.

'The murderer? You have found another to blame for the crime?'

'As I said, Sir John. The murderer. The dean and precentor have been informed of the circumstances and provided evidence, though we lack one item that is, I believe, in your possession.'

'And what is that?'

'A small book of accounts kept by Ronan, stolen from the chancellor's hall by two of your men, Porter and Diggs.'

The archbishop had been making a slow progress through the crowd, pausing to speak to select folk. He reached them in time to hear the names.

'They are Crispin Poole's men, I think,' Alexander said as he held out a small hand burdened by his ring of office for the three men to kiss.

All three made their obeisance.

'The two were in Crispin's service,' said Owen, 'but no longer, Your Grace. They resumed their place in Sir John's household once his party arrived at the palace.'

The archbishop glanced at his brother with annoyance. 'Is this true?'

'I do recall now, yes, they brought me the little book. A curious thing. Have you forgotten?' Sir John raised a brow to his brother.

Alexander turned to Owen. 'The book has to do with the vicar's murder? A man has confessed?'

Owen nodded.

'Where is he?'

The dean stepped forward. 'The miscreant is being held at the castle, awaiting the decision as to his fate, Your Grace. Although Captain Archer kindly stepped in to assist us at the request of Master Adam, the chapter precentor and the one responsible for our vicars choral, I feel that as the crime occurred in the minster liberty we should defer to you on the matter of the resolution.' He gave a little bow as he took a breath and tore his gaze from the chilly hostility emanating from the archbishop. 'There is a – complication, Your Grace. If we might retire to a more private place to speak of it . . .'

Alexander raised his hand and from the shadows stepped his secretary Leufrid.

'Cousin,' said Brother Michaelo with a little bow.

Lady Maud looked between the two with interest, the one most courteous, the other gracelessly pretending not to hear.

A small smile played round her mouth and eyes. 'What is the nature of this complication?' she asked.

'This matter is not your concern,' said Alexander. 'Leufrid, have some wine brought to my parlor. Four cups – I have matters to discuss with the officers of the chapter.' Nodding to Owen, he took his leave, the dean and precentor following, the latter glancing back with a look of pleading.

For his part, Owen was relieved. His work was done.

'And what of the spy Ambrose Coates?' demanded Sir John. 'When will he be brought to me?'

'Ah, but he is no spy, husband,' said Lady Maud.

'No? How did you come to that conclusion? Your niece?'

'My lady is correct,' said Owen. 'Ambrose is under the protection of Prince Edward. I will be handing him over to Sir Lewis Clifford as soon as he arrives in the city.'

Sir John grunted. 'Clifford. You are known to him?'

'He was in Princess Joan's party when she paid a visit to the late archbishop,' said Owen.

'Ah yes, you were Thoresby's man – steward and captain of his household guard.'

'I had that honor.'

'Have you heard we found Pit's body floating in the Floss this morning?'

'I have.'

'Two of my best men drowned in your treacherous waters. And your bailiff has arrested another two for the murders.'

'May God forgive them their sins,' Lady Maud whispered, crossing herself.

'For Pit's murder, not Gareth's,' said Owen.

'They are my men,' said Sir John, his eyes cold but his color deepening.

'They committed a crime in the city of York. Two witnesses came forward. The bailiff did his duty. You can take it up with the sheriff.'

'You can be sure I will.'

A courtier interrupted them, and Sir John stepped away with a glare.

Lady Maud rested a hand on Owen's arm. 'Be of good cheer, Captain. My lord knows it would not serve his interests to cross either the prince or the Percys. Your family and your friend are safe.' Her smile was warm, her eyes kind and knowing. 'And now the prince and the city depend on you,' she said more loudly as Sir John returned his attention. 'You carry much on your shoulders, Captain Archer. May God watch over you.'

She reminded him of Princess Joan, a gracious facade, kind heart, and iron will.

'We will talk again anon,' said Sir John with a cold smile.

Owen bowed, taking his leave of them. He forced himself to stroll across the hall and out the door, aware of Sir John's eyes upon him all the way to the steps. As soon as he reached the yard he picked up his pace. Despite Lady Maud's assurances he wanted to see for himself that all was well in his home.

Lucie greeted Owen and with a hug and a finger to her lips. But she had no need. He had heard the singing from out in the garden. *Lullay, lullow, lully, lullay, / Bewy, bewy, lully, lully, / Bewy, lully, lullow, lully, / . . .*

'Dame Marian is here?' he whispered.

'She came by barge from St Clement's with Lady Neville. The novice-mistress accompanies her. They will be summoned when it is time to return. She wished to thank us, and tell us how it stands with her. But Gwen drew her away to fulfill her promise to teach her a carol.'

As Lucie spoke, the refrain was repeated slowly by Gwen and Hugh, with Dame Marian assisting.

'They learn quickly,' said Owen.

Lucie laughed. 'It is the third time round. Listen!'

Lullay, baw, baw, my barne, / Slepe softly now. / Lully my child, / Sleep softly now.

'I see what Michaelo meant about her voice,' said Owen as Dame Marian repeated the lines with the children. 'Surely that is the voice of an angel. Has there been any trouble?'

'None. Sir John and His Grace were informed that Dame Marian is paying us a visit with Lady Maud's blessing. Now come.' Lucie took his hand and led him into the hall, where Kate, Alisoun, and the children sat round with their backs to the fire, listening to Marian sing a verse of the carol. Then she gestured to the children to sing the refrain.

Lullay, lullow, lully, lullay, / Bewy, bewy, lully, lully, / Bewy, lully, lullow, lully, / . . .

Garbed in a simple gown, wimpled and veiled, Marian sat beside an older sister. Her eyes alight, her pale face seemingly bathed in a beatific glow, Owen shed any last doubt of her innocence. No dark secrets shadowed her heart.

Owen and Lucie settled on a bench a little away from the others, listening, watching. Dame Marian's hands danced in the air as she sang a verse, marking a rhythm, the highs and lows, the gestures as graceful as her voice. The children repeated the refrain. Gwen made it through without a stumble. Hugh managed almost as well. Emma sang her own tumbling melody. Dame Marian sang another verse. *A maiden mother, meek and mild, / in a cradle rocked a boy-child / That softly slept; she sat and sang . . .* This time she sang the refrain with the children. At the end, she noticed Lucie and Owen.

'We must pause here,' Marian said to the children.

'Will you teach us another before you leave?' Gwen cried.

'If I have the time, of course, my love.' Kissing Gwen on the forehead, then Hugh and Emma, Marian joined Lucie and Owen. 'I have a message for you, Captain. Lady Maud says to beware her husband, he poisoned a maidservant at Cawood for helping Master Ambrose, and he has his eyes on you. He will not rest until he knows what brought the musician to England.'

Lucie touched Owen's arm. Of course she felt the threat.

Thanking Marian for the warning, Owen said, 'I have something for you.' He drew the prayer book from his scrip and handed it to her.

'My choir of crows!' Tears welled in Marian's eyes as she ruffled the pages, then pressed it to her heart. 'How might I ever repay you for all you have done?'

'Pray for us, Dame Marian,' he said.

'I will. Always.'

'Will you return to Wherwell?' Lucie asked.

'I will accompany Lady Maud south. I must at least see Dame Eloise. But her health no longer permits her to carry out her duties, and Bishop Wykeham's protégé has taken her place. I—' Marian blushed and looked away.

Having long experience of Bishop Wykeham, Owen could well imagine the arrogance of anyone considered his protégé. 'You might not stay?'

'I am not certain. Lady Maud says Archbishop Neville will accept me back into the order to appease my uncle, but Mother Isabel believes Bishop Wykeham should be consulted as he heard my vows at Wherwell.'

'Wykeham might prefer you beholden to Neville,' said Owen, 'so that his protégé is not threatened by your return.'

'All that is out of my hands,' said Dame Marian. 'I am theirs to command.'

'And if you are accepted back into the order but find the situation at Wherwell difficult?' Lucie asked.

'Mother Isabel is of a mind to have a trained cantrice at St Clement's. Lady Maud has told her she could find no one better trained for such a position than I have been. Dame Veronica, the precentrice, welcomes the possibility of lightening her duties.' A little smile.

'How wonderful for us,' breathed Lucie.

EIGHTEEN
A Prayer for Harmony

B rother Henry welcomed Owen into the abbey infirmary
with a serene smile. 'The fiery-haired Gabriel has been
claimed by his lord, a not entirely cordial reunion. But
you will find the musician deep in conversation with your
friend Dom Antony. A most learned man, your friend. Sir
Lewis Clifford and Sir Thomas Percy were here as well,
much moved and angered by the lengths to which the
French have gone to protect themselves from the prince's
military prowess and the love he inspired in the Aquitaine.'
All serenity had vanished as the infirmarian led Owen to
Ambrose's bedside, where Dom Antony sat on a stool beside
the sleeping man making notes on a wax tablet, unaware he
had company.

'Well met, old friend,' said Owen.

Antony glanced up. His eyes warmed and a smile softened
his chiseled features as he rose to embrace Owen. 'All in the
realm are indebted to you, my friend,' he said. 'The information Ambrose brings us is inestimable. Though perhaps too
late to benefit the prince's health.'

'Too late?'

'Ambrose tells me Dame Magda is uncertain that the effects
of such a poisoning with mercury can be reversed after so
long a time. I believe she is right.'

Difficult to hear. 'When would have been soon enough?'

'When the prince began to weaken. Long before he returned
to this country.'

Ambrose had opened his eyes. 'All my hopes come to
naught,' he whispered.

'Ah. You waken again.' Antony resumed his seat beside the
pallet. 'No, my good man, no. His Grace will see that God is
not punishing him for his work, but that it was men who cursed

him. That will be a comfort to him, his family, and all whom
he has served, and who serve him.'

Owen watched as Antony worked his magic, easing
Ambrose's concerns, assuring him that the king and all the
realm would thank him for his selfless act in bringing this
information from the French court.

In a little while, Brother Henry insisted that Ambrose be
permitted to sleep, he was still weak.

'Bless you, Owen,' said Ambrose.

'Be well, my friend.'

Antony pressed Ambrose's hand. 'I will return.'

Brother Henry hastened the two away, promising them they
could return on the morrow.

As they stepped outside, Antony mentioned that Ambrose
had confided in him about his lover. 'Denis has joined
our party. A steadfast love such as his is to be admired and
respected.'

Owen smiled. 'I am glad. He will need your protection if
His Grace is indiscreet.'

'His temper, yes. I had thought of that. France will wish to
silence both men.' Antony cleared his throat. 'Ambrose asked
whether I knew anything of Martin Wirthir.'

'Do you?'

'The king's men hunt him in Wales. He proves elusive.'

Not surprising. 'Did you tell Ambrose?'

Antony nodded. 'He grinned, as you just did.'

'Did I?'

Antony grunted. 'Sir Thomas wishes to thank you for
protecting his ward. Are you in a hurry to be elsewhere?'

'No. I would like to meet him.'

Owen and Antony were shown into the abbot's hall. Sir Thomas
Percy turned from a window and cleared a scowl from his
face to greet Owen with warmth, expressing his eternal gratitude for protecting his ward.

'Marian has been through a terrible ordeal,' said Sir
Thomas. 'Though I seem to recall she once dreamt of traveling about with a company of minstrels.' An impish smile
that surprised in the scarred, square-jawed face, and then

faded as he condemned the brothers Phillip and Rupert for all they had put her through. 'I cannot thank you enough for shielding her from those who would use her as a pawn. Lewis Clifford regrets your offending John Neville, but I applaud you. The man thinks far too much of himself.' He motioned for them to sit with him, calling to a servant to bring wine. 'And I apologize for the oafish Gabriel. The young man needs humbling. A battlefield, I think.' He nodded as if to himself.

And so it continued, Sir Thomas managing to carry on a conversation of one, until Owen excused himself. Antony walked out with him.

'As you can see, the Percys are grateful to you. However, the Nevilles might prove less cordial, though Sir John values all you discovered about the murdered vicar. He knows to keep an even tighter grip on his brother the archbishop.'

'What I know of Alexander Neville suggests his elder brother has failed to control him in the past.'

'Indeed.'

'Am I to be chastened for annoying Sir John?'

'It is true that the prince wishes you to walk softly round the Nevilles, else you will hear nothing of their movements. But the circumstances warranted your actions. There is time. I have arranged for a dinner after the enthronement, before Sir John and Lady Maud depart. I pray you and Lucie attend.' Antony paused. 'Let me correct that. I insist that the two of you attend.'

'How can we refuse?' For his part, Owen looked forward to watching Antony handle Sir John Neville. And he welcomed the chance to introduce Lucie to Lady Maud.

Four women gazed down at the wonder of Muriel's long-prayed-for baby, a sweet, chubby girl with a tuft of fair hair and long, dark lashes.

'Lucia Swann,' Muriel murmured, 'you are the image of your handsome papa. God blessed me with such a remembrance in you.' She looked up at Lucie, Alisoun, Lotta, and Magda. 'Is she not the image of my beloved Hoban?' Her husband, viciously murdered less than two months earlier.

'She is very like,' said Alisoun, offering the baby a finger to tug on. 'You have indeed been blessed.'

'I confess I find it difficult to see a man's visage in this delicate child,' said Lotta with a laugh. 'Though she be almost as bald as my George.'

'Dame Magda? What do you say?' Muriel asked.

'Magda sees a child who will bring great joy to thee and thy betrothed, and bring new life to thy grieving kin.' The Riverwoman's eyes were kind, her hands gentle as she retrieved the infant and coaxed the new mother to lie down and rest. 'Thou hast endured a long, difficult labor and now, if thy milk is to continue to flow, thou must eat well and rest often.' She handed the baby to the maidservant. No wet-nurse for Muriel. Having waited years for this experience she wished to savor it fully.

'Thank you all for coming to celebrate my daughter's birth. And to you, my dear Lucie, and you, Lotta, for standing for her at her christening.'

Both women assured her they were moved and honored. Lucie was to be first godmother, Lotta Hempe second, and Peter Ferriby, a prominent merchant and the husband of Lucie's friend Emma, was to be godfather. Strong alliances for Muriel's daughter among the merchant class of York. A clear sign that although she had wrested her betrothed from the archbishop's grasp, she was well aware that for their businesses to thrive Crispin needed such alliances. Lucie prayed that this child brought a fresh chance to both her parents. She had expressed her gratitude for Crispin's part in moving Marian to safety and promised that word of his courage and compassion would spread to those merchants who could be trusted to befriend him for it.

'I do so wish I might be churched in time to attend the enthronement. Crispin says that Dame Marian will sing a hymn to the Blessed Virgin during the processional.' She looked to Magda, who shook her head. 'I will pray that she chooses St Clement's as her home.'

The York Tavern was rowdy this night, Crispin Poole buying drinks for all and sundry to celebrate the birth of Lucia Swann. He and Muriel had pledged their troth.

'Blessed be that Dame Muriel was safe delivered,' said Bess as Owen arrived. 'She deserves much joy.'

'Here's the captain!' Crispin shouted, clearly on his way to a good drunk. He waved Owen over, calling out the news of his role in the baby's hours-old life.

Folk pounded on Owen's back, eager to hear about Carl the murderous musician and poor Will the silversmith now imprisoned in the castle. Owen tried to smile over the bitterness of losing that battle as he made his way to the back table where George Hempe sat with Alfred and Stephen, off duty for this special occasion. He wished no gloom for Crispin's celebration. He had just lifted his overflowing tankard to his mouth when a hush fell over the room and all eyes turned toward the men in the doorway.

With a flourish, Dom Antony bowed to Tom Merchet, his deep voice carrying through the room as he introduced himself and his companion Sir Lewis Clifford. 'I have long wished to meet you, Master Tom. Your ale is by far the best in the land.' Antony paused for the cheers. When they died down, he said, 'And we have brought the finest crwth player in the land to entertain the house tonight in celebration of young Swann.' Stepping aside, he revealed Ambrose Coates, resplendent in his gorgeous cloak, repaired by Jehannes's talented Anna. Denis stood beside him, carrying a leather case.

Tom made room near the fire, providing a stool. Lowering himself onto it, for he was still weak, Ambrose took the crwth from Denis's hands, lifted it to his lap, and began to play.

AUTHOR'S NOTE

A few years ago, as part of a fundraising event for the Medieval Women's Choir,[1] I raffled off the chance to appear as a character in my next book. To my delight, the woman who won the raffle asked me to use her daughter, our fabulous soloist and assistant choir director Marian 'Molly' Seibert, a dream subject as she's talented, smart, personable, striking in appearance, and a good sport. The wheels in my head began to turn . . .

I relished sharing insights gleaned from performing medieval music as a member of the choir – nothing teaches like hands-on (or voice-engaged) experience. I had been planning a reappearance of the musician Ambrose Coates, a character from *The Lady Chapel* (book two in the series), and the singer and the musician seemed the perfect combination. With Molly as catalyst the tale began to take shape.

If you're reading this before reading the book (I wish you wouldn't!), I assure you that *A Choir of Crows* is *not* a dissertation on performing medieval music, but rather a murder mystery that happens to touch on aspects of the music and how it was learned and performed as that relates to the tale. Now turn back and read the book first, because I can't promise there aren't spoilers below!

Early in *A Choir of Crows*, Ambrose guesses that Matthew, a talented member of the company of musicians and players he's joined, received his musical training in a religious house because he uses the parts of his hand to memorize a melody. He's using what is called the Guidonian hand, a mnemonic device in which each portion of the hand represents a specific note within the hexachord system used for chant.[2] A youth

---

[1] https://medievalwomenschoir.org/

[2] http://www.medieval.org/emfaq/harmony/hex1.html

learning a song by listening to the others in a company of musicians would be unlikely to have the habit of using his hand so.

The youth also toys with melodic embellishments appropriate for the mode in which Ambrose set a song they are rehearsing. The modes of melodies are the sets of pitch intervals similar to a modern musical scale.[3] I was once fortunate to participate in a workshop at a medieval studies congress led by a member of Anonymous 4. We learned two modes, singing the pitch over and over until we internalized the mode, then learning pieces of chant in those modes that were familiar to all of us who listened to early music, particularly sacred music. The third step was learning to do just what Ambrose finds Matthew doing, embellishing the melodies yet retaining their harmony by limiting the notes to the mode in which the piece was based. I'm simplifying this, but I hope it suffices to show why Ambrose believed that Matthew received his voice training in a monastic setting.

One more wee bit. At a recent rehearsal our artistic director Eric Mentzel[4] used Hildegard of Bingen's neumes (notations) to illustrate one of the challenges of performing medieval music, which I feel also explains its emotive beauty. As choir member Michelle Urberg, PhD, puts it, 'Before we had notation in the middle ages that looks square and is written on a set of horizontal lines and spaces, music was notated with sets of symbols indicating where to raise or lower a pitch in a melody. All of the information about the note (pitch or movement up or down) was kept in the symbol and duration was

---

[3] 'Modes are sets of eight pitches arranged around whole and half steps. A whole step is the distance between a C and D or a G and A; meanwhile a half step is the distance between E and F or A and B-flat. Modes are similar to modern musical scales in that they have a defined set of whole and half steps that are used in a given piece of music and privilege certain pitches (e.g. D mode privileges D and A). The arrangement of notes make modes like modern keys in that they give a mode a particular sound or timbre (not unlike associating major keys with happiness and minor keys with sadness).' Michelle Urberg PhD, personal communication.

[4] https://medievalwomenschoir.org/artistic-director/

determined by the text, rather than dividing that work out discretely between the note, time signature indicating measured and rhythmic duration, and staff lines.'[5] These symbols are neumes, inflective marks that describe the shape of the music as it dances with the text, leaving the performers to improvise with counts, measures, and pitches. All depends on the text; the music works for the text.

In medieval religious houses, the cantrice or cantor used the methods I learned in the workshop to lead the nuns and monks in singing the daily office. The cantrice's duties included the upkeep of liturgical books, the choice of chants for specific occasions, the creation of chants if necessary, and the setting of tempos and pitches in the performance.[6] A challenging and important position. The best of them modified the music to suit the voices available for the choir. That Marian was learning these skills at Wherwell Abbey was a tribute to her talent.

Another aspect of the book involves the ill health of Prince Edward (popularly known today as the Black Prince). Although the disastrous Battle of Nájera is often cited as the beginning of his disabling illness, I'm inclined to believe Michael Jones's claim that Edward's health started to decline a year after that battle, in the autumn of 1368.[7] If that's the case, the common claim that it was dysentery, which never made sense to me, is unlikely. When I was working on my novel of Joan of Kent (*A Triple Knot*, published under the pseudonym Emma Campion) I developed my own theory about the disease that eventually killed him, that he was slowly being poisoned with mercury. Mercury, or quicksilver, was used for medicinal purposes in the Middle Ages and after – the sale of over-the-counter medicines containing it was not banned in the UK until 1955.[8] In various forms it was known to be an effective antibacterial and was used for a wide range of health issues including scurvy, ringworm,

[5] Personal communication.

[6] Yardley, p. 58.

[7] Jones, p. 329.

[8] Emsley, p. 46.

boils, syphilis, eye and skin complaints, and as a laxative. It's still used in some Chinese and Ayurvedic medicines, albeit in small amounts. We now know that human ingestion of mercury damages the kidney, brain, liver, reproductive system, and other organs. Small amounts over a long period of time might have caused many of Prince Edward's physical and mental symptoms. In the book I mention Pierre de Manhi, a surgeon in Bordeaux, who is known to have received payment for services from Prince Edward in 1368.[9] I used him for the purpose, though I may be taking his name in vain. I apologize to his descendants if this is so. I created a fictional character, Ricard, as the physician who joined the prince's household in Bordeaux and returned with him to England to continue the gradual poisoning.

December 1374 was a perilous time for the English royal family. With both King Edward and his heir in physical and mental decline and the prince's son, Richard, still a child, the great houses were understandably concerned about the succession, a situation that was the perfect Petri dish for conspiracy theories. One of the most popular such theories was that John of Gaunt, Duke of Lancaster, was plotting against his nephew the young Prince Richard, intending to ascend the throne himself. Aside from these theories, the great houses, including the Percy and Neville families of the North, were competing for influence in the realm. The enthronement of Alexander Neville as Archbishop of York, the second most powerful churchman in the realm, was a coup for the Nevilles. A brother as Archbishop of York added to the power of the patriarch of the family, John Neville, Knight of the Garter, Admiral of the North, and Steward of the King's Household, already an impressive man. From all accounts Alexander would never have risen so far in the Church without his family's backing. As I mentioned in my author's note for *A Conspiracy of Wolves* (book eleven in this series), Alexander was a petty, arrogant, aggressive man, and his new role did nothing to ease those tendencies. In short, he's a gift to a writer, a deliciously hateful character and a contrast to his predecessor, John Thoresby.

---

[9] Jones, p. 425.

Owen chafed at Thoresby's power plays, but compared with Neville he was a saint.

Works Cited

Emsley, John. **The Elements of Murder**. Oxford University Press 2005.

Jones, Michael. **The Black Prince**. Pegasus Books 2019.

Yardley, Anne Bagnall. **Performing Piety: Musical Culture in Medieval English Nunneries**. Palgrave Macmillan 2006.

Additional Reading

Colton, Lisa. 'Languishing for provenance: Zelo tui langueo and the search for women's polyphony in England', in **Early Music** vol. 39, 3 August 2011, pp.313–325.

Duffin, Rose W., ed. **A Performer's Guide to Medieval Music**. Indiana University Press 2000.

Greene, Richard Leighton, ed. **The Early English Carols**. Oxford Clarendon Press 1977 (2nd edition).

Haines, John. **Medieval Song in Romance Languages**. Cambridge University Press 2010.

Mullally, Robert. **The *Carole*: A Study of a Medieval Dance**. Ashgate 2011.

ACKNOWLEDGMENTS

As mentioned in my Author's Note, Marian 'Molly' Seibert, soloist and assistant choir director for the Medieval Women's Choir, is the inspiration for her namesake in this book. Not only that, she helped me along the way by brainstorming with me at the beginning, suggesting appropriate pieces of music, reading the finished draft, and simply being her fabulous self. Dr Michelle Urberg, a fellow member of the choir with a PhD in medieval music from the University of Chicago, was the third part of the brainstorming team, generously loaning me books and suggesting others from the library as well as the music used in the book; later she read and commented on the finished draft and contributed to the Author's Note. I am so grateful to both of them! I take full responsibility for any errors that crept in despite their care.

Deep thanks to my friend Dr Louise Hampson for fielding questions about scenes in and around York Minster and all things medieval York, as well as reading the final draft with an eagle eye watching for errors that might have crept in.

As ever, I am grateful to Dr Mary Morse for a careful edit of the complete manuscript and thoughtful comments. Professional editor, professor of medieval literature, manuscript scholar, musician, and good friend, she swept through the manuscript at the end, asking insightful questions and helping me tidy up.

I count on my agent Jennifer Weltz to read through the manuscript as a staunch advocate for my characters and the series. She's always right, and I couldn't be more grateful.

Huge thanks to my editor Kate Lyall Grant for her support, enthusiasm, and thoughtful questions and comments, and to all the team at Severn House.

On a sad note, I lost a dear friend and partner in crime, Joyce Gibb, on Christmas Eve 2019. First reader for almost all of my books, Joyce never held back when she thought I was going astray. There is more than a little of Joyce in Magda Digby. I miss her sorely.

For his beautiful maps and patience throughout the year helping me with systems issues, travel, and whatever comes up, I am always and forever grateful to Charlie Robb, my anchor, my best friend, the love of my life.